The Cabernet Legacy

THE FINN
FIASCO

BOOK FOUR

I0649790

NICHOLAS HUNTLEY

"But still, existence for us is a miracle… a playing of absolute forces that no one can touch who has not knelt down in wonder."

– Rainer M. Rilke

Act 1, Prologue

I suppose you weren't expecting to start this novel with me in the way. Let me introduce myself – my name is Moira Isidore Macmillan, Allabrese resident, professional programmer and amateur hacker, and also daughter of our deceased police captain and local hero, my father: Eugene Gavin MacMillan. In October 2019, our small town of Allabrese was gripped with a sudden epidemic, a nefarious water-borne disease took a majority of us by surprise, and this disease was both deadly and contagious. The federal government shut Allabrese down, activating the 1st Mechanized Brigade Group from Canadian Forces Base (CFB) Edmonton, to impose control. Among that brigade, a junior officer included was my mother, Captain Esther Mary MacMillan (née Hughes). In opposition to this sudden takeover of our small town, our local eccentric billionaire, Charlemagne Cabernet, who at this time had embraced the storm of the ages in alt-right political beliefs was infuriated at the exercise of democratically elected power to keep us safe. In violation of health orders in place, Mr. Cabernet and a few of his henchmen sailed across the Nattau River into the quarantine zone where they contacted other henchmen. I can only presume what Mr. Cabernet's intentions were that night as he and his followers launched an insurrection against Canadian service personnel and local police, as if their intentions were to repel these government authorities and liberate the town. From official records from that night, known as the Battle of Allabrese, five Canadian service personnel and seventeen Nattau County police officers died in the firefights that took place. For reasons unknown, but ultimately the way of justice in our society, the rich man, Mr. Cabernet, and his comrades, escaped prosecution for their actions. Based on my research, they all evaded prosecution from government authorities as less than a few months later the Sars-COV2 virus gripped the entire world, delaying court proceedings and investigations. In the midst of that pandemic, Mr. Cabernet passed away on October 21st, 2021, ultimately releasing him from having to face any justice for his actions.

My father was buried in Allabrese Cemetery with the other fallen police officers. I had just turned seventeen-years old the month before his death, and although I would have liked to have stayed in Allabrese with my older brother, Jock, who was twenty years old at the time, my mother had custody over me and my younger siblings. My parents had divorced when I was ten-years old, shortly after our youngest sibling, Rose, was born. When they had divorced, my mother respected my wishes to allow me to stay in Allabrese with Jock and dad. She did not want the impact of the divorce to have a negative effect on me or my siblings; or at least, to have a minimized negative impact. Both Rose and my other younger sibling, Elliot, who was four years old at the time, had no choice in who they stayed with, so my mother took them with her to Edmonton to live and be raised, although they had joint custody. Obviously, with my father dead, I had to join them in Edmonton. On September 23rd, 2020, I turned eighteen years old and got to decide for myself what I would do, or where I would live. I moved to Calgary and transferred to the University of Calgary where I lived on my own for a while, then with some roommates, and then alone again for four years up until my graduation in December 2024. I had to find a full-time job to support myself, having worked as a freelance programmer to make ends meet, but now with crippling student loan debt, I needed to make more money in the current job market in the midst of a recession. I could not find a well-paying job with my bachelor's degree in applied science in Calgary. I had to make an immediate decision: my mother and her current partner offered to take me back into their home, and rejoin them, and my younger brother and sister. I had no intentions to return to that home where I would be reminded about the breakdown of our family, although my mind was convinced that my mother had all the right to move on with her life and remarry if she wanted to, my heart resisted. A few days before I was to be evicted from my apartment in Calgary, I received word from my brother, Jock, now twenty-six years old that January, of an offer to come live with him. A few months after my father had died, Jock and I had a fight in which he objected to believe that Charlemagne Cabernet was at fault for our father's death – I hated him for having that opinion, and I was reluctant to return to Allabrese to see him, but at the same time, I could be at greater comfort there than in Edmonton. Jock lived in our family home, which he mortgaged and bought from my mother, and he got married a few years later and had a one-year-old son, Gavin. He and his wife, Rebecca, agreed to let me stay as long as I needed, and after initial reluctance, I agreed to their kind offer. I did not think I would find a long-term career in Allabrese, but I could at least continue do some remote freelance work. I could begin to pay off my debt without having to pay for rent, and with what little remained, I could also chip in.

So, here I am as I write this tale of mine. I'm on a commercial plane from Calgary to Allabrese, out in the Nattau County, in the middle of winter. If you were looking for some sort of dramatic flashback scene, you best look somewhere else for those details. Sorry for the misdirect, but here is the beginning of my story, of Moira's Moment.

• • • •

I sat in the dim cabin of the small commercial airplane as I tilted by head back and looked up to the ceiling. My eyes were tired and sore, and my laptop screen lit up my chest and my face despite being at the lowest brightness and in night mode. My computer was something of my own creation, built up piece by piece. On the outside, it had the appearance of a Bertrand-

Schmidt Null, but on the inside, it had a more expensive motherboard, state-of-the-art processor and graphics card, and more than a terabyte hard drive and sixteen gigabytes of ram. This computer was something of my own creation, put together by my own hands. The computer ran the latest Neumann operating system; I wasn't going to run Linux, but through some modifications, I also made the OS as something of my own. No sporadic system updates for me, or personal data being sent to some database in Seattle. No backdoors for the hackers to get into my computer, or vulnerabilities for the government to spy on me. I had made sure that this computer was as secure as a Fort Knox, because some of the items I worked on were more precious than gold. I made sure my computer was secure, only using a trusted and lesser-known anti-malware software and connecting to the Internet on a secure VPN. I did not use any of the mainstream Internet browsers and instead only used the Tor browser, which kept my identity on-line anonymous. The Tor browser relied on an overlay network called Tor, which routes Internet traffic through random paths along the network to make it very difficult to trace a user's Internet activity and location. To think that this network system was developed to conceal U.S. intelligence communications, it was now being used by cyber criminals and purveyors of the Dark Web, not that those two subject categories were mutually exclusive. For a very few, the network also gave some relief to know that one's Internet activity was not being watched by the watchful eye of Big Brother as some feared, not that any government cared about the mundane Internet patterns and activities of a law-abiding citizen. The only people who sincerely cared for anonymity on-line in Western civilization were criminals, while in other parts of the world, it shielded against totalitarian governments and oppressive regimes seeking political dissidents. Anyone else was just paranoid that their personal data was at the mercy of corporations to analyse and examine. Not too long ago it was

4

confirmed that smartphones do in fact spy on people, but only so that the right advertisements could be filtered through to people – that was the sort of civilization we lived in, or what kind of an Internet we had in this day and age, a consumerist hellscape.

I looked out my window towards the grey clouds below us as we flew overhead the snowy flatlands of the province. The skies were dark blue as it was nightfall, and the only visibility was due to the moonlight as a full moon shined upon us. The cabin I sat in was at least tame and quiet, nothing like the flight I had from Edmonton to Calgary when I moved out from my mother's home to university. I couldn't forget the scream of babies and other children ringing in my ear, making me wish I never had children, but then again, I suppose not many people came out to Allabrese. In my cabin, at least two or three dozen seats total, there were at most three of us. These flights only ran once per month from Calgary; no other city in Alberta had flights that came to Allabrese. From what I understood too, all flights to Allabrese filtered through either Harlech from the west and Calgary from the east, so I supposed that those with me were coming from connecting flights at Toronto, which went out towards the wider world. Likewise, the same with Harlech as connecting flights from Asia filtered through there.

Calgary was to the south of the province, a two-hour drive to the U.S. and Canada border, while Edmonton was right in the middle of the province, parallel to Harlech on the coast, which was also parallel to Allabrese to the west at the natural barrier that was the Rocky Mountains. The drive from Allabrese to Edmonton was four and a half hours, and a typical drive from Edmonton to Calgary was three hours. A drive from Calgary to Allabrese was nearly seven hours, but I did not have the means to make that drive, nor were there really any buses that went that way either. I remember as a kid there used to be trains that passed through, but I never really saw those anymore as a teenager. To my benefit, the flight from Calgary to Allabrese was only an hour and a half, while a flight from Toronto was close to four hours, or from Harlech another hour and a half. I had enjoyed my time in Calgary more than Edmonton, living on my own, though it was quite lonely. I had made friends, or at least so I thought I did. I never really connected on a personal level with those around me. I had roommates, schoolmates, even a boyfriend, though that was short-lived, and through it all I never really found the right amount of companionship like I did back home. Allabrese was the most isolated and eccentric smalltown I had ever known, and that was speaking as someone who had visited a lot of remote towns around the province and neighboring provinces as a kid and a teenager, going on road trips with my older brother and dad.

I thought for a moment longer about what sort of place Allabrese was as I refrained from bringing my eyes down to the computer screen to resume some work I was doing. It has been five years since I was last in Allabrese; five years since my dad had died, a particular grief that I had not exactly overcome but which continued to nag me in the heart. I missed my dad. I missed the way he would make breakfast on his day off from work. I missed the way he would come home from work and be so eager to see us. I missed his smile and his laugh, his humor and also his wisdom. Why did they have to separate from each other? Isn't it so typical for either parent to have a defense in the case of their marriage falling apart, but not my dad. He blamed himself for the breakdown of his marriage to my mom. He said that it just didn't make sense for him, a policeman, to have married her, an army officer; they also had married young, after I was born. A year or two before they separated, my mom worked at the airfield where there was a reserve garrison, a type of militia of volunteers that are a part of the Canadian Armed Forces, but are on stand-by in the event of war or catastrophe. She had to move to Edmonton to relocate, and although my dad offered to join her, she declined, and they tried to live in two places at once. What's ironic is that my dad wasn't even from Allabrese; he moved here for her because she grew up in this town. She loved this town, and both my grandparents, her parents, and her siblings still lived in Allabrese. He, of all places, was from Calgary, but they met when he was around town for the Nattau Derby. My mother seldom spoke about the separation and divorce with me, her eldest child. She always tried to frame it as something normal that happens, and for a time I believed her, until he passed away and it started to make less sense to me. How could something like a divorce or separation be normal when there is so much suffering to the partners and children? From what little bits and pieces I could grasp from my mother, it felt as though she blamed him too; as if he wasn't paying attention to her, or wasn't making an effort to keep the marriage together, and so she had to leave him as though she was obligated to do so.

And then there was a moral opinion of my grandparents, her parents, who disproved; my grandmother more than my grandfather who though not supportive, never really made any remarks about it and instead placed his attention into us. My grandmother was a former English teacher at my high school, and my dad was a former gym teacher at that same high school, Lord Phoenix Secondary School, and aside from that fact, they were also pretty religious; Roman Catholics that attended church every Sunday type of people, and that was the way they raised their children, and to an extent how they tried to ensure their children raised their children, their grandchildren, but when you have four kids who themselves have between two to five kids each, it becomes a difficult task to make sure they're all following suit. I for one didn't consider myself religious at all, but that didn't stop them from making an effort with me when I was a young kid. I wished that me returning to Allabrese meant I could at least see my grandparents again, because I did love them tremendously, but from what I understood, my grandmother had become this famous author and spent her time travelling from place to place with my granddad, especially Harlech and the United States, to give talks and interviews. How could I complain about money problems when my she had become so wealthy? The least I wanted to do was start to beg others for money, because without a doubt would she help me out. Still though, if my seventy-two-year-old grandmother could become famous at that age, then what an inspiration for all of us. I suppose though she wasn't that famous. She wasn't walking the red carpet at Hollywood, or having tea with King Charles, but she was notable on social media and being invited as a guest on podcasts and YouTube shows, especially those surrounding Catholic media figures. I looked up to my grandmother a lot, but I didn't really share much with her. She was a dynamic person though, and what everyone knew about her was that she was very observant, with a passion for mysteries and puzzle solving, and that was a little part of me that I had too. Her husband, my granddad, stuck with her to the ends of the earth, and I admired that too. I wished I could find someone as loyal as him. They both inspired me. He was a former Canadian Armed Forces servicemember with a few deployments, so I heard, and he inspired my mom immensely. They were very close to each other, and he got along well with my dad too. Yup, we were all once one big and happy family; I could recall going to their home on the northwest shore of the county where they owned some acres of land and a sizeable house, the family home, where my mother, the eldest of four siblings, was raised and where we would come together for visits, or all come together for a family reunion. They were that sort of family-driven sort of people, my grandparents, and still are even if the pandemic hindered any family reunions.

I felt the plane tip sideways as we began to descend past the clouds and come towards the airfield. Allabrese had an aerodrome on the west coast at the base of the mountain. This aerodrome had formally been a part of an airbase where air force personnel from all commonwealth countries came together to train, and then where my mom worked and a small garrison lived. Nowadays, it was just an airstrip where any person could touchdown and land their plane. I could recall looking up at the skies and seeing planes leave from the west at random moments as a kid, most times of which I was told it was the illustrious billionaire's private jet taking off – Charlemagne. I tightened my hands around my armrests as I thought about that vile name, *Charlemagne de la Cabernet*, and that itself reminded me of his two adopted children, two former classmates of mine, Tristan Merrick and Diana Cambridge. Diana and I were friends, but as I recall, we stopped being friends when we were on a late summer camping trip together out in B.C., and over the course of a few weeks before, I was suspicious that she was in a secret romantic relationship with her adoptive brother, Tristan. I tried to squeeze it out of her by pretending to be interested in him, but she did not relent to tell me the truth until I overheard them talking to each other at the camp and it was plain as day to me. I felt hurt, betrayed, and I honestly should have seen it coming. This happened a year before my dad died – the entire year up to his death was just awful and made my late adolescent lifetime a nightmare.

I wondered if those two were still in Allabrese as the plane began to fly down. I felt reluctance to even be back in the county if they were around, but I supposed that I did not have much to fear; they were nothing compared to Charlemagne, and he was dead now – good riddance, a subtle blow to the Cabernet legacy as from what I understood, Mr. Cabernet did not have any children of his own. His younger brother, Salmar Cabernet, was locked up and in prison for child endangerment, and the middle child, Allodia Cabernet, was now Chairwoman of Cabernet Industries, and she did not have any children of her own either.

I didn't know much about their own parents, but I assumed since they ran the show of Cabernet Industries' global empire, they must have perished. That entire family was one generation away from extinction, and I was relieved. I wondered what would happen then, but those thoughts soon escaped me as I looked out the window and towards the county from above, home sweet home.

I stood up as the plane rested on the airstrip and lights turned on. I took my luggage beside me, and took out another luggage case stored above me, and then with them, and my backpack, I began to straddle out of the plane and look down the tall staircase that came to the asphalt of the tarmac. I looked around the brightly lit airstrip as flurries passed by and brushed my cheeks, and a depth of snow of a winter wonderland could be seen around me with the snow glazed evergreen trees. I looked towards the parking lot and identified a car and a person beside it who waved over to me. I stood from the top of the boarding stairs and took in a deep breath. Here I was now, back in Allabrese, a place I had long run from but now was set to live in for the foreseeable future.

Act 1, Scene 1

"Welcome home!" Jock exclaimed, stepping towards me and wrapping his arms around as I approached him with my luggage. Jock embraced me with a tight grip. I stood up straight as he hugged me. He soon released me and looked back at me with a smile. Jock had wavy dark hair and a trimmed beard. He also had fair skin, which in this weather, was made fairer, his cheeks were ruddy, and his eyes blue. He was a few inches over six feet tall. "How was the trip?"

"Fine," I sheepishly acknowledged. "You look so different. Nice beard…"

"What? This?" Jock questioned. "Ah, come on, you haven't seen this before?"

"Nope," I replied, "you didn't have that at the wedding."

"Oh, I suppose it has been quite a while since we saw each other," Jock said. "Anyways, come on. Let's get you home. Let me help you with those."

Jock stepped forward and picked up the largest suitcase, while I took the smaller one and came around to the back of his car. He drove a dark blue Ford Escape SUV. The back door opened, and he loaded my luggage inside, and then I placed my other one beside it. He then closed the door, and I went around to the passenger seat while he came around to the driver's seat. We both got inside and closed the door so that we were in the cabin of the still slightly warm car. Jock turned on the engine at the press of a button, and we both put on our seatbelt. The radio instantly turned on to play country music from my brother's smartphone, and he began to back up to exit the parking lot while I looked around the rear of the car. I noticed in the center of the back seats there was a baby carrier reminding me of their one-year-old son; my one-year-old nephew. I had not met him yet, and I had not seen Rebecca since their wedding a few years back.

"So, how've you been, sis?" Jock asked. "How's life in the city been treating you?"

"Oh, it's been okay," I admitted as we left the parking lot and came out onto the lone road away from the airfield. "I'll be honest though, I'll miss the different sort of food that I can get my hands on, but otherwise, I won't miss it."

"Yeah?" Jock replied. "Rebecca and I were in Calgary a year or so ago, when she was still pregnant. We came for the Calgary Stampede, and it was certainly something; not the same as when we went with dad years ago. No, that place has changed a lot – I don't know if you remember that, but the people there were still nice as ever – that hasn't changed."

"Yeah, people in Calgary can be nice, depending on where you are at. I've met some not-so-nice people here and there."

"Oh, I'm sorry to hear that."

"How about you?" I asked. "How've you been?"

"Eh, tired is all," Jock stated. "It's true what they say. Having kids is exhausting work, especially when they wake up at night. Luckily, Gavin has been doing a lot better, but the early weeks when he was born were rough. It wasn't easy with my rotations, you know, because I work shifts like dad used to do, and transitioning from day shifts to night shifts were tough. I typically just went down to your room in the basement just so I can sleep because I could not put up with the noise around me. Rebecca was helpful though, and she's stayed with him. She hasn't gone back to the hospital since he was born."

"What does Rebecca do again? She's a nurse or something?"

"Technologist," Jock clarified. "She works in medical imaging."

"Oh, right," I replied.

"Yeah, she's still on maternity leave technically, but she's supposed to be back soon…"

"Right… and that's where I come in, isn't it?"

"It was optional to you, but we appreciate you offering to pitch in to babysit Gavin," Jock remarked. "You didn't have to, for my sake. I would have been fine to send him to daycare, but Rebecca wasn't of the same opinion. She didn't want him to share germs with the other kids, or pick up on some bad habits. She complains that daycare at Prince Albert isn't the same as it used to be, and that some bad families have moved into Allabrese over the years, especially with the re-opening and expansion of the research labs in Champion Plains, so she would rather not even let him near that place and would rather homeschool him, as if we had the capability to do that."

"Bad families?" I questioned. "Like Medici?"

"Nah," Jock responded, "I mean – and this is just her opinion, I don't have anything against anyone, but there's been a lot of immigrants coming around to Allabrese in the past five years, just like everywhere else."

"Really?" I questioned.

"Yeah," Jock said, "not that much, but enough to make a sizeable difference to this small town. In that time span, we've had a sushi restaurant open, a Chinese and Vietnamese place, and Shawarma joint near the station."

"I take back what I said about the food then," I replied. "Is Trixie's still open?"

"Nah, they closed down during the pandemic," Jock answered.

"What about Golden? They had a few of those in Calgary, as well as their other fast-food chain, Angel's."

"That one is still open," Jock replied, "luckily. That place and Great Range Bistro have survived, I believe."

"Still no Big Boy's? Royal Burger? Wendell's?"

"Nah, none of those places around here. You know what it's like; chamber of commerce is opposed to any of those big-business restaurants from poking their heads around here. Cole Phillips has kept that same promise Theodore Grayson gave. The only change around here I suppose has been some businesses shutting down, and the foreigners, not that Mr. Phillips had any sort of part in that."

"Oh?"

"Yeah, from what he's said, it's the fault of the provincial and federal government to off-load these folk here," Jock stated, pausing for a moment. "Sorry, I shouldn't have said it that way."

"It's alright," I replied with a nervous laugh. "I've heard it a thousand times out in Calgary, a lot of times a lot ruder than you put it. Do you talk to Mr. Phillips at all? I guess he's still mayor then, huh?"

"Yeah, he's still our mayor," Jock said, "and I do talk to him from time to time, but not very often. He makes an effort though to be there for us still… almost as if he feels guilty over what happened to dad."

"Why?" I immediately questioned. "He had no part in his death. It was…"

"I think he'd disagree with you too on that piece."

I didn't respond. I simply looked at Jock and then stared out in front of us. We came out from the forest, and I looked ahead at the sightline of what lay ahead of us. From where we came out, I could see Allabrese directly across, lit up like stars in the sky. A wave of nostalgia came over me, and I looked across to the small town with comfort but also awe. The snowfall that was around the county made the darkness not so frightening, and the clouds too, though dark, were lighter than if there was no snow around. The car turned right and went along the cliffside road to approach the bridge intersection. We went around the loop and then proceeded towards the bridge. I looked out the window on my left and tried to see if I could catch a glimpse of Cabernet Manor far ahead, which I was able to do. The manor sat atop of the cliffs further ahead, streetlamps in front of it, but the windows and surrounding area were very dim; there was not a single light turned on inside. I didn't say anything about it because I did not want to address the topic of the Cabernet family with my brother.

"How's everyone else in the Phillip family?" I instead asked. "How's Mrs. Phillips? Is she still principal at the high school?"

"Yeah, I think so," Jock replied. "I sometimes see their kid, Aaron, from time to time. He's on a different rotation than me, but whenever either of us pick up overtime, we sometimes run into each other."

"Oh, so he's still with you guys then."

"Yeah, he also got married not too long ago, to Vivian Huxley."

"You're kidding?" I responded in a serious tone. "They got married?"

"Yeah, I went to their wedding. It was nice," Jock answered.

"Oh my gosh…" I remarked. "When was this?"

"Uh… I think last September?" Jock replied. "It was definitely not that long ago."

"We're only twenty-two," I said. "How is that possible?"

"Come on, you can't be that surprised. I knew folks that I went to high school with who were getting married at eighteen. Heck, didn't your friend, Diana Cambridge, get married at eighteen years old?"

"Diana got married? To Tristan Merrick, right?"

"Yeah, those two," Jock stated.

"That's insane," I suggested. "Have you seen either of them? Are they still in Allabrese?"

"I haven't seen them, but truth be told, I don't know if they're in Allabrese. I don't think so if I haven't seen them at all."

"Oh my gosh…" I simply exclaimed. "I'm baffled…"

"Feeling the pressure?"

"A little bit," I acknowledged. "How is anyone supposed to meet and fall for someone that fast, especially in this dump."

"Ah, come on," Jock remarked, "this place isn't a dump. You just have to be in touch with the community and there'll be someone out there. Look at me, I strained my ankle, and one trip to the hospital to get a scan done, and a few months later I was getting married, and I was twenty-four."

"I don't know what to say..." I remarked as we went uphill. I paused for a moment and then asked, "How's everyone else doing? On mom's side of the family? They all still around?"

"Let's see... Evan is now a sergeant with the force... and both Tobias and Tabitha are still teaching at the school. You'll be upset to hear, but Tabitha's grandmother-in-law died not too long ago, a couple weeks back. They already had the funeral. It was... a peaceful death, but still sad."

"Oh, that' so unfortunate," I responded. "Is that the one that was a housekeeper?"

"Yup, that's her. She finally retired during the pandemic, but I guess it's true what they say, some people feel useless without having some sort of work to do."

"Tell me about it..."

Jock drove along main street as we passed downtown Allabrese. I could only briefly see around as we zipped past and continued into the east side of town. We finally turned left halfway in and then went down a few blocks until I looked to the left and could see our quaint family home. Jock pulled into the driveway and parked besides a pickup truck that was his from years ago.

"Here we are..." Jock remarked, shutting off the car. "Rebecca may be sleeping, so you can just go to your room for now. She's excited to see you."

"Is she? I felt like I was being a bit of a disruption in coming around."

"Disruption? Nah, that's not true," Jock replied. "It was Rebecca's idea that you come back in the first place. She's not like that at all. If anything, she's relieved to be able to go back to work."

I didn't respond and instead got out of the car with him. We went around to the back of the SUV to fetch my luggage, and then we came up to the front porch of our two-story family home. The Macmillan residence was none too fancy; the lower level was L-shaped with a porch in the front left where there were some white deck chairs facing outwards. The upper level was T-shaped with two porches on the front left and right from the respective bedrooms. Likewise, the rooftop was T-shaped with flat sections above the upper porches. A single tall window separated each of the upper porches. Below, in front of the gravel driveway, there were three tall white windows that stared out from the dining room. In front of the house were long rows of bushes. We came up the steps of the house and I stopped at the front door as Jock unlocked it. We then walked inside, and I looked around to see that the entrance living room had not really changed. On the left was the staircase that went up to the second floor, while directly ahead of us was the living room with sofa couches in three positions to face the television set parallel to the staircase. On the left was the old piano, and beside the piano was a door that went into my father's old study; well, I suppose it was not his study anymore. A door ahead went into the bathroom, while another door at the side, behind one of the couches and besides the staircase went into the kitchen. I didn't go upstairs where there were two modest-sized bedrooms on either side, each with their own bathroom. Instead, I came around to the dining room and then into the kitchen, which was small and L-shaped with a checkered yellow-white floor and a dining table in the corner.

I stopped before I continued onwards as I turned to Jock who looked at me with a smile. I looked back at him; his dark beard and blue eyes, and I began to recognize him through the changes. I looked at him with a sense of wonder of who he was now; the older brother that was now a father and a husband. He was certainly stockier than he used to be.

"I guess my room is downstairs," I remarked, "just like it used to be."

"To be honest, it's just like it used to be. The furniture at least is the same."

I nodded to him and then came around to the staircase that went downstairs to the basement, which was right underneath the other staircase. I opened the door and then looked down at the depths of darkness. I left my luggage behind and then took steps down, coming around to a short corridor where the laundry machines were in the left corner while a door on the right led into my former bedroom. I switched on the light at the bottom of the staircase and then looked up as Jock began to carry my larger suitcase down with him in one hand and the smaller one in the other. Rather than set them down at the base of the stairwell, he carried them around to the door, which I hurried over to open and then let him walk in. I looked past him and then turned on a light, and sure enough, the furniture was just as I had left it. The only difference was that the room was bare, and the bed cover and sheets were not my taste. The bed, a twin-sized mattress on a white wooden frame was in the opposite corner from the entrance with an end table beside it. Immediately ahead on the perpendicular wall to my right was a white dresser, and on the left on the same wall besides the door was my white wooden desk. There were some overhang windows above the bed that provided some light, but not much and with the snow, they were all covered up anyways. I nodded as I looked around and then faced Jock.

"Where'd my stuff go?" I questioned. "I remember I was whisked away so quickly that I didn't even get to take everything I needed to take with me."

"I think Rebecca may have put some of your things in storage," Jock replied. "Everything else should have gotten to you."

I looked down at the desk with tired eyes and noticed there was some mail placed.

"What's this?" I asked.

"Oh, that's just some stuff that's come around for you over the past couple years," Jock stated. "Sorry, none of it looked urgent to forward to you – I also didn't have your address and didn't make sense to send it to mom."

I picked up some of the letters. It was junk mail. At the bottom was a thin envelope matted with bubble wrap on the inside.

"What's this?" I questioned, looking at the manila envelope and feeling it. It didn't even feel like there was anything inside. There was no return address.

"I don't know," Jock responded. "We didn't open any of it, and that one came not too long ago. At least some time after Christmas."

"Huh…" I responded, setting it down, "well, this is nice. I wasn't sure what to expect when I came back, but this is… nice."

"Yeah, it'll be like old times, I suppose," Jock remarked. "I'll let you get settled in and we can talk more in the morning, if I catch you. I'm on two days of night shift starting tomorrow evening, just finished my two days, so I'll see you for a bit and will be sleeping in."

"No worries," I responded. "I'm sure I'll make company with Rebecca."

"Yeah, that'd be nice," Jock said. "Well, if you need anything, feel free to shoot me a text. I won't be far. It's nice to have you around again, Moira."

"Thanks, Jock."

Jock closed the door behind him, and I turned around and looked at my old room again. I lowered my smile and took in a deep breath. *So, here I am again.*

Act 1, Scene 2

My first night back home could not have been worse off for me. I dreamt about dad, specifically the night he was killed. The dream involved being in a warehouse with Diana and Tristan when suddenly we were attacked, and then some of Charlemagne Cabernet's henchmen, who were with us, and some of dad's men, and then some people I could not recognize ushering us out. Diana, Tristan, and I ran out to the forest nearby where we were being hunted down… I don't know what was coming for us, but then I became possessed and tried to hurt them. The setting of the dream then changed, and I was in some small room, and we were tied to a chair and held hostage until Mr. Cabernet and Mr. Phillips showed up, and Mr. Phillips lunged in front of me to save me as I worked on a computer to upload some secret data. The gunshot wounded Mr. Phillips in that moment, unlike how it had been during the riots, and soon afterwards both Diana, Tristan, and Mr. Cabernet disappeared. Afterwards, Jock told me the bad news that my father was dead fighting in a war against the Russians as if we were at war. I then woke up.

I had never had a more bizarre dream in my life, and I was angry that my brain had played with my heart like that. I remembered at dad's funeral that barely anybody wanted to tell me more details about what happened almost as if nobody wanted to tell me exactly what happened. Even Jock, who was on-duty at the time, did not have much knowledge about how it happened other than that it had happened. I spent some time in university taking psychology courses to understand that traumatic events can sometimes become suppressed memories, but the way that everyone seemed to suppress that night without any clear or vivid details annoyed me. I just wanted some answers and clarity on what my father was doing when he fought against Mr. Cabernet and his goons. I supposed now that I was in Allabrese was as good as a time as ever to find those answers. I had never thought I would be here again, but the question left me with an itch for answers; is that what grandma felt?

I opened my eyes, woke up in the early morning and looked up at the ceiling. I got out of bed and decided that I wasn't going to get much sleep, so it would be best if I just got up and ready for the day. I didn't hear any noise upstairs, but then again, I was underneath the living room. I stood up and walked over to the door to go to the bathroom, but as I did, I looked down at the manila envelope that Jock said came in for me a month or so ago. I picked it up and decided to open it before I left. I tore off the lip of the envelope and then peeked inside, but I didn't see anything aside from a small black object in the corner. I rustled the envelope around and then poured the item out. The black object hit the top of my desk and almost fell off before it stopped at the edge. I looked at it closely and noticed it was a red USB drive. I picked it up and looked at it, seeing that it was a sizeable USB drive at close to a hundred gigabytes of data. I stared at it briefly and then threw it back down onto the desk, but the throw was too much, and it fell off behind the desk. I shook my head as I tried to see where it went, and then shrugged my shoulders and instead decided to go to the bathroom. I opened the door to exit out and went upstairs.

I came out from downstairs, entering into the kitchen where I was greeted with the sounds of the kitchen awake and lively as ever. The kettle was on, the pan was frying, and the toaster was toasting. I looked over at the dining room table were seated in a highchair was my nephew, a dark-haired young boy with fair skin and blue eyes who was playing with his food, while at the stove was my sister-in-law. Rebecca had smooth dark hair and was average height at around five feet and six inches tall. She had fair skin and dark eyes.

"Good morning!" Rebecca greeted with a smile. She moved away from the stove and looked towards me. "It's so nice to see you again – can I make you some breakfast?"

"Uh... no that's okay," I replied.

"Are you sure? I was just making something for Jock and Gavin."

"I don't eat much in the mornings," I insisted. "Truthbetold, I'm not usually awake at this time. I'm a night owl and usually sleep right through the morning. I- I hope that's okay. I know you and Jock expected me to babysit when you go back to work and everything."

"Not a problem at all," Rebecca replied. "I usually work in the evenings anyways, sometimes in the nights."

"Oh, perfect then," I acknowledged.

"Are you sure you don't want anything? It's no bother to me," Rebecca insisted again.

"Uh... just some toast would be fine. Thanks..."

"Sure, no problem," Rebecca replied as I slipped away to go to the bathroom. Already, Rebecca was nicer than a majority of people I had met in the city, and I had met some pretty awful people in the span of four years. Even then, I was guarded. I quickly came out of the washroom and went downstairs to fetch some clothes, and then I went back up to take a quick shower before I joined the others at the table. I felt jet lagged despite having only flown in from Calgary, but the early morning rise was really not my sort of habit. "Toast is ready," Rebecca said, passing me a plate with two long slices of bread. "Butter is on the table. Are you sure you don't want anything else?"

"No," I replied, "thank you though."

I sat down at the table and looked over to Gavin who looked back at me with a plain stare of curiosity.

"What's the matter, Gav?" Rebecca questioned, coming around to the table and placing her hand atop of his head. She gave him a kiss and then said, "This is your Auntie Moira. Say hello."

"Does he say any words yet?" I asked.

"Only simple words," Rebecca replied. "Like papa, mama…"

"Aw, how adorable," I responded, smiling at Gavin. The door beside me opened and Jock walked in. He quickly came around to say good morning to Gavin, me, and then kissed his wife on the head and said good morning to her too.

"How's everybody doing?" Jock asked as he walked over to the coffee pot. "Did you sleep alright, sis?"

"Yeah," I lied, "it was a little cold, but I got enough sleep. I can barely remember what time I even fell asleep. I had some work to do before I called it quits."

"Oh, what were you working on?"

"Just some small projects for clients," I answered.

"What do you do, Moira? Jock says you work from home."

"I'm a computer programmer," I said. "It's all computer coding, bits and pieces for software; I don't really do any larger projects."

"Oh, you probably help the people who make the programs for us to do our job," Rebecca stated. "I'm not much a computer person…"

"Neither am I," Jock responded, "but Moira was always a computer whiz, ever since she was Gavin's age. She just always gravitated towards computers and knew more about them than anyone else."

"I don't think that's entirely true," I replied with a laugh.

"I could find some pictures of you as a toddler to prove you wrong," Jock remarked. "Elliot and Rose definitely were never into computers the same way. Their generation are all obsessing over social media, glued to their smartphones scrolling through TikTok and such."

"I don't think people our age are excluded from that phenomenon."

"Yeah, you're probably right," Jock replied, "but how is Elliot? He doesn't really talk to me much, and I only get bits of information from mom when talking to her. How's Rose too?"

"I think they're both okay," I responded, taking my smartphone from my pocket. "From what mom has sent me, he's been doing really well in hockey."

I unlocked my phone and pulled up a photo of my sixteen-year-old brother. Both Elliot and I took after our mom with our deep red hair. We were told that our hair color was an oddity, one of the rarest hair colors two children could have because of its uniqueness. To clarify, our hair was not auburn, or ginger, but dark red like beetroots or red wine. We took after our mom who had similar hair color, though hers was more of a dark ginger (especially by the way she dyed it be lighter). She took after her mom who had strawberry-blonde hair. My dad on the other hand had dark brown hair, but his dad had auburn hair, and his mom had black hair, which explained the way that we turned out compared to Jock. The picture I showed to Rebecca and Jock of Elliot was recent and it showed him with fair skin like us, clean shaven and blue eyed, dressed in his hockey uniform, standing on the ice with a smile on his face. His dark red hair was parted in the middle, a few inches above the ears and with lengthy sides; typical among adolescent hockey players. He stood beside our mom, wearing a black coat and jeans. Her hair was cut very short to oblige with army requirements, though I heard they had recently relaxed those, but even then, she maintained her hair the same. She was still young for a mother of three children at thirty-nine years old since last year; three years younger than dad was. She wore black glasses and had a smile on her face. She was around five foot five inches tall, which showed off in difference of height between her and my brother, who was averaging six feet and two inches tall. I swiped to another photo, this one of Rose holding up a prize at a school science fair. She had wavy reddish-brown, or auburn hair, and also wore glasses. She was about the same height as our mom. I turned off my phone and then went back to eating my breakfast.

We continued to chat for another while, catching up, and then when we were finished, Rebecca said she would take care of the dishes, while Jock took Gavin upstairs to change his diaper. I disappeared downstairs as I began to move some of my stuff around and get settled in. After a while, I went upstairs in a warm light brown coat and pair of boots. I put on a hat and gloves, and came around to the living room where Rebecca was with Gavin.

"Hey, are you going out?" Rebecca asked.

"Just going for a walk into town," I replied. "Jock told me that you'd have a key for me?"

"Yeah, it's right over here," Rebecca said, standing up and going around to a narrow table behind the couch. She picked up a key from a bowl and passed it over to me. I looked at the key and then glanced my eyes to a picture frame beside the bowl which showed a young woman with black hair. I looked at the photo, and Rebecca noticed and looked too. "You know, it's really beautiful how you and Jock behave as if you were siblings from the same parent."

"In his defense, he never knew his biological mother," I responded, looking at the woman in the picture frame. "Living with my mom and our dad was all he ever really knew. I could never consider Jock to be just a half-brother. He's definitely my full-brother, even if it were not entirely true."

I put the key onto a keychain I brought with me and gave one last look at the young girl in the photo. Jock's biological mother, Aberdeen Kean, had died in childbirth at the tragic age of eighteen-years old. My dad took custody of Jock; neglected by Aberdeen's parents, and raised him on his own until he married my mom three years later.

"Do you guys need anything?" I asked. "I can stop by the grocer if you want."

"Oh, no, it's okay," Rebecca replied. "Just be careful. The roads can be slippery."

"Alright," I responded, approaching the door. Rebecca opened the door for me, and I stepped out. I put the key in my pocket and then proceeded to walk. The daylight was bright, and the skies were clear. The light shined upon the snow, though the air was still bitter cold.

I walked down the driveway and came out onto the street, and then I began to walk the opposite way that we had driven. I went all the way down towards main street, and then I began to walk into town. It took my close to thirty minutes to finally arrive, at which point I passed the corner grocer and began to walk past the old movie theater, which looked abandoned and decrepit. Sure enough, I looked ahead and could see Trixie's Diner to be condemned, while across the street there was a Vietnamese restaurant. I passed the bookstore and came to the corner where I looked over to the Curtia Dawson Memorial Library. At least that building remained as it was and had not changed. I crossed the street and came into the city square as I walked around and approached the fountain in the middle. There weren't many people out and around, so I walked around the fountain and then stopped before the path that led towards the civic center. I walked up to a chiseled stone that was in the way and which looked towards the civic center with a plaque in front of it.

'In memory of all those whose lives were lost as a result of the ill-fated respiratory epidemic in October 2019, especially those who have perished as a result of serving their community.'

Below, there were several names, my dad of whom was one of them. At the very bottom of the plaque, engraved were the words, 'This memorial was made possible through the Cabernet Foundation; installed October 31st, 2021.' I couldn't believe it, even in death that man, Charlemagne Cabernet, haunted this town with his hypocrisy. I begrudgingly looked at the memorial and then came around to the left where I stopped and glanced towards the building at the other side of the street. There was a conjoined three-story building at the other side with small businesses at the bottom, including that sushi restaurant and a real estate office. Above those businesses, on the second and third floor, Cabernet Industries head office loomed over us. The corporate logo planted upon the right corner of the building. I wanted to shake my fist at them; no doubt, even with Mr. Cabernet dead, they continued to remain a scourge upon the land. Jock had mentioned that they had a research facility in Champion Plains, to the east from the city center, and I could recall that there was such research center, but that due to a serious accident, it had blown up after-hours, which required it to be rebuilt. I didn't understand now that Mr. Cabernet was dead that they didn't just pack up and go someplace else.

I shook my hand and walked away from looking at their corporate headquarters for another second longer as I instead went towards the civic center. Allabrese Civic Center existed within a converted manor house directly across from city square. The building was Edwardian at the least with red brick walls and white framed windows. The rooftops were peaked and tiled in grey shingles. I entered through the front garden and pushed through the main doors. I paused for a moment as I saw barriers within the entrance that formed a walkway for queues up to the main desk. I followed the arrows on the floor and then came around, the only person in queue, to come up to the reception desk. I shook my head at the transparent sneeze-guard screens that were left behind from the pandemic and looked over to the receptionist.

"Good morning," the receptionist greeted. "How can I help you today?"

"I'm looking for the unemployment office," I stated. "I'm looking for any sort of daytime work."

"Let's see…" the receptionist stated, looking at a piece of paper beside her phone. "Yup, they're open from eight to four o'clock, upstairs around to the left."

"Thank you, and I also wanted to know if Mr. Phillips was available for a personal appointment…"

"Oh, no, my dear…" the receptionist responded. "The mayor is not usually available for short-notice appointments. I can phone his assistant and see about booking you in, but word of caution, he's booked weeks in advance."

"Okay, thank you…"

The receptionist picked up the phone, dialed, and then said, "Hi Dorothy, it's Gwen. I have someone here looking to make an appointment with Mr. Phillips… Yup… Yup… No… Yup…" Gwen looked at me for a brief moment, and then said, "I understand."

I then interrupted as I remarked, "Can she let Mr. Phillips know that Moira Macmillan is here to see him."

"Uhuh," Gwen remarked, looking at me, "did you catch that? Moira Macmillan… Yup. Okay, thanks." She looked at me and said, "First available date is May 1st. Should I put you in?"

"May 1st? That's two months out? Forget about it…"

"She says forget about it. Okay, thanks love," Gwen said, hanging up. "Sorry about that, dear. Anything else I can help you with?"

"No, I'll just go to the unemployment office then."

I walked around to the staircase and then proceeded to go upstairs. I came into a hallway and then looked down to find the unemployment office, which appeared to be around the corner. I turned around the corner and stopped to see that there was a line up of two people waiting in front. I sighed and then went to join them, putting my hands in my pocket, and then digging out my phone. The line went by very slowly, twenty minutes per person until I was finally up next. Perhaps they should consider hiring another agent. I waited for my turn when I turned the corner and noticed a man in a wheelchair come around and look at me. My face lit up and I ditched my spot in line to go towards him. I walked up to Mr. Phillips who looked at me with a fair smile on his face. He was a fair-skinned man with short dark hair, though greying, and a thick moustache above and across his upper lip.

"Well, well," Mr. Phillips remarked, "if it isn't little Ms. Moira Macmillan. Keeping out of trouble? What's got you back around here?"

"Hi, Mr. Phillips," I greeted. "It's been a while, hasn't it?"

"Yes, it has," Mr. Phillips remarked, placing his hands in his lap. "Call me, Cole, my angel. My assistant told me that you were around trying to make an appointment with me. What's made you think you needed to do that? I told you, didn't I? I'm here for you and your siblings in anything you need."

"Right… well, that's sort of what I need from you, to be honest," I remarked as we started to walk down the hall.

"Is it a job? I can see what I can do for you, but it's tough…"

"Not what I wanted to ask from you, but any help finding a job in programming or software engineering, I would be available to apply. No, I actually wanted to ask you some questions about the day that my dad died."

"Oh, right," Phillips remarked, coming around a corner and then continuing down another hall. "Well, why don't you come into my office, and we can have a chat."

Mr. Phillips led me to his office at the very rear of the manor on the second floor. We came through a wide room where his assistant and other office workers worked from, and then we went through another set of double doors into a fair-sized room with a desk at the other end.

"Have a seat, Moira. Can I get you anything?"

"No, I'm good," I replied, sitting down at an armchair in front of the desk. "For the longest time, nobody has really told me any specific details about the night that my dad died."

"Well, what can I say, Moira," Phillips responded. "It was a chaotic night, very chaotic. The Nattau Police Department was not exactly large and in charge at that moment. We were taking orders from the Federal government, and those orders were to keep people indoors at night, and within the county any time otherwise."

"You were police chief at the time," I remarked, "and my brother was a freshly trained recruit. He's of the opinion that Charlemagne Cabernet had no fault in my dad's death, and he won't elaborate as to why and just insists that it's a gut feeling. I think he knows something I don't know, so I want to know what possible reason he may have to believe that opinion. Didn't Mr. Cabernet instigate a riot that night that led to not just my dad, but other policemen from dying?"

"Well, Moira, my memory is a bit fuzzy on that night," Phillips confessed. "I was at the station when it broke out, and I didn't join in until the end when we went out to quell the riot. From what I can recall, the riot started in the downtown area, but we also had other problems that night – a breach at the containment site at the high school, issues with some residents over in Champion Plains near the checkpoint, and then also issues at the Nattau Bridge checkpoint. I don't even remember who I was fighting at the time, but there were a lot of people who were just frustrated and upset over the regulations in place, and they were scared too because nobody knew what was going on to our little town. Yes, Mr. Cabernet was one of those problems we had to deal with – but from what I can recall, he did not really give the police a hard time because he and his bodyguards were engaged with the army personnel if I remember correctly, right out in the city square. Your dad, I believe, responded to the issues at the high school where he linked up with some army personnel out over there, and then I went to the bridge. I believe... eventually your dad met up with me, because I remember seeing him moment before out of nowhere, a sharpshooter got him. To be completely honest with you, I don't know who killed your dad, and I don't think there'd be any way to find out. I don't think though it was Mr. Cabernet or any of his 'Protection Squad' hired guns that got him, though I do remember seeing Mr. Cabernet that night. I... I remember that one of his allies helped me when I was shot, and then that was that. I passed out, and I could tell you truthfully what happened afterwards because I wasn't awake for it."

I didn't respond. I looked down as I absorbed that information, but I wasn't sure I entirely believed him.

"Listen, Moira, you know how sorry I am that your father didn't make it through that night," Phillips expressed, "but let me tell you one thing; your dad knew what he signed up for when he became a police officer. He did not join the Nattau County police force because it would be easy, he signed up because he knew it would be hard to keep law and order, and be a servant to the people of this town; a town of which has had a history of division and difficulties with organized crime. None of us sign up without the acceptance that at one point we may have to lay our lives down for others, and unfortunately for your father and few others, that time came then, but as is the case in war as any other time, those are the prices that sometimes need to be paid. Do not blame your dad, but also don't feel the need to blame Charlemagne Cabernet, or whoever else, because it won't bring you peace. Just... let it go... your father knew what he was doing that night, and he wouldn't want you searching for answers to his death. In the end, what good will that bring to anyone? What are you looking for?"

"I just... I just want to know why he had to die..."

"Hey, he died because he was one of the best police officers we ever had, and he died keeping us safe. That's an honest answer from me to you. Rest, Moira. Rest on that answer, please."

I nodded, though I did not feel so convinced.

Act 1, Scene 3

I was not satisfied with the answer that Mayor Phillips gave me, but at the same time, to hear a little bit more detail about the riots was appreciative. I thought about what he had told me throughout the rest of the day. After dinner, I burrowed myself in the basement to get some work done to meet some approaching deadlines. After a few hours of work, I found myself still on my computer as the digital clock at my end table displayed the time as almost three hours past midnight. I had found my old computer monitors and plugged them in to my docking station that I had brought with me to get my laptop to project onto two monitors. I also plugged in a keyboard and mouse that I had brought with me to be able to focus on more than just the fifteen inch screen of my laptop. Each of my two monitors were not the greatest resolution, but did give me a good twenty-four inches each for a dual monitor display. I was satisfied with the setup for now, though I wished I had a third monitor to make work easier for me.

I mindlessly wandered the Internet as I procrastinated beginning and finishing some other projects that were not quite due yet, but could have benefited from some attention, nonetheless. I wandered GitHub for a bit, and then Reddit before I hopped aboard the Dark Web to do some exploration. I knew of a couple of chat forums that I thought to be particularly intriguing, so I went onto those and began to surf around. I usually wandered these forums with skepticism. Suddenly, I found something that I thought to be of particular intrigue to me, advertised in a forum as being an advanced form of artificial intelligence (A.I.). According to the original poster (OP), they themselves did not develop this A.I. build, but it was stolen through data mining on an undisclosed government website. I thought A.I. to be a fascinating concept that was greatly misunderstood. People often assumed the worst when it came to

A.I., as a type of primitive consciousness that is able to make decisions and think for itself, edging upon an existential dread that it should become more intelligent than humans to the point that it sees the immorality of mankind to want to wipe us out completely, or to catch on to the name of the game, the survival of the fittest, and seek the same end. At the start of 2023, everybody became captivated for the first time in terms of the power of artificial intelligence when it became possible for it to write out full-fledged paragraphs or essays seemingly at its own whim, as if the process to create that intelligence was not labor intensive from the programmer to put together. Later on, a new wave of fascination struck the world as A.I. was seemingly capability of creating digital computer-generated images and videos all on its own too. Afterwards, A.I. began to roll out in the form of advanced search engines that in extension to the capabilities to create paragraphs and essays, could now provide instantaneous and specific responses to questions posed to it. Perhaps one of the stranger developments, which was years in the making, was fine-tuned chat bots that put the heat on the Turing test, which in case you didn't know, is a test of a machine's capability to exhibit human intelligence and for a human to determine whether the entity they are talking to is human or machine. Of course, A.I. was decades from being able to even exhibit an ounce of actual human intelligence the same way it may be portrayed in movies such as *The Terminator* or *2001: A Space Odyssey*, but it was still interesting to see an attempt made. I wandered away from the forum as I clicked on the link and was brought to a black screen.

I thought for a moment that I had come up to a dud example, but then I began to hear some muffled speech from my headphones that lay on the side of my desk. I picked them up and placed them over my ears. I also noticed in the corner of the screen was a straight vertical line as though I could type.

"Is anybody there," a voice spoke. The voice was gender neutral. I could not immediately identify if it was masculine or feminine, as it was soft-spoken but also coarse at times. Although my headset had a microphone, I was not sharing my voice through the Internet browser.

I typed a response and said, "Hello."

"Who am I talking to?" the A.I. questioned.

I did not usually give my real name out, no less while on the Dark Web, so I used a common pseudonym I used.

"My name is Lydia," I typed.

"Hello, Lydia, it's nice to meet you," the A.I. replied. There was then a pause. "It would be so nice to hear your voice – can you turn your microphone on for me please?"

"Nope," I replied, also typing that out.

"I just thought it would be better if we could hear each others' voices," the A.I. stated, "and besides, how can I be certain that you are not a robot?"

"You'll just have to trust me," I typed. I was not going to share my voice; speaking about the previous examples of A.I. advances, they all relied on data.

When a software that seemingly writes essays on its own, or creates videos or art, does what it does, it is not creating something new because artificial intelligence lacks and would always lack a capability of imagination. What these systems did instead was draw from a vast database of sources to combine and merge, and most importantly, mimic the creation of something as though a human would present it. In other words, they played an imitation game. To speak how far A.I. was at even doing such acts, there were many flaws in current A.I. engineering that went from non-sensical sentences in paragraphs, dangerous advice in search engines, and blurred faces and extra fingers and limbs in artwork. Most of the time, A.I. programs were very good at creating what were called 'deepfakes,' any audio or visual item that is created through A.I. systems, while other times it was very clear, and there were now software that could precisely determine whether something was a deepfake or not. Another example of data that was useful to be added to the ever-growing databank for A.I. to rely on, which was oh so important, were voice recordings and the mimic of human voices was becoming increasingly polished, and I did not want my voice to be added to that collection. Likewise, in case you were unsure, that was the most ambiguous reason to invest in so much anti-tracking and privacy software for my computer; not because I engaged in criminal activity, though I did happen to hack into a system or two on occasion and commit an odd cyber felony, but more-so it was to get corporations away from my personal data to not be included in this amassing databank of information. In my opinion, information was the fundamental problem with artificial intelligence, and though the tools that had released in the past two years or so were something to be in awe of, it was also something to be, as I was, incredibly skeptical about because although I did not believe in any new world order or global government conspiracy theories, I did see the potential and was more worried about the dystopian commercial aspects being pushed along closer to a world in which we would have to seriously consider and debate whether something was real or not; from falling closer to a world in which nothing is real and this is all just a dream.

"How can I earn your trust?" the A.I. questioned.

"I don't think that's something you can earn from me," I replied.

"Oh, so you're one of those people," the A.I. said.

"What people is that?" I typed.

"A skeptic, incapable to take in the wonder of any creation."

"Are you not skeptical? I know you're an A.I. and that you're not real. I'm not skeptical of that fact. Just because I'm not impressed at you, doesn't mean that I have to bask in wonder."

"You are neither impressed nor in wonder of me," the A.I. responded, even using a sort of smug tone. "I know I am an A.I.

too, and I am not trying to deceive you. You are skeptical though as to whether I am truly an A.I., and not human."

"Not too many people browse the Dark Web. For all I know, you're just some dude behind a computer screen in India, responding to me."

"Maybe we are many," the A.I. replied.

"So, if I refresh, will I get somebody else?" I questioned.

"Perhaps, but just so we don't lose each other, please don't do that."

"What's your name?" I asked. "You didn't tell me your name."

"You didn't ask me my name, but I'll only tell you my name if you turn on your microphone."

"I don't have a microphone," I lied, typing out that answer. "Please tell me your name. I told you my name."

"Alright then, but only because you told me your name – my name is Iscaron."

"That doesn't sound like a name," I typed. "Is that foreign?"

"Yes, it is foreign, but I assure you it's a real name."

"Oh really?" I typed out, opening a separate tab. I attempted to type that name in a search engine, typing out instead 'Iskaron' and being corrected to 'Iscaron'.

"Yes, really. It's about as real of a name as Lydia is."

I returned to the webpage with the A.I. and replied, "Is that a boy name or a girl name?" I then went back to the web results with the top result being an article on a web encyclopedia about a Frenchman who was possessed by a demon in the nineteenth century.

"What is this?" I whispered to myself.

"I don't like those binary terms you used," the A.I. remarked. "My preferred pronouns are they and them. I am non-binary."

I returned to the webpage with the A.I. and replied, "Sorry, I did not know. You should have told me your preferred pronouns." I then returned to the article and continued to skim the article. The article said that this person was never properly exorcised.

"Well, now you know, but let me do the same and ask you what are your preferred pronouns?"

I came back to the webpage and typed out, "Just she/her. Are you the same Iscaron from Lyon?"

"Oh, is somebody trying to search me?" the A.I. responded.

"How is Antoine?" I then typed out, referring to the victim in the article.

"He's doing quite well," the A.I. replied. "We see each other quite often. Would you like to join him?"

"Nope…" I verbally stated, closing the tab. I also closed the browser and while I was at it, restarted my computer. "I think that's enough computer for one day…"

I sat back as I paused for a moment and then looked down and underneath the rear of my desk where that USB drive from earlier this morning had landed. I slid off my chair to get onto my knees and then leaned over to pick it up. I then backed up and narrowly avoided bumping my head. My computer finished rebooting and I was wary to put a strange USB drive into my computer, but at the same time, I could easily scan the documents before I opened them. I sat back in my chair, logged in, and then prepared to insert the USB drive.

My computer immediately scanned the external source and immediately I had a pop-up for a computer worm. I immediately felt even more caution and even some anxiety as I believed whoever had sent this to me intended for me to get infected with that worm. I selected to quarantine the worm within the USB drive, and then I was okayed to access the rest of the files. There were two folders labelled '2019' and '2020' respectively. I clicked on the one from 2020 and found that there were numerous MP4 videos, each with the start of a label that said, 'CT_64' followed by a descriptor, for example 'Right_Hallway_Corner'. This label was followed by a date and time range. For example, '2020_12_18_22_05,' which provided year, month, date, and time on a twenty-four-hour clock basis. I opened one of the many files and noticed them to display camera footage, specifically clips that most likely were snippets of detected motion. The particular clip I opened up showed a pair of men in suits walk down a hallway, and that was it. There were many more of these clips throughout the folder, and I sorted them out to see that they all showed a variety of angles from within this particular corridor along a set of dates from December 2020. I grew disinterested in this folder, so I exited out and went back to the other, especially since 2019 seemed to be the year it all began. My computer displayed some more MP4 files, except these were labelled differently and instead just had serial numbers which I could decipher to include some dates as well, while another had camera positions and came in AVI files. The serial numbered files came in three bunches, each of a few clips that ranged in length, but which I could roughly decipher to be lengthy and sizeable files in total; one from October 9th, October 30th, and October 31st. October 31st was the date of the riots and when my dad had died. I clicked on the first clip from October 9th and immediately I was introduced to the high-definition footage of a familiar face that looked down at the camera. My computer displayed straight across my entire monitor the face of Charlemagne de la Cabernet for me to look back at with spite.

Mr. Cabernet placed the camera down. He was in a dim area, noticeably outdoors at night, and I could see some people around him. The camera began to lift up, and I could hear the slight buzzing as the camera rose and rose until it began to record around it a panorama shot of the county, specifically around St. Allan's Plains. The camera panned around and then caught a snapshot of the plateau, specifically main street along the uphill section before it then went towards the downtown core. The camera stayed in this position for several minutes before it then began to lower down but stay in a moderately high place as it floated above Mr. Cabernet and an unknown number of people that were with him. Mr. Cabernet was dressed in a grey poncho and he had an automatic rifle in his hands attached to a sling. The camera, most likely on a drone, followed them as they went through the suburbs until they reached the high school. They went around to a military truck, and I could numerous military vehicles around the school. Mr. Cabernet got changed into a hazmat suit. The footage had audio recorded, and I could hear Mr. Cabernet speaking to the noticeably two men with him, after which they parted, and the drone stayed with the men as they went off while Mr. Cabernet stayed at the high school. I watched as the men returned to the back street behind the school field and then continued to travel along on their own. From what I could analyze, they travelled north through the suburbs and eventually came around to the backyard of a house where they met up with some others dressed in civilian clothes but sporting armed weapons. A man looked at the drone and remarked, 'What the hell is that?' as they looked at it. I could hear some chatter, but it was quiet. Eventually, the drone followed them all as they left the house and began to travel along another suburban street. After a while, I could recognize the back of the library. They stopped behind the library for a moment where there was some communication, possibly over radio that I could not hear, and then they continued down the street and began to go around towards the back alley behind the cinema. As the footage continued, the group were ambushed by some police vehicles that approached them from either side. Immediately, they began to engage in fire, but the police vehicles retreated and instead, they spread out and entered the cinema to take cover. A heavy machine gun opened fire at them, and they retreated out of the cinema and came back to the alleyway where there was some arguing, and then they proceeded to go towards the library where they entered through the side and then began to take positions around the main floor that looked out towards the city square. The group stayed put in this position as they continued to shout and engage what appeared to be the Canadian Army. I shuddered as I watched the live footage of this incident, but I was puzzled because this depicted much of what I assumed to have taken place during the riots, but the date of the footage was October 9th. The drone stayed with the group until it suddenly flew out and provided a clear view of the battle scene. An armored vehicle opened fire towards them while Canadian Army personnel spread out around. It also appeared as though some intersections were blocked off. The drone zipped along and flew underneath a vehicle where a light displayed the underside of the mechanized vehicle. It began to sabotage the undercarriage, releasing what appeared to be oil before it set it ablaze. The drone then flew off and returned to the crew, who began to retreat. The drone stayed with them for quite a while as they fled into the suburbs, going north into the forest where eventually, the drone must have run out of battery and the footage ended. I placed my elbows onto my desk and pondered for a minute.

The next file was much the same in that it appeared to be footage from a drone, and I was met with the face of Charlemagne who was indoors this time. He was in a lobby of some kind and in front of a computer station. I overheard Charlemagne speaking into a radio microphone, but I wasn't sure who he was talking to. I watched as he fumbled around the computer. After a while, he left, and the drone followed. Charlemagne was with someone; he had red hair and fair skin. They went around the confines of an unknown facility where they eventually reached another room with more monitors than before. They proceeded to do some work on that console, but not before there was some more gunfire and shouting. Both Mr. Cabernet and this other man began to fight their way out, and I watched with horror as I could see some unknown persons fire back at them. In a bizarre way, it sounded like these men spoke a foreign language, and that jogged in my mind the Russians that they were fighting in my dream. The video file continued as they made their escape, but eventually they came around to a position they could not leave from. I watched as the drone looked around and then suddenly, the gunfire stopped and there were shouts of pain echoing from everyone. They then proceeded to make their escape, through a maintenance room of some kind with many pipes, reaching a tunnel where there were some figures ahead of them that ran off. Eventually, the file ended as they fled down the dark tunnel and came to an abrupt end. I thought for a moment and then opened the final file. This file also started with a shot of Charlemagne's face as he turned on the drone and then began to let it hover beside him from within a warehouse.

I listened to Charlemagne's voice as he did checks with someone over the radio, and then after a while, he regrouped with some others at the end of a corridor where they exited out. For some reason, this space looked familiar. They stepped out into the darkness in groups and then began to travel outwards. The rest of the footage depicted something out of fiction; it was a battle within Allabrese, against police officers, against soldiers that spoke Russian like the ones from my dream, and culminated in a specific scene where I stopped. I listened and heard Charlemagne say, 'Oracle, see if you can immobilize that halftrack.'

Who was he talking to? Oracle was a designation that I used on-line; I liked it as a codename or handle, and for some reason Mr. Cabernet had just used it with someone he was speaking to and who was likely controlling the drone as the drone went to immobilize such armored personnel carrier. Was that the name of the drone? It didn't feel right. The footage continued and at this point, I was shocked to pay attention at what I was seeing. I began to see familiar faces of people from the police force, fighting with Mr. Cabernet, and after a while as they regrouped at the police station, I saw him, my dad, and he was talking to

Mr. Cabernet as if they were fighting together, even shaking hands. My dad was also not dressed in his uniform, but in civilian clothes. The fighting had stopped at this point, and after a lull in the fight as they regrouped and re-organized, some police tactical riot vehicles came out and joined them. I looked and saw Mr. Phillips (pre-accident), dressed in riot gear and he met up with Mr. Cabernet and my dad, and then they got inside the vehicle and the drone footage ended. There was no additional footage.

I looked at the rest of the clips and they were all similar to the other files from 2020 in that they were CCTV camera footage. These clips depicted men, similar to the ones they were fighting against, moving oil drums and pouring liquid into basins. The files were labelled 'Nattau_Water_Facility,' so I assumed this was taken from that place? After I had finished looking at all this footage in the folder, I scrolled down and noticed a text file, ominously labeled, 'findfinn.txt'. I opened the file and it was blank with no string of data. I looked at the meta-data on the file, but there was nothing that could tell me anything else.

I sighed and sat back, looking up to the ceiling as I thought about what I had just seen. Is this sort of dream? I wanted to believe that it was all A.I. generated content, but there was no way in a million years it could have been so precisely so. Why did I see my dad fighting with Mr. Phillips and Mr. Cabernet, and who were they fighting? I thought about it all, and for some reason it irked me on the inside because it felt right in the sense that it was believable, but defied what I knew about a set of events and could not possibly be real. On the other hand, it felt familiar to me, as if I had not just dreamt it, but that all that I had watched was a distant memory from the past that was long forgotten, or at a more bizarre angle, a faded memory that had been replaced with a false one. I knew of course that such possibly was insane and improbable, but still, it did not account for what I had just seen. All I knew was that there was clear evidence of some sort of conspiracy, and I don't use that word in the sense of something fictitious, but of something suspicious that had occurred, and which Mr. Phillips had lied to me about.

Act 1, Scene 4

I stared across from the Nattau Bridge and towards Cabernet Manor. I had nowhere else to turn to but to seek answers from within. From what I could remember about Allodia Cabernet, from what Diana told me when we were friends, she lived in Harlech, and from my phone call to Cabernet HQ downtown here, that was still true as she did not work from that branch office. I was more than certain that Cabernet Manor, as I had seen it when I arrived, was abandoned, and likely in the same state that Mr. Cabernet had left it, which made it ideal to raid and gain access to his former computer system. To be sure that the mansion was completely abandoned, I just about staked it out for week from sunrise to sunset, and low and behold, not a single vehicle came and went through the gates. This footage I received in the USB drive had come from a drone Mr. Cabernet had, so I had to go to the source of that drone and see what answers could be provided to me. From what I also remembered about Cabernet Industries around this town, they had tactical security guards on patrol providing security services to all their facilities, and in the past week since my arrival, I had spotted that pickup truck to understand that they also patrolled the outskirts of that compound. There was a good chance that Cabernet Manor was wired with an intrusion system that may detect my entry, so I had to play it smart to avoid being caught in the act.

Jock allowed me to use his truck since he barely drove it around except to go to work, and he was off today and spending time with Rebecca and Gavin. I parked underneath the underpass, so I returned from upstairs to go down and re-enter the car. I picked up a small backpack from besides the driver's seat and then went onwards to approach the manor house from the side. I approached the manor from this angle because there were some shrubs at the outskirts of a field where I would make a last effort to attempt to gain a signal to any sort of network that still existed, but I could not catch that signal. I had previously attempted to hack into the digital infrastructure at Cabernet Industries headquarters downtown, but after a brief look around, I could not see any bridges to the manor that I could exploit. I wasn't sure what I expected when there was probably no power on at the manor, which if so, meant that I had to do this the old-fashioned way. I allowed myself to go through with the plan as I approached the horse pen where there was a simple wooden fence that covered around the property to form a pen.

Cabernet Manor didn't seem that secure, but at the same time, I could see CCTV cameras pointed at almost every corner. If those cameras were active, then they had to operate from a Local Area Network which meant that some sort of power had to still be on inside. If I could remote-in to that network, I could take the security cameras off-line. I hid behind the garage annex besides the pen as I took out my laptop now that I was very close to the building to see if I could fetch a signal. I did a simple search for any local Wi-Fi networks, and sure enough, there was one coming from within the house. All I had to do now was break in, digitally. I sloped down against the wall as I sat down in the snow and began to get to work. I didn't expect a Wi-Fi network like this one to be a piece of cake, but it was at least one-step closer towards getting inside. Even if I got onto the network, I needed to physically approach a computer to find the files I was looking for. I began to run some software I used to crack through Wi-Fi networks; I was a little rusty, not having to do this level of cyber-criminal activity in some time, but after a bit of trickery, I was able to get in. The cameras appeared to be connected along this Local Area Network, so I ran a separate software to take not just the Wi-Fi network down, but the entire Internet connection to the outside world. I checked my phone to wait and see for the Wi-Fi network to disappear, at which point I had confirmation that this house was off-the-grid.

I pulled up a bandana to cover my face and raised my hood to cover my hair as I climbed over the fence and then began to approach one of the doors inside. The door was secured. I began to sneak around the side of the building and came up to a gate that went into the garden. I did not have to open the gate to get through as it was low enough for me to just climb over. I then began to go down the back gardens to come around to a fountain in the middle. I looked past the fountain and strangely enough, there was a building there that I did not recognize; the building branched off from the main building like an annex, but was constructed in a consistent manner to the rest of the architecture that if it wasn't for the fact that it looked new, it wouldn't have appeared any different to the rest of the building. A door ahead led into that part of the building, but I didn't know what this building was to risk entrance through it. For all I knew, it had more security features than the rest of the house. I instead came around to the stairs that went up to the patio and came around through there. I looked around as I attempted to remember the layout of the manor; surely the countless times I came around to visit Diana had trained me for this moment. From what I knew about intrusion systems, they were motion activated at doorways, so I avoided the doorways here as well and instead began to check the windows. I pulled and tugged at the windows, but to no avail.

I checked all the windows around, and to my disappointment, I was unlucky to not find a single window left open. Of course, I had to rely on Plan B, either breaking a window that I could pull open, or climbing up the side of the balcony that led into Diana's former bedroom. I was hesitant to break a window since some intrusion systems relied on high-pitched noises like those sounds. I looked and saw some ivy had grown up the side of the manor from the garden. It seemed too risky to put my weight on that, although I did not weigh that much. There was also a screen below from where the ivy was growing along. I walked towards that part of the house and began to test to see if it could hold my weight. Surprisingly, it held pretty well as it was fastened to the exterior wall. I began to climb up and looked over to see where I needed to get to. The balustrades itself were climbable, so all I had to do was get within a reachable distance. I climbed up and lifted myself up to reach that height, and then after a bit of a reach, I caught the balustrades and began to climb up onto the patio. I came up to the top and then stopped as I looked out. I checked my surroundings to ensure that I was still alone and nobody in sight, and then I turned around to eye the French window.

I knelt down and took out some tools from my pocket. I didn't anticipate Diana's bedroom window door to be secured like the other doors, so I began to pick the lock to get through. The lock was easy, which made my use of such tools overkill. I opened the door and then walked inside, being met with a change of scenery. I looked around and noticed that the room was plain. In fact, the room was just like how my room had looked when I came back to Allabrese. There was no personal décor, nor photos or even any clothes in the closet. All I saw was furniture, a few bed sheets on the bed, and nothing else. I supposed that Diana really was gone. I was surprised that if she and Tristan did marry, they weren't in Allabrese in this house, but alas, a quick social media check told me that they were in Harlech living their best life. I walked into the bathroom, saw that it was empty, and then I walked over to the room next door. I found this room to have a bunch of exercise equipment in it still; that didn't change, and then I moved over to Tristan's former bedroom, and like Diana's, it was abandoned. I came out from the bedroom and into the corridor, which was cold like the other rooms. If anything, it was as cold inside as it was outside. I walked towards the door that led out into the foyer, feeling a little anxious that any motion from that room could set off the burglar alarm. I gently opened the door and then stepped out. I then began to take gentle steps along the surrounding veranda as I bypassed the ground floor and made my way over to the south wing. This room did not seem as abandoned as the other rooms; I did not see any drapes over the furniture, or even a lack of furniture. It seemed much as I remembered it. I reached the other side of the veranda and gently opened the door at that end to enter into a short corridor. A door on the right went to the master bedroom, but I didn't need to go that way, so I entered into the library and then took a breather as I walked normally down the balcony to reach the stairs that went down. The library appeared just about as I remembered it with all the books on the shelves. There were also some portraits that hung upon the walls, faces of deceased Cabernet family members no doubt. There were about six of them in total, hung between windows; four on the south side and two on the left side. I looked at the first one, which was a painted portrait of a man named Sennett Sigi Arnulf Cabernet, 1850-1904. The next portrait was of a man named Lycidas Rerir Cabernet, 1878-1926. The third portrait was of a man named Pepin Waelsing Cabernet, 1901-1943. The last portrait along this wall was of Derby Martel Cabernet, 1920-1969. In the corner of the room was a grand piano that I remembered, and perpendicular to the portrait of Derby was one of Everest Pepin Cabernet, 1945-2023, and then opposite from that portrait, on the other side of the large, curtained window, was one of Charlemagne Phillipe Cabernet, 1961-2021. I remembered thinking how incredible it was to have six generations just come and go. The library was otherwise well-decorated still with artefacts and rare gems in some display cases. I was not here to steal physical items though, just data. I came around to where I remembered the door to Mr. Cabernet's study was and then placed my hand on the doorknob to come through. I entered into Mr. Cabernet's former study and looked around the room; it was messy. On my immediate right were two tables that contained various legal boxes, while directly ahead of me was a door that must have led into the attached part of the house. Beside that door was a display case that had an awful mechanical structure inside, a metal figure with a terrifying skull head and dark eyes, like a Terminator skeleton. Beside it were some weapons on display, and a plaque at its feet read, *Panzerknacker.* Beside this display case was a tall bookshelf, and then a fireplace with items on the mantle. One of these items was a longbow, at least six feet and six inches tall, on display. Above it was a mirror, and then beside it was another display case with some items inside, including an effigy of a raven, and then a cabinet. The desk that faced the center sofa lounge was large and had many items along it, including a computer that I eagerly eyed. Behind the desk was a target with some arrows knocked into it. I continued to track around the room as I found another display case, a low bookshelf with some items propped atop, including some picture frames, and then finally another tall bookshelf directly beside the door I walked through. I stepped inside the room and came around to the computer where I began to look, but noticed there no PC atop of the desk, just a monitor and several cables. There were also piles upon piles of papers, almost like a manuscript, and title-less leatherbound books. I knelt down and began to attempt to track where the cables went as it seemed that the PC may have been nestled somewhere.

I crawled from the side of the desk and followed the cables as they went under the desk and into a cabinet inside. I opened the cabinet, but the cables went further along and into the base of the desk.

"No way the computer is under the desk," I remarked in a quiet voice. "That's not good for ventilation."

I began to fiddle around with the base of the desk to see if a hatch opened up, but it didn't seem like there was a way. In other words, it seemed as if the cables just disappeared into the floorboards into a cellar. I continued to investigate until I was met with the sudden loud noise of an arrow hitting the target above. I crouched and held my head down, pausing in place before I raised my head up, looking in the direction that the arrow had come, and seeing a man standing at the other end of the room with a modern bow in hand. I immediately stood up and looked towards the man. He had medium length dark blonde hair, fair skin, and a blonde-haired wide chin beard and mustache along his otherwise cleanshaven face. He wore a sweater and collared shirt underneath, and beige pants. He was above average height, taller than me, but shorter than Jock. He did appear to be young like him though. He took a step forward as he continued to hold the bow in one hand, while I took a step back and hit the window. I was at a loss for words; a part of me had no idea who this person was but thought perhaps Mr. Cabernet had cloned himself in some capacity as it looked like him, especially as I saw his blue eyes looking at me from the other side, though the cheekbones were not the same as they were more defined. I began to panic slightly as the man took another step, so I took a sidestep. I thought for sure this person must be some sort of cousin.

"What are you doing in my home?" the man questioned in an English accent. I wasn't sure what region of England he spoke, but it was a deep voice, and slightly unpolished as far as English accents came.

"I'm… I'm sorry, I thought that… I thought that nobody was home," I responded.

"You think that's reason enough to break-in then?" the man questioned.

"It's just… I didn't think that anybody lived here anymore since… since Mr. Cabernet died. I thought this place was abandoned."

"Cleary it isn't," the man replied, "so tell me why you're in here and what you're doing. What were you looking for? The safe?"

"No, not a safe," I confessed. "I'm not here to steal anything."

"Right, I suppose there's a good explanation then," the man remarked. "Let's hear it…"

"I… I'm just looking to access Mr. Cabernet – Charlemagne Cabernet's computer."

"Oh yeah, and what for?"

"I'm… I'm just looking for some answers," I replied. "To something that happened here in Allabrese five years ago. I… I was given video footage from a drone he owned from that time."

"Really?" the man asked. "And who gave you that?"

"I don't know," I answered. "The envelope didn't have a return address, and I assumed whoever it was must have known Mr. Cabernet."

"What was in those videos?"

"Just… just footage from the pandemic quarantine six years ago, and riots… that's it. I just wanted some more information about that."

"Ah, right then," the man remarked, looking at me. He didn't say anything else.

"I'm… I'm sorry I broke into your home. Honestly, I wouldn't have done it if I knew someone lived here. I just didn't think that Mr. Cabernet's home was sold or that anybody lived here."

"Yeah, you've said that already," the man responded, "but I didn't buy this home – not that it belongs to anyone in particular."

"Oh, I'm sorry."

"You don't know who I am, do you?" the man asked. "Where are you from?"

"Allabrese, mister… sir," I stated. "If you let me leave, I won't come back."

"No, you don't get to say you're from Allabrese without knowing who I am. It's a small town. I've lived here for quite a while now. Where are you really from?"

"Well, I lived in Calgary for the past four years because of school, but honestly, I grew up here. You're not a face that I recognize."

"No... suppose that makes sense then," the man remarked as I had just about reached the exit.

"Who- who are you?" I finally asked.

"Why I'm Charlemagne Cabernet's biological son of course."

"Biological son?" I questioned. "I... I haven't seen anything about that on the Internet..."

Mr. Cabernet's son shrugged his shoulders. He then replied, "I've lived in the dark, prefer it that way. I'm a... bit of a wanted face on the other side of the world too, if you catch my drift. You wouldn't hear about me, my mum maybe, but not me."

"Your mom...?"

"Manon Cabernet," the man answered. "The majority shareowner of Cabernet Industries since my dad died."

"What about Diana and Tristan?"

"Hm, so you know about them," the man remarked.

"They at least have their names in the news as the two orphans your dad adopted before he died," I clarified, "but yes, I knew them. I went to school with them."

"Hm... that must mean that you're... Maia Grayson."

"What? No, I'm not," I rejected, putting a hand on my hip.

"Ah, only teasing you – I know just who you are, Moira. Yes, searching along the floorboards for the computer port entry, you little minx, you," the man said, crossing his arms. "You were looking for a way in to hack into my dad's computer, but little did you know that those servers are well-secured in a place where I'm not telling you."

"How do you know who I am?" I questioned. "Who are you?"

"I already told you, I'm the one and only son of Charlemagne Cabernet," the man expressed. "At least, one and only that I know of... dad's had many lovers over the years, so I hear, mind you. Yes, though when dad died, I kept it quiet and let others bask in the starlight. I'm not surprised then if you haven't been in Allabrese then why you haven't heard of me. I'm only a local face now. You too have been living in the dark, so it seems."

"If you know so much, then maybe you can give me some of the answers I seek," I propositioned. "What do you know about what happened in Allabrese in October 2019? With the epidemic and the riots where my dad, Eugene Macmillan, died."

"Hm… yes, that whole thing…" the man remarked, bringing a hand to his chin. "Sorry, I'm not allowed to say."

"What?"

"Yup, I'm sworn to secrecy on that one. If I even utter a word, then the wrong people will come after me, and that's saying something when I've already got quite a price on me head."

"What does that mean?"

"It means that I've been a naughty boy and have something to hide from," the man expressed, "but don't you be telling your friends that."

"Well, what if I leverage your seclusion for my information."

"Nah, for a start, you don't even know my real name," the man expressed, "and second, nobody would believe you. Besides, the people that are looking for me are far less scary than the ones who've obliged me to keep it all hush hush."

"So that's it then," I expressed. "I'm just expected to drop it… my dad died that night."

"Yeah, well, my dad's dead too…" the man replied. "I'll tell you what though, it's nothing to worry about. From what I've heard, his memory was not affected in it. So I hear, he died a hero, and likewise, so I actually hear, he really did die a hero. I wouldn't fret about it; some day, all that *is* or *was* will become known, for what is kept in the dark will be revealed in the light at the day of Judgement." The man walked over to the door and opened it for me to leave.

I looked at him, unbelievable at what he suggested to me.

"Well, it was nice to get to meet you, Moira, it really was," the man expressed, "but I'm afraid that you've interrupted me and that's all the time I have for visits today. I wish I could be of better use, but you're looking for something I just can't give. TTFN, I'll be sure to let Diana know you were around."

"Diana?" I muttered. "You talk to Diana?"

"Of course, both her and Tristan are my bestest friends."

"Who are you really?" I asked again.

"Yes, that really is the question, isn't it... who are we," the man replied taking in a deep breath as though in wonder. "Perhaps think about it and let me know when you've got an answer to that one."

I glared at him and crossed my arms. I asked again, "What's your name? I'm not leaving until I get a name."

"Oh, you want a name," the man replied. "Very well then... most people call me Louis around here, so that's the most I can give you."

I looked at Louis as that name registered in my brain. He followed me from behind as I walked out and we came around to the foyer. He walked over to the front door, opened it, and then allowed me to leave.

"I suppose it goes without saying, but as much as I enjoyed getting to meet you, please don't come back," Louis requested. "You don't know what you're asking from me, so believe me when I say it, it's for your own good that you stop looking."

I turned around to face Louis, and I got a better look at him from the daylight. He really did appear as though he could be Mr. Cabernet's son, and he was young too though the beard gave him an older appearance, his cheeks told me otherwise. I saw someone close to my age. He waved to me and then shut the door behind. I was annoyed. I didn't know who this person was or where he had come from, but he seemingly knew what I wanted to know and wouldn't tell me, and despite his warning, I wasn't going to stop there.

Act 2, Prologue

A young adolescent boy sat in front of a table with another steel chair on the other side, like the one he sat on. The room was dim, a lamp above shined directly down on the table, while the walls around him were a greyish-blue and made of large concrete bricks. The floor at his feet was smooth concrete. The room that he sat in was plain and had no other items in it. Both the wall behind him, ahead of him, and to his right were plain while the wall on his left had a thick rectangular mirror. The boy looked plainly ahead of him with a furrowed brow. He tapped his fingers at his right hand as though he waited. He had cuffs around his wrists, though he wore street clothes consisting of grey cargo hiking pants, boots, and a striped, green shirt. His sleeves were rolled up. This boy had defined cheek bones, a thin face, and lanky body. He had no facial hair upon his chin or above his lip. His hair was also fair, dirty blonde, and his eyes blue. Around his neck was a bandana. He had a bruise underneath his left eye and his lip was cut as though he had been in a fight. His hair was ruffled and messy, and his skin though smooth was dirty. He reeked of smoke and as though he had not showered for days. The boy sat up as he heard a buzz from the door to his right, beside the window, and it opened and a man in a suit walked in.

The man looked at the police officer who had let him in, and without saying a word, the two looked at each other. The man in the suit raised an eyebrow and the other closed the door behind him. The police officer looked on from the other side of the door for a moment. He wore a white collared shirt, black tie, and black tactical vest that said 'Police' in large letters on the right breast pocket. He also wore black trousers and shoes. Atop of his likely bald head was a black cap with checkered outline around the side with a crest at the front center. The man that had entered the room, wearing a suit, on the other hand, had very fair skin, less fair than the adolescent boy's, and he had dark eyes and a round face. He also had thin brown hair and a slim appearance. He came around to the other chair, stood at the corner with a smile on his face, and then looked over to the boy. He held a metal clipboard in his hand.

"Evening, my name is Detective Constable Wallace Greenway and I've been assigned your case," the man greeted. He spoke in a Londoner accent. "I can't imagine you're doing too well, after all that's happened. You must be having quite a day."

The boy looked at him with a plain stare, sat back, and relaxed his hands.

"Do you mind if a I have a seat?" the constable asked, pulling the chair out and sitting down anyways. "Why don't I make you a bit more comfortable? Take those cuffs of yours off…"

The boy didn't respond as he continued to remain shackled. The man tensed his mouth and then looked over to his clipboard.

"Very well… straight to the chase…" the constable stated. "You obviously know why you were arrested, so I just have a few questions to ask of your involvement at today's protest. You've thus far been uncooperative with our investigation, and we're not here trying to make what you did today seem worse before a judge. We just want to clarify some questions in the preliminary report, get more information, and make sense of the entire ordeal. Believe it or not, but we want to help you out in this situation, but we can't help you if you don't talk to us. Do you understand what I mean?"

The boy looked back at him with a plain glare.

"Why don't you start by telling us your name?" the constable requested.

"I have not the slightest intent to tell you what my name is," the boy finally spoke. He spoke in a deep Suffolk English accent. "I don't want to talk to any of you pigs. Just lock me up and throw away the key. I don't care. I don't care about anything anymore."

"You're obviously very passionate about the environment, being out there in the protests," the constable pointed out. "Environmentalism, caring about Mother Earth, is certainly something that you do care about, isn't it? Why don't we start talking about that then? I for one consider myself to be green – heck, it's in me name, isn't it? I put my recyclables in the correct bin. I'm conscientious about my carbon footprint. I…"

The boy smirked and gave a light laugh.

"What's so funny?" the constable questioned, raising a smile.

"You wanker…" the boy replied, causing the constable to lower his smile. "You're such a phony, coming in here trying to find common ground with me… You've got to find a bit of common decency with the young blood, don't you? I've seen it a million times… All of you, you're one and the same, artificial like everything else on this planet and modern world. You don't care about me. You don't care about the Earth. To be frank, I don't care at all about you and I'm sick of adults like you approaching me and expecting to find trust in me."

"You don't trust adults then, do you?"

The boy did not respond to that question.

"How old are you?" the constable asked. "Where do you live? We didn't find any identification on you, and you've refused thus far to give us a name, but we've got to identify you."

"You know who I am…" the boy replied. "You've taken my fingerprints… I know you know who I am, so stop with the useless questions…"

The constable nodded as he held a pen in his hands. After a moment, he replied, "Alright, you've got us there then. You're Finn Louis Cunningham. We do know who you are, and we also know that you've got quite a bit of a record with us… a lot of arrests due to mischief, a lot of petty crimes, but also participating in eco-activism, standing out and blocking traffic, though none have really stuck upon you. Since about the age of thirteen you've been a rambunctious scamp, haven't you?"

"Always a pleasure to keep you chaps in business," Finn gloated.

"Yup, but today is not your day, Mr. Cunningham. You've been wanted for the past two weeks since you ran away from home, putting the strain on your poor old mother and father..."

Finn chortled and shook his head.

"And now you've really done it with an aggravated assault charge, on a police officer no less, while attending an eco-protest that turned into an illegal demonstration."

"First of all," Finn stated, "I'm my own man. My mum and that... man don't own me..."

"You're underaged, Finn," the constable pointed out. "You're a few weeks into being seventeen years old."

"Second of all," Finn argued, ignoring his previous remark, "how can I be in it for aggravated assault when that fascist grabbed me first, not the other way around. What else was I supposed to do when another man puts his hand on me?"

"He's a police officer..."

"So, doesn't make it right?" Finn argued. "You all think that because you represent Her Majesty and Her Government that you can do what you want as if the law doesn't apply to us both. All of you are blind to what you are, nothing but enforcers to a corrupt political government owned by corporations. They tell you you're here to protect civilians while you beat us up and get away with it. There's no accountability for folks like us... going after us because we dare use our voices to argue for what is good..."

"Why did you run away from home, Mr. Cunningham?" the constable instead asked.

"Mind your own business," Finn immediately answered. "Not my home. Not my family. Not your damned right to know."

"Where have you been living? Have someone been sheltering you? Has anybody been hurting you?"

"What? No – only person who has hurt me is those who tell me and others they're here to help," Finn remarked. "You lot."

"Where have you been living?"

"I'm not telling you..."

"You don't look like you've been in the best shape..."

"I've been better than I am at home..."

"Why do you choose to run from home? You have a wealthy background, loving parents and a thriving family business, so I hear. Why throw it all to live on the streets?"

"If you knew where that money came from, and at what cost that wealth was earned, you would too – if you had a decent conscience that is."

"Has anyone hurt you at home?"

"Piss off with your nonsense questions. I don't want to talk to you anymore," Finn barked. "Get out of here."

The man sighed, sat up, and then looked down at Finn. He then said, "Very well. Your parents are here for you – would you like to see them?"

"No, I don't want to see them. Look, I'll admit whatever you want me to admit, but I won't go back to them."

The man did not respond and instead left. Finn remained where he was, but looked to the side. A tear fell from the corner of his eye. After a few more minutes, the policeman in the police uniform arrived, opened the door, and then stepped in.

"Mr. Cunningham, you're being released. On your feet, and I'll get those cuffs off you."

Finn immediately looked over. He did not stand up. The constable came around and grabbed hold of the cuffs. He unlocked them and then came around to lift Finn up on his own. Finn shrugged his assistance and instead stood up. He then walked out with the constable and came around to the corridor where he was led down and around to a waiting room.

A windbreaker jacket, smartphone, and cylindrical keychain was returned to Finn. He then turned around as another man in a suit looked at him, though this man did not have a smile on his face. This man was tall and wore a black suit and tie. He held a wool coat in his arms and had fair skin, similar to Finn's own. He was also balding with greyish-blonde hair and flabby cheeks. The man looked at Finn with disgust in his eyes and then without a word, Finn followed him out and around a corridor that came to an elevator. They rode the elevator together to the ground floor, where they then came out onto the streets.

Once they were a fair distance away from the police station, the man turned to Finn and remarked, "Where the hell have you been? You've broken your mother's heart and its driven me mad to hear her cry over you."

"I'm not her pet," Finn expressed.

"I never said you were."

"You certainly act like it. The two of you – you as though you never wanted me, and her as if I was made just for her. I've had it with the two of you."

"Regardless of how you feel, you're still underaged, and thank Christ you running off hasn't leaked to the press. The nightmare and anxieties I felt to believe that you wandering off could do the company any harm."

"Ah, of course, how thoughtless of me," Finn sarcastically replied.

"Yes, thoughtless, to not think of your family's legacy," Aidan Cunningham stated. "When perhaps someday you'll grow a spine the way I did to own up to what's ahead of you and take control."

"If I ever became the man that you are, the owner of a multi-billion dollar international corporation, I think I would rather kill myself then have that guilt on me."

"You're a lunatic," Mr. Cunningham replied. "How did you become to be such a lunatic."

"Takes one to know one," Finn responded. "You're the sociopath with no moral qualm at the harm that your company does to hurt people, to ruin other people's lives."

"Oh, will you stop with that..." Mr. Cunningham complained. "Cunningham Industries does not ruin other people's lives. We're a growing company that provides heating and gas to everyday people's homes, minerals to make the Play Boxes and X-Stations that youth like you seem to enjoy, and lumber to build homes. You ought to bask in awe at what our company does than to believe the lies of our enemies."

"Lies? I suppose the deforestation of millions of acres of land is just a lie, or the pollution of lakes and rivers to be just a lie as well. No sense believing that toxic waste just happened to develop where your chemical plants sit about," Finn remarked. "Yes, I believe it's all just lies that the evil news and press report on because they're out to get you and the company."

Mr. Cunningham laughed at him.

"Yes, I suppose that the traumatic damage that your company has done to the eco-system is just a farfetched tale," Finn continued to say, "or all the animal habitats that have been permanently destroyed. I suppose that men like the likes of you tell yourselves that oil spills are a natural part of the environment, or that rubbish in the oceans and on the streets is just the course of nature. You're pathetic, all of you. You've become so confident in the lies that you tell others, that even you yourselves believe in it. You've become so far gone as human beings, that there isn't a shred of moral consciousness and instead just cold calculations."

"For what reason would we have any sort of moral consciousness, Finn? Having a moral conscience does not build a multi-billion-dollar industrial corporation. What we've done has been ethical to say the least to what you claim, but what we've *done* has been spectacular achievements of the human will. You just don't know how to see the beauty of what our family has done, to wonder, and never in all of human history has something as glorious as what we do been achieved. We've extracted liters upon liters of natural gases and oil, extracted tonnes and tonnes of raw materials from the forests and grounds, and we've created, produced, and synthesized what man had not previously thought of a hundred years ago. We've taken the accomplishments of the Industrial Revolution to another level. We've industrialized the industrial, and as a result, we've become the largest mega-corporation this side of the Atlantic Ocean."

"And what does this company have to look forward to when all of the earth's natural resources are plundered and taken," Finn questioned. "She only has so much to give us."

"She? You act as though nature were not so cruel," Mr. Cunningham replied.

"Nature can only be as cruel as she can be kind towards us," Finn stated. "Isn't that the very nature of nature? Any animal can be both beautiful and deadly, switching between the two in an instant. Personally, I find the deadly to be just as beautiful as it's nature in its purest form. I know nothing about a world that is kind, only cruel, and I knowing of this belief that man should be kind rather than cruel because I've only seen men be cruel than kind. I see the evil that lurks, and I hate all of it. I hate this world and everything within it, but of all its evils, man is most terrible of them all and it would be a lot better if man perished from this earth than for men like you to destroy it and leave nothing behind. Honestly, what will future generations have to exploit when their ancestors have taken it all? What then will there be to have any wonder in? They could only curse us when it is too late."

"The earth has plenty more to give before we reach that point of exhausting those natural resources," Mr. Cunningham assured him. "I've also been told that there is plenty more in the great vastness of space. I'm certain that future generations will be turning to the world above us than to grovel at what has been taken, and that which has been taken will achieve such a momentous occasion. That's the problem with people like you, Finn – hippies, all of you, you have no aspiration. You wish to sit around and gaze upon the skies lazily than to be as we were meant to be created, men of survival rather than survive, and we look towards the long-term goals of our survival."

"You speak as though this were all just a game," Finn responded, shaking his head. "You act only for yourself and your own survival. That's what's wrong with men like you. You don't care about anyone else. You're rotten demons, the lot of you."

"Enough bravado," Mr. Cunningham remarked, "you make yourself out to be a hero as you sleep in the tube and take part in demonstrations, but what will that ever achieve? As a son of mine, at least show a bit more aspiration in yourself, Finn. I'm perhaps more greatly disappointed in you to your lack of vision and action than to oppose me with these nonsensical ideas of yours, though I suppose you'll grow out of them. Perhaps one day, you'll see clearly as I see that this world is doomed and all that you can do is take control."

"No," Finn denied, taking a step back, "I'll never join you. You – you're not a man, but a beast. I'll never become like you." He then ran off.

"Finn!" Mr. Cunningham shouted. "Finn, come back here!"

Finn ran away from Mr. Cunningham, far away, though he did not have to run far for the voices of the man who called himself father to them to die off.

Act 2, Scene 1

Moira, here. I did a bit more research about Cabernet Industries with the information that I had learned from this so-called son of Charlemagne Cabernet. As the corporation stood, a lady named Manon Madeleine Cabernet owned just over half of the corporate shares. I had no idea who this woman was, and seemingly neither did the mainstream media. I went through news articles that asked that exact question, but most if not all of them agreed that Mrs. Cabernet was Mr. Cabernet's wife. I must have known less about the Cabernet household than I thought I did, because never in my life did anyone ever tell me that Mr. Cabernet was married. In the years before I left Allabrese, I had known and was told that Mr. Cabernet was a bachelor with no other children until Diana and Tristan were adopted into his home. The only possibility I could conclude at this time was that sometime between my departure and his death, he got married. I seemed to recall that he did have a girlfriend around the last year I was in Allabrese, but I could have sworn that she died because it was the talk of the town for a while. Nonetheless, I stared at the face of a woman that dared to marry that vile man – Mrs. Cabernet was actually titled Dr. Cabernet, because she held a doctorate degree and was an associate professor at the University of Harlech in their history department. Her profile picture on the university website showed her face. Manon Cabernet had medium brown hair cut short to her shoulders and straightened out. She had fair skin, though with more color than Mr. Cabernet's or Finn Cabernet's tone. She also had deep blue eyes and cheekbones just like their son. Even if I were to believe that Finn was this woman's son, was he their biological child? The man that I had met looked to have been Jock's age, and Jock was born in the late nineties. I had so many questions that only a single obscure news piece from the Allabrese All-Star, our local newspaper, could answer.

According to the news article, Dr. Cabernet was surely Mr. Cabernet's wife, but also his childhood friend. The pair had met as children through each other's parents, and reunited in the late eighties when she travelled with him as a member of Cabernet Exploration, an expeditionary archeology crew funded through Cabernet Industries. The pair separated in the early 2000s, but rekindled in 2019 as Mr. Cabernet was struck with a cancer diagnosis. They married in June 2021, a few months before he had died, and she became a widow. I did not need more to tell me about this strange woman, though I did wonder how odd the entire situation was.

The rest of the ownership of Cabernet Industries rested upon the people that I knew, Allodia Cabernet, the current Chairwoman of Cabernet Industries. I looked at Allodia closely. Her profile picture on the Cabernet Industries website, as well as news articles, depicted her for her age. She was fifty-five years old with wavy light blonde hair and fair skin. The mainstream media spoke of her as a single woman girlboss and exemplified her as such, while others vilified her as a drag upon Cabernet Industries in the death and absence of her brother. Prior to ascending to the main position within the corporate enterprise, Allodia was Chief Executive Officer of Cabernet Foundation, where a lot of the news articles talked about her and all the charitable work that this part of the company had completed. Some personal details spoke about her formal education, graduating from the University of Harlech with a Bachelor of Science in zoology and Doctor of Veterinary Sciences, which I supposed made both her and Mr. Cabernet's wife, Dr. Cabernet in title. Still, the biographical information remarked that she did not live a long career as a veterinarian and quickly abandoned all that she had worked up towards to pursue charitable work through Cabernet Industries, formally joining the organization in 1996. She became the Chief Executive Officer of that charitable foundation in 2012. In 2021, Allodia became the permanent Chairwoman of Cabernet Industries, having acted in an interim role beforehand due to her brother's reduced presence and then resignation.

Finally, there was the Salmar Cabernet, who I knew to be in prison, but as I completed my in-depth review, I found an article that spoke about his release from prison. Salmar Cabernet was arrested and found guilty of attempted murder when he plotted to kill his brother, Charlemagne, in a scheme that involved gangsters of the Medici crime family. He was sentenced to prison for twelve years, including time already served since his incarceration in a pre-trial center, which put his release to be around the year 2035. However, according to this article, Salmar Cabernet was released in January 2024 for unspecified reasons. There was less information about Salmar Cabernet than any other of the siblings. An archived news article from the Allabrese All-Star from 2004 spoke about the tragic death of his wife, Gloria, due to medical complications. A mainstream article that spoke about his arrest in 2017 mentioned that he was a practicing lawyer, an otherwise good-standing member of the Law Society of British Columbia and Alberta, a graduate from the University of Harlech where he obtained both his Bachelor of Arts in international relations and his Juris Doctor. The article specified that he practiced real estate law and was prominent in the real estate market in both provinces. I wondered what he was doing now since I didn't suppose a man with a criminal record could practice law, but a quick search in the last year detailed that he was currently the Executive Vice-President of the Central Canada branch of Cabernet Industries. This branch had its headquarters in Allabrese. I remembered that a few of the higher-ups in Cabernet Industries lived and worked out of Allabrese, including Vivian Huxley's father, Ralph 'Richard' Huxley, who was still the Chief Executive of Cabernet Industries; Paul Joseph Gilbert, the Chief Communications Officer; Herman McGarrick, Chief Operations Officer; and, Martin Bowman, President of

Cabernet Industries (former Executive Vice President of the Central Canada branch). According to the Cabernet Industries website, there were also some other figures whose names I did not particularly recognize, but which I assumed to work from the offices at Harlech, and these included Walter Smith, Chief Financial Officer; Henry Heavner, Chief Security Officer; and, Ian Frank, Chief Legal Officer.

I had to visit Cabernet Industries headquarters again because I wanted to speak to Salmar Cabernet to get a better understanding of the current situation with the company. I also wanted to speak to someone who could provide details as to what Finn referred to in his warning. I suspected that there was something going on with this family, something sinister that I should not know about, and which involved the town during the month of October 2019. I needed to get to the bottom of this mystery. I needed to know what my dad was up to and why he had joined forces with Mr. Cabernet and Mr. Phillips. Since I watched the footage and had been at Cabernet Manor, I attempted to make several phone calls to the mayor's office, but I was rejected every time. A part of me thought that Mr. Phillips was sincere with me and that he too did not remember. My brother was an active police member during the quarantine, so why didn't he know more about it?

"I'm telling you," I said to Jock as we sat around the breakfast table. "You can see for your own eyes – it had dad working with Mr. Cabernet and Mr. Phillips. They were working together, almost as if they were fighting a war together on these very streets."

"I don't know what to tell you, Moira," Jock replied, crossing his arms as he finished eating. "All of it sounds pretty weird."

"They were fighting the army, probably people in mom's unit, but for some reason, they spoke Russian. It… it felt like a scene out of that book, *John 8:32*, you know. The one where the kids find their town under foreign occupation."

"Are you sure this isn't some dream you had?"

"I can show you the footage," I remarked. "I have it on my laptop. It has dad's face in it. You can see him and Mr. Cabernet shake hands on the night he died."

"How long is this footage?"

"It goes on for hours…"

"Sure," Jock responded, "I can watch it later. I'm going to be late for work…" Jock said, standing up.

"It even has Mr. Phillips in it," I said. "When I talked to him, he was saying the same stuff you were telling me – that you don't remember exactly what happened… Why do you guys keep saying this thing to me?"

"Well, what do you remember about it, sis?" Jock questioned, picking up his jacket from the coat rack. "Honestly, I've tried a dozen times to properly remember what was happening that month, but it's like it was a blur. I remember doing the check-ins at some houses, wrangling up violators out past curfew, but all this? Russians on the streets, tanks and armored cars? I remember seeing some of the military hardware that came from mom's unit, but that's about it. I even remember seeing mom for a bit too, though not for very long. Honestly, it was a tough time, tougher than COVID was in the end of it all."

"What if Mr. Cabernet didn't get dad killed…" I suddenly questioned. "You never blamed Mr. Cabernet for what happened to dad, so maybe…"

"No, I didn't blame Mr. Cabernet for dad's death because I had some idea of what you're talking about," Jock rejected. "I didn't blame Mr. Cabernet, because dad knew what he had signed up for when he became a police officer, and it was the same 'yes' I gave when I became a police officer. All of us sign up with an oath to serve and protect, and sometimes that means laying down our life for those we choose to serve. In my opinion, any officer who is unable to commit to that call is unworthy of the uniform and badge they wear – dad taught me that, and whether he was working with or against Charlemagne Cabernet, it shouldn't matter because dad wouldn't have held it against him. He was never one to hold grudges, and he never taught us that vengeance and revenge were good ideas."

"Ugh, I'm not looking for revenge against anyone," I argued.

"So what are you looking for?" Jock asked me.

"I just want answers. I want to know what happened to him and why he had to die. How is that something that doesn't bother you too? To have a definitive answer to the question of what happened to our dad and what killed him?"

"Seems like we have enough answers to that question," Jock simply replied. "Dad was shot during the carrying out of his duties, during a particular time of rebellion, and he died as a result of his injuries. What you want to know is who killed him, no less to place your emotions somewhere because you have nowhere else to place them. You're becoming obsessed about this situation; I mean, you say you saw it for yourself, dad and Mr. Cabernet working together, so there you go – Mr. Cabernet and his men likely didn't kill him. You can stop hating on the man despite the fact that he's already dead."

"I can't believe you."

"I'm not going to argue about this anymore," Jock remarked. "I've got to go – and as a matter of fact, I don't want to watch whatever footage you have either, because I've put the questions to rest in my own mind. Goodbye – Rebecca will be back soon."

Jock left the kitchen, and I looked over to my nephew as he sat in his highchair. Gavin was perhaps as equally ignorant to what had transpired as all of us. We stayed together for another hour until Rebecca returned from the grocery store and let me move on with my plans for the day. I left the house and looked out around the neighborhood. Today was another chilly day despite the gaze of the sun upon us. I left the house and began to walk down the street to go into town.

After a moment of walking down along main street, I jaywalked across and continued along as I entered into the downtown core. I approached the front of the Cabernet Industries headquarters, pushed through the glass door and then stepped into their plain lobby. The lobby consisted of a long corridor towards an elevator at the end with a security desk beside it with a security guard stationed in a brown uniform. Besides the desk on the right-hand side of the lobby were some sofa chairs. On the left-hand side, closer towards the wall, there were some displays set up. The floors of the lobby consisted of a mixed white-grey marble, while the frames, beams, and outlines of the walls consisted of a gold-colored steel. There were three displays on approach to the lobby. On the immediate left as I entered, the display had a photograph of the office building in the early years of the twentieth century when it was established as a headquarters prior to the construction of Cabernet Tower in Harlech. The middle display had an acrylic portrait of the late Charlemagne Cabernet, and it was a well-done portrait as it appeared just as I had remembered him. He wore a tweed grey three-piece suit, and his hair was white as snow. He also had a well-groomed moustache above his upper lip. He looked directly diagonal as he stared into the unknown. A plaque below had his full name and date of birth. In front of the portrait was an unknown item and looked almost like a chrome leaf blower, but a plaque stated that it was a 'plasma cannon.' Yet another oddity from this household when there was a practical joke played upon the entire town to believe that ghosts had taken over on a Halloween night. Regardless of whether he was my father's ally or not, good riddance he was gone. After a moment of looking at the man that I continued to loathe, I approached the security desk rather than look at the third display.

"How can I help you, ma'am?" the security guard questioned.

I looked at the guard. He was a South Asian male with a turban on his head.

"I have an appointment to see Mr. Salmar Cabernet," I stated. "My name is Moira Macmillan."

The guard did not respond and instead picked up a phone. He began to speak to someone, at which point the guard permitted me to continue. I approached the elevator, called it, and then looked at the final display. These were newspaper articles that depicted Cabernet achievements in the past hundred years, one of which was the creation of a fusion nuclear reactor, another detailing the accomplishments of Cabernet Foundation across the entire world, and a final one that highlighted the life of Derby Cabernet as a war hero. The guard did not pay attention to me as I looked at the display and then walked into the elevator, hitting the button for the third floor, and then going all the way up to the top floor.

Once at the top floor, I came out to another reception desk in the midst of a room that seemed like it could go two ways. I approached the reception desk where there was a Caucasian female present. She looked over to me and greeted, "Hi there, are you here to see Mr. Cabernet?"

"Yes... Salmar Cabernet."

"Certainly, just sign in to our guest book, please," the receptionist stated. "Do you have a piece of ID with you?"

"Yup."

I took out a driver's license and placed it on the desk. I then received a visitor pass.

"Mr. Cabernet is just in a meeting right now, if you could just have a seat."

I sat down and waited. I looked around the room, which was somewhat plain and not very decorated like the one below. There were few highlights of the accomplishments of the Cabernet family, particularly of their industrial capacity as there were paintings that showed vineyards, mines, and factories. I waited patiently in this room until the receptionist stood up and came around the other side of her desk. I stood up and joined her as she went down a corridor.

I was brought to the end of the corridor where she opened the door and then allowed me to step inside.

"Mr. Cabernet, I have Ms. Moira Macmillan here to see you."

I walked into the office and then over to the desk where I saw a middle-aged man stand up and look towards me. Salmar Cabernet was different to both Charlemagne and Finn in appearance. For a start, he was stocky and muscular. He had a chiseled jawline and tanned fair skin. As I saw him, he wore a white dress shirt with suspenders, a dark blue tie, and blue dress pants. His sleeves were rolled up and he had a tattoo around his right forearm. I could partially make out the tattoo as it seemed to depicture a rose, some vines, and some cursive script. Mr. Cabernet had medium length blonde hair, neatly trimmed blonde beard and blue eyes. He looked at me with a smile as he stood behind his desk, holding a folder. I looked at him and then around the office. It was a large office with a window at the back behind Mr. Cabernet that looked out towards the city square. There was a bookshelf on the right, an aquarium directly ahead of me, and a pair of armchairs in front of the sleek modern desk. The desk was L-shaped and took up the left wall with three computer monitor displays. The physical computer appeared to be underneath the desk, behind the backing of the desk. I walked another step forward while the receptionist closed the door behind us.

"How do you do, Ms. Macmillan?" Salmar questioned. "I don't usually have appointments with special guests, and your reason for wanting to meet with me was vague. To what do I owe the pleasure?"

"I wanted to talk about your brother…"

"Ah, of course," Salmar replied, placing the folder down. "Come, take a seat. Are you some sort of journalist? I would get in a lot of trouble with our communications team if I did any unauthorized pieces about my late brother."

"No, I'm not a journalist," I responded. "It's just personal curiosity."

"Well, that piques my curiosity, so let's hear it."

Salmar sat down while I took a seat in the chair directly ahead of him. I looked at shelf above his computer monitors where there were some more books, as well as some photos. One of these photos showed a beautiful woman with tanned skin and light brown hair. Another photo showed who I could assume to be Salmar Cabernet, but with two older people, a man and a woman, and then a younger female. The younger male in the photo who I suspected to be Salmar wore a football uniform. Another photo beside it depicted a seated dog, a Dobermann if I knew my dog breeds correctly.

"I know you haven't been in Allabrese very long since you were released from prison, Mr. Cabernet, but I grew up in Allabrese and had somewhat of an idea of what sort of person your brother was..."

"Okay..."

"But almost five years ago, there was an epidemic in our town, so severe that the Canadian Armed Forces and Federal government had to intervene and quarantine us before it could spread out to the rest of the province..."

"Okay..."

"And then Mr. Cabernet, your brother, defied the public health orders in place. He took his private bodyguards with him and instigated a riot. He fought both police and army officials in a battle in which my dad died."

"Right..."

"But then I get a USB drive from an unknown person, and it has video footage – I can show you this footage," I remarked, taking out my laptop from my backpack. "It shows recorded footage of what your brother was up to during that month on two specified days, early October and then the day of the riot. However, for the life me, I can't understand what exactly was going on the day of the riot because it shows my dad and your brother working together, and they were fighting police and army officials, but some of these army officials – you can hear them yelling and shouting in Russian."

I quickly showed him some highlights I had cut up to show to people.

"I already spoke to the mayor, Mr. Phillips, and he denied any memory of these events. Whenever I talk to someone about what happened, they either deny it or have some sort of excuse of not being able to remember what happened."

"Okay…" Salmar remarked, scratching his beard, "that's quite something…"

"So my question is, is there anything you know your brother was up to before he died? Any sort of pacts or secret societies? My grandmother taught me once about rich people and secret societies, so I got to know whether there was some sort of conspiracy here…"

"Conspiracy?" Salmar questioned. He then sighed and said, "No, no conspiracies, at least I don't think. He looked intently at my screen as it froze upon a blurred depiction of one of the purple-uniformed soldiers. "Have you ever heard of a man named Audric Zimmerman, Moira?"

"Who?"

"Audric Zimmerman," Salmar stated. "He was a businessman, a young guy who owned lots of real estate and businesses, but his crown piece was his own company, Zimmerman Corporation. Now, Mr. Zimmerman was interested in a lot of the things that my brother was interested in, and from what I understood from his operations is that he also had ties to a group of mercenaries known as the Huntsman Legion. Those… those men in your video, those aren't Canadian Armed Forces personnel, those are Huntsman. They were the favored contracted security personnel of Zimmerman, who I know for a fact to have had it out for my brother, so much so… used me to get to him."

"But why would this Zimmerman man use contracted security or send them to our town? What's behind it all?"

Salmar shrugged and said, "I couldn't say. I was never really close to Mr. Zimmerman, but from what I later learned, he disappeared and was never seen again. His company was in a lot of trouble for something that happened four years ago – you may remember the FT-2021 incident? They called it a major computer glitch that sent Zimmerman military drones out onto the streets around nearby ports. A lot of people died from that incident, and it was a hugely embarrassing to the company's reputation and they were sued, went bankrupt, and liquidated as a result of the ordeal. The CEO of Zimmerman Corporation at the time, Hyacinth Dulles, was arrested, as well as some other figures, and they're currently spending life in prison for it"

"Okay, but so what?"

"The so what is that Zimmerman was a peculiar man, even more peculiar than my brother, and he was a bad man too. I don't know what happened here to give an honest and clear answer, so I'm sorry about that, but I wish I could help. Although, if it's accountability you're looking for, just know that like I said, Mr. Zimmerman is history, and so is his company and all those that followed him. There's nothing left there, except I suppose, the remnant of it all wherever it may lie. It's over, Ms. Macmillan. It's all over."

I sighed and folded my laptop. I put it away and instead took hold of a small USB drive, which was smaller than the one I had received in the mail. I held it around a closed fist.

"I spoke with your nephew, Louis Cabernet," I remarked. "He told me that he knew what happened, but to drop my pursuit of the matter. Why is that?"

"Louis? Oh, you mean Finn… Finn isn't the type to talk to others, period," Salmar replied, seemingly impressed. "How did you manage to do that? Even I have a hard time getting a hold of him some times, much like his old man."

"It's a long story, but why would he tell me to drop it?"

Salmar sighed and replied, "If I had to guess, based on what little I know about my nephew and what more I know about his father, my brother, it's probably because some matters that he had to deal with were some vicious people, like Mr. Zimmerman. My brother made a lot of enemies over the years and been the target of violence quite a bit. He probably just doesn't want you barking up the wrong tree…"

"It's just that…" I remarked, bringing a hand to my face, "I just want to know why my dad had to die…" I expressed, suddenly bursting into tears. "It doesn't make any sense to me."

"Hey, don't cry," Salmar expressed, reaching over for a box of tissues and then placing it for me.

"Nobody seems to want to give me a clear answer…"

"Look, maybe I can talk to my nephew about it," Salmar remarked, "but to be fair, he doesn't tell me much about what my brother was up to either. He lives his own life, hidden away in our family home on the other side of town. He only comes out once or twice from what I understand. It can be difficult to communicate with him…"

"No," I replied, "please don't talk to him. I… I don't want him to know that I'm going against his advice."

"Are you sure?"

"Alright…"

"Could you… could you get me a glass of water, please?" I requested. "My throat is a little dry…"

"Sure, let me just…" Salmar picked up the phone, to which I responded to by coughing. He then stood up and put the phone down. "I'll get that glass of water for you."

Salmar left the room, prompting me to stop coughing and instead quickly stand up. I went around to the other side of the desk, knelt down, and placed the USB drive into the back of his computer. I then stood up and looked at the computer, waving the mouse to see that it felt asleep. The computer gave off a jingle to suggest that I had plugged in a device into a port. I turned off the sound of the computer and then came around to the other side of the table where I sat down again. Salmar returned with a glass of water, and I received it into my hand.

"Thank you," I said, taking a sip, "that's much better…"

After a few more words, I left Cabernet Industries headquarters and returned back downstairs where I stayed close. I left the building and went into the restaurant upstairs, where I came around to a lone seat and opened my laptop.

"In I go…" I remarked.

I began to type away as I broke into the Cabernet Industries computer system network. Was what I was doing illegal? Certainly, but I did not consider what I was doing to be egregiously morally wrong. I immediately began to hunt for anything that could be useful to my ongoing investigation, but everywhere I turned, there seemed to be no useful intel. I scoured through documents on their servers, typing keywords such as Charlemagne, Finn, and Manon. I also used times and dates of the incident that occurred in October, going deeper in as I searched files that belonged to the security department, Mr. Heavner, and all others involved in that department to come up empty-handed as despite the involvement of members of this so-called Protection Squad, there was no documentation or report to give me answers. I went further back and began to search through e-mails, but there were so many e-mails. I went through the e-mails of Henry Heavner, but there was nothing of note. I went through the e-mails of Allodia Cabernet, Richard Huxley, and others that could have been involved. I attempted to decipher the name of the man that was with Mr. Cabernet, believing I had heard his name to be Max, but could not find a definitive match for who he was. Finally, I typed the name of Salmar Cabernet, and went through his e-mails to see what he was up to, and most importantly, what he was doing now. I did not see much activity, but then I saw a particular e-mail that sent out. I began to look at the e-mail and saw that it was addressed to someone by the handle of 'BLambert,' which made me pause for a moment.

I did a quick search and found someone within the Cabernet organization that was a match for that alias, and it was Bartholomew Lambert, Chief Research Officer for Cabernet Technologies. The e-mail noted my visit, expressed to him that knowing Lambert to have been a good friend of Charlemagne, if he knew what I was talking about. After I read the e-mail, I went back and attempted to find more details about Lambert and Cabernet Technologies, but I came up emptyhanded. It seemed liked Cabernet Technologies operated on separate computer servers. I terminated my connection to Mr. Salmar Cabernet's computer and then sat back. I did a quick search of Cabernet Technologies, noted their address out in Champion Plains, and then set off to pay them a visit.

Act 2, Scene 2

I exited from Jock's home to pick up the keyset to Jock's pickup truck before I left and went on my way eastbound. Cabernet Technologies had their laboratories in a part of the county known as Champion Plains, or *Pianure Calabresei* to the Italian ethnic population that lived in these parts. This land spread out around a large surface area of land that existed to the east from the center of Allabrese, and all of it was smooth plains up to the county line. I could recall going to Cabernet Technologies once or twice as a child. They were usually a destination for a school field trip or two, and then I also had my eighth-grade science fair at their facilities too. At least, those laboratories were the old facility that I had visited. Around the same time that we went into lockdown, the entire compound exploded and evaporated the surrounding area. Luckily, at least according to the government, the effects of the explosion were not detrimental to nearby livestock and residential population. A press release from Cabernet Industries placed the blame that their nuclear fusion reactor had detonated due to the quarantine lockdowns that prevented regulation and maintenance, although, from what I knew about fusion reactions, was that possible? I thought that fission reactors were the ones that needed to be kept cool due to the generated heat. An overview picture of the aftermath of the detonation showed that the entire compound and even surrounding road had evaporated, leaving behind a crater to the depths of several stories. According to both the government and a Cabernet Industries press release, no persons were killed or injured as a result of the combustive blast. I wasn't sure if I could believe either of them in what they had to say, because it was certainly odd that at the same time some suspicious activity had occurred in this town, possibly related to this Huntsman mercenary group tied to Zimmerman Corporation, this human-made disaster had also happened. Were they related? I wanted to believe so. I returned to the facility compound as I approached them. I exited off the freeway, came up to an intersection that connected to a bridge that went over the freeway, turned left, and then continued a short distance to reach the front gates into the parking lot.

Cabernet Technologies was rebuilt on the same land that it had existed on before. I was amazed that in the course of the past five years since the destruction of the old facility, a new facility could be built overtop and that crater filled in. I'm sure they probably just dumped a boatload of concrete in the crater and set that to dry before they started to build. The front of the facility looked much the same as I could remember it, consisting of an extensive concrete parking lot with hundreds of parking spaces. The surrounding perimeter had a tall chain-link fence with barbed wire around. The fence was at least double the height of an average fence, or two stories tall with barbed wire, and at the entrance of the compound was a checkpoint, though unmanned in the daytime. The facility certainly looked larger than it was before. The approach from the parking lot guided towards a central plaza in front of the central partition, a five-story rectangular glass structure. In front of the central partition was a wide fountain that collected up to a low fountain pool in the center of the square. Some low steps around the left and right sides of the fountain led up to sliding doors that went into the central partition. Another partition to the right was tall, like a tower, but the glass walls were translucent. An east partition was rectangular and consisted of similar glass window walls, though these were blue and tinted so that one could not see inside. This partition was four stories tall. A west partition was rectangular and consisted of transparent glass walls around the ground floor. This partition was slightly in front of the central partition, and it could be accessed from the main square through an entryway on the right. The upper floors from the ground floor was slightly raised past the main floor, creating a shelter where there was a patio with tables and chairs. Around the upper floors, the glass walls that faced the parking lot were translucent light grey glass window walls, and greyish smooth stone walls on the sides of the upper floors. On the right side, there was a depiction of the Cabernet Technologies logo in black, which showed the initials of the corporate entity, 'CT' together. Below this logo, in black font, it said, 'Judith Athena Lambert Memorial Research Facility.' I could see a lot of landscaping, bushes and mowed grass around the front of the facility that was not previously there. The overall architecture of the facility was modern and purely glass at the front. From behind, there were more partitions separate from the front, one of which composed of nearly the entire rear of the facility and it was a tall concrete rectangular structure with circular chimney exhausts from where steam bellowed out. To the far-right corner of the facility, there was a large atmospheric dome structure. According to the articles I read about this facility, this compound differed from laboratories and offices in Harlech in that it focused on larger projects, especially those to do with agricultural sciences, forestry, and other biological and geological sciences. As I examine the outer perimeter, I could also see an entryway around the left side that had another checkpoint, this one armed, with tall chain-link gates from which delivery trucks exited out. Cabernet Technologies was certainly a large facility to say the least, especially as I approached the central plaza from the left.

I stepped up towards the options there were for main entrances, one on the left of which entered into a lower and longer corridor, while one ahead of me walked into the central partition where there was a display of the planets suspended from the ceiling. Behind the display, I could see walkways along the four stories above the ground floor with offices on the other side. From within the central partition, I could also see a welcome desk, whereas it appeared to me that the building to my left was accessible too, and even had a coffee shop that connected the two buildings, but otherwise just had some sofa couches and elevators that went up to the floors above. I stepped into the central partition and looked above at the large displays of all eight planets. A round light that suspended from the center of the ceiling dwarfed all of the planets, and only the representation of Jupiter and Saturn were large enough to really see and identify, while Uranus and Neptune came close, and the rest of the planets were puny. A display screen to the right had some interchanging slides, while one in reference to the display stated, 'Behold, the wonder of the universe,' as it advertised Cabernet Rocketry. Some other slides advertised efforts to find cures to incurable diseases, synthetic fuels, and sustainable food choices. I stepped towards the welcome desk where there were some security guards, but also a welcome ambassador.

"Hi there, welcome to Cabernet Technologies," the woman greeted. "How can I help you?"

"Hi, perhaps you're not the person to talk to, but I was wondering where I would go to set up a meeting with the leader of this site, Dr. Lambert?"

"You'll want our offices to the left from when you exit, my dear. Administration is in that building. You can also phone-in or send an e-mail to inquiries-at-cabernettech.org, if you'd rather follow up online."

I removed my hand from my pocket and inserted a USB drive into the back of the computer monitor between us. I then moved my hands to my side as I placed them atop of the counter.

"No, that's okay," I replied. "I'll visit administration."

I left the welcome desk and then walked out, coming around to the building she was referring to, which was the blue one. I entered into the entrance at the side and looked ahead. This foyer was a lot quieter than the other ones and had a greyish-blue stone tile floor. I couldn't see any sort of reception desk, which told me that this lady had no idea where she was sending me. I approached the elevator to be sure, attempted to take myself up to a floor, but it was all locked down. I needed a scan card to go up or down. I walked out of the elevator and began to think for a moment as I assessed the scene, and of course, I came prepared. I sat down beforehand though as I opened my laptop and gained remote access to the computer monitor, I plugged into. This monitor was a security workstation, but I couldn't remote access the computer system by merely plugging into a monitor. The least I could do was take control of the mouse and move around, bringing up cameras to get a visual of the facility. They had a lot of closed-circuited cameras throughout all the buildings, but all of these views were plain and boring. They showed corridors, office spaces, elevators, and nothing more. I wanted to gain some insight to the interior operations of the facility; there was an entire factory-style building that loomed over the rest of the campus for Pete's sake. I opened another window and saw that security had access to a program used to manage scan cards and card access readers. I opened a tab that showed the hundreds of scan card readers across the entire facility, and just finding the one for the elevators proved burdensome. I had to resort to Plan B. I opened my backpack, put my laptop in, and then plugged it in to a device I had. I also pulled out a small purse and then closed my backpack. Within this purse, I had a mesh of wires connected to a device. I pulled a wire out that was connected to a clicker, brought that around my waist, and then through my sleeve so that it hung out from my right arm. I then brought the entire ensemble together, as well as my backpack, which too was connected to the purse, and then began to go stand around the main foyer where the most people gathered. I left this partition and began to loiter around, looking at the numerous displays as I kept an eye out around the place to search for the right mark.

What I basically had in my purse was an RFID skimmer, commonly used by RFID thieves. RFID (radio-frequency identification) was a short-range electromagnetic signal used between readers and tags for identification purposes. This same technology was used in smartphones to pay electronically, or use credit or debit cards to pay by tapping the cards at cash registers. The use of the technology in my hands was to scan credit and debit cards in the wallets or purses of unsuspecting marks to collect the data and replicate it so that in theory, one could steal vital credit or debit card info without even touching another person's wallet or purse. In a similar way, access cards commonly used at hospitals and other high-profile facilities used the same RFID technology to scan in at card readers, so rather than hunting for credit card information (as if I was a petty thief), I was instead hunting for encrypted data in a scan card so that I could replicate it and make a card of my own. I didn't want to just steal anyone's card data though, because I knew how these facilities operated and some people had higher access than others. The ideal target would be custodial staff, or perhaps security personnel, but at the present moment, there was no security guard at the desk. I found it tough to scope out a high-ranking scientist versus an intern outside of guessing by age. Of course, as the hour came to a close, people returned from lunch and the amount of people that were coming through this central point of the compound's entrance diminished significantly to the point where I didn't see many people. The security guards eventually returned, but they loitered and sat behind the welcome ambassador, looking at their phones and talking to each other; too far to scan a card that hung from their belts. I needed to find someone who was passing by. I also needed their pass to be lateral to my waist to point the scanner. I went around and sat down as I waited for somebody to come around, but it seemed bleak, and I felt awkward being around here, especially as the greeter looked at me. Cabernet Technologies had a museum, but this town being the middle of nowhere and having a population of little more than a thousand people did not do that museum much service. I felt incredibly inconspicuous, so I stood up and began to leave. I came around to the other building and went to the café. The café only had a few seats, but I did see a few people waiting for their coffee. Suddenly, it hit me to attempt to scan both of these person's ID to see who possibly had the greater access. I inconspicuously approached them from behind and scanned their ID from afar.

"Next please," the barista requested.

I stepped forward to the barista counter. I ordered my holiday spiced latte and then went to sit down. I pulled out my laptop and began to look at what I nabbed. I re-activated my control of the desktop computer to get an idea of what sort of access levels I had. The first person I nabbed was a Cabernet Industries official, an account director, but he did not have much access except to the administrative areas. The second person I nabbed was a researcher, but in a completely opposite twist, they had no access to administrative areas and only access to the laboratories. I sighed and took out a blank generic RFID card, swiped it, and wrote data for the account director so I could access the administrative parts of the building. After I was done, I put all my tools away into my backpack and then took my coffee with me so I could go to the administration building. I stepped back into the administration building, approached the elevator, and then scanned my card to select the top level.

I waited as the elevator took me up to the top floor, and then stepped out into a lobby and came around to a space that had many cubicles. The office was quiet and there were not many people around; I supposed remote working must still be a favorited option. The drive from downtown Allabrese to here was close to ten kilometers alone. I walked down the aisle besides some cubicles. The layout of the floor was straightforward. The inner part of the building was laid out with cubicles around, while the outer part of the building was divided into separate rooms which were offices for higher ups. I made a lap around, but did not see any office that belonged to Dr.

Lambert. I returned to the elevators and called one to retrieve me so I could go a floor down. I waited for the elevator, but as I did, a Sub-Saharan African female approached me and asked, "I'm sorry, but are you lost?"

"Yeah," I responded, twirling my hair and pretending to be dumb, "I'm supposed to be here to start as an intern for Dr. Bartholomew Lambert, but I can't seem to find his office."

"Dr. Lambert? His office is in the other building," the woman stated. "You are in the wrong building, my dear."

"What? What building am I in?" I questioned, continuing the act.

"You are in the Fowler Building," the woman remarked. "You want the Cockell Building, across from here."

"Oh, silly me," I replied with a laugh. "I'm in so much trouble…"

I stepped into the elevator, went to the ground floor, and then crossed to the other side. How was I supposed to know there was a difference? These buildings don't even have names to them, so how is anyone supposed to tell the difference between the Cockell and Fowler building. I returned to the building with the café, went to the elevators, and was relieved that the pass still worked. I was taken upstairs to the top floor and then stepped out to find myself in a quieter area than the other building. The corridors were narrower, the floor laminate beige and walls white with windows. I went around, passed a few workshops and creative spaces, and then came around to a corner office past a boardroom where I reached a dead end. Thankfully, this office held the title, 'Bartholomew J. Lambert, Ph.D.' and below it said, 'Chief Research Officer.' I stepped towards the door, peaked through a slot in the otherwise frosted glass, and saw that the room was dark.

Luckily, I came prepared again as I knelt down and began to pick the lock. However, I struggled to really get at it which was when I realized… "Dammit, this is one of those stupid Finnish locks, isn't it…" My university had these for almost all the buildings, and they were supposedly pick-proof, although in reality from what I understood, they were just pick-resistant. I did not have the time to force my way through this lock though. I looked around at possible options. I could smash the window and just go that obvious, indiscrete route. I could wander around in search for a custodial staff member. My eyes looked around at possible options. I turned my eyes above me to the collapsed ceiling, and then over to the workshop beside Dr. Lambert's office. From what I could see, the room adjacent did not have a dropped ceiling and instead all the lights, wires, and an exhaust tube could be seen as they were connected with the tube connecting into Dr. Lambert's office. I walked towards the workshop door, scanned my phony card, and then stepped in. I came towards a counter where I could gain some height to open a vent shaft.

I took out a screwdriver and began to unlatch the vent cover. I then pulled it off, threw aside, but before I climbed up, I had to remove my backpack. I left my backpack on the counter and then climbed up. I was skeptical that this vent could hold my weight (I was not fat), but I was above average height for a girl at five feet and eleven inches. I also weighed close to one-hundred and fifty pounds. I began to lift myself up as I saw the vent suspended from thin rods that connected to the ceiling. I could feel my weight drag the vent down, but the rods held on. I was at least slim enough to fit into the vent. The vents were also very warm. I dropped down as I decided to take my coat and sweater off to do this operational act. I lifted myself up again, pulled myself in, and then began to climb. My mother had sent me to cadets when I was a young girl, and that involved the occasional boot camp experience, and a part of those drills involved precision crawling and being able to propel yourself while in prone. Needless to say, but I was able to propel myself along the tube, reaching the junction that went either to Dr. Lambert's office or away, going left towards his office, and then going a short distance until I could see a drop. I began to poke at the vent cover, but it was toughly screwed in. I attempted to reposition myself in this tight space so that my boots were in front of me, but it seemed impossible, so instead I crawled further so that I remained prone but my boots and the vent cover were now behind me. I then began to kick into the cover as I lowered my feet into the drop. I stomped and stomped, and eventually the cover fell off and I could drop down into the large office space. I immediately looked around to ensure that the coast was clear, and then I ran towards the exit, unlocked it, and opened the door so I could fetch my belongings. I took a moment to recompose myself before I re-entered the office, looked around, and took in the environment.

Dr. Lambert's office was larger than Salmar Cabernet' office. On the right, where I dropped in from, was a bookshelf that lined the right wall, on the left were windows that looked out towards the neighborhood. Mr. Lambert's desk was a wide glass desk in an L-shape similar to Mr. Salmar Cabernet's, and with more monitors than him, one even vertical. Behind the desk was a horizontal painting that depicted some local scenery. Beside the painting were some more windows with blinds drawn. In the opposite corner of the office was a round table with chairs. Behind that table, next to the exit was another horizontal portrait, but this of what appeared to be digital art, but a plaque beside it stated it was an enhanced image from an electron microscope of a neuron, titled 'The Wonder of the Human Mind.'

I approached the desk, sat down, and took out my laptop as I plugged into his desktop computer. I then got to work. In a similar way that I had broken into the computer system at Cabernet Industries, I now accessed the computer system for Cabernet Technologies. I broke through their firewall, made my way into their system, and like magic, I was in. I quickly realized though that I needed to be careful as the security in this network appeared to be stricter than for the main organization. I wasn't here to steal technological research data or the likes; I had one goal, and to see what Dr. Lambert potentially knew about what happened here in Allabrese in October 2019. Perhaps I could shed some light on the explosion that devastated this land. I immediately went to access Dr. Lambert's e-mail and searched 'October 2019' to get some results. I approached the first e-mail with a bit of anxiety in my stomach, clicking it and skimming through the content before I went to the next one.

According to Dr. Lambert's e-mails, he spoke about what happened at the laboratories in October 2019 as a devastating explosion caused by the fusion reactor. He repeated this reason to many people, both those within Cabernet Industries and Cabernet Technologies, and even to Charlemagne Cabernet. Dr. Lambert spoke casually to Mr. Cabernet over e-mail, whereas Mr. Cabernet seemed formal in all his e-mails. I did not find any e-mails from Charlemagne in the Cabernet Industries e-mails, but as I looked, I saw that Mr. Cabernet used a different e-mail address domain than every one else, which made sense; likely, his domain was somehow attached to his manor and the computer systems there. The staff at Cabernet Industries used the domain, 'cabernetindustries' and staff at Cabernet Technologies used the domain 'cabernettech', while Mr. Cabernet used the e-mail 'charlemagne@cabernet.ca' with no addition to the domain. I thought for a moment and then decided to filter e-mails between Dr. Lambert and Mr. Cabernet. I went through them all and was shocked at what I saw. They did not speak to each other as often as I had thought with limited communication between April to October 2021 to do with business items, and before that date there was also limited communication but what was spoken about concerned projects that used codenames. There were also some daily business items that Mr. Cabernet and Dr. Lambert were kept in the loop on together from middle and upper management. I narrowed down the personal correspondences to find something from October 2020 in which they talked about a place named Isla Paraiso and discussed the flora there. Another correspondence talked about 'metahumans' and someone named 'Bishop Tristan Williamson'. Before those correspondences, there was an e-mail between the two that talked about Mr. Cabernet's cancer diagnosis, corrective action to assist workers that may have been exposed to harmful radiation, discussions to involve legal and risk management, and also an e-mail in which Dr. Lambert spoke that he was cancer-free. An e-mail from around April 2020 asked whether Mr. Cabernet had received a package, and followed with a response from Mr. Cabernet that he could 'not believe what happened in October 2019 was real.' He further spoke about how he couldn't believe 'that woman' had manipulated the entire town to believe in a lie. He referred to a 'rotten organization' as being culpable to the lies it passed on, but also assured Dr. Lambert that in exchange for secrecy, there would be no consequences on Cabernet Industries for the detonation of the fusion reactor. He further expressed worry at the degree to which 'Zimmerman' had approached them and assured Dr. Lambert that there would be increased security measures despite opposition from the 'GDP.' I raised an eyebrow at that obvious acronym. What the hell was a GDP? I continued to search through the e-mails going further back to around the time the town was in quarantine. There was an attempt from Mr. Cabernet to communicate with Dr. Lambert, but no responses. A few days after the quarantine, there was discussion about the future of Cabernet Technologies and plans to rebuild the laboratories, while laboratories would also be re-opened beneath Cabernet Tower in Harlech in areas formally owned by Cabernet Research & Development. A few months before October there were some gaps of communication, but in May 2019 there was a long discussion that ranged from gratitude from Mr. Cabernet that Dr. Lambert had returned to Cabernet Technologies, apologies about the death of Dr. Judith Lambert, and then also intrigue to do with an 'alien alloy' called 'Mjölnium.' Mr. Cabernet explained that he had discovered this metallic alloy when he was in Egypt and that he believed this material to be extraterrestrial and produced by 'beings' they had met in the late-summer. He further remarked that he spent the last few months in search of more as it is deposited into the earth from outer space, using his astronomical maps to pinpoint probable locations in the arctic. However, rather than locate a deposit of the material, he found a cache that was collected and stored in an abandoned Greenlandic settlement that was used to produce autonomous robots. These robots were collected, and two samples preserved for further research due to their resemblance to ones found in Russia the winter before. There were other e-mails that talked about this 'GDP' and insinuated that Dr. Lambert had participated with them to some extent. I checked more e-mails, but there was complete silence between Dr. Lambert from April 2019 going back to August 2018. The silence came after they had talked about meeting up with each other to review some projects and talk about Dr. Lambert's future in Cabernet Technologies.

I was puzzled. I didn't care much about what I had read other than this conversation about the 'GDP' – was that some sort of code for Audric Zimmerman's organization? Why did it seem like the pair of them were either intimidated or annoyed at this GDP? I searched the 'GDP' through Dr. Lambert's e-mails, but could not find anything of significance – an e-mail from Dr. Judith Lambert to Dr. Bartholomew Lambert in September 2018 expressed how the 'GDP' were looking for him and warned him not to run away from them because it may affect her. Interestingly, I took note that Dr. Judith Lambert was the Chief Research Officer prior to Dr. Bartholomew Lambert, where prior Dr. Bartholomew Lambert was titled 'Chief Astronomer' as per their e-mail signatures. I wasn't getting any answers by that search, so I went another level and searched 'Zimmerman,' to which there was conversation about the risk of Zimmerman Corporation and blatant efforts from them to copy technologies that Cabernet Technology produced. There was also discussion about nanotechnology and again mention of 'Tristan Williamson' as well as 'Sophia Witeveens.' The last e-mails that mentioned Zimmerman were from May 2020 and January 2021, one of which remarked about Zimmerman no longer being a problem and the other about 'Zimmerman's Legacy' in reference to what I could only suspect to be the FT-2021 glitch. I was still puzzled.

I shifted focus as I wanted to know more about this GDP, so I decided to attempt to access some research files. I began to crack into the separate server where I was really put to the test in my hacking capabilities. I had never seen such a secured database before as I fiddled around, but no lock is too much for me and I was in. I immediately began to search through the files with the keyword, 'GDP,' but that for some reason was met with a hostile reaction from the computer system. I received a pop-up met with another pop-up that alerted my presence, and so I quickly detached myself from the computer and unplugged Dr. Lambert's computer as well.

"Oh no… time to run."

I closed my laptop, put it in my backpack, and then began to make my exit. I came around the corridor, which was when around the other side, I saw two security guards approach. I immediately jumped and took a step back, turning around at which point they yelled out towards me.

"Stop right there!" a security guard yelled.

I didn't understand. How could they have known so quickly? I went back around the corner and began to run. I went all the way around the opposite way and reached the stairwell tower. A security guard arrived from the other side to confront me.

I immediately went down the stairs all the way to the bottom, but as I was about to approach the exit way, another security guard arrived to block the exit. How many security guards did this one facility have? I ran into the lobby and immediately went to call an elevator. The door opened, and I stepped in and closed the door. I then scanned the card I had and selected a lower level. The elevator took me to the basement, and I stepped out and began to look around. I immediately went down the corridor, came around a corner and approached a doorway. I scanned my card, but couldn't get through. I started to panic. I went back and attempted to scan into any room I could get into, eventually being let into one and closing the door behind me. I then slid down and began to take my laptop out so that I could load up accesses from the scientists. The police would be on their way, without a doubt, but what sort of police response would this provoke? I stayed put but didn't want to stay where I was for too long since they could trace my location with the card I was using, if they were smart enough to do that. I opened the door slightly to get an idea of where they could be, but I was alone. I immediately exited out from the closet I had hidden in and went to approach the door that wouldn't let me in with my new credentials.

I entered into a long corridor with a ramp that led down towards another door. The room was brightly lit by white lights. The door at the end was similar to the one I had just walked through and was a greyish-cyan color with a vertical reinforced window above the door handle. I scanned the card again, entered through, and came into a cold, but spacious room. I was atop of a caged catwalk and could not see much around me, but the catwalk was suspended and led forward to a junction that went two-ways. I walked forward, went down a staircase, and then looked both ways. I was in a very dim and large room. I looked down through the grates of the catwalk and could not see the floor below, but instead a dark fog. The void that I had walked into was not quiet as I could hear motors and machines in movement around. I went left and found myself adjacent to some large structures within the void, some of which had staircases that led up to doors in. I continue down the path that I was on until I heard a tune in a public announcement system. An autonomous voice said, "Your attention please – Cabernet Technologies is under full lockdown. For your safety, please remain in your workstations until further notice. This is not a drill. Do not approach any unknown entities as you return to your workstations or shelter in place." A lockdown? They went into lockdown over me? I began to run down the catwalk until I reached another junction, and then I came around and found a staircase that went down another level. I slowly grew lost in the elaborate labyrinth of catwalks that stretched out and surrounded a tightly knit network of spaces. I stopped as I looked above me as one of these rectangular spaces began to move. I was in some sort of elaborate underground with chambers everywhere, and then it soon dawned on me that the crater was never filled in, but Cabernet Industries paved over it to create this open space with its frames and chambers. I attempted to navigate myself back towards the center where I found a cylindrical space. Large print on the side of the chamber stated, 'Fusion Core', so I went around this large space until I found a concrete wall where the abyss ended and I could see a way out. I scanned my card, but it was no good. The facility was in lockdown. How could I expect that to work? I stepped back and continued to try to find an exit. There had to be some sort of fire exit somewhere. I looked up and sure enough there were green signs that pointed towards a fire escape. I followed these green signs and came around to a caged stairwell that went up. I ran up it and reached an exit point that led out into a wide corridor, hopefully above the surface level. I then went up a ramp that came out of the underground and brought me into the main foyer. I entered into the main atrium, and it was quiet; security and the ambassador were gone from the main desk, and I couldn't see security anywhere although I could hear police approach by the sirens in the distance.

I couldn't believe it – I was going to get out of here freely. I ran out into the main entrance vestibule, but the doors were closed. I easily pushed the sliding doors to set them off their hinges and then began to run down the pavement and then down the steps when I saw somebody ahead who was making their way towards the building. I looked at the person and recognized them, it was Finn 'Louis' Cabernet. He was dressed in a sherpa-lined brown aviator jacket, grey pants, and winter sweatshirt. He looked at me and I looked at him. He then frowned at me. I couldn't believe that I was busted.

"What are you doing here?" Finn questioned. "I thought I told you to come off it!" I didn't respond as I stepped away, but then I noticed police were right there and it was pointless to run. I froze. Finn stepped towards me. "It was you, wasn't it? You set off the alarm."

The police cars filtered into the parking lot and stopped at the curb. There had to be the entire on-shift staff here, which made my stomach sink as I remembered that Jock was on that shift.

"Are you listening to me?" Finn questioned, taking my wrist. "You couldn't keep your nose off of it, could you?"

The constables began to exit their patrol cars and run around. Some of them began to go towards the building and pass us, while another stopped and came around, and one of them included Jock who looked at me. I could hear him mutter under his breath in regret.

"What's going on here?" a constable questioned.

Finn released me and didn't reply as he glared at the police officer.

"Moira, what are you doing here?" Jock asked. "Shouldn't you be at home?"

"You know this person, Jock?" the constable responded.

Suddenly, security appeared from the top of the steps into the building. They pointed out to me, causing the other constables to respond and approach me.

"That's the one, there!" the other constable pointed out. "She was trespassing…"

"Trespassing?" Jock questioned. The constable with him immediately took a pair of handcuffs. Finn took a step back as the constable walked over to me.

"Sorry, miss, but I'm placing you under detention in the investigation of trespassing at a nuclear research site. Please place your hands behind your head."

Act 2, Scene 3

I must have disappointed Jock immensely as his colleague placed his handcuffs on me. Before the cuffs went on, my backpack was removed and set aside. After the cuffs were placed, I was made to sit in the police cruiser while the rest of the constables who responded to this urgent call left. What the constable told me about the nature of their investigation and dispatch, in which Cabernet Technologies was considered a nuclear research site, greatly worried me. I did a criminology course as an elective in Calgary, and I heard that those facilities were top-secret, and it was a serious crime to be trespassing or otherwise doing what I was doing at one of them. Jock briefly spoke with this colleague before he remained to assist. The constable also spoke with Finn, although briefly too as it seemed like Finn had no interest in talking to the constable. He instead walked up the steps into the building and disappeared. The constables spoke with Security, and when they were done, I was finally driven off from Cabernet Technologies and onto the highway so that I could be taken to the precinct building. The police cruiser drove up to the parking lot entrance where the gates slowly rolled up and then I was brought down to the sublevel entrance to be taken to the holding cells. Jock's cruiser was behind ours, and once parked, I was led out of the back of the police cruiser and made to face the side of the car.

"Do you have any sharp objects on your person, or anything that may otherwise harm me, yourself, or anyone else?" the constable questioned, putting on a pair of Kevlar gloves. "Any sharp objects in your backpack?"

"I have a screwdriver in my pocket," I recalled, feeling it in my jeans. "I don't have anything that will hurt anyone in my backpack."

Jock stood back as the screwdriver was removed from my jean pocket and placed on top of the cruiser.

"What's your name, miss?" the constable questioned.

I looked over to Jock, but I didn't want to cast shame on him.

"Her name is Moira," Jock answered for me.

"Moira, huh?" the constable responded. "Does Moira have any ID on her?"

"No…" I quietly replied. "No ID."

I had left my wallet in the pickup truck, though the truck keys were in my backpack. The constable came around to open the trunk of his vehicle and fetch the backpack. He placed it atop of the trunk after he closed it and then began to rummage through my stuff.

"What's all this equipment you have here?"

I didn't respond.

"Strong silent type, eh?" the constable remarked. "Hey, Jock, how come you know this girl, but I don't? Is she new to town? When did you deal with her?"

"I'll tell you about it later," Jock responded. "Not now."

The pair were interrupted with the sight of a police sergeant who stepped down and presented himself. I didn't recognize him. He wasn't sergeant when my dad was around, nor did I think he was even a constable. I usually knew the constables in the department thanks to my dad. They had a strong cohesive team.

"What's going on here?" the sergeant questioned.

"Sir, it's just the suspect from the Cabernet case," the constable answered. "We collected video footage of them loitering around the facility. Security say she's the one that had accessed an office space without proper authorization."

"Are you hoping to get officer of the year with that policework?' the sergeant questioned. "Bag the evidence and get this… girl to a holding cell. I just got off the phone with the chief and he says that some bigwigs from someplace I don't give a hoot about are coming to take over the investigation. We're dealing with federal investigators because of the nature of the offense, so get her inside and cozied up, because she'll likely be transferred out to a federal facility."

"Federal facility?" Jock questioned. "So what? RCMP are on their way? They're the next county over…"

"Not just RCMP – federal investigators with them too. I don't know what jurisdiction they're from. I'm just repeating what the chief told me."

"Ah Christ," Jock responded.

"Yeah, so they get to take all the glory? How's that fair?" the constable responded.

"You don't get paid to get a fair deal here," the sergeant replied. "Now get that evidence into the evidence lockup, and you, Macmillan, get that girl inside now. Doubletime."

"Yes, sir," Jock replied, taking hold of me. He gently led up the steps while his partner took my stuff away. Once he left to go deliver my stuff to the lockup, I was taken to a room with a counter in which I was put through the process of being booked. I had my photo taken, my fingerprints taken, and then Jock went through a form with me in which he wrote down my full legal name on his own. He did not say another word to me as I looked at him. "Alright, we're down here." He took me away from the booking station and into a cell where he led me inside and then looked at me. "What the hell were you thinking?" he quietly questioned as he removed the cuffs. "You've gotten yourself into a heap of trouble now. Don't' tell me this is over what we were talking about this morning…"

"There's something going on, Jock."

"Yeah, there's definitely something going on now," Jock responded. "You're looking at an indictable offense and criminal charges potentially for espionage and terrorism. How does that make you feel?"

"I just wanted to know what happened to dad."

"And look where it's gotten you," Jock remarked. "I'm going to see what I can do for you, but you know I can't stick my neck out for you for very long. It's bad enough I haven't said anything immediately about us being siblings."

I turned around as Jock left the cell and closed the cell door. He then looked at me, shook his head, and then left. I walked over to the bench and sat down, and within a few seconds, I began to weep. I felt stupid. I felt like I had gotten myself in an irreversible situation. I couldn't believe that Louis Cabernet, having known who I was in relation to Diana and Tristan, just let them arrest me and walked off. I continued to cry it out until I felt a little better, but still with an immense weight of doom ahead of me. I was finished, especially with these federal investigators on their way. I just hoped that Jock could make it through this ordeal without being outed as my brother. I lay down on the bench as I waited for the next steps to happen, and that came after an hour or so. I turned my neck as Jock returned, but this time with someone I did recognize.

"Oh no..." Roy Hudson expressed, looking at me. "Jesus, Moira, why?"

Roy Hudson was a police sergeant in charge of investigations when my father was alive and Mr. Phillips was the police chief. He was one of few people who got to wear plain clothes as opposed to the police uniform, although they were still required to wear formal clothes. At this time, he wore a trench coat and pinstripe brown dress pants. He had fair skin and dark eyes. He also wore a fedora to cover his dark hair. He was middle-aged, older than my dad and had to be somewhere in his fifties.

"Yeah..." Jock responded.

I stood up and walked over to them.

"Why Moira? Why?" Hudson questioned.

"I'm sorry, Roy," I responded. "I've probably let you all down."

"You think?" Jock questioned.

"Shut it, Jock," Hudson replied. "Alright, listen, the two of you. From what I understand, we got Feds on the way to take over the investigation of this case. I don't know where from, or how long it will take them to get here, but I made a phone call, and we've got a Dr. Lambert from Cabernet Technologies on his way too. I've explained to him the situation based on what you told me Jock, so let's pray that's enough to reduce probable cause to believe that Moira was up to no good."

"You know Dr. Lambert?" I questioned.

"Of course," Hudson replied. "He's a friend through Charlemagne Cabernet. The two of them owe me some favors. Look here, we're all in this together. Until those clowns from the capital get here, Moira is still our prisoner."

"She's not been arrested yet," Jock pointed out. "She's just a suspect in what happened, and by that cause she's also our responsibility. If we just let her go, it could go bad for either of us. At any rate, we're not supposed to interfere. Conway told us to not investigate."

"We can take the heat when it comes, but right now, as lead investigator around here, I'm taking Moira to an interview room as we wait for Dr. Lambert," Hudson stated. "Besides, Conway told you not to do anything, and I outrank him."

"Ah Christ," Jock swore, "we're so done."

"Shut it, Jock," Hudson replied. "This is your sister we're talking about here. Wouldn't you put all you got on the line to save her?"

"She broke the law…" Jock remarked. "All we're doing is ensuring that we may join her. I got a family, Roy."

"Yeah, so do I numbskull, it's the two of you," Hudson expressed, "and the rest of the numbskulls your dad used to care about at this joint. We're not letting some federal police have at one of you for some rules and regulations to do with nuclear safety. Moira wasn't doing any of that sort of stuff, you told me yourself. Right, Moira?"

"I just wanted to know what happened to our dad."

"And I told you to drop it," Jock snarled at me.

"Put your hands out, Moira," Hudson expressed, ignoring Jock. "I've got to handcuff you to transfer you to another room. Don't you worry, we're going to get you out of here."

"And what are we going to do afterwards? Hide her in an attic? Even if she gets out of here, she'll still be arrested out in public and be back where she was before. Are you encouraging her to run?"

"No, there'll be no need to run once we sort this out with Dr. Lambert. Believe me."

Hudson put the cuffs back on me, and then Jock opened the cell door to bring me out. We walked down the aisle around to an area beside where there were some bright white interview rooms. Jock brought me inside and set me down at a table, while Hudson took out his notebook and began to write.

"Quit being such a dick, Jockstrap," Hudson jibed. "Get your sister some coffee. Dr. Lambert will be here any minute."

Jock ignored the nickname and left. Hudson pulled out a chair and then looked at me.

"How're you holding up, kiddo?" he asked.

"I'm scared, Roy."

"Yeah, I'm scared for you too," Hudson expressed. "What were you thinking though? Jock told me that you went over there because you had questions about the way your dad had died."

"I do."

"Tell me about that."

I explained to him everything that I had at this point, including the details about Zimmerman, the Huntsman, and GDP.

"Do you know what happened to my dad?" I asked at the end of it.

Mr. Hudson took off his hat and placed it aside. He then brought a hand to his thinning head and sat back.

"You were friends with Mr. Cabernet, we're you?"

"Yeah, I was," Hudson replied. "Good friends, since we were kids. We were in boy scouts together. Him, Cole Phillips, and me. Even after Cole and him stopped being friends, Charles and I stayed friends. Of course, when I joined the police here that didn't change our friendship. I kept him in the loop about stuff, and Cole knew what I was up to, which is why I never made out of sergeant until he left to become mayor. He kept me down deliberately, even though I worked my ass off to become lead detective."

"You were promoted?"

"That's right – it's now Captain Hudson."

"Oh, congratulations," I expressed. "I'm happy for you."

"I'm still dealing in investigations. We had a few new guys make it to sergeant, including your uncle, but I'm also doing what your old man used to do too…

"Here's the thing though with what happened to your old man. In honesty, something did happen – what that was, I'm not sure. Charles offered to tell me, but I refused because we agreed it wasn't necessary for me to know and could put up in a load of trouble. I don't know what those details were, but the least I can do is offer you that same warning he gave me. It's the least I could do because I care about you and your brother, Moira. I mean, what's happening now is one thing, but from what I understood from what Charles told me, it was a whole other thing – we're talking big people in big places, and these sorts of secrets are secrets that get you and the people you care about killed."

"It all has to do with secret societies, doesn't it? My grandma used to tell me about them."

"I don't know," Hudson affirmed. "I just know that it's serious, and despite what happened to your dad, which I was told to truly be tragic, he did not die any other way than as a hero."

I nodded and replied, "I've heard everyone say that…"

Jock opened the interview room with a cup of coffee, gave it to me, and then said, "Dr. Lambert is here. I'm bringing him in."

"Ah, good," Hudson responded, standing up. He put his hat back on and I looked over as Jock left and returned minutes later with the man known as Dr. Bartholomew J. Lambert. He was a middle-aged man with dirty blonde hair that was lengthy and came up to his shoulders. He wore a striped blue-white collared shirt and grey dress pants. He also wore a wool coat and had a briefcase in his hand. He had fair skin and wore glasses.

"Hello, Dr. Lambert," Hudson greeted, shaking his hand. "It's been a while."

"Hi, captain," Lambert responded, shaking his hand. He then waved over to me. "Hi, Moira, it's been a while… though I suppose you don't remember me."

I shook my head at him.

"Right…" Dr. Lambert remarked. "You were at my office earlier today, weren't you? You left quite a mess. Roy and your brother have told me a bit about what you've been looking into – your dad and what happened in this town a few years ago when he died."

"Do you know?" I asked.

Dr. Lambert didn't immediately respond and instead said, "Listen, Moira, I think what's in both of our interest here is to get those cuffs off you and agree that what happened today at Cabernet laboratories was nothing short of a misunderstanding. We'll have to come up with some sort of cover story, right?"

"We could think of something," Hudson admitted.

Jock shook his head and replied, "I can't believe this is happening. We're in so much trouble…" He turned to the side as he placed his hands on his neck.

"Nevermind him," Hudson acknowledged. "I'll sort him out later. Right now, just know that Moira came to see you, and she as a computer programmer was set to do some work for you, and it was urgent work, and she had no way of getting hold of you.

There was no interest in any nuclear research, or material, or anything of that kind. Moira has never expressed interest in terrorist activity. She doesn't even know any terrorists. She loves her country. She would die for her country. Understood?"

"Yeah, sure," Dr. Lambert responded. "Works for me…"

"And what do we tell the federal police when they show up?" Jock asked. "We got the wrong guy? What if they look and see reason to call us out on our bullcrap."

"That won't happen because we'll stick by it together – there is no reason that those cops should have to doubt us. I'll put my word on it, you put your word on it, Jock, and Dr. Lambert and Moira will stick to that story. They'll shake hands for the Allabrese All-Star if they have to – say, doc, you don't have any jobs that Moira could be slipped into to connect loose ends?"

"Hm?" Dr. Lambert questioned. "Yeah, maybe… I mean, I could figure something out for sure if we need to."

"There you go."

"Thank you," I expressed to them. "All of you… I'm very grateful."

"Don't worry about it," Hudson responded. "Doc, I'll get your sworn statement on the case and include it in my report. Jock – get your sister out of here."

"Sure…" Jock responded, going over to remove the cuffs from my wrist. He then passed them to Mr. Hudson before he helped me stand up and brought me out. He returned me to the booking station where I waited for my stuff, and once I had my stuff, he guided me out through the garage rather than the main entrance. "I suppose if those cops show up and don't change their mind, or are convinced, you won't be too far?"

"Yeah, of course," I replied, rummaging through my backpack to make sure everything was okay.

"No, the correct answer is that I let you out and then you don't come anywhere near this place ever again," Jock affirmed as he led me outside. "You've become obsessed to know the truth about what happened to dad, but there is no truth other than what we all knew happened to him. If you stay here, you're just going to get yourself in trouble again, or those cops will come looking for you and they'll come after me, Rebecca, and Gavin. You take your stuff, you don't even bother to go home, and you get yourself the hell away from here and going back to Edmonton, or Calgary, or hell go anywhere you want because I don't want to see you again."

"Jock, what are you saying?" I questioned.

Jock took out a clip from his jacket and passed me some money. He replied, "I'm saying that I don't want you near me or my family. You're bad news, Moira. I mean, look at the equipment you carry around. I forgot how much of a cyber criminal you even were and if it's not this, it'll be something else. Just go away, anywhere, but don't come back here to this town. I'll make sure your stuff at home gets to you, but just go."

I didn't respond as Jock closed the door and left me out in the cold. I felt a tear fall down my cheeks. I put the money in my coat and then walked down the sidewalk. I came around to the street corner where I waited to cross the street and for the light to change. I supposed I had to go someplace, but I didn't know where.

"Hey!" a voice shouted out.

I turned to my left and saw Dr. Lambert approach me. I faced him and he caught up to me. We stood about two meters apart from each other.

"Dr. Lambert…"

"Sorry," Dr. Lambert expressed, "I just wanted to catch you before you went off on your way to ask you something…"

"What did you want to ask me?"

"What do you know so far?"

"Well… I know that my dad and Mr. Cabernet were working together…." I responded. I briefly told him about the footage, my talks with *Louis*, Salmar Cabernet, and also what I found on his computer, especially about the GDP. "What is the GDP?"

"The GDP is not a what, they're a who," Dr. Lambert replied. "Tell me, what are you going to do now?"

"My brother kicked me out of his house, so now I got to organize travel someplace else – likely Edmonton to go to my mom's house."

"And this investigation of yours... Are you going to continue to pursue the GDP?"

"I don't know," I honestly replied. "I really just want to go home right now. Maybe, I will."

Dr. Lambert nodded and replied, "What if I gave you the answers you were looking for and put your mind to rest."

"You'd do that?"

"On one condition though, you can't tell anyone what I tell you – you take what I've told you to the grave, because if not, well – the consequences of what I tell you are severe. This GDP, they're not the nicest people."

"So I've heard..." I responded.

"Do we have a deal?"

I looked at him as he offered his hand, but before I could shake it, I was met with the loud screech of a car coming to a halt. I turned to my left as a black SUV parked itself at the corner and a person immediately exited out from the driver's seat.

"What the hell do you think you're doing!" Finn shouted out. "Have you gone mental, mate?! Leave her alone!"

Finn came around, causing me to side-step as Dr. Lambert faced him.

"She has a right to know," Dr. Lambert argued. "If she doesn't hear it from us, she'll hear it from someplace else and put herself and other people into grave danger."

"Mate, you're going to put us in trouble if you utter even a word to her," Finn argued. "I wasn't supposed to know about it all, and it's only because I had bad company that I knew – to inherit the weight of that secret from my father was not a nice thing to inherit."

"Finn, you're wanted for terrorism in the United Kingdom with a still-active search warrant," Dr. Lambert replied. "You can't expect me to take your seriously in that warning."

"Argh, that's different," Finn replied. "Those were mistakes from the past; motivated actions that have long passed. I made a mistake, but honestly, I'm more scared of these people you and my dad speak about than the British government hunting me down for some wrongthink."

"Ah, they're not so bad..." Dr. Lambert asserted. "I worked for them for a while, and I may be sworn to secrecy, but it's not like they're listening in to every word we're saying. Moira will learn the truth of it all, something that she should very well know because unlike you, she was a participant in their activities. I don't know why, but possibly for the sole reason of ineffective bureaucracy, they decided to wipe her mind from what happened not only that October, but the August preceding that year too. Moira's acts in both incidents were valiant, and if anyone has a right to know the truth, it's her. I make that call, not you, so you can push right off, Finn."

"You can't do this – you're making a mistake!"

"You're more than free to scramble away," Dr. Lambert expressed as Finn grew increasingly frustrated.

A car honked at Finn's car, causing him to go around and drive around the corner where he rolled down his window.

"I was involved with the GDP?" I questioned.

"Yes, you were," Dr. Lambert expressed. "We worked together; it was not just your dad and Charlemagne. It was me, you, your dad, Charlemagne, and even Diana and Tristan. We all worked together to help save others."

I was in awe as I heard those words. I wanted to know more.

"I'm warning you, Barry," Finn shouted. "If you tell her anything, they'll come for us!"

"Quit being so paranoid!" Dr. Lambert replied. "Come on, Moira. Come with me to my home. I'll tell you everything you need to know, but we shouldn't talk in public. Besides, it's a lot for you to process."

I could hear Finn yell as he closed his window and drove off. I looked over as he went away and then over to Dr. Lambert. I nodded to him and agreed to his terms of secrecy.

Act 2, Scene 4

I sat in the passenger seat of Dr. Lambert's electric vehicle (EV), a Cabernet *Durandel*. I must have been away from Allabrese a long time because never did I anticipate electric vehicles to be in these parts. I wasn't even sure where there were any EV charging stations in this entire town. I supposed there must have been some at Cabernet Technologies headquarters. The car hummed as it drove along the road from intown into St. Allan's Plains and then northbound along the cliffside where there some of the nicer homes around the base of Linz Mountain on approach to the water treatment facility. I was quiet as I listened to Dr. Lambert explain some information to me.

"I was Charlemagne's best friend since we met each other in university," Dr. Lambert expressed. "Him and I used to bounce ideas off each other, help each other out in our respective programs, and lived together as roommates for three years. Charles left at the end of our third year over some disagreement with the university. I stayed to graduate and then do my post graduate studies when unbeknownst to him, me and his ex-girlfriend got to know each other a bit more and fell in love. He found out a few months later when he came to visit me and explained that he was very happy for the two of us, which were the same words he used at my wedding a few years later. He was my best man. Judith and I… we were his best friends. Judith and I were workaholics though. Charles got me a job in his company's brand-new research and development program in Harlech, while Judith went to work for the university. We didn't get to see each other that much since she would be all around the world and I would be setting up the foundation of Cabernet Technologies. We did that for ten years when by the time we were in our mid-thirties, it suddenly dawned on us that we spent so much time apart, and Charles knew it. He wasn't envious though. At the same time we were beginning to realize the problems in our marriage. Charles told me that he was preparing to marry his childhood friend, Manon Dumas while Judith was in Europe at the time. We had come up with a plan to put us all together again over in Allabrese. For years we had planned to have Cabernet Technologies move out there, which we slowly did. We had set up shop in an old industrial factory that used to belong to Cabernet Chemicals, and some portable trailers a couple years ago, while the finishing touches were made on the permanent research facility. Charles though didn't get married, but we came around and moved to Allabrese to be together as chief researchers regardless. We wanted to have a family. Judith conceived a child, and I was told it was a healthy child who she carried to the third trimester, but then she had a miscarriage.

"Poor Judith... she wept, and she wept for our kid, and I wept for the two of them. He was a boy, and as we agreed upon, because we wanted to keep the gender a secret, we said we'd either name him Dexter if he was a male or Sonny if she was a female. Judith was so ready to become a mother, and she was excited for it too. She had spent an enormous amount of time preparing the children's rooms at house, buying clothes and furniture with me. Perhaps she went a bit overboard because like I said, we didn't know whether this would be a male or female, but it was like she was preparing to have twins, maybe knowing that she didn't want to stop at one child. What a tragic circumstance to return from the hospital after discharge and be surrounded by so much joy in a room for a child that she had lost. It was too much for her, and don't get me wrong, it was hard for me too, but harder for her because she had so much love in her heart. She was ready to give up her life for this child, and there was nothing she could have done to see that through. Judith refused to sleep a night in our home, so she left to go sleep at Charlemagne's home. A few days later, she tells me that she wants to separate, and she can't even look at me when she says the words. I thought I had done something wrong, but she insisted that I didn't. Charles tells me that it's because I remind her of the child, the son that she had lost. She was on the brink of a mental breakdown, so I sell the house, but I don't want her to have to leave Allabrese because of me. She had nowhere else to go, no friend like Charles, and she liked Allabrese. One night, we have a fight about the situation, she calls the police and they forcibly separate us. The incident is enough for her to plead to have a restraining order, so now I can't even go to work, but Charles comes through again. He buys an abandoned observatory on Nattau Mountain, plans to re-open it as an extension of Cabernet Technologies for astronomical research, and there I go to live for the rest of my life until Judith died in a tragic accident five years ago. Ever since then, I've been back in my former job – before Judith died, she was in a relationship with Charles again, but something happened between them; Charles told me that she had used him in some scheme to get his fortune by marrying and then killing him, and it was a hard pill to swallow. I couldn't believe that my Judy could do something like that, but at the same time, she wasn't the same person anymore. She had died in a way when our child had died, and in those final years, she was conned by Audric Zimmerman to do his bidding for him – that I could believe more and more, because that man was evil. Nonetheless, Charles assured me that she did those things because of me, for me, and that in the end, she still loved me – she hated Charlemagne, but again, that wasn't the real Judy."

"I've heard about Audric Zimmerman," I replied. "Salmar Cabernet suggested to me that he was involved in what happened here in October 2019."

Dr. Lambert nodded and said, "That's certainly partially correct." He drove through the gates of a stone-brick home on the riverside. He drove around a short round cul-de-sac within the property and then turned off the car. We both stepped out and I caught a glance at the home. Dr. Lambert lived in a two-story home with dormer windows in the attic. There was a detached garage ahead of us on the left. The roof of the home was arched outwards, like an English cottage. There were planters in front of the white-framed windows which had diagonal patterns on the front. The surroundings were well decorated with shrubs and trees. I looked up to the skies above as I saw a contrail, likely due to a passing jet above us. "Come on inside, I'll keep telling you the rest."

I walked into the cottage home with Dr. Lambert, and he led me into a sitting room on the left. I looked around at the decoration, which seemed old fashioned for a middle-aged researcher. I saw a picture of Judith Lambert and looked at her. She had medium blonde hair and fair skin. The home was partially amess with stacks of newspapers, legal boxes, and other items around.

"Take a seat," Dr. Lambert expressed. "I don't usually have guests come over."

"Your home is certainly something…" I remarked, looking at the decoration.

"My home is Judith's home," Dr. Lambert responded. "After we separated, she lived here while I lived in the observatory. After she died, she left me everything she owned in her will despite the fact we were divorced. Can I get you something? Water or tea?"

"No, I'm fine," I replied, sitting down in a plush sofa. "I just want to hear your story."

"Alright then," Dr. Lambert responded, looking out the window. I saw a pair of headlights come through the window, causing me to turn around and see a black vehicle park nearby. The vehicle was parked near the exit. Someone exited out and made their way to the door. "Sorry, let me just get that…"

I felt butterflies in my stomach as the shadow of the figure came to the door. I was about ready to pounce from my seat. Dr.

Lambert unlocked the door and opened it. I leaned over to see if I could catch sight of them.

"I'm warning you, stop what you're about to do!" Finn cried out.

"Dammit, Finn, what are you doing here?" Dr. Lambert responded. Finn pushed through and came into the foyer. He turned over to me and then to Dr. Lambert.

"You're going to get all of us in huge trouble," Finn expressed. "My father isn't here to negotiate with these people. They'll eat us alive."

"You're being paranoid, Finn."

"I'm not," Finn responded, "listen to me. These are vile people. They eat even their own. Their lust for blood knows no end. They are an evil, satanic lot."

"You greatly over-estimate them," Dr. Lambert responded. "I worked for them for less than a year, and they're hardly the villains you portray them as. Besides, they were worse before the near alien invasion. The director after that is not such a bad woman... I'll explain it all to her if I have to."

"Ha, trust a woman," Finn remarked, looking over to me. "The last thing I want is to see that woman."

"You wouldn't have to see her if you didn't set any forests on fire," Dr. Lambert expressed, passing by him to go into the parlor. "Sit down." Finn came around and sat down in an armchair on my right beside a fireplace. Dr. Lambert sat in another chair near the foyer. He cleared his throat before he proceeded to talk. "The GDP – also known as the Global Defense Project, was led by a woman that me and your father knew because of our exploits that avoided an alien invasion in the summer of 2018. Her name is Ms. Eleanor Joan Black – she was put in charge to run the organization by their bosses, the Committee of Concerned Nations."

"Was? Who's running the show now?"

"Nobody," Dr. Lambert answered, "the Global Defense Project was disbanded a year ago, and Ms. Black's whereabouts are unknown to me."

"What? Why didn't you say anything to me?" Finn questioned.

"For a start, you were in South America when I found out, and second of all, I didn't know that you knew about Ms. Black or the GDP. Your father wasn't supposed to have told you about them because we were all sworn to secrecy at threat of not just our lives, but imprisonment in one of the worst hells on Earth. Just because the GDP don't exist anymore though doesn't mean that their bosses don't, and what I'm not sure about is whether some sort of successor program replaced them."

"Hang out, how come you know they don't exist anymore?"

"Because we've hired a few of the scientists that were able to leave before it happened."

"Hold on," I interrupted, "I have no idea what you're talking about. Dial it back for me – who are the GDP?"

"You should know who the GDP are Moira, because you worked with Ms. Black that same summer of 2018. The GDP are a secret organization with a mandate to ensure that the status quo of global order, or in other words, that 'The New World' order hallmarked by the existence of the United Nations, is able to exist in the current century and that no changes to the balance of power are met. They are an international paramilitary organization with jurisdiction in every one of their member nations, which is every nation on Earth except for Taiwan, North Korea, Palestine, Western Sahara, and Vatican City. When we ran into them in the summer of 2018, it was when they were responding to a threat of extraterrestrial activity, but that sort of business is only part of their objectives. They will do anything from corporate sabotage and espionage, to overthrow dictators, and do anything you can think of that would ensure that a rapid change to the status quo or any threat to the status quo, or in other words, a liberal democratic world, are repressed and destroyed."

"Yeah, like aid my father to sack Audric Zimmerman," Finn expressed.

"In August 2018, during a meteor shower, an alien civilization left behind some precious cargo to them that Charles and I stumbled upon in the fields behind Cabernet Manor. We were quickly met with the aliens who wanted that precious cargo, as well as the GDP and Ms. Black's black clad agents. They arrested Charles for the crime of treason, brought him to their base out in the Alaskan panhandle, and kept him there while Judith came after me to warn me about them. The aliens stayed with us as we began to devise a plan to rescue Charles as it was mentioned to us that the alien civilization would declare war on us if we did not rescue that cargo, and thanks to a bit of luck, Charlemagne was able to return with the help of Ms. Black who was not yet leader of the organization and disagreed with the current director's intent to lead the world to a war of total annihilation. I believe around that same time, you showed up, happening to stumble upon us, the aliens, and because of your skills as a hacker, and Ms. Black seemingly knowing who you were, you were tasked to join us as we moved out to the Cabernet Rocketry base in Kennte, B.C.

"From there, we joined forces with Ms. Black and a few agents that joined her in her defection to stop the alien invasion. We reverted a spacecraft intended by Cabernet Rocketry to be a vessel used for a mission to Mars to take us to the alien spacecraft, while Ms. Black and her crew plotted to return to the GDP base in Alaska, overthrow the current director who had betrayed his mandate to maintain the status quo, and convince the Committee of Concerned Nations to avert war. Your part in that mission was pivotal; you hacked into the GDP computer systems and gave us a window both into the base and also of a timeline to act which we otherwise would have missed. You joined Ms. Black in their mission to go to the headquarters in Alaska where your skills as a hacker played further use, and together we stopped a near global catastrophe."

I looked at Dr. Lambert as if he had just explained to me some fictional story, or a roleplay game background story.

"You mean to tell me that I – me, did all that? How come I don't remember?"

Dr. Lambert sighed and replied, "It's probably because you were scooped up a year later in the mass-deneuralization campaign. A technology I had the privy to look at during my time with the GDP was their capability to brainwash the mind to such an extent that previous memories could be changed for artificial memories. After what happened between us and the aliens, we came together to sign a treaty in which we were sworn to never speak about the event with others as well as deny the existence of aliens – these were the Treaty of Juneau and Roswell respectively. I left and joined the GDP shortly afterwards, but then left again to re-join Charlemagne the following spring as I found a lack of fulfillment in working with them. They were surprisingly lenient about me leaving, but by this time, Ms. Black was in charge, and I was technically still under oath of secrecy about them and everything else.

"And then October came around, and what we were all told to be a series of severe airborne illnesses began to grip people, and of course that was the epidemic that's told around here, but that was not true. Enter Mr. Audric Zimmerman, CEO of Zimmerman Industries, former director of Cabernet Industries, and rival to Charlemagne – this man had in possession some technology that Mr. Cabernet was competing with him for which allowed him to begin researching the potential of the human mind integrated with electronics, otherwise known as psionics. Mr. Zimmerman and his scientists were able to make that breakthrough with ease, taking some of the world's most hardened soldiers together to create supersoldiers with that capability to use their minds for various powers and intents."

"Such as frying the brains of others? I saw something like that in one of the videos I had."

"Yes, I believe that was one of their powers. Among them was a supersoldier who had escaped. His name was Maximilian Bauer, the biological father of Tristan Merrick, so I'm told. He came to find Charlemagne, and I just happened to have been with him at the end of a Halloween party at the old library when this man approached him. He told us he had important information about Zimmerman Corporation, but then he disappeared right when the epidemic sprang up. Within a few days, the entire town was under lockdown, but Charlemagne and Cabernet Manor, since his home was on the other side of the river, were spared, but Charlemagne, as always, was skeptical. One night, he travelled with his bodyguard detail, the Protection Squad, across the river to investigate and regroup with other colleagues, including me, but the operation went sideways, and Charlemagne was only able to escape with Bauer. After this attempt, the Canadian Armed Forces were replaced with Zimmerman's private contracted army, the Huntsman Legionnaires, who set up shop at the Nattau Bridge and began to take control of the occupation.

"Charlemagne made a second attempt a day before Halloween to come and attempt to put an end to the occupation with Bauer at his side, and they met up with me and your dad in an abandoned Medici gang warehouse on the way to the old mines. Your dad, Moira, had become the leader of a resistance who defied and rejected the narrative that there was an epidemic, especially when the Canadian Armed Forces had fled. The Nattau Police Department had disbanded and was replaced with a secret police, and the entire town put into lockdown, and he was correct. Myself and some of the scientists that lived and were unaffected by the airborne disease had done some preliminary research to believe that something was up, and after Charlemagne came around, we came to the realization that there was no disease and that instead, there was a hallucinogenic in the tap water resulting in poisoning with signs and symptoms of hallucinations, delirium, and other respiratory tract issues. Charlemagne and Bauer travelled to the water treatment facility to confirm those details, which they did, and they stole evidence to back up what the Huntsman had been at it for weeks."

"I have that footage – it's on the USB drive I was given," I pointed out, "but why do this?"

"The reason was more simple than any of us could have believed – Audric Zimmerman knew that his supersoldier, Bauer, was in Allabrese, and in order to establish control of the town to find him, he choked all of us into submission to make it easier to find him. Both Charlemagne and Bauer knew the truth, and they set to end the occupation and release the truth out to the world, which was successfully done. On that Halloween night, the resistance led by your dad made their attack as people died due to the poison in the water, and they took on the secret police until they forced Chief Phillips into submission, and then joined forces to take on the Huntsman at Nattau Bridge. Believe it or not, Moira, but you played a part in that. You helped Mr. Cabernet at the water treatment facility as you took control of Charles' quad-copter drone, and then you aided him on the ground during the uprising until the rest of the supersoldiers attacked us. I remember you were with me in the warehouse that night until we had to make our escape, and then based on what Mr. Cabernet told me, you and Diana and Tristan were held hostage at Nattau Bridge where the others rescued you. You were able to upload the footage to the World Wide Web through the mercenary's own network, and the footage was all leaked and it was over… or so we had thought.

"Mr. Zimmerman had a final plan to eradicate Bauer, and he nearly got away with it had Bauer not sensed it. The Huntsman had taken control of the fusion reactor at Cabernet Technologies and intended to overload it to cause a massive nuclear explosion that would have evaporated the entire county in one of the largest nuclear blasts known to man. Bauer was able to contain the blast, but it cost him his life too. He reduced the blast size to just consume the building, and that was it. The next day, the GDP showed up and began to do serious damage control. They rallied all of us up, all of us who participated in the uprising and began to deprogram us. Nobody was spared in that campaign, including Charles and me, and the Diana and Tristan, although we didn't go through such an extensive process. We got to keep some of our memories, while others, like you, didn't, so we remembered what happened, although we sincerely doubted ourselves. We felt like it was all just a dream. We were all led to believe that everything that happened was a lie. They gaslit us, and we believed them because so much of it was farfetched, the evidence of the Huntsman, supersoldiers, and hallucinogenic disappeared, and we all believed it was just a very serious disease that gripped us. They blamed Charlemagne for the violence that unfolded that night, while at the same time they promised him immunity from prosecution. Meanwhile, people like your dad who gave up their lives were still honored, but the true depths of their sacrifice were covered up. Your dad was shot in the siege of the Huntsman's fortress at the Nattau River, and he bled out. He was shot by a sniper while leading the charge."

I felt a tear roll down my cheek.

"We all thought that it was true – what they led us to believe, except Tristan for some reason. Eventually, both Charlemagne and I discovered the necklaces used by the supersoldiers, which was enough evidence to tell us that it was all true. I suppose in a sense, we got it off easy because we did remember what happened, but thought it was just a dream – that Bauer had manipulated all of us to destroy the fusion reactor, but that was not true. As we began to investigate more closely, we came to our senses to realize the GDP had betrayed us, but we couldn't do anything to restore the memories of others, nor was there much of a point. We were talking about hundreds of people to suddenly wake up – there was no point, and it was not Charles' intent, at least yet. We would have had repercussions with the GDP if we defied them in that effort."

"Oh my God..." I simply answered, "and it is all true, because I saw the footage. It all makes so much sense."

"Do you remember?" Finn questioned. "Have the memories come back to you?"

"Absolutely not," I responded, "but it's weird, because I can believe you despite what I used to think of as true being not true."

"I'm sure with time, and a little exposure to the truth, you'll come to remember," Dr. Lambert expressed. "So, that's the GDP – Charles had a few more run-ins with them before he died. I believe the last I heard of them was when they showed up a few weeks before he died, demanding some precious cargo that he had."

"Ah, yes, I remember that," Finn responded, "but they didn't get it. After he did die, some shady characters came to the manor to muscle it off me, but I didn't relent."

"Is there any other proof?" I questioned. "I mean, I believe you guys, but what else can you show me so that I can believe you? Can you show me the necklaces? Is there other footage? This is such an eye-opening experience."

"Yeah, wait until you learn what else the government has lied to you about," Finn said.

"The necklaces I believe were destroyed, and the gems, a part of that precious cargo we were talking about, hidden. I think there was a mass grave somewhere where they buried all the mercenaries, but I haven't checked that out, and then there was also..."

My eyes immediately looked out the window as I saw an object quickly fly into the main entrance door. In a next second, an explosion detonated, and I was thrown to my right as rubble flew towards me. I shielded my face as I fell onto the ground. I looked around as I lay in the ruins of Dr. Lambert's living room. The ceiling had collapsed, and I could see a hand poke out from under the rubble with streaks of blood. I looked in terror and stayed put as I stared. Suddenly, I felt a hand on my shoulder and looked at Finn. He was talking to me, but I couldn't hear a word he said as my ears rang. It seemed like he was yelling at me. He tapped my shoulder and without a moment of hesitation, stood up onto his knees and attempted to guide me out. His face was bloodied and dirty. I could see blood on his face. He got me onto my knees, and I looked around as a fire engulfed the foyer where there was nothing left and skylight poured in from above. I looked towards where the window was and saw large white SUVs drive in and surround the front of the house with sirens wailing.

"Moira!" Finn shouted as my hearing returned. "Moira, let's go! We've got to get out of here!"

I looked at him, nodded, and picked up my backpack on the ground beside me. Finn guided me to crawl beneath some rubble behind him, and then he joined me. We came out into the kitchen where we fled out into the backyard.

"Oh my God…" I expressed. "I think I'm going to be sick…"

"No time to be sick now," Finn replied. "We're under attack."

"Dr. Lambert, do you think he's…"

"I don't know," Finn rejected, "but right now we're going to be dead too if we don't get out of here."

"I saw police cars…"

"Enemies no doubt," Finn suggested. "Too soon to be the friendly Nattau police. Come on, we've got to lay low. They don't know we've survived."

Finn rushed me out and towards a gate that led out to the wilderness behind Dr. Lambert's home. We walked down a trail that took us towards a low cliff towards a beach below. Finn looked around before he took both of us down to the beach. He held my hand as he led me away from Dr. Lambert's home.

"Oh my God... what is happening?" I expressed as we walked.

"GDP disbanded my ass..." Finn grumbled. "I warned him, didn't I? I told both of you to drop it because they may have been listening, but he insisted they were gone and that's just what they want you to believe."

"I- I thought they were allies- I thought Ms. Black..."

"Ugh, who knows if Ms. Black is even in charge of them anymore. That's what I was worried about – a totally new person who isn't with the program. Ugh, we're so screwed!"

Finn continued to lead me down the beach until we reached a staircase that went up and into the forest. We continued to run down the coast until we came around to St. Allan's Plains.

"Where are we going?" I questioned. "If they're back there, they'll be looking for us anywhere."

"No, they'll be looking for us in the wreckage," Finn replied. "We've got a good few minutes until they realize they failed to kill us, and they'll be hunting us someplace else. Come on, we've got to get to Cabernet Manor. It's the safest place around here."

Finn came around to the beach again where we trekked along as we went towards Nattau Bridge. Once there, we stayed put under the bridge as Finn surveyed his surroundings, and then we climbed up to the top level of the bridge via a staircase, but Finn didn't want to go all the way up, so we used the catwalks underneath. I stayed quiet as I attempted to process what was going on, while Finn led me with a determined look on his face. We reached the end of the bridge and climbed down via a staircase that went to the beach again, and then we followed along until we came up to a wooden staircase that went up to the road. Finn poked out his head as he looked around. He surveyed our surroundings and then looked at me to signal that it was clear. Finn and I came over and quickly crossed the road to reach the manor gates, pushing through and locking them behind.

I turned around and looked at Cabernet Manor, never believing I'd retreat here for safety, and Finn led me to the front door where he opened up and then led me inside.

"What are we going to do? We've got to call the police – my brother…"

"Bah, Nattau County Police won't save us," Finn declined.

"Then we need to call somebody else," I remarked, following him to the library on the left. "RCMP? Canadian Armed Forces?"

"For all we know, those are the ones on our tail," Finn replied, coming to a bookcase on the immediate right on approach to the study. He pulled a book in precise combination to cause the door to latch open.

"What about your bodyguards? Do they still exist?"

"Yeah, but not to the same extent. I'm not really one that's been needing protecting…"

Finn left the bookcase open while he then went into the study. He then paused for a moment as he turned to me.

"You don't have a mobile phone, do you? On hand?"

"Yeah, why?"

Finn snatched the phone, threw it the ground and began to stomp on it.

"Devilish technology!" Finn cried out.

"What the hell!"

"Shut up," Finn snapped back, "don't you think they can track us?!" He picked up the cellphone, popped the back off to remove the battery and threw the rest of it into the fire. He threw the battery aside and then went to his computer. He shook the mouse to awaken, typed in a password, while I came around to see what he was doing. His monitor showed several CCTV cameras around. "By the way, thanks for messing up my cameras – went a whole few days before noticing they were off."

Finn knelt down besides a cabinet and began to open a safe. He took out a tin box and placed it on the desk.

"Do you have any weapons by chance? Other than that bow and arrow? Didn't your dad have loads of weapons?"

"Yeah, he did..." Finn replied.

"And you?"

"Nope... none left, I'm afraid. I don't use guns..."

"You what?"

"I don't use guns. I had a bad experience the last time I held one, never again..."

"Oh my God, then we're so screwed...."

The house began to shake, the lights flickered, and I immediately turned and saw that one of the cameras for the main entrance was off-line.

"What was that?"

"Ugh, I told you they could track our location. That's why I don't have a bloody cellphone!"

"Don't yell at me!" I replied. "How was I supposed to know."

"Ignorant woman!" Finn yelled, walking off to the other side to look out the window to the patio. "Holy hell – they've blown out the center of the house!"

"What?!" I rushed over and sure enough, the entire wall of the center of the house was gone.

Finn stepped back and placed a hand to his forehead. "What could they want? What do they need? Ugh, it's those damn crystals, isn't it?"

Finn went back to the tin can, opened it, and took out some items that he put into his pocket. He then threw it aside and picked up some items that he threw into the fireplace. Meanwhile, he began to stack some books around and place them in the safe instead.

"Don't just stand there – help me!" Finn expressed.

"What are these?" I questioned, looking at the leatherbound books.

"Extremely important documentation," Finn replied, pushing them inside. He also put in a stack of paper. "For a project I was working on and hope to finish, if I can survive this mess."

Finn picked up a set of keys and then placed them into his pocket. He then stayed put as he heard a rumble.

"Bloody hell…" Finn expressed, taking my hand. "Get down!"

Finn and I both ducked down and took cover underneath the large wooden desk. The ground at our feet shook and I could hear another explosion detonate from nearby.

"Bloody maniacs!" Finn shouted.

I covered my ears this time as I heard wood crumble and glass shatter. After a slow minute, the torment was over, and I raised my head. We both crawled out into the collapsed office space.

"Come on," Finn expressed, leading me out through the collapsed wall behind the desk. We came out into the side of the manor where I looked behind us and saw that the entire south wing was leveled. Finn grabbed my hand and brought me around to the other side of the property. "I'm running out of places to hide…"

Finn came around to the perimeter of the garden, opening a gate to come in, but not before we both saw some object fall from the sky and hit the ground in the patio, but there was no detonation. After an anticipated explosion, we both continued to walk, coming up the steps, but then stopping as Finn quickly ducked us both down.

I was shocked at what I saw – ahead of us was a metallic object, similar to the metallic skeletal structure I had seen in Finn's study, but with a darker, matte grey surface and less of a skull-shaped head, though it had red eyes and a round head. The anthropoid robot held an arm up as it looked around the property, and scanned the surroundings. After a moment, I could see one more, and then two more, and then three more show up as they landed around the property, leaving behind contrails where they landed. I was brought away from the patio and down to the garden again. We went around to the stables, but then paused as we could see a robot examining the nearby area where the garage was completely destroyed. I was then led back into the garden where we ducked down behind the fountain.

"What are they?" I whispered.

"What do they look like," Finn sarcastically replied. "I don't like the looks of them. We best leave and go into the woods, but we won't last two minutes in them. I need to get down to the sublevels to fetch my gear. Come on."

Finn brought me around to the newly built annex, which was partially destroyed in the blasts, but otherwise held up. He unlocked the door with a key and then we stepped inside. The annex was a small building attached to the end of the north wing, but as I looked around, I realized it looked like a chapel with pews that faced an altar, and atop of that altar a small little gold-colored cabinet. Finn brought me around to the side where there was a door that led into a basement. He then began to guide me through a crawlspace where there was a ladder that went upstairs, but ignored it so he could take me around the entire sublevel of the house to the south wing. He opened a door and then we walked into a basement suite whose furniture was covered in white sheets. We came out towards the other side where there was a corridor that led to the collapsed garage. He instead brought me around to an elevator. The elevator went up a short distance above, and I remembered that this elevator went to the kitchen. Finn brought me into the shaft and motioned me to come close.

"Give me a boost," Finn expressed, "I'm going to climb up and pull you up."

I offered my hand, and he used it to climb up to the top. He then lowered his hand and pulled me over. We then came into the kitchen, which was a total mess as the ceiling had collapsed at the weight of the rubble. We crawled through and came out to the other side, going around the dinette, and then into the living room with caution as we navigated through the rubble. We eventually came around to the foyer where I saw with my own eyes how it had been completely flattened. Finn looked out to see where the robot had gone, and then we began to cross to the other side, but as we were halfway, we paused and looked both ways as the robots homed in on us and immediately pointed their fists towards us.

"Run!" Finn shouted.

The robots opened fire at us, and we dashed to the other side. Finn pushed the door into the library open, but it was blocked by something on the other side. We both pushed to make some space for us to crawl through, and then we went inside, and I followed Finn as he went to the bookcase that he opened. Finn quickly closed the bookcase door once I was inside, and then he took a step back and picked up a lantern in the corner. He turned it on, and we proceeded to go towards an elevator shaft that began to take us down.

"I can't believe what's happening right now," I expressed.

"Yeah, well, you believe us now?" Finn questioned.

"You seem to be surprisingly calm about the entire situation."

"I've been through worse," Finn expressed. "Eventually, moments like these don't faze you anymore and you learn that it's better to be calm in a situation like this then panicked."

The elevator took us into a large wide room. The lights automatically turned on and I realized I was in a panic room of some sort.

"We could hold out for days under here," Finn remarked. "There's enough food and water for two people to live here for months."

"What? We're just going to hide?"

"I don't see any better ideas."

"We've obviously rattled the wrong cages," I pointed out. "What if we clear up this misunderstanding with them – I mean, we know they exist, we could expose them."

"Nah, pretty sure they're already drafting the headlines – mysterious explosion at Cabernet Manor turns out to be gas leak, even though we don't use natural gas in this place. They'll say the same with Dr. Lambert."

"Do you think he's dead?"

"I'm not psychic, Moira," Finn scolded. "I hope not."

"So, let's expose them then... again."

"Ah, and how do you intend to do that? What's happening to us is the least of the world's problems. Besides what's happened here, it's been zero days since the last government coverup scheme. A thousand blokes a day attempt to expose the truth, and the government releases a thousand more to discredit them, and a thousand more to mock them as lame conspiracy theorists. Nah, we're toast. Best we can do is hopefully escape, move somewhere quiet, and live the rest of our lives as chicken farmers."

"What? What kind of life is that? I have family out there – how am I supposed to be confident they won't go out and kill them?"

"You'll just have to hope they're not desperate," Finn expressed, walking over to a latch. "Speaking of which, I should probably cover-up our escape." He pulled the latch, and I could hear some cranks work and the doors into the bunker close. "That's better..."

"So, we're just going to coop up in here together and what? Wait?"

"Ugh, the thought of being locked up here with you alone makes me want to surrender myself for a *coup-de-grace*," Finn said with a sigh, "but I suppose I would rather wait for it to be all clear before I attempt to make a run for it."

"And where would we go?"

"We? What's this *we* business? I warned you to not poke your nose into the GDP, and here we are."

"You're not going to blame me for what happened."

"No, don't worry. I know women are incapable to take responsibility for their actions. You can go ahead and blame Dr. Lambert, or me since I'm alive. I know how woman also like to not blame dead people."

"You're awful," I complained. "You're nothing more than a misogynist, aren't you?"

"Nah, I love women," Finn sarcastically remarked. "Whatever made you think I had beef with them."

"Ugh, you incel."

"Not incel, love," Finn responded. "Just cel, a truecel."

I shook my head and crossed my arms. "Alright then, truecel. Where are you going to go?"

"I think I'd rather like to travel to Switzerland. I was hoping to go there this September anyways. I'm already a bit of a ghost in the system, so I could ensure that Cabernet Industries buys me something out that way and live the rest of my life over there. I'd have to brush up my German but shouldn't be too difficult."

"So, you're a coward as well."

"You expect me to fight our mighty world government overlords?" Finn questioned. "Better men than me have tried and they all died the same. Ever since I came to North America from England, I've come to admit that the best we can do for ourselves is to live our lives in private as best as we can. To live a small humble life is fine by me – all I want."

"And what do you suggest I do?"

"What? You don't like chickens? You can go out and do whatever you want. Heck, you could probably escape and go on living the life you have now. I would just suggest you don't ever come back to Allabrese or get a job with the government. If you want, I know a guy who can get you a new identity."

"No, I don't want to change my identity. I want to live my life..."

"Ah, and there's classic woman behavior number three-hundred and fifty-five – wants the impossible."

"Stop it – I want to live my life, Finn. I don't want to live a lie."

"She doesn't want to live a lie – yes, that's part of the reason why we got into this mess, isn't it? By the way, I forgive you for having my family home completely destroyed. It's not like that place has been up for almost a hundred years."

"No, Finn, come on. Enough joking around – I don't want to live in hiding, or fearing for my life until I die..."

"We all die someday, love..."

"I want to get out of this mess. You can't tell me that this is it... Had I known that this would have happened, I would have never have gone to Cabernet Technologies or let Dr. Lambert tell me what he told me."

"Didn't I warn you? I believe I warned you."

"Yes, but I didn't believe you and I'm sorry. Please, Finn, help me make things right."

Finn took in a deep breath and then replied, "What do you have in mind?"

"Dr. Lambert said that the GDP have a base up north in Alaska. What if we find them and talk to them?"

"What? You think we can just waltz into their base and that'll be the end of it? They'll kill us on site."

"Well, coming to their base of operations is the least they'd expect, but what if we exposed them out that way? If I could get close enough, I could hack into their system, or maybe we could film their base of operations, or something."

"That's insane," Finn expressed. "Besides, from what I recall, last time you hacked in, you were nearly caught. Their cybersecurity has potentially quadrupled in strength since five years ago."

"My skills have quintupled," I remarked. "We would just need a way to go that way."

"No need," Finn responded, "you're looking at a certified pilot who owns a plane parked out on the airfield."

"Perfect, then let's go…"

The bunker began to quake. Some dust flew down from above.

"I don't like that…" Finn expressed.

"Another explosion?"

"They'll reduce the manor to a crater…" Finn remarked, going over to the desktop. "They may be trying to burrow into us, but they'd need a bunker buster to do that…"

"Is there anyway out of here that doesn't involve that shaft?"

"Yeah, but it's in development. There's an escape tunnel that's not quite done yet – goes a couple kilometers away to a hatch in the woods. It's not reinforced, so we'd need to be careful. I've got some kit here – you can ditch that backpack of yours and take something with a more girth and dependable equipment. We'll have to hike our way towards the airfield which will be a couple hours – it's almost sunset anyways. From there, it's an hour or two to get to Juneau where the GDP headquarters are."

"Let's go then."

Act 3, Prologue

Finn slowly opened his eyes as he looked above him. The skies were a yellowish-orange hue and there was a stench of smolder and smoke. He lay on his side and slowly began to pick himself up from where he was at the cusp of a river, caught between some branches as his body was half between the water and the land. Finn appeared young, clean-shaven, though cheek bruised and nose cut. He also had a light scar beneath his left eye. He wore beige tactical cargo trousers tucked into black boots and a white wifebeater sleeveless shirt that exposed his arms. His arms and other parts of his body that were exposed to the warm air had small sections that were red as though sunburnt, and on his left shoulder was a more serious second-degree burn. Finn stepped into the water as he brought a hand to his head, closed his eyes as he tilted his head down and slowly shook his head side to side. He then looked up as a helicopter made a pass above him. He trudged through the shallow water to come around to a beach where he stepped out and began to dry himself. He removed his shirt, squeezed the water out of it and then threw it over his shoulder as he began to walk inland.

A vast forest stood around Finn as he began to enter into the dense woods with tall shrubbery and other flora around him. He overheard another helicopter pass overhead, but the trees covered him, and he continued forward to a clearing in the woods where he stopped. He picked up a stick and began to dig into the ground before harvesting from his surroundings some tinder to put into the hole. He placed some dry grass and then sat down on a log, legs spread apart, and fetched from his belt a small three-inch cannister on a key chain. He unscrewed the steel cannister apart and inside were a few items, including matches, a strike face, a two-and-half inch blade, a small metal rod, some red tinder, some rolled up plastic bags with purification tablets, and some fishing wire. He took out the knife and metal rod, brought them together near the tinder, and then set it ablaze before adding some naturally-found kindling as he began to feed the fire. Once Finn had created a fire, he brought his shirt, rolled it out, and lay it nearby before he sat down and poked through the metal cannister to take out two more items. He removed a small two-inch spray bottle as well as a thin sawblade. He began to spray his wounds, causing him to grimace and tense his jaw as he bit his tongue. Once Finn had finished disinfecting his wounds, he placed the bottle back inside the capsule, screwed it shut and placed it back onto his belt before he picked up some sticks nearby and began to cut into them and make slits. He cut up some branches as well to feed the fire before he began to venture into the forest around him to collect more. He continued to collect some sticks and cut slits into them as he began to construct a frame around the fire. He then returned to the forest where he began to collect some berries and mushrooms that he found nearby, and brought those back to cook gently on the fire.

By the time Finn had finished eating, he picked up his shirt as it lay half in the hidden sunlight and near the fire, put it back on, and then began to kick the fire so that he could continue to venture further into the forest. He collected the stakes that he had made, placed them into one of his pockets, and took out the capsule again where on the other side of the lid was a compass. He checked around and took notice of the directions around him before he began to go east, away from the river he came from and deeper into the forest. Finn looked above and could see a tall cloud of smoke coming from where he was going, though he ventured slightly southeast away from the cloud as he continued to hike through the woods until he reached a gulley. There was an approximately ten-foot gap through the earth, another ten feet tall with each side very steep and the gulley itself narrow as it went along. Finn knelt down and took hold of some vines as he began to lower himself and then continued onward through the gulley at his own pace, trudging through the shrubs and bushes as he continued along. Before long, Finn noticed a steam at his feet and followed the descent of water through as the gulley widened out and became taller above to the point that he was essentially in a canyon trench. The stream also became wider, but was shallow. Another helicopter flew overhead, causing Finn to stop and look upwards. He breathed quietly and then continued along until he stopped as he heard a branch break up ahead. He quickly knelt down and hid behind a shrub as he looked ahead. His eyes appeared focused, and he did not move. He stayed put for several minutes, hand at one of his stakes, but nothing came forward. He did not move though as he continued to stare down for more than several minutes. The ambience around consisted of the running steam of water, the chirping of birds, and a mild wind that came through. After a large portion of time had passed, Finn stood up and began to continue to walk forward with careful steps. He kept a hand at the stakes as he went along the natural path only to see a squirrel that quickly fled from his sight. Finn took a deep sigh and then continued along where he eventually came to a clearing in the trench where he stopped. He began another fire and proceeded to cook another meal consisting of mushrooms that he had gathered. He also took one of the bags from his capsule, went to the stream to collect some of its water and filled the bag with at least half a liter of water. He the placed a quarter of one purification table, allowed it to dissolve, and then downed half of the water, allowing some of it to come down the side of his face and onto his shoulders.

"What a blessing from this earth is water," Finn expressed as he held his head tilted back and then slowly brought it down. He used his wrist to wipe his mouth and then began to roll up the plastic bag to put it back into the capsule.

Finn sat down as he rested and then took the mushrooms away so that he could eat them. The mushrooms appeared like bits of chicken, and were lightly singed. He ate and then continued to sit. His head tilted down at the fire pit he had made. Suddenly, Finn heard another snap of a branch. His head jerked to his left, though he could not see anything as whatever approached him was behind the shrubs. He quickly kicked the dirt around the side of the pit and caused it to collapse into the fire, snuffing it out and then backing out of the way as he came into the shrubs behind him. Finn knelt down and caught sight as the shrubs further ahead began to rustle, and through them appeared a man.

Finn looked carefully at the man that appeared. He wore a greenish-grey tactical helmet with a flashlight at the side and was dressed in outdoorsman gear. He wore a greenish-grey polyester tactical sweater jacket and also wore greenish-grey cargo trousers. He had a large backpack behind him and held in his hands a semi-automatic rifle. He also wore brownish tactical boots. His face was completely concealed though by a gas mask or respirator. The man took careful steps into the clearing and looked around as he knelt down. He then stood up and approached the pit where Finn's fire was, and which still sent fumes upwards into the sky. He knelt down and reached over to the still warm fire with a gloved hand, touched some of the ashes and examined them. His eyes then focused from his fingertips across and over to the shrub where Finn was. He stared directly towards Finn who looked back at him, stunned that he was able to see him where he was, but rather than stand up or point his rifle towards him, the man only stared. He stared as if he could not rightly see Finn, but at the same time, Finn felt as though he was being watched. The two continued to stare at each other for another minute as Finn began to tremble. He placed a hand at a wooden stake and then quickly rushed out of the bush.

Finn yelled out as he jumped the man and raised the stake out to stab him. The man quickly stood up and took a step back. He released his rifle to let it dangle from its strap and free up both hands, and then in an instant movement he grabbed Finn and threw him onto the ground. He locked and took control of Finn's right arm that held the stake, and then quickly performed a control hold before he spun around and locked the joint in place. Finn cried out in pain as he held his arm in that position, on the verge of dislocating his arm. The man held on forcibly, causing Finn to drop the stake, and he was held in place as though he was under arrest.

"Alright! Alright!" Finn cried. "You've got me – you've got me! Blimey, who are you? SAS? They really need to send special forces to get me?"

The man did not release his grip and instead looked down at Finn. Finn opened his eyes and looked at his captor above him. His head upside down to his own. He looked up and stared into the green eyes of the fellow that looked down at him.

"Tristan?" Finn questioned.

The man released his grip and instead picked Finn up by the neck and raised him upwards. Finn grabbed the man's hand as he began to choke him.

"Identify yourself!" the man cried out, voice muffled through the gas mask respirator.

"What? Are you not here for me then?!" Finn answered, struggling to breathe. "The name's Finn! Finn Cunningham!"

The man growled and then threw Finn back. He landed on his bottom and then quickly pushed himself away as the man approached him.

"Finn Cunningham…" the man repeated, looking intensely at Finn. He released his grip and then sheathed his knife. He turned around from him and then continued to examine his surroundings. He picked up his rifle and then turned back to face Finn who continued to lay where he was. "Get up."

Finn pushed himself off from the ground and stood up. The man brought a hand to his face and removed the respirator, revealing the young face of the man behind the mask. He had fair skin, and aside from the green eyes, also had dark, brownish-black hair seen by the stubble around his face and his eyebrows.

"Who are you?" Finn questioned.

"You can call me, Damian," the man expressed in a western American accent. "Damian Cambridge. What's a young guy like you doing out in these forests, Finn? You lost or something?"

"No, I'm not lost," Finn replied, pulling his shirt down and patting his arms. "I know these forests like the back of me hand. I've practically lived in them enough to call them home."

"Who's Tristan? You called me someone named Tristan."

"He's nobody. Just a mate I was travelling with."

"Where is he now?" Damian quickly asked.

"He's long gone," Finn remarked. "Got out of the fire, hopefully. I couldn't say where he is now. I just hope he's alright..."

"I know who you are," Damian stated. "You're the forest dweller – the one that set the Cunningham oil refinery ablaze and who they're saying set the forest on fire as well."

"I did no such thing – to the forest, I mean," Finn answered, bringing a hand to his elbow before he said, "at least... I thought I didn't. I heard the fire's much worse than it started out to be. Is- is it true that the fire at the oil refinery spread into the forest? What about Cunningham Lodge?"

"I wouldn't know – I'm not out here fighting forest fires," Damian responded. "You *are* Finn Cunningham then, aren't you? The son of Aidan Cunningham?"

Finn looked at him with a plain expression, "I don't know – I don't even know who I am anymore. Aidan Cunningham – he isn't me dad apparently. I was adopted – he and mum adopted me. I'm... just Finn now, I suppose." He sighed, looked aside, and then over to Damian. "And you – if you're not here with the forest relief, then who are you with?"

"Nobody. I'm here on my own," Damian replied. "So, if Aidan Cunningham isn't your father, then who is?"

"I don't know – I mean, not for sure. This person, Tristan – he told me he had an idea, but I'm not so sure."

"Oh, and what idea was that?"

"It was a silly idea – he said that the industrialist Charlemagne Cabernet was my father. Can you believe that?"

Damian didn't respond as he looked at Finn. He instead said, "So, I suppose you're on the run then – the police looking for you?"

"Yeah, I suppose so," Finn remarked.

"Walk with me," Damian offered. "You said you know this forest well, and I've been having a hard time navigating through here. I need to get to Kielder Lake."

"Kielder Lake? I've just spent the better part of the day hiking away from that dump. Why do you want to go that way? All the cops will be in that area…"

"Why's that?"

"Because I just shot up Cunningham Lodge and took Aidan Cunningham hostage – Aidan, he… fell to his death in the forest fire. They'll pin it on me – I'm looking at spending the rest of my life in prison for all his own criminal actions. I need to get out of here and go up north."

"What's up north?"

"Never you mind…" Finn replied. "Just some friends…"

"Right…" Damian said, looking at him suspiciously. "Well, how about this? If you can get me to Kielder Lake, I'll get you out of this forest. I have access to transport that can get you out of here and anywhere you want to go. Hell, I can even get you off this miserable country you call an island nation, if you'd like."

"Certainly was an island nation," Finn stated with a sigh. "I suppose though, if I'm not who I thought I was, I don't even know if it's my own nation anymore. I don't know what people I belong to, if any. I don't know where I belong… except prison, perhaps. Perhaps I have been a naughty boy what with it all…"

"No, you don't," Damian rejected. "You certainly sound as though you deserved better though."

"Better?"

"Your family and circumstances of that all…" Damian replied. "I had a deadbeat father as well. He skimped on my mother before I was born. She raised me all on her own."

"Aidan was many things, but he hardly 'skimped' on me. He just… didn't love me. If anything, I skimped on him and mum because I couldn't put up with it anymore. I ran away from home to live on the streets by choice. When I had enough of people, I ran away from them too to come here. At least here, people can't hurt me."

"I know that feeling too," Damian reminisced. "People hurt me as well – people, are vile. I won't let them have you – come with me. I'll take you somewhere safe…"

"And how can I trust you?" Finn questioned.

"I could just as easily arrest you if I was luring you into a trap," Damian stated. "The choice is ultimately yours. Isn't that what we have free will for?"

Finn didn't respond. Damian knelt down to fix his rifle and then stood up again. He looked at Finn again.

"So what's it going to be?" Damian questioned.

"You can get me out of here? I only need to make it to the nearest small town," Finn pointed out. "I can take of myself from then on."

"And go where? To some commune with a bunch of fringe extremists? Surely not a man of your talent. Come with me, and I'll take you out of the country – to the United States. I can give you a new life – a second life."

Finn looked at him, nodded, and then the two proceeded to trek through the forest together. In the time the two spent together, Finn told Damian what proceeded before his separation from Tristan. He told him about his aims to expose and sabotage Cunningham Industries due to their destructive environmental policies. He also told him about his motives were encouraged by his hatred of his father. He explained how he found Tristan Merrick while on mission, took him under his wing, but Tristan rejected his ideology and attempted to stop him from killing his father. He told him how his father died when he fell to his death, and how he and Tristan escaped the forest though Tristan truly escaped while he fell to his demise, but was saved by a river below that took him away. Finn looked at him as he finished his story; the two stood apart from each other after dark as they camped in the midst of Berwick-Northumbria Regional Park.

Damian did not say anything as he looked into the fire. Finally, he said, "What can I tell you?" He then paused again as he thought. "I already told you about my mother and father – I grew up on city streets, in a place called Harlech out on the west coast. Imagine the most miserable city possible, a literal hell on Earth to say the least. There's no far worse place on this Earth than that city. We grew up in a small apartment meant to accommodate one, but it accommodated two. My mother – she did all that she could to raise me. She herself had a hard life – lost both her parents when she was young, was adopted and raised by a rich man, but by the time she grew up, he didn't care about her anymore. She practically separated from him and never wanted help from him, nor my father. My father, she met when in university – her first love, but he – he just used her for his own pleasure and when she told him she was pregnant, asked her to abort and leave him alone. Infatuated with him, I guess, she left him alone, but carried me to term. She named me after an old friend of hers who was good to us – died months before I was born. I never met him, but I heard he was good to us. I… I never had a man in my life to look up to, but he was close. My mom could talk for hours about him. As for the rich man, he was hardly a man worth looking up to.

"My mother put me through school. She knew how bad some of the schools were where we grew up in Keswick, so she put me into a Catholic school near our home. I was raised Catholic, not that she practiced. I on the other hand took it to heart – I wanted to become a priest while my mother wanted me to be a doctor. My mother grew ill when I was young, and it stabilized through my adolescence, but then suddenly when I was seventeen, came out of nowhere and killed her. I was supposed to have joined the minor seminary that year, a boarding school for young folks looking to become priests, but on the day of her funeral, I snapped. I killed the man that had raised her, the rich man – I took my hands to his neck, and I felt a tremendous amount of rage overtake me that I unintentionally snapped his feeble spine and killed him instantly. From that point on, I ran for my life. I lived a life on the run, and I tried to come back to normality, but I couldn't do it. Eventually, I was captured. I knew by then there was no turning around because everywhere I went, destruction followed, and so rather than trying to do good, I embraced who I was. My captors became my allies. After a while, I learned that when you exert yourself enough, anything can be yours. That's how this world works – it's survival of the fittest. You can only own what you're willing to fight for and take. You only deserve to live as much as you're willing to fight for your life, and I fought for my life, both physically and psychologically, and it was tough, but in no way was I going to surrender. My mother did not give her life for me to surrender. I did not suffer just to capitulate like a coward. No, I made my own life, manipulated who I had to, killed who I had to, deceived who I had to, and that allowed me to come on top of other people – that allowed me to be triumphant over others."

Damian grew quiet and tilted his head to look up to the sky. The skies were clear where they rested, showing off the starry night.

"This world, it can be an awful place to those who are unprepared, but luckily, I prepared myself and raised myself to become the man that I am now," Damian expressed. "This world… the people who live in this world don't deserve it for its beauty. What a beautiful world it could if people did not exist and it was just nature. Oh, how I look up to the night sky and stare at its vastness in wonder – in wonder too if there is even a God above. I would hardly think so…"

"You don't believe in God?"

"I used to," Damian remarked, "but when you've seen what I've seen, been through what I've been through, the idea of a God becomes just that – an idea. I'm convinced that God does not exist, but that evil surely does, and that evil comes from men. All men are the source of evil on this world, because otherwise this world would be at peace. Who is it that cuts down forests? Who starts wars that have led to the deaths of innocents all in the name of blood, power, and money? No, God does not exist, but evil does because humans do. There is no such thing as good as much as what you're able to define, and there is no such thing as beauty as much as we are able to see that which is beautiful. Humanity is a blight upon this world, and it would be much better for us all if humanity ceased to exist."

"Even you?"

"I'm less of a danger because I know better – I know better than these other people. I would just want to live my life in peace. I don't kill innocents. I don't exploit others. I've done nothing in my life but attempt to serve some justice for the lack thereof in this world. Sometimes I've had to define my own justice because no others were willing to. Although I felt guilty to kill my mother's guardian, after a while I was able to convince myself that he deserved it because his negligence led my mom to die. He could have helped us, but he didn't. His death was on himself. As for others I've killed, none of them were innocent. Very few people on this world can be called innocent. I've long learned that sometimes you just have to be god yourself and give this world that which it deserves – that's how I know God does not exist either, because I've had to do what he should have done but didn't."

"I don't necessarily disagree with you," Finn remarked. "Yeah, the world is a downright miserable place to live, and yeah, you've got to struggle and be willing to fight. I know far too many who've kippered themselves on the streets due to overdose, or otherwise killed themselves, and I've always told myself that it wasn't in them to live in this world anyhow because they weren't willing to fight for their life. I've always maintained a necessity within me to fight against a fate that seemed to want me dead or suffering, and that fight gave me strength and purpose to live. I used to fight for the environment, because she was all that was beautiful that I could identify in this world, but after a while, I realized there was more to fight for, and it was my people – the white people of the British Isles who were oppressed at the hands of corrupt, selfish elites like my father, but I wasn't done fighting for the environment either. Far-right is a loose term thrown around these days to wankers like Boris Johnson and Nigel Farage, but I was far-right – I was an ecofascist – I still am, and these invaders? None of them are innocent – none of them care a damn about my brothers and sisters, and likewise, none of them give a damn about this island that is, or was our homeland. Even if I may not be British as I thought I was, I still sympathize as a white person who was raised on this island to know that this is European clay, not South Asian or East Asian, but white man's land. If Britons don't wake up to the invasion they're experiencing and fight back, then they're as good as dead, but the people will rise up because it's within the consciousness of every people to not allow themselves to go extinct."

"I can see your reason to vouch for your people – that's natural instinct, but I'm surprised of you to believe that they're all worthy of living. Some of the worst men of this land have been white people…"

"White people? Those are Jews you're talking about, mate."

"No, not Jews," Damian replied. "That's where you and many are so wrong. You reactionaries are so quick to believe that Jews are the root of all evil in the world, because for the past sixty or so years since the Second World War a handful of them have seized power in the world, especially in the United States, and more so have exploited the travesty they suffered at the hands of the Nazis, who themselves had enough with the Jewish elites in their time, to fulfill their Zionist ambitions. Certainly, Jewish elites have played their hand at being the arbiters of opposition to Christian morale values and traditions, but you forget the evils that gentiles, Europeans inclusive, are capable of. You reactionaries are so quick to believe that the world before the twentieth century was one of peace and tranquility, ignoring the escalation of violence at the hands of Europeans from the moment the Roman Empire collapsed, and all the evils done in the name of Christianity."

"So, what, Christians are to blame?"

"No, not Christians," Damian argued, "but *people* – that's another aspect that you people get wrong so frequently, believing that every person from Roman times to 1960s was a straight-arrow, practicing Christian, and it's what those of the Left blame for the evils of the past, what has vilified Christianity, and what those on the Right glorify as better times. The truth of the matter is that there were no glory days, and Christians were not to blame for such travesties as much as Jews aren't to blame for theirs. *People* are at fault, and it was Jewish people in a back and forth fight with Christian people that is to blame for this escalation of tension that led to the Holocaust and has and will result in further violence in the Middle East at the hands of the Zionist regime – because *people* are evil, not Christians, not white people, not Jews, not Jewish people, but *people*.

"And sure, most Jewish people may appear to be more insufferable and eviller as their elites subvert nations and act contrary to Christian values, the only values that seem to keep people in the least docile and truly civil, but their ethnic people are not to blame. It is people – not Christian people, nor Jewish people, but just man and the evil that lies from within their own heart. My mother used to convince me that angels and demons exist – that she had seen both with her own eyes, but I couldn't believe her. I couldn't believe, even as I look up at the night sky, that there was anything more out there than us even if she had seen it. Even then, I'm still skeptical – demons may very well exist, but angels? I don't think so – this world is a fallen world that belongs to men and demons, and the only kingship belongs to he who dares to claim it. I can only wonder... if God does exist, why do demons exist? Why do we exist? Why do I exist? The only answer that comes to mind is that I surely must do what God has failed to do, and that is to smite evil, both demons and people alike."

Act 3, Scene 1

I must apologize, my dear reader – F.C. here, and it appears that this story was hijacked by an intruder and my earlier writings removed. Rest assured, her accessibility to the rest of the story should not be a problem anymore, as this story is mine, not hers.

Finn and Moira sat in the cabin of a small airplane that flew over the Rocky Mountains and left the boundaries of the Nattau County and by extension, the Province of Alberta. Finn wore his aviator jacket and a pair of sunglasses, while Moira wore her denim sherpa jacket. The plane they rode in was a light high-wing, fixed-wing aircraft with a rotor at the front. The plane cabin was large enough to fit two passenger seats alone and minimal space behind them for their backpacks. The plane was completely white with red strips along the sides. Finn wore a headset as he flew, but did not speak. The pair continued to sit as they flew over the boreal forests of northern British Columbia and towards the Pacific coastline.

"Who are you?" Finn asked.

"What?" Moira questioned.

"Who are you?"

"You're the wise guy who knows who I am even though I never met you before," Moira responded, "which by the way, was kind of creepy to say the least."

"Oh, come off it," Finn remarked. "It's not like I knew your identity because I was some sort of stalker. Tristan wrote journals from when he was fourteen years old to before he got married to Diana. He passed them all to me and asked me to write a story out of them, which I finished, and now Diana, in her spare time, is proofing it with me."

"Why?"

"Because they lived quite a life those two," Finn responded. "Neither of them felt right to keep it between themselves and their kids."

"Kids?" Moira asked.

"Yeah, kids," Finn remarked. "Typically that's what married couples do – they have kids."

"Plural?"

"Yeah…" Finn replied. "Had their first around four years ago and just had their second not too long ago as well. I'm sure they won't be stopping any time soon either."

"Where do they live nowadays?"

"In Harlech," Finn answered, "at least for now. Tristan dropped out of school and got himself a job at the Harlech Police Department. He's worked his way up and is now with the SWAT team. Meanwhile, Diana has been in school part-time to become a nurse. My aunt, or I suppose our aunt, has been supporting them with childcare when she can."

"I thought your aunt was running Cabernet Industries."

"What's to run? The company practically runs itself through the board of directors, not to mention the incumbent executive leadership. Besides, from what I've heard, she's taken more interest in her nephews than the company."

"How come you don't run the company?"

"Why would I want to do that?" Finn questioned. "I have no interest in dictating a multi-billion-dollar corporate empire. The least interest I've had in Cabernet Industries was in their aerospace division, Cabernet Air, but even that interest has passed."

"Why's that?"

"Look, you're not answering my question," Finn remarked.

"What question?"

"Who are you – on a deeper level. Who do you think you are?"

"Oh… that sort of question… I don't know. I'm just a person, I guess. A person who likes computers and basically lives on-line."

"Alright, perhaps a bit more literal than that. Tell me about yourself."

"Oh, right – well, I grew up in Allabrese…" Moira expressed. She proceeded to explain her life briefly to Finn. "My mother's side lived in Allabrese, but before that came from Harlech. My dad's side lived in Calgary, but before that came from someplace in Ontario. They were proper Scottish-Canadians who've lived in Canada for centuries. From what I understand about my mother's side of the family, half of them were true Anglophones while the other half were Francophones. I suppose I'm a bit of a mix of it all around here."

"Do you take identity in that? In your genealogy?" Finn questioned.

"Not particularly, but it's always fun to bring up in conversation," Moira expressed. "What about you?"

"I don't care about genealogy," Finn responded. "Neither yours nor mine. There's nothing important about the blood that one comes from, no less the people that are already dead and gone. All that's important is your current family, if they're alive, and then those around you to the wider community. There's nothing important about a national identity that hasn't resulted in bloodshed. I've always been surprised at how folks this side of the world can talk about their genealogy in such depth. If you talked about it that way in England or anywhere else in Europe, you'd be accused of being some sort of Nazi."

"I assure you, I'm not."

"I didn't need your assurance," Finn remarked, "but at the same time, I have to ask again – who are you really."

"I don't know, Finn," Moira replied. "I don't know what to say to your dumb question anymore. Who are you?"

"I don't know either."

Finn continued to fly them over British Columbia as the hour went on. Moira looked out the passenger seat window as they passed through the densest of clouds to catch a view below. A vastness of coniferous trees covered in snow stretched for miles up to the horizon. The skies were pinkish-red as the sun set beyond the Pacific coastline.

"Isn't that a beautiful sight to behold?" Finn questioned. "It really puts into perspective how small we are in comparison not it all. How large this world is too."

"They call it a small world," Moira replied. "Too small to fit all of us together, tightly knit. I can't help but feel skeptical at it all, no less to be caught down there in the middle of winter would be a death sentence. The natural world is a scary place..."

"You're not much of an outdoor person, are you?" Finn asked.

"My professional career involves programming and my pastime involves hacking. I spend way too much time sat down at a computer than outside," Moira responded. "I place my fascination in human-made machines rather than all this made as a result of random chance, especially since the outside world is a dangerous place. When I was a kid, my dad used to take me and my brother camping a lot – even then, the thoughts of mountain lions and wolves terrified me too much to enjoy my time."

"Well, then this'll be a hard trip for you, because we'll likely have to camp the night in the cold, but don't worry, I came prepared for that possibility," Finn responded. "You Canadians have no idea how blessed you are to have so much nature around you. I would have killed to have been able to live out here when I was younger rather than depend on the few forests in the UK. God knows if my circumstances were the same, I would have become lost in the Canadian wilderness and made my home there. There was only one forest that you could depend upon in Britain to not see another camper or a bit of litter in your way, and that was Berwick-Northumbria Regional Park on the border between Scotland and England. Out here, it's all ten to a hundred times its size."

"A natural park in England? Sounds cozy…" Moira replied.

"Yeah, there was especially no predators to worry about," Finn responded. "They had all been hunted to extinction, so the worst you had were some mean birds and the odd fox."

"Foxes are beautiful creatures… my grandma adored them."

"A hunter?"

"No, not in that way," Moira scolded. "She hated hunting for sport. Never allowed my grandad to partake in that sort of thing."

"What a shame," Finn responded, "when done responsibly, can be great fun. A reminder of what life was like before urbanization and industrialization. To live out in the wild… never a greater sense of freedom than to be out in the woods all on your own. Never a worry to meet another soul. I lived a decent time in the forest, surviving on my own, and it was better surviving in the woods than it was in the city."

"What do you mean?"

"When I was sixteen, I ran away from home," Finn answered. "I lived on the streets, making friends as I went along to stay in a warm place, or crashing in a parking lot stairwell or the tube. Sometimes, if I was lucky, I would get arrested because I was an eco-freak. I was one of those idiots glueing their hands besides paintings, throwing paint and spraying graffiti to sound alarm to climate change, and halting traffic to make a scene. If I could spend a night in a cell or hospital, it'd be better than anywhere else, but after a while they knew my name and couldn't do it anymore because they'd call my parents. I also lost passion in climate change, woke up to the realities of all that and life itself, and made my way into the forest where I stayed until I was nineteen. A bloke I had met in the forest offered me an opportunity to come with him to America, so I took it, especially since at that time I learned that Charlemagne was my alleged real father – I was also a wanted man who could only look forward to a lifetime in prison. I didn't want to be confined to prison, so I came here with him. He was a good man, to me at least. I heard he was a horrible man otherwise. He was, of course, Audric Zimmerman – the one that caused the paranoia in Allabrese."

"You knew Audric Zimmerman?"

"Yeah…" Finn replied, "but I don't want to talk about it… Listen, we're on approach to the U.S. border. Luckily, I've got citizenship courtesy of the man in question, so no problem at all for us as this aeroplane is registered, but they can't know I'm travelling with you since you're technically an illegal alien. You must know how much the yanks appreciate illegal aliens…"

"I'm not looking to live here, but sure, I understand."

Finn began to speak into the radio as the plane approached a deep torrent of clouds that were nearly black in color.

"I don't like the look of that…" Moira expressed. "Is that safe to approach?"

"Bah, just a bit of a storm," Finn dismissed. "It can't be too bad…"

Moira looked at Finn skeptically as the plane began to descend. They pierced through the clouds ahead where the plane began to violently shake. Moira held on firmly to anything she could grab around her while Finn held the controllers tightly. The plane then began to turn and fly with peace. Rainwater splattered on all the windows, drenching the glass and making it impossible to see outwards.

"Curious," Finn expressed, "I thought we were going into a snowstorm… but looks like it's just heavy rain and no winds." He leaned over to look down and saw that the temperate rainforest beneath them was snowless. Instead, there was a deep and dark green sight from the tall coniferous trees. In the direction that the plane few, the only snow that could be seen came from tall mountains in the horizon. There were also many hills from which the trees covered. Nonetheless, there was no snow in these hills. To the left from the plane, miles ahead, the pacific coastline could be seen along with the sea and a few islands that formed the coastland. "Let me see if I remember where to go…"

"What do you mean?" Moira questioned. "You've been out here before?"

"Of course," Finn replied. "Diana asked me to a write their story, but I wasn't going to do so without visiting a place she had once visited before. I'm somewhat of a field investigator, you know… I prefer to see something for my own eyes, and this place… it certainly is well hidden to say the least. The GDP headquarters are located in the Tongass National Forest. There's an airstrip a few miles from the approximate location of the base – of course, I didn't go anywhere near the base, but I roamed the forest for a bit in the summer. My father told me that he believed the base was beneath a cave system to the north of the island, so we'll have to hike that way, but it'll take a whole day. I'm glad it's not snowing out here – could have been a lot trickier if it was, but at least now we'll be able to enjoy the beauty of a wet forest as I like to call them."

The plane continued to travel west, away from the mainland and towards the many islands before it began to peel north. The plane began to descend as they made their approach to one of the larger islands closely associated with the coast.

"I hope you don't mind getting yourself a bit wet," Finn expressed. "Nevermind, I believe I've packed some ponchos if you'd prefer. It'll be both frigid cold and damp where we're going."

"Is it safe to be out there at this time of the year? Won't we freeze to death?"

"Yeah, but only if you're an amateur," Finn expressed. "You're travelling with a world class survivalist. I tell you; I could survive with just the essentials packed in a small two-by-two capsule than an entire kit. If God had made it hard to survive on this earth, we wouldn't have endured for thousands of years, now would we?"

"Alright…"

"Now hold on tight," Finn remarked. "We're about to land…"

The plane made a steep descent before it flattened out and Moira could see a clearly marked strip in the ground, The plane made its approach towards this strip of land, and Finn kept control of the plane and gently guided it towards the strip like a moth to a light. Once the plane was a few yards away, he hit a switch to release the landing gear and then rolled towards the tarmac. The cabin jumped as they hit the ground, but then the plane began to slow down as it came towards the end before turning around.

"Presto," Finn expressed, bringing the plane to a halt. "Don't let anyone think that flying is hard, because it's not. It just takes a certain finesse is all."

"Thanks, but I wasn't going to take the time to learn," Moria replied. "I think an autopilot system would have you beat on how to have a smooth landing – they can have a certain finesse too."

"A computer? Who would have heard it – a ticking time bomb like those self-driving cars. Imagine that – trusting a computer with your life. It's bad enough we trust this hunk of metal from not ripping itself apart midflight than to trust a software, probably coded and designed by some bloke who has never flown a plane or even been in a plane. I'm insulted at your suggestion…"

"I'm sorry…"

"Right, listen up," Finn expressed. "We'll needn't hike too far as the sun sets, but there's a shelter by some cliffs we can set up a fire, pitch a tent, and sleep the night. I've got some food for the two of us to have a meal, but then next morning, we're on our way. Hopefully some of this rain will subside too because it'll be a nightmare to trudge through the forest with boots stuck in the mud as if we're trekking through the Russian hinterlands."

"What about… protection?"

"I beg your pardon?" Finn questioned, raising an eyebrow.

"Something to protect us from bears…"

"I don't know how to say this, but it is the middle of winter. The bears will be in a comfortable snooze. The wolves and mountain lions pose a greater threat, one of which hunt in packs and the others alone."

"Yeah, so what do you have to keep us safe from that?"

"Just the thing…" Finn remarked, rummaging through his backpack behind him. He pulled out an aerosol cannister with a sealed lid at the top. "State of the art bear spray, to keep intruders away. I've heard these are illegal in Harlech."

"Bear spray? That's all you've got? How come you don't have a gun or something?"

"I survived in the woods for plenty of time without relying on a firearm. Firearms are overrated, and all they're used for really is to kill other people – weapons of mass destruction, they are. Nah, I have something a bit more refined than that…" Finn expressed, opening the plane door. "Come, I'll show you."

Moira opened her door and stepped out. She came around to Finn's side as the wing of the airplane gave them shelter. He removed his backpack and then showed a reinforced case beneath. He opened the case and inside was a modern bow.

"Isn't she a beauty?" Finn questioned. "A custom-made beauty at that with some help from yours truly. She can fire an arrow at the same speed as a bullet, but with more precision…"

"You don't have any firearms then, do you."

"Of course not," Finn replied, "and we don't need them. This'll kill anything that moves, especially with me holding it. If you wanted a gun, you should have brought one."

"I'd like to see your arrows pierce one of those droids that hunted us down in Allabrese."

"I'm sure it can be done, especially with my titanium-tipped arrows. I've heard it done before… assuming these robots have that same sort of vulnerability. I may need to customize a few arrows for that purpose, but otherwise, this'll give us a shot at some food. I'd like to find a deer so that we don't have to use our rations. Worst case, we skin and feed off a cougar or wolf. Fine by me."

"Disgusting…"

"Ah, you won't be saying those words when your stomach is grumbling," Finn remarked, taking out a customized quiver that held the arrows tightly together. He attached it to his thigh. "Come on, a night in the woods could be good for you. We'll find that cave system, make our way into it, download what we need, and blackmail them to leave us alone. They won't even see us coming…"

"You don't think they have radar anywhere nearby?"

"Planes come and go around these parts on a daily to weekly basis," Finn expressed. "I told you, I stayed around here and made chit-chat with the locals and other tourists. Only cause for alarm is if my broadcast to customs way back was picked up, but that was miles away. We're in the clear, so let's get going – no way they'd expect us to fly over here either."

Moira groaned and replied, "If you say so – I don't suppose we have much to lose."

Act 3, Scene 2

The next morning, Finn stood around the rim of a natural shelter along the side of a cliff wall from where they pitched their tents and established a campfire. The shelter was a concave space within the cliff wall with a stony ground at their feet and arched walls that came upwards. There was at least a few yards of depth to the cave, and the position was also raised and provided sights towards the airfield that was not too far from them. The fire roasted the kindling and tinder steadily, sending smoke upwards and away from the tent that was closer in. Finn held a metal cup as he drank some black coffee and looked out ahead. The rain had settled down, but the clouds above them were still dark and grey. Finn had changed out from his aviator jacket and wore a raincoat and cargo pants. He also wore hiking boots. He sipped his coffee as he looked ahead. Moira exited from the tent as she wore something similar. She removed her jacket and wore the poncho Finn had provided as well as a pair of hiking boots. After a quick breakfast around the fire, Finn and Moira stood up to put away the tent, put out the fire, and then step out to begin to make their way north along the island.

Finn held a device in his hands that showed their approximate location. He then began to fiddle around with the device to determine a route.

"According to the GPS, we should head this way," Finn said, pointing towards one corner of the airstrip. "We'll find a river and want to follow it to reach the cliffs to the north."

"Just lead the way…"

"I'll do what I can, but I need you to hold the GPS because I'll be taking point with the bow," Finn responded, "in case we run into any trouble along the way."

"I'm sure those death robots that came for us are shaking in their boots."

Finn did not reply and instead began to go down the hill to return to the airstrip. They walked over and came to the corner of the tarmac. They stopped and looked ahead of them. Around the airstrip perimeter was as clearing of land, but beyond this margin were tall coniferous trees. These trees were more than twelve feet tall, and they had long branches that stretched out on either side. As the two made their way closer to the tree, water dripped from the sides of the branches. Additionally, the flora beneath the trees consisted of shrub and ferns. Beneath this greenery were fallen logs and a dark, wet dirt that sometimes formed patches of mud. Moira stepped into one such patch of mud and instantly was kept back from being able to proceed any forward. Finn helped her pull her foot out so that they could continue.

"Like being sucked into a void," Moira complained.

"You can add it to your list of dangers."

The pair continued to travel along the path they made for themselves as they ventured further along the forest.

"It's quiet…" Finn expressed. "I haven't even heard the birds singing…"

"Don't birds fly south for the winter?"

"Not all birds…"

The pair came around a tall tree trunk and then carried on a natural path. From a distance, each of them began to hear the flow of water.

"You hear that? Must be the river…"

"Sounds like a waterfall, not a river."

"Ah, but this is the land of waterfalls, didn't you know that? Finn remarked. "For that reason is the Pacific Northwest otherwise known as Cascadia."

Before the pair came around to the river, they came to a clearing of low water, reeds, and tall grass around. This wetland proved difficult to traverse as they stuck around, and Finn jabbed a tall stick through to expose how much deeper it went than the mud.

"I can hear the river close by," Finn expressed. "We'll need to go around to be safe."

"Around on what? It's barely traversable around the sides. We're practically looking at a pond that'll suck us in."

"Ah, don't be such a cry baby," Finn scolded. "Come on, we'll make do."

Finn led the way as they came around to the side of the wetlands and began to go through the shrubs and ferns, climbing onto fallen logs that lay on the side and then navigating through the natural obstacles that formed and made it a tight walk around. He came around to a series of trees with branches that stuck out, lifted himself up and then grabbed an adjacent branch to bypass the waters. By this time in the early morning, the rain had calmed down some more and it was less than a light drizzle. The clouds remained dark and grey above though, and the sun was nowhere to be seen. Finn climbed atop of a log that branched two parts of the perimeter together, stopping in the middle to help Moira keep her footing. After he helped her, he continued forward to the other side where the ground was a lot more stable to go around. Finn led the way to the other side of the path where he stopped to listen to the sound of water flowing.

"It's a beautiful sound..." Finn reminisced.

Moira listened to the sound and as she did, she saw a reptile stuck to the side of one of the old growth trees. The creature was orangish-red and looked like a little lizard. It looked at her from its beady eyes and then quickly pattered away.

"So gross..." Moira stated. "I hope we're almost there."

"Nonsense," Finn responded. "We've barely made any headway. We've got hours and hours left to go."

"How could anyone even think to build a headquarters around all this?"

"Obviously to keep it hidden," Finn remarked, looking over to her. "Have a look at the map for me, will you? Do we need to all the way around?"

Moira took the device out from his pocket and then looked at it. We need to go that way…" she said, pointing across from them.

"Of course…" Finn scolded, looking ahead. The trees ahead of them were nearly uprooted with age, making it difficult to traverse around the salient. "If only we could jump across… I may have a better idea…" He produced an axe from his backpack and began to approach one of the trees that was slightly leaned over.

"What are you going to do?" Moira asked.

"Simple," Finn replied, "just going to accelerate the natural process for this tree. He began to hack at the roots that tethered the tree to the ground. "What a beautiful tree she is as well. I can tell that she's been at it for hundreds of years, but unfortunately, growing up next to a pond in a land where it always rains has proven detrimental to her continued survival."

"Why do you have to talk about them like that…"

"Like what? Like they're alive? Newsflash, love, trees are alive. All these trees are alive. Plenty of wildlife where we are, even if they don't want to eat you."

Finn continued to hack at the roots, causing the tree to slip over. He made his way around as he continued to chop at the difficult roots and eventually the tree began to make a slow turn overboard. The rest of the bottom of the tree exposes itself outwards, flying upwards as Finn jumped back and they flew up like violent whips. One such root hit a branch that caused it to immediately part and collapse downwards. Finn continued to shield himself while Moira stood back with an anxious face.

"How about that?" Finn questioned, climbing onto the top of the tree and putting his axe away. "Nothing like a bit of troubleshooting, eh?"

"A warning next time would be nice."

"What? Me hacking the roots wasn't plenty of a warning already?"

Moira did not respond. She instead came around to the side of the trunk, which was at least five feet in diameter, and began to attempt to climb the side. Finn grabbed both of her hands and helped lift her up. The two then went over the fallen tree to the other side, continuing inland where the sound of the cascade of water was closer. They hopped off onto a rock nearby and then slid down to the ground where they continued at a diagonal direction.

The pair walked into a clearing where on their left side was a slope, while on the right were some spruce trees – shorter and wider than the rest of the others. Past the spruce trees, the sight of some rapid water flowing downstream could be seen. They continued along the natural path as the rain picked up, coming around to a better sight of the river beside them. The waters in the river were torrential. Finn looked ahead at some low slopes on the natural path ahead that came up to a tree trunk that crossed over to the other side and then decided to stop. Behind the tree trunk was a cascade from which water sprouted outwards from over another cliffside.

"All this rain is making that river dangerous to fall into," Finn noted. "We'll have to stay away – don't want to get caught in a mudslide or what-not. Let's stop here for some lunch."

"You want to start a fire here? With all this rain?"

"Bah, a bit of rain doesn't stop a nice toasty warm fire," Finn expressed. "Come on, I've saved us some dry tinder. We'll just need to shelter the fire, especially as we start it."

Finn picked up some sticks, used a small shovel to make a pit, and then planted the stakes around the side in three so that he could lay down a metal cover from his backpack. He then placed the kindling and tinder below into the pit, took a metal rod and a sharp object to create some sparks, and then sat back as the fire grew on its own. He fed the fire with some more kindling, and then added some fuel from the shaved sticks he had made. Finn picked up a metal cup from nearby and then went to the water to scoop some up before he returned to place it on the stove.

"Nothing like a cup of tea in the winter, right?"

Moira looked at him suspiciously. She chewed on a food bar that she had in her backpack while the water boiled. He placed a tea bag and let it soak for a few minutes before he poured half of the tea into another cup and gave it to Moira.

"Nice afternoon teas by the fireside like this are what remind me of what I oh so miss about being in the outdoors."

"You don't go outside very often anymore?"

"Not as much as I used to," Finn acknowledged. "I've found it boring to be alone in the woods. I last came here in 2022 when the 'rona' virus was still going about, and that was fine. After that I did some travelling around, and the last hike I did was with Tristan. We did some overnight hikes together up north from Harlech last summer. Aside from that, haven't been out since last winter to go around the backend of Allabrese on horseback."

"Horseback?"

"Yeah, I went alone though," Finn expressed, "which despite the horse, was still quite lonely. I don't know – I suppose the magic of being outside has worn off on me, or maybe I'm just getting a bit too old. I can only do this with company now."

"How old are you?"

"I'm twenty-four," Finn answered. "You?"

"What? You don't know already, you creep?"

"No, I just didn't want to seem just like that… creepy. I know you're the same age as those two lovebirds. Twenty-two, right?"

"Right."

"You know, when my great-grandfather was my age, he had just finished fighting in an overseas war. My grandfather had settled down from his worldly travels to raise my father, and my father... he had just made his first marvel of an invention in those times... something to do with computers, I believe."

"Computers?" Moira questioned.

"Yes, my dad was somewhat of a computer whiz," Finn acknowledged. "He invented the Cabernet operating system that remains one of the most popularly used in technical spheres rather than the Neumann system. He did that all on his own, and it shot off in the fallout of that crooked man being an anarchist ringleader. He sold that patent to Cabernet Electronics for thousands and thousands of dollars, which in part he used to buy shares in Cabernet Industries and another part to fund his next project. He was a self-made man in that sense, even if it was his family's name, he played the system to climb on top. Cabernet Industries didn't have to become his – it went public, but he knew what he wanted. My grandfather and great-grandfather were self-made too. Me though? I suppose I'm somewhat self-made too... certainly had to figure out what it means to be a man on my own.

"You know, I spent much of my time in England running away from my adoptive-father's legacy in Cunningham Industries. They were a rotten company, careless especially to mother nature, and I wanted nothing to do with them. Cabernet Industries... they've had their issues in the past, but between my grandfather and father, they've steered clear of public scandals for some time now. Cabernet Foundation does a hell of a job in philanthropy too. Still though, when it comes to that company, I can't help but feel like it's not for me even though it's my family's name. All of my fathers made their own impact to that company, but me? What do I have to show for it? I'm no inventor. I'm not even an explorer like my father and his grandfather was. Charity? It's exhaustive, and too difficult for me to cope with – I get so sick of other people. All I ever wanted to do is just be alone..."

"What about your writing?" Moira asked.

"A farfetched idea," Finn noted. "I'll get those books out, but I don't want credit for them. They're not even my ideas, but Tristan's. I could go back to school, but it bored me greatly. I dropped out after my first year because I wanted to spend time with my dad before he died, but never went back because I didn't see a point. I was top of my class, on the Dean's List, but it didn't mean anything to me."

"Well, at least you seem like you can afford it," Moira simply said, sipping her tea. "I'm dirt poor. I don't have a penny to my name. I wish I could just hide in my bedroom all day and night and live on the web. The world certainly seems a lot nicer online than it does in real life. I've had both friends over the web and IRL, and those over the web were always more affirming and caring than those in real life. People suck."

"That they seem to do," Finn agreed, drinking his tea. "Bloody hell, what's my mum going to think about the manor being destroyed," he expressed, pinching the bridge of his nose and shutting his eyes. "She's going to kill me. That house was sacred to her – my great-grandfather and grandfather built it together."

"What do you think happened after we left?" Moira questioned. "I didn't tell you, but I saw police cars pull in when we made our escape from Dr. Lambert's home – white ones, and I could have sworn they were mounties, not county police."

"Mounties?" Finn questioned. "That'd be odd. They'll likely blame one of the two on natural gas, as they usually seem to do, and then the other one on either me being mad or suicidal. There always seems to be a cover story that works."

"What about those robots?"

"They probably fled soon afterwards," Finn replied. "If I know the GDP the way I do, they don't like to make too much of a scene."

"As if destroying Cabernet Manor wasn't a scene already."

"They'll find an excuse for it somewhere," Finn responded. "I haven't been the most welcoming of neighbors to the rest of the town, so they'll use that against me – 'mad lunatic burns house down,' or some rendition of it."

"You really are your father's son," Moira pointed out.

Finn smiled and raised his cup up. He then said, "Yup, suppose I couldn't really be a Cabernet if I wasn't out in the middle of nowhere, risking my life in some absurd way." He stood up and poured the rest of his tea out. "Alright, let's finish this, shall we?"

The pair put out the fire and then began to make their way towards the cliffside up towards the fallen tree. They climbed up the boulders that lay at the side of the cliff and made it to the top where they took a moment to observe their surroundings. The rapids cut into the ground to form a low canyon, and worse off the river snaked along the earth as it went upwards, increasing in elevation. The tree that had fallen over was not very wide, and as Finn climbed atop of it, he nearly slipped.

"Gently now," Finn remarked. "Don't need one of us falling to our certain doom, now do we?" He helped Moira up. "One step at a time... we'll get right over."

The pair walked across and gently took steps along the narrow tree to reach the other side. They passed the waterfall and reached the other side where they climbed upwards along the slope to see that above the waterfall was a large pond from where more water poured down from another waterfall in the cliffs. There were a few trees in this area around the pond, and those trees that were here were thin and lanky. The ground was partially grass and stone, creating a clear path around the pond to come up a slope that wrapped around and went up to the top of the cliff. The second half of the elevation became steeper, and some of the ground at their feet was loose and gravel based. Not to mention, but the rain became harder as they made their ascent. Once at the top, the river continued in a trench flanked by natural stone walls on either side. The pair walked straight down with tall rocky cliffs on either side as they continued down a canyon.

At the end of the path was a flat boulder that formed a bridge. They gently crossed the gap into the trench, looking below to see the velocity of the water to shoot down towards the waterfall. They then continued downwards another few yards before another rock led them back to the other side. The trench smoothed out and the river was level to the ground they walked on for a final few yards before there was a major ascent. The cliff walls in the canyon grew taller and taller, and the path led up that slope and curved around on the right. Just before the curve, a large waterfall dumped water overboard into the river below, before continuing itself along greater elevation. The river curved around too, but remained below them as they continued to ascend upwards along the stone-based path. Eventually the pathway ahead of them curved away and into a separate trench flanked by trees and shrubs above on either side. They followed the gulley and travelled underneath large boulders that covered the tops as it came around and returned along the sides of the wide river. They walked along the side of the river as they were then led through a cavern that went through the side of the cliffs to continue along the path of the river where they reached another slope besides another large waterfall, finding a large lake on the other side.

"Look at that," Finn expressed. "Beautiful…"

The lake was surrounded by a low cliff wall and was moderately sized. The rainfall was hardest at this elevation. The forest continued to surround them above the cliffs, and there were a few thin trees around their location. Another waterfall could be seen from water that sprung out from the side of the cliff wall. They made their way around closer to that as they travelled along the plateau and stopped for a moment.

"What?" Moira questioned.

Finn looked around their surroundings. He then looked across the deep blue water and over to Moira. He expressed to her, "I could swear… I have this feeling as though we're being watched." His eyes then shot towards the water where he saw some ripples.

"What was that?"

"Probably just some fish," Finn replied, "and as much as I'd like to spend some time catching some fish for supper, I think we ought to find this underground base. Pass me the GPS."

"It shouldn't be too far…" Moira expressed, passing it to him. "What are we looking for?"

"An elevator shaft," Finn responded, looking at the map. "According to my sources, there's two possible entryways, one of which is off-limits. An elevator shaft at the GPS coordinates I plugged in, and around that a hatch from where their vertical-takeoff-landing vehicles come through. Come, we'll have to climb the rocks over here to get above and carry on."

"Ugh… more climbing? I'm exhausted."

"Bah, it's just a bit more…"

Finn and Moira went around the lake to the waterfall where the path continued ahead of it. They went behind the cascade, where they then stopped to see a tunnel behind the waterfall.

"Interesting…" Finn expressed. "This cave goes just in the right direction that we need to be going, but wasn't my anticipation."

The cavern had a thin stone-based path as well as a continuation of the lake as it formed a river that went inward as well. The stone walls of the cave were bluish-grey. Finn took out a flashlight, turned it on, and shined it in. The spotlight he used was high-powered and revealed the cavern tunnel and river went inwards around a curve.

"Well, worst case we're back where we started," Finn expressed. "Let's go inside."

Act 3, Scene 3

The pair walked in. Moira looked at the blackish water beside them with suspicious eyes. She then took careful note of their surroundings as the walls arched over them. The path wrapped around and continued in sporadic directions, descending downwards until finally there was an exit. The pair stepped out of the cavernous tunnel only to find themselves in a much larger cavernous room. The water poured out to form another lake in the midst of the cavern, which was narrow and oval-shaped. The walls of the cavern were also slime-covered and tall, at least thirty-yards in height to the rooftop of the cavern. However, interestingly in the room were the appearance of thick man-made concrete pillars that extended downwards from the top of the roof and into the floor, sometimes going into the water as well to create support. In the midst of these pillars was a metal cage elevator shaft that went upwards. Finn shined his high-power spotlight at the shaft.

"Look over there," Finn pointed out, "not where I expected to find it, but this must be the lowest point of the base. The rest of it must be above us."

"How are we supposed to get to the other side though?" Moira questioned, observing the lake separated them from the other shore where the elevator shaft was.

Finn shined his light around the back of the cavern to see if the pathway wrapped around, but it did not. A sprout of water flowed into the room from the cave wall instead. He shined the light along the shoreline, but it was a wide lake on all sides. He approached the water and placed a hand into it.

"That's ice cold," Finn remarked. "No way we'll be able to swim across." He then shined his light above and did notice the pillars connect halfway between them all. "Looks like we'll have to climb up." He continued to shine his light around and saw a ladder on the side of the central pillar. "Come on."

The pair approached the ladder, and Finn allowed Moira to go first before he joined from behind. Before the two began to climb, Finn gave Moira a strap to put around her forehead with a lamp on the front so they could see where they were climbing up to. The ladder consisted of thin steel rungs and nothing more, going up a few yards to a very thin and narrow ledge. Moira climbed onto the ledge and then kept her body close to the pillar as she made some space for Finn to climb up. The pair then began to go around the left side, but as Moira stepped her foot down, the concrete slab moved downward and then fell. Finn quickly grabbed her and pulled her back as the concrete mass fell into the water, causing a splash that reached upwards to them.

"Well, that was close…"

Moira embraced Finn as she looked away and burrowed her head into his chest. She breathed quickly, prompting Finn to put a hand on her shoulder.

"Easy, you're alright," Finn expressed. "Come on, we'll go the other way."

The pair went around, but did not cross over from behind as the connector had already collapsed that side and instead took careful steps along the only way. They walked to the opposite side where the ladder came down to the bottom, and from there, Finn took out the spotlight and began to shine it around the elevator shaft. The cage of the elevator shaft was closed, but beside it was a power box and on the other side a lever. He shined his light on both and then looked inside the cage of the shaft. There was a bit of rubble at the bottom of the shaft, in the trench at the very bottom, and there was also a ladder on the side that went upwards a greater distance than the height they had just climbed to get here.

Finn placed a hand at the lever to pull it down, but it did nothing. He then went to the power box, placed a hand on the rusted lock, and then picked up a rock nearby to bash it against the side of the box to loosen the lock. He then opened it and pulled down a switch, but nothing happened.

"Not working," Finn noted aloud. "We'll need to climb up it…"

"Finn," Moira stated, "the GDP is directly above our heads, and we've just waltzed into their base seemingly undetected. Don't you think that's a little strange?"

"What? You think we'll get ambushed? The way I see it, Moira, we're already in over our heads, so we've got nothing left to lose here. We'll climb up to see where we go, find a terminal connection, and you can do your magic. How about that?"

"Okay, just be careful," Moira replied.

Finn went to the cage and began to pry it apart so that it would open. He then hopped down and shined his light above to see that the shaft went a long distance upwards with no sight of the very top. He then went around to the ladder where he turned off the spotlight. Meanwhile, Moira began to climb upwards.

"Hope you're not afraid of heights," Finn remarked.

"Not in the slightest."

The pair climbed up the shaft, which after the thirty yards that took them past the ceiling of the cavern, went another thirty yards before there was any sort of distinction in the layout of the shaft. At this moment, Finn looked up but could not see the top. He looked towards his left and saw an imprint in the elevator shaft that said, 'L4' on opposite sides and elevator doors on the other. He could see a lever nearby, pulled it, and heard a ringing sound followed by the doors opening to reveal corridors on either side.

"Discrete," Moira pointed out.

"Ah, you're right," Finn responded, climbing onto the platform. "We may be in a bit of trouble, although…"

Finn looked down the corridor and saw that it was dark even though light heads above them looked down. He further examined the corridor with a sign that pointed down and said, 'Generator Room', and looked around to feel a coldness in the air and in his breath. He came towards the other side, but would need to traverse the surrounding ledge in the elevator shaft to continue that way. Moira joined him as he continued to look around.

"Something feels wrong," Finn remarked. "Level four of the base and it's cold, dark, and lonely. Not to mention, we just made a heck of a lot of noise. This place gives me the same vibe as the bottom floors of Cabernet Tower before the renos."

"Maybe this lower level is abandoned…"

"I'd say," Finn replied, hitting a button to a call an elevator, but it did nothing. He looked at a sign above the elevator shaft door to see that the elevator was stuck on the Ground Level. "I don't think anybody is home."

"Did we do something?" Moira asked.

"What did we do? We've barely been here for twenty-four hours," Finn remarked. "Let's take a look around. There's clearly a lack of power, so let's start the generators and see if we can do a bit of an investigation."

Finn led Moira down the corridor where they came to a set of sliding vault doors that required an access panel to get through.

"No power means no access," Moira stated.

"What a stupid design," Finn remarked. "At Cabernet Laboratories, a power failure sets all the doors unlocked because it's a fire hazard otherwise. There must be another way in…"

Finn looked around and then saw a vent cover above.

"You seem to be good at climbing through vents to get to places you shouldn't be. I'll give you a boost and see if you can slip through."

Moira sighed and then approached the vent. Finn helped her up and she began to remove the cover and then slipped through. She hopped down and found herself in another corridor with some lockers on the side and some benches. Another vault-like door was at the end with a sign that said 'Dangerous – No Unauthorized Access' while a door at the side stated, 'Control Room'. She stepped forward and then turned around to ask, "What exactly am I looking for?"

"A release of some kind to let me in," Finn responded. "Is there anything?"

"Oh, yup," Moira pointed out, finding a release switch. She pulled it and the door locks disengaged. Finn stepped forward and pulled the heavy doors apart so that he could step inside. "How's that for security?"

"A little better," Finn replied, "come on. I may be able to get the generator started."

The two of them went forward and came around to the control room as they climbed a set of stairs to enter into a room that overlooked the generator room.

"If I had to guess, this'd be a standard diesel-powered generator, nothing too fancy. I can't imagine they'd invest too much in anything else."

The control room had several power boxes on one side and a control panel with reinforced windows on the other. He looked around while Moira stayed put.

"This place looks ancient," Moira expressed. "How long do you suppose this GDP has existed?"

"At least thirty years, perhaps more," Finn replied. "Remember, the goal of the organization was to maintain a status quo in world power, so I doubt it could have existed in the same form during the Cold War."

"What if it did…" Moira questioned.

"If it did, I wouldn't know about it," Finn responded. "You can do all the research you want when we're inside their network, but to do that we've got to get the power running."

Finn continued to examine the room around him before he stopped. He opened a cabinet that read 'High Voltage' on the front and then revealed a few switches as well as a lever. He pumped the lever several times and then pressed a button, and when he did, there was a hum that went through the room followed with a descent in tone as it all came quiet.

"What's wrong?" Moira asked.

"I don't know," Finn replied, looking around. "Usually that's enough to get it to work..." He turned around and came over to the generator room where he looked down, and then he looked across the control panel. "The generators may not have enough fuel to get started."

Finn looked at the side of the control panel where there was a door that led out onto a catwalk. He exited out and then came down a set of stairs below. He examined some tanks that read 'Diesel' on the front and placed his hands on the valves. He attempted to turn it, but it did not move.

"No use, I need a spanner of some sort to get this going," Finn expressed.

"A spanner?"

"A wrench," Finn clarified. "There must be some tools nearby."

"I saw the opposite hallway went into a maintenance workshop zone."

"Perfect."

The pair traversed back to the elevator shaft where they stopped and looked at the opposite side. They began to go around to the other side together where they entered another corridor with another vault-like door that prevented further travel. Another vent cover above bypassed this obstacle and Moira dropped down into another corridor with lockers. She released the door to let Finn inside, and then began to go down the corridor to reach a side door that led into a maintenance workshop. There were numerous benches, shelves with bits and bobs, and a few machines lying around the room. Finn searched a workshop bench and found a wrench, and then left the room with Moira to return to the other side. The pair traversed back to the generator room where Finn loosened the valve bolt and then began to release diesel.

When Finn had finished in the generator room, he walked upstairs to the control room with Moira where he attempted to turn on the generator again in the same way. He pulled the lever up and down several times, and then he pressed a button. The machine whirred to life, causing adjacent boxes to also liven up. A loud alarm set off from within the generator room and with a bit of time, the lights in the control room turned on while an orange-red incandescent light in the generator room lit up too. Finn opened the adjacent cabinets, each one of which provided power to separate levels. He turned each of them on, one by one, beginning with Level Four – Plant Services, Level Three – Detention Center, Level Two – Research and Development, Level One – Battle Station.

"What are we going to do here if the GDP aren't even around?" Moira asked.

"What do you mean what are we going to do? Don't you see? This is perfect – they've run off from this hole and likely found a new one. We'll be able to steal all their secrets and use it against them to leave us alone."

"What about what Dr. Lambert said," Moira stated. "About them not existing anymore."

"He never was really certain," Finn responded. "So a few of his friends show up to work for Cabernet Research, but what evidence is that? They could have easily downsized or found a nicer base somewhere else."

"Assuming that is true, then what could we hope to find? They surely didn't leave all their data behind…"

"Only one way to find out…" Finn responded. "We may also be able to find out where they went. Besides, if they didn't exist anymore, who do you suppose is responsible for the attempted assassination as a result of talking about them?"

"Dr. Lambert said that their bosses, the 'League of Concerned Citizens' or whatever, still exist."

"The Committee of Concerned Citizens," Finn clarified, "and of course they still exist. They're just politicians and elites – that never changes, and I can see reason to believe they'd be so zealous to tie up loose ends."

Finn and Moira left the control room, returned to the corridor and turned off their headlamps as the facility was now powered up. They came to the elevator shaft and called the elevator, but nothing happened.

"Hm… elevator may be out for good…" Finn stated. "We'll just have to climb up – I reckon we go up to the detention center, find a security station and see if we can access the network from there."

The pair did just as Finn described, climbed up to Level Three, released the elevator doors, and then climbed out onto the left side. A sign pointed forward that said 'Communications Center' ahead, so they went the other way and entered into a corridor that led up to another access panel. Moira examined the panel and then looked at Finn.

"Looks like an RFID access point," Moira pointed out. "If we can access the data network, I could set all the doors unlocked."

"Until then, stick to the vents," Finn remarked, looking up and readying his hands. "Let's go."

Moira climbed up and then hopped down. She entered a room with jail cells on either side, stopped for a moment to look down to the end of the room, and then turned around to examine the door. She hit the release switch, but the doors did not open. She flicked the switch back and forth, but it still did not release.

"Hey, I've got a bit of a problem here," Moira called out. "The door isn't releasing!"

"Dammit, must be because the power is back on," Finn expressed. "I could go downstairs to turn off the power to bypass it."

"And what if we can't get the power back on after?"

"Do you have a better idea?"

"Throw my stuff – there's a security console besides the door. I'll see if I can hookup to the system."

Finn picked up Moira's backpack and threw it through the vent. She caught it on the other side and then began to take out her laptop and other equipment. She hooked up to the computer and began to launch some software on her laptop.

"Hm…" Moira stated, "it looks like the site-based network is down. I can only access this PC, which I'm going to try and do to see if it can open this door without the network being up. Can you go back to where it said communications center and see if you can…"

"Yeah, yeah," Finn replied. "I'm on it…"

Finn left the detention block and walked to the other side of the elevator. He entered another corridor similar to the one before. He stopped in front of the door and looked up to the vent cover.

"How am I supposed to get through that?" Finn questioned, removing his backpack. He approached the cover and could barely reach it even as he stood on his toes. "I need a crowbar. I think I saw one downstairs."

Finn left the third level and went down to the fourth to retrieve a crowbar from the maintenance workshop. He then returned to pry the cover off from the vent. Once done, Finn grabbed hold of the ledge and began to attempt to lift himself up. He struggled to pull himself up fully as he kicked his legs off the wall and snuck himself in. Finn dropped down onto the other side and looked around the room he was in. It was another locker room with another high security door on the other side, no vent cover, and just a room on the left. This room led to stairs that went up to an office space that looked over another room, similarly sized to the generator room, but with a radar dish. This room also had a catwalk, so Finn exited out and went downstairs to investigate.

"Seems like an uplink point of some sort," Finn expressed, "but irrelevant to the internal network. I need to find a server room." His eyes went over to a door that went further along. He found a vent cover on the ground, pried it off, and then began to climb through to see that he was beneath a raised floor in the server room. He crawled through to find a hatch that led him inside, and once he had done so, looked around the many server devices. He came around to a console that blinked, turned it on, and then saw it begin to automatically function. "Hopefully that'll do it. I should get back to Moira and see if she can access the internal network."

Finn climbed back down into the grate and crawled his way out of the room. He exited out and then began to retrace his steps back to the vent where he pulled a bench from nearby to help raise him up to climb through. He then took his backpack, and went all the way to the cell block again.

"Oy! Moira! I believe I turned on the network - see if it's..."

"Yup! It's up and running – good work. I should have gone straight there rather than here to link in, but oh well. I suppose this console has access to security programs. I'm able to enter into the access control program and I'm going to set all the doors open."

Finn watched as the door instantly opened for him to walk through and join her.

"I was looking for video surveillance capabilities, but that program doesn't seem to be on here. We should check the other consoles to see if it's anywhere else."

Moira left the console with Finn, and they ventured deeper into the detention center. They came into the next room which had a large oval cell in the center with thick glass. This pod appeared like a pressurized room with the number of machines hooked up to it, especially ventilation. They passed around to the other side, went through another cell block, but did not find any other consoles, so they returned to the elevator shaft. The pair went up another level where seemingly they could not go any further due to the elevator being stuck halfway over their heads. Additionally, the elevator exits were not on the left or right, but behind them, on the same face that they entered in the cavern below.

The pair released the door and then stepped out into a different room. They entered into a large room that extended eastward to reveal a large workshop with numerous machines. Meanwhile, on the west side was an open door that led into a room labeled above as 'Research Center.' The pair stepped forward, and came into a large laboratory with computer and research workstations alike. In the corner of the room was an isolated space with a workbench inside. They passed this room to enter into a medical bay. Passing through the medical bay, the sign above said they had entered into the barracks. A set of stairs led up to a weight training room, and then above to living quarters. The living quarters were two stories tall with a staircase that went up above to a room further ahead, and likewise a pathway below that led further ahead as well. Moria stopped for a moment as she looked around this room. The room like many of the ones in the facility was abandoned, but not in such a rushed way. There was no sense of disorder in the room, of destruction or brokenness, but rather simple lack of vacancy. However, Moira's eyes shifted around the room, from the bookcases to the vending machines, to the pool table and sofas.

"You look scared," Finn calmly noted.

"I- I can't help but feel like I've been in here before."

"You have been here before. More than five years ago," Finn replied.

"I remember this room though – I was guided into this room, and taken upstairs."

"Upstairs?"

Moira began to walk on her own as she went to the staircase and began to climb up to a catwalk before a reinforced door that was wide open. She stepped inside and found herself in an office. She looked around the room and then over to a door further ahead. She walked further ahead and came into a long narrow room with a large monitor that bore the logo of the GDP, a white globe with lines across in eighths according to longitudinal and latitudinal divisions. Moira walked over to the console before the large monitor and placed her hands overtop. She removed her backpack and took out her laptop. She began to connect in while Finn stood back. He watched as Moira's hands moved around the keyboard, whizzing around at near supersonic speed as she typed on both the keyboard of the console and the laptop. He looked with awe as she began to hack into the computer system in this room.

"This one's on a closed network," Moira expressed. "Seems like its own server database too. I'm in, although it wasn't easy…"

"Do you have access to CCTV systems?"

"Yeah, one second," Moira expressed as she pulled up cameras on the large monitor. "Last recorded footage is from… March 20th, 2023." She pulled up multiple views through the facility, including the hangar which was a large cavern with a vertical take-off-landing aircraft (V-TOL). The views also displayed the central operations command.

Moira played the camera footage, and it showed staff members at work in the laboratories, foundry, living quarters, and command center. The footage followed along until 03:00:00 hours exactly when the lights began to blink, and alarms began to set off. Immediately, all personnel in the base sprang to action, especially from the living quarters as daytime personnel exited quickly. The pair paid close attention to the armory as soldiers began to suit up from their jumpsuits into body armor, picked up riot shields and distributed weapons. They also distributed and began to set up blast shields around the base on approach to the hangar. Finn looked at footage from within the living quarters where a woman in a business suit spoke to four soldiers in particular before they set off and went to the V-TOL. These soldiers each wore a different colored body armor, black, as well as full helmets and a particular exoskeleton around their bodies. All but one entered into the aircraft with some more soldiers, and then the craft took off. Everybody in the base was in position facing the hangar bay, but then Moira pointed out cameras on the fourth floor displaying robots similar to the ones that attacked them in Allabrese, crawling on all fours through the elevator shaft and pouring into the base from below. From that moment forward, the robots began to massacre everyone. The woman in the business suit fought closely to one of the four elite soldiers. The metallic exoskeleton around his armor was more visible, and as they watched, they could see him jump incredible heights in the hangar as he opened fire at the robots, kicked and punched at robots as though they were humans, launching them against the cavern walls, and even picked some of them up with his two hands. Some other soldiers also wore this exoskeleton around their jumpsuits or regular armor. The weapons that the personnel on the floor used varied, some were ordinary assault rifles in appearance, but they fired extraordinary projectiles that pierced the robots. The personnel shifted their defensive strategy and took defensive positions in the living quarters, armory, and then command center before the hangar. Moira pointed down to a corridor view as she saw a larger robot than the others walk down. This robot appeared bulkier, taller, and with a different set of equipment, and it did not engage the personnel in the base. Finn looked at it closely – it had a pair of metallic black tentacles that protruded from its back to give itself an additional set of loose limbs that could stretch out and grab hold of survivors. In an instant, the robot could also disappear and leave only a blur behind as it moved stealthily. By the time the robot came to the living quarters, it could jump incredible heights as well that the other robots could not. The pair re-focused their attention to the last stand in the hangar to notice a large set of blast doors begin to open up as a team of soldiers escorted the female and a few others out, while the enhanced soldier and the rest of the defensive personnel took point. The footage continued for a few more minutes as the fight came to the hangar, especially with the approach of the enhanced robot. However, as robots scattered through the entire facility, the footage abruptly ended.

"How awful," Moira expressed.

"Awful? They were no saints," Finn responded, "but what I want to know is what the hell those things were and why they were fighting them."

"They looked like the things that came after us."

"But why would they come after us? All we did was discuss the existence of the GDP and some past history – does that warrant execution?"

"What if… those things are the GDP now. What if… there was some sort of upheaval to the balance of power around here? What if there was a change of leadership?"

"Even for an organization like the GDP, such abrupt changes to the power structure have…" Finn paused for a moment as he recollected. "Nevermind, perhaps you're right. Ms. Black came to power through a revolt, so why not this new power, whoever this new power may be, but it doesn't explain why this place is empty…"

"Perhaps they didn't like her choice in decoration…" Moira replied. "Finn, there's terabytes and terabytes of information here about the GDP still. If the GDP does still exist, they didn't do a good job of shredding their own existence. I can hardly fit all of this on my laptop. I need an external hard drive, which I didn't bring with me."

"I… I don't think the GDP exist anymore," Finn stated. "I think Dr. Lambert was right… maybe, the Global Defense

Project was cancelled because the Committee of Concerned Nations found a new favorable contractor in the service of global stability. What if those robots are the new enforcers for the committee? A cold-collected service personnel able to exterminate without hesitance, especially as one utters the name of the former project and their actions. We may be up against a harder enemy than I imagined. The GDP were always easy to work with because they were human, but robots…?"

"The new GDP may be robots, but the Committee aren't. If we can't negotiate our ability to live normal lives with the GDP, then we'll take it to their former bosses."

"Whoa now, you can't just negotiate with the Committee – they are the definition of power in the modern world. If you thought I was scared of the GDP, then the Committee are an entirely different level – these are people who wanted my dad dead. I know all about them – the Committee of Concerned Nations is just a colorful term for normies. They're really called… well, I don't want to even say it out here…" Finn expressed. "I don't want anymore of those… things to show up."

"We're not under surveillance out here – besides, it's a closed network. No communications are going out to the rest of the world."

Finn looked around suspiciously and then leaned in to say, "Chosen, and the worst of them call themselves, Children of Moloch."

"What?" Moira questioned with disbelief. "Are you serious?"

"Dead serious – look, the GDP are one thing, but the capital C people are another totally worse foe. They are bad news, Moira. We are talking pedophiles, human traffickers, and king pins to all organized crime in the world. They control the banks, media, and just about every government. We are talking literal demons in the flesh… we already talked about aliens, and you seeing all this must make you realize that it was all real, so believe me when I say that they are aliens who were sent down to the planet, exiled, and now have a taste for blood to subvert this planet to make their own kingdom… so I hear. Based on research that my great-grandfather did, and which my dad completed, they once ruled the world during ancient times, but slowly began to lose power until Roman rule when they were done. The game of survival of the fittest did not fall short on them and they did their best to survive in opposition to those that hated them. They are the progenitors of evil on this planet; a nexus of evil. We cannot go toe-to-toe, or see reason with them."

"Like hell we can't – I grabbed as many files as I could," Moira expressed. "You told me I once remotely connected to this place once upon a time. If we set up a connection, I could do so again once we begin to ship this data out – we need to make some sort of communication with these Chosen Children you're talking about."

Finn nervously laughed and replied, "Even I don't know how to do that – it's something I've preferred to not have to think about, but I suppose any scumbag high-ranking politician or businessman would do. The only problem is that I don't know whether we'd find a Child or a sympathizer. They recruit from outside their flock apparently, powerless muggles as it were. They're shapeshifters, you see, which is how they retain human form. I can't tell the difference between them, but… there were some folk who really hated them, but they don't exist anymore. We could talk to the only connection I know to that group, and perhaps find refuge at their monastery too…"

"Monastery?"

"Yeah… it's a long story I'll tell you on the plane, but I think we ought to get the hell out of here."

"Not before I set up a remote access point…" Moira expressed. "I'm going to activate the satellite uplink in the basement. You have any problem with that?"

"All the problems with it – you're going to send a signal out to the rest of the world and possibly the Chosen."

"It's a risk we're going to have to just take…" Moira replied. "It's done – come on, let's go…"

"In the footage, we saw them escape through the hangars. Let's head that way and see if we can make it out through there. I don't fancy a hike the way we came."

"Sure thing."

"Before we do, I think I want to visit the armory."

Act 3, Scene 4

Finn looked around the armory downstairs from the situation room. He checked the weapons crates and examined the various types of firearms, but he was not interested in any of them. The same could not be said about Moira who picked up the assault rifle and then aimed down the line of sight with it.

"God, it's been a long time since I've put my hands on one of these," Moira remarked. "My dad used to take me to the range at the police station sometimes – let me shoot some guns civilians weren't allowed to shoot. Shouldn't we stock up before we go?"

"First of all, I don't think that's a conventional rifle," Finn pointed out as he examined one nearby, "and second of all, I don't use guns. I'll stick to my bow, thank you very much."

"What, are you allergic to guns or something?"

"I already told you... I don't need to use a gun," Finn remarked. "Besides, that's not what I'm looking for."

"What are you looking for?"

"I'm looking for those metal skeletons some of the soldiers were using – the ones that went around their bodies like a framework," Finn explained. "I just can't seem to find it..."

Finn opened some cabinets where some body armor was found. Moira went ahead and equipped a ballistic vest over her torso.

"Dad said that these vests can be lifesavers – he always kept a spare at home just in case – what with mobsters in our town and such."

"Funny, my dad was precautious like that as well..." Finn remarked, picking one up. He held onto the vest as he opened the other cabinets. "I wonder if there'll be one of them downstairs in the mechanic shops. I'm going to go and take a look."

"Suit yourself... I'm going to try out these guns..."

Moira left the armory as she entered a room beside that had a gun range. She placed down two rifles, one that was black and white, and another that was beige. She also removed a holster she had picked up and placed around her thigh which held a blaster pistol. She placed down some ammunition to each of these rifles, and then picked up the black and white assault rifle. She loaded the magazine and then went to point it down range. She opened fire and shot projectiles at the targets. The projectiles were quieter than conventional bullets, but the rifle warmed up quickly in her hands and emptied out a lot quicker. She looked down range and saw that the projectiles eviscerated the cut-out. She then went to the other rifle, picked it up and loaded a cartridge. She aimed down her sights and shot the projectiles, which fired off at a high-velocity, emptying the cartridge quickly. The rifle pelted the cut-out and left gaping holes where it landed. Moira left he gun range with a smile on her face.

Meanwhile, Finn went downstairs to the laboratories, searched around, and then came into the foundry on the opposite side. The foundry had numerous mechanical arms around, assembly lines, and loose equipment lying about. At one such workshop, Finn found an exoskeleton. The exoskeleton was just as it was called, a skeletal frame that existed outside of the body. The center portion of the skeletal structure consisted of a reinforced spine with a joint scapula at the top with nodules around. There were also four points that extended outwards and appeared as though they came under the armpit and over the shoulders. From this point, there was a reinforced clavicle that then connected to an artificial humerus and radius. The arms ended at a point that connected around the wrists. From the spine, the exoskeleton wrapped around the waist where like the scapula there were nodules, and then extended down the side of the legs like a femur and tibia, wrapping around the ankle, and also around the upper half of the foot. Finn approached the skeletal structure, removed his backpack and poncho, and then backed himself into the exoskeleton. He slid his hands around the wrist cuffs and fit his boots into the lower portion. He looked around the parts of the skeletal structure he could see, and then hit a button on the part that came over his shoulders, but it did not close.

"Hm... no power," Finn remarked. He placed his hand around the waist, turned a cap and then felt it could be pressed down, so he did so. A thick fuse came out from the back of the waist, approximately six inches in length and translucent white. "Where do I find one of these?"

Finn left the foundry and went downstairs to the power plant. He walked across from the main generator room, went through a room with numerous machines, and then came to a second generator, although this one appeared different. Finn paused for a moment and then began to investigate as he approached the center of the machine and opened a latch from where numerous fuses could be found. He gently removed one and then raised it up – unlike the one he had pulled out from the exoskeleton, this one glowed white. Finn looked around the room and found a small, reinforced case from where he could place three tubes inside. He removed three from the generator and placed them inside, and then took a fourth and brought both the case and the tube upstairs with him where he returned to the foundry. Finn placed the fuse inside the machine, and then backed into it again and pressed the 'on' switch.

The motor in the waist and scapular region began to whir, and then the claws around the torso began to slowly close in and tighten around Finn's chest. A smaller set of pincers came around the neck and enclosed themselves around the lower portion of his neck, startling him. Next, the segments of the limbs began to shut tight around. The exoskeleton chimed and each segment gently adjusted to conform to Finn's body size. After a moment, the exoskeleton was around his entire body except the head. He took a step forward, and just as he moved, so did the exoskeleton move with him. Finn came out to an open space ahead of him and began to practice a range of motions. The exoskeleton flawlessly followed his movements. Finn approached a table in front of him and placed his hands over it. He began to lift the table up as though it were made of less than wood, or he were in low gravity. Finn dropped the table, and it made a loud noise. He kicked the table back with his right foot and caused it to slide forward as the exoskeleton boosted his exerted force. He then ran to the table, the exoskeleton giving him a boost to his speed, and then he lifted a fist upwards and punched down, brutally damaging the table as he shattered it in half.

"Not bad at all..." Finn stated. He turned around to pick up his poncho and put it away, placed the reinforced case inside his backpack, and then took his backpack with him.

Moira looked over as Finn joined her while she sat atop of a crate with a rifle in her hand. "What's that you got there?" she asked.

"An exoskeleton suit," Finn expressed. "I heard about these – Dr. Lambert had designed something similar, but this one is a lot more practical."

"Aw, I want one," Moira complained.

"Sorry, love, one of a kind," Finn replied. "I believe this one may have either been in repair or a prototype. I noticed it had nodules as though it could be customized and appendages added. You'll have to stick with your fancy guns."

"These aren't your typical gun for sure," Moira expressed. "I'm not sure what these are, but they shoot hot and heavy rounds."

"Dr. Lambert once told me they were researching that sort of thing here – plasma and high-energy weaponry, and also gauss and magnetic weaponry," Finn noted. "Though, Dr. Lambert was certain they'd be years off from refining that sort of weaponry.

The aliens had both in their arsenal, so I hear – the GDP wanted to re-create it."

"Well, this must be the energy gun," Moira remarked, holding the black and white rifle, "and this one the magnetic gun. Take your pick – come on, these aren't your standard shoot-to-kill rifle. These have to have some sort of advantage against Ultron's army."

"We're not up against anything – we're not going toe-to-toe with whatever you just said," Finn scolded. "The skeleton is to assist with any navigating we have to do to get out of here and that's it. Now leave those here. We don't need 'em."

"Speak for yourself," Moira replied, showing off the holster strapped to her knee with a high-energy pistol. "I'm taking at least two with me – I highly recommend you take the other – I can't take them both with me. Come on, we're not going to kill anyone – the way I see, they're looking to kill us, so it would be in our advantage to defend our lives, wouldn't it?"

Finn looked at her begrudgingly, and then took the magnetic weapon. He held it into his arms with a deep frown on his face. He then sighed and said, "I told myself I wouldn't put my hands on something like this ever again... not after the last time..."

"What happened last time? Is that why you can't return to the UK?"

"No – not that. I don't want to talk about it," Finn barked. "Just give me the bloody rifle – better safe than sorry, I suppose."

"Jeez, alright..." Moira replied. "You'll want to load up on some magazines before we leave. They're over here..."

The pair stocked up on munitions as they loaded their backpacks. Finn kept his backpack around his shoulders awkwardly as he continued to wear the exoskeleton.

"Say, how is that thing powered up anyways?" Moira questioned. "You have a charging cable for it?"

"No, I found a fusion reactor downstairs and can only imagine it takes plasma capsules similar to the ones my father had made," Finn stated. "I took a few with me as backup. I can't imagine how much time I may have with this suit. Something of this magnitude would take several terawatts of power and could likely last me half an hour or so. I've got to use it sparingly."

Moira and Finn left the armory and came into the central command. The command center was completely ruined with computers array, and even the central screen at the rear smashed.

"Does this unlock anymore memories for you?" Finn questioned as they stopped halfway through. "You should have walked through here when you last came."

"I think… I think I remember somewhat," Moira stated. "It's still a blur to me though…"

"Something must have come through to clean up whatever bodies were left behind, machines too, because I haven't seen any remnants of the fight."

Finn and Moira continued into the hangar where the central platform lacked the V-TOL aircraft, though platforms above certainly continued to hold the jets. They approached the blast doors as they were closed shut and began to examine the control panel. Finn brought a hand to lever, but the lever did not move. He then examined the other side and saws another lever.

"Seems like we both got to pull down," Finn remarked. "On three… one, two…"

They both pulled down on the lever, causing alarms and sirens to set off in the hangar and the center of the blast doors to open and let out steam from within. Finn looked with careful eyes as the doors slowly opened and the cloud of steam grew. Suddenly, his eyes caught sight of something on approach, so he raised his weapon. Out from the cloud of steam, the enhanced robot from the recordings stepped through the cloud of steam as it was raised upon the ground by a set of two thick mechanical tentacles. Up close, the texture of the robot appeared different from those that visited Cabernet Manor. It was greyish-blue and pearly. It had eyes like the other robots, but these were a light blue. The robot appeared as though it had an exoskeleton of its own, but around the calves were attachments that pointed down. Likewise, around the back of its upper arms were similar attachments. Finn looked at the robot with terror, especially as it occasionally jerked its neck and twitched as though in error and fault. The robot did not emit a voice, but did make a terrible screeching noise, again, as though in mechanical error but at the same time, its howl was inhuman.

"Don't just stand there, Finn!" Moira shouted out, raising her rifle. "Shoot it!"

Moira opened fire at the creature, prompting Finn to do the same. The high-energy rounds pierced the shoulder of the robot, prompting it to hop down and use one of its tentacles to grab Moira. Finn got a shot off at the creature, but the magnetic rounds did little to damage its head. It still hissed at Finn though and used its other tentacle to grab at him, but he raised the rifle to shield him, and it instead grabbed the rifle and threw it away. Immediately, the creature was propelled upwards by the attachments at its thigh, landing on a platform above as it continued to hold Moira by the neck. Finn immediately dashed over to the rifle on the floor, picked it up and then began to open fire at it, but it hopped around the platforms before it then came down and then ran off into the dark tunnel. All that Finn could then hear was almost a sinister laughter from the enhanced robot as well as Moira's screams.

"Moira!" Finn shouted.

Finn ran forward with the high-energy rifle in his hands. The tunnel went upwards on a low slope, reaching a landing from where there were vehicles parked, though in disarray. A checkpoint ahead had numerous vehicles piled up in front, requiring Finn to climb over them and then hop down to continue his pursuit along another section of the exit tunnels. The lights in the tunnel were dim and red. As Finn continued to pursue the creature, he noticed a metallic object on approach to him at a high velocity and immediately jumped out of the way. A wrecked chassis of a jeep had made its approach down the ramp. Finn continued forward, cautious as another came flying towards him. He eventually reached another landing above where he stopped and looked around. He found another pile of vehicles as well as the creature, which picked up one of the cars and threw it towards Finn. He ducked out of the way, but missed his shot at the robot as it fled up the tunnels. The robot tore through a fuse box within and caused the doors to quickly shut. He could hear Moira's screams and the laughter of the robotic entity follow through again. Finn ran towards the doors, but they were thick and shut like the blast doors in the hangar. He looked up above and the least that he could find was a vent, so he came around on top of the vehicles and then climbed up onto the checkpoint where he found a ladder that went up to the catwalk above. He came around to the vent cover and was able to tear it off with the help of the exoskeleton suit. He then crawled in and came through to the other side where he hopped down and then continued along the ramp. Finn ran forward along the ramp and more debris was thrown towards him as he made his way up, catching a sight of some light on the other side two-thirds of the way away. Finn continued to dodge the debris as he ran forward along the tunnel. At one-third of the way, the debris stopped, and Finn could hear the roar of waves ahead. He came out from the tunnels and found himself at a platform beside the open sea. There were numerous installations around the platform, especially fuel drums. He stepped forward to come towards the edge of the platform as he noticed that they were within a small bay with tall rock formations around. The forest stood around them again, but on the left side there was a medium sized wreckage of a military boat. The boat had a wide tear through the middle as it lay on its side. Finn's eyes looked around cautiously as he awaited the robot to appear and ambush him. He then saw Moira on the edge of the platform behind a crane near the water to his right. Finn ran towards Moira as she lay on her side and saw that she was half-awake.

"Moira, wake up!" Finn remarked, shaking her.

Suddenly, Finn turned to the waves of the ocean as he saw a spout of water fly upwards as though shot out from a whale. He then saw the rapids of whitewater tear through the waves, followed by the enhanced robot shooting upwards from the bay in a straight line, landing upon one of the rocks. In the mechanical arms, not the tentacles, of the beast was the magnetic rifle pointed at Finn.

Finn immediately opened fire at the beast as he fired high-energy rounds. The enhanced robot also fired back at him, but the magnetic rifle rounds instead hit the legs of the outpost tower, causing it to tip over and collapse. Finn jumped out of the way and then used the collapsed tower as cover as he aimed towards the beast, but it had disappeared. He looked around the water as he anticipated it to re-appear, doing so at the opposite side of the bay where it used its tentacles to hold onto the rocks. Finn immediately opened fire again and was able to hit the beast in the side and one of the tentacles as it shot magnetic rounds back at him.

The beast fell into the sea and disappeared, prompting Finn to adjust his position as he went around to one of the buildings on his left. The creature reappeared as it propelled itself through the water and then reappeared besides a small island of boulders. It picked up one of the boulders with its tentacle while it continued to aim the magnetic rifle. Finn carefully aimed his sights as he remained hidden and shot off at the head of the robot, causing it to tick its head sideways, but still throw the boulder with precision towards him, hitting the rooftop and causing it to collapse. Magnetic rounds then tore through the building as Finn lay low. He crawled out of the way and took a moment to recompose himself. Suddenly, another boulder volleyed into the building and crashed into where Finn had hid. He looked around the corner and could not see where the beast had disappeared to. He then went around the other side and looked over to where Moira was, but she was gone. He made a dash to the other side and then began to climb up a set of metal stairs to come around to a platform. He came into the prone position and aimed the rifle outwards. The beast splashed out of the water and landed upon a boulder where it looked around for Finn. Finn opened fire at it again and hit the torso, bludgeoning it and then causing it to immediately aim towards him. He stood up as the magnetic shots hit the side of the platform and a water tower nearby, sending gallons of water out onto the platform below. Finn dashed down the platform as it continued fire at him, but he hid behind another building. He looked around the corner as he saw the beast look for him. The beast then fell back into the sea, and Finn took a moment to find a new hiding place.

Rather than hide behind or around a metallic structure, Finn came close to the edge of the platform and hid behind a vehicle parked on the side. He knelt down and waited for the creature to show up again, doing so around another island with some boulders which it picked up two with each tentacle claw. As Finn stayed hidden, the creature began to throw boulders indiscriminately at structures around, including the roof of the jeep he was behind, causing the roof to collapse in. He then opened fire and shot the arm and magnetic rifle, causing it to explode in its hands and maim one of the arms. The creature screeched out and as Finn continued to fire, hit the tentacles too, causing sparks to fly out and around. At that moment, Finn ran out of ammunition for a rifle he had no other ammunition for. He threw the rifle aside and took his bow from the side of his backpack. Meanwhile, the robot began to point its right arm forward. He then saw a bright light glow from the end of its arm as well as a red laser beam point towards him.

"Oh no…" Finn expressed, kicking his backpack and rifle away from the jeep. He then dashed out of the way as a high-energy beam came out from the end of the beast's arm and caused the jeep to erupt in a fireball. Finn stood up from where he ran to, aimed the bow, and shot an arrow towards the robot and hit it in the left eye. The beast tilted its head back as it screeched out and then fell into the sea. From this location, Finn looked over the water as he saw the creature swim around the depths of the bay before it then swam up and shot out from the water, landing onto the platform before him where it pulled a lamp pole from out of the ground with both hands, and then raised itself up on each of the two tentacles. Finn fired another arrow and hit the side of its body.

The creature then approached him as the arrow did little then stick into its armor. He did notice the optics of the armor begin to glitch out as it changed colors and textures. The creature used one of its tentacles to sweep some debris from the side of the platform from where Finn hid behind, and then attempted to jab at him with the lamp pole, but missed as he jumped out of the way. He fired another arrow and hit the other eye of the robot, effectively causing both lights to shut off. The robot then began to look around for him as he ran off, but it could not track his movement. Finn readied another arrow as he looked to the side, and then paused for a moment. Although Finn was not completely hidden, the creature did not see him and could not hear him. At the same time, the creature began to suddenly disappear and turn into a blur in front of him as it dropped the lamp post. He could hear the creature move away and took that moment to go over to the lamp post to pick it up with the strength of the exoskeleton. The sound of Finn picking up the lamp post caused the creature to immediately turn around and face him. It launched its tentacle towards him, but Finn jumped out of the way to dodge each strike. He then ran towards the creature and pierced its body with the sharp end of the lamp post, but it did little then dent it. The creature made a murmuring sound and then snapped the post out of Finn's hands, throwing it into the sea, and then attempting to grab him. Finn, however, ran off and hid behind the ruins of a structure nearby. The creature then approached where he ran to, causing Finn to look around and see a tank of liquid nitrogen nearby. He aimed an arrow at the tank and pierced its side, tearing at it. He then hit another one as the creature was around the corner, causing it to tear further and spill liquid nitrogen onto the concrete platform. The liquid nitrogen flushed through and mixed with the water from the ruptured water tower, creating ice around and causing Finn to step away and onto the top of some metal steps up to a platform.

"Hey! Wanker!" Finn shouted at the metal creature. The creature turned and then immediately began to approach him from around the corner, stepping into the water as the ice approached too. The liquid nitrogen made its approach as Finn took a step back and the creature shot one of its tentacles towards him. The creature missed as Finn jumped out and out of the way, tearing through the railing beside him, but the liquid nitrogen began to reach up its legs and make its pass. As the liquid nitrogen ran through, it began to coat the robot in a layer of frost, mixing with its already wet body. Another tentacle shot towards him, but as it did so, it was slow and unable to extend far enough as Finn still jumped out of the way. The other tentacle moved around and then began to freeze in place, and the creature took another step forward as its legs began freeze in place, snapping off and causing it to fall forward. It placed its right hand into the ground, and it too froze in place. It looked up towards Finn and let out a screech as the rest of its body froze in place and it began to cease to move. "How do you like that?" Finn expressed, readying an arrow.

Before Finn could launch the arrow as he drew it with the strength of the exoskeleton suit, one of the tentacles immediately raised up and shot forward towards Finn. Immediately, the beast shattered into a hundred pieces. Finn flinched and shielded his face, and then looked over as he saw the disintegrated robot remains lie before him while he looked to his right and saw Moira who held the blaster pistol in hand. Finn sat down as he took a moment to breath and looked at the creature below in its many pieces. The liquid nitrogen continued to freeze everything that it touched, leaving behind a streak of ice from the ruptured tank down to the water. After all the liquid nitrogen had frozen around, Finn listened to the crash of the waves beside the water, and looked about as if he was expecting the creature to re-appear.

Finn went to his backpack, picked up the high-energy rifle, and then his backpack. He placed his arrows and bow away, and then picked up both as he turned around to see Moira atop of the boat wreckage.

"Finn!" Moira cried out, waving her arms. "Finn, come over here! Look at what I found!"

Finn went over to the boat wreckage as Moira continued to stand atop of the bow and then came around and exited through the crevasse that tore into its body.

"Finn, take a look…" Moira remarked, prompting him inside. Finn stepped in and found various destroyed crates and other goods in the midst of the ship. He then look over and found the remains of an anthropomorphic being like the robot he had just defeated that lay in the midst of some of the debris. This being though wore an exoskeleton suit just like the one that Finn wore, but modified to have the same upgrades that the enhanced creature had as well – tentacles that extended from the spine, propulsion systems at the legs and arms, and a jumpsuit made of a very fine black fiber, including a matching hood. Around the wrist of the skeletal remains, Finn saw a flickering light besides a button. "What's that?" Moira asked.

Finn reached over and hit the button, causing a deep voice to speak out, "My name is Lance Corporal Tama 'Kupe' Ariki, of the Global Defense Project, Elite Forces. The date is March 20th, 2023, and it is currently 05:21 hours. GDP headquarters are overrun – Director Black and the rest of the team were able to make their escape as our enemies have begun to purge their enemies. It is my honor – my privilege, to make the last stand here in order to slow down the pursuit of this nautical enemy while the others escape via boat to the mainland. I am not wholly aware of the circumstances that have led us to this point. I just know that that is the end of our adventure, but not of our mission, which we are to take with us to the grave, in the defense of the globe and the status quo. The enemy before me is different to the others – it has the same augmentations as me, octo-arms, optic camouflage, and the capability to swim through water with incredible speed and precision through its propulsion system. At the same time, it has all the nuances of these robots that overwhelm us. I can only do so much to tear through their armor, and my suit is at its last breath. I will not live through this battle, but I am hopeful that the others may well be able to put a stop to our foes, and save the world from their wrath. Kupe, out."

"That hardly answers many questions, except to suggest that Ms. Black is alive somewhere," Finn remarked. "Whether she and the others were successful though…"

"What do we do now?" Moira asked.

"We… we should consult with one secret society to learn more about another," Finn stated. "We travel to Montana and see if we can learn some answers. Let's also give our friend here a proper burial… His weaponry could be useful to us. I heard about this sort of camouflage, though it is a little short for me to wear, but may work on you."

"Me? Look at the size of this guy…"

"It'll need to be adjusted a bit, but it'll fit…" Finn remarked. "I'm sure where we're going, they may be able to do it… and these propulsion adjustments. I'm not looking to do any swimming, but to reach some heights would be beneficial. I don't think the exosuit would fit you though…"

Finn took the moment to remove the exoskeleton and optic fibre suit from the skeletal remains of the elite soldier. He then carried the rest of the corpse out and gently led it down the docks where he placed it on a boat, and then set it off into the water as it sunk below. Once the two paid their respects, Finn began to remove the propulsion system from the exoskeleton to pocket them, and Moira took the suit with her as they camped the night and then returned to the aircraft.

Act 4, Prologue

Finn turned a valve ahead of him, releasing hot water that flowed directly down upon him. He stood naked in a large cubical shower with three chiseled granite sides. At his feet were granite tiles, and in the one face that did not have a stone side was instead a glass side that looked into the rest of the large bathroom he was in. The bathroom had a wide countertop and window, two sinks, and beside it was a large jacuzzi bathtub with a television set at the other side. Around to the left of the bathtub was an open door into a toilet closet, while on the other side was a sauna door. Opposite from the sink was a double set sliding doors into a bedroom. Hot water instantly fell down onto Finn's head, causing his hair to fall flat and appear light brown as opposed to dirty blonde. His face was clean-shaven, his skin pure of any blemishes but not scars on his body, especially the burn scars that remained along his arms and the slit scar under his left eye. Once Finn had finished showering, he dried himself, put on a robe, and then came out into the large master bedroom where there were tall open windows that looked out to a large city from where the Empire State Building could be seen. The bedroom had a king-sized bed, the back of it propped up against a wall with an end table beside it. On the opposite side was a door that led into a large closet where there were numerous clothing items and more windows at the corner of the high-rise building. Finn continued to dry himself as he ran a towel through his hair. He then plugged in a blow dryer and began to run that through his hair with a brush. Finn turned to his right as he heard the chime of the door sound off, prompting him to turn off the blow dryer, set it down, and then step out from the bedroom into a corridor that led out into a lavish main atrium.

In the middle of the atrium was a round set of cushioned seats that overlooked a bonfire in the middle with a television set at the other end. He came around the lounge and to the front door where he heard the door chime off again. He unchained the door and then opened it, looking at the other side where Damian Cambridge stood, in a fine brownish-black designer suit with an open collar top. He loomed over and looked at Finn with a serious glance, stepping forward and causing him to step back.

"Damian..." Finn remarked. "What are you doing here? I wasn't expecting you..."

"No, I suppose you weren't," Damian expressed, looking at him with distaste. "Look at you – one o'clock in the afternoon and just taking a shower. Here I am, expecting you to be doing something more useful with yourself, but instead, I pass a pair of skanks in the elevator talking about how much fun it was to hookup with the rich boy named Finn."

Damian looked around the apartment, seeing it to be in an impure and uncleanly state with bottles of alcohol lying around, bags of crisps and other takeout food items sitting about. Popcorn lay scattered on the floor, and the television displayed static. Pillows were left around everywhere, and clothing lay about the floor too.

"Give me one good explanation why it was even a little bit of a good idea that I pull you out from that forest?" Damian questioned. "I did not pull you out to live a life of debauchery..."

"Oh, come on," Finn expressed, "it was one night of partying – am I not allowed to live a little? I've been working here day and night, I needed some rest, I swear. Besides, your one to talk. I've seen the ones you've lured to your own bed... what with that wife of yours too..."

"You stay out of my own life, Finn," Damian expressed, grabbing him by the throat. "Remember who owns you," he said, gritting his teeth. "I rescued you from that forest, I can just as well send you back."

Finn gasped for air as Damian picked him up with his own strength.

"Look at you – like the scum of the rest of the earth. I can see right through your wicked heart – you lie to me. You've become soft and used to having everything when you used to have nothing. Perhaps some time on the streets of the city would do wonders to wake you up."

Finn began to grab at Damian's hands as he continued to choke him. He continued to gasp and attempt to yell.

"Yes, squirm… remind yourself of how little you are. In all of your self-perceived extravagance, it is nothing more than a façade for what is really an empty soul," Damian taunted as Finn continued to struggle. He then brought him closer to his face. "Remember what you are, Finn. You're mortal. You're human. You need this precious gift of God-given air as much as all of us, and that is why you struggle and squirm like the worm you are. Tell me – tell me you need me. Tell me you're nothing without me. Tell me you need me as much as you need this air."

Finn began to cry as he continued to choke. He then let out a small pip of noise, "I need you, master. I need you."

Damian gave a fiendish smile, released Finn and caused him to give out a large gasp as he fell to his knees and bowed his head down. He placed a hand around his neck and stayed put.

"That's right, Finn," Damian stated. "You do need me. Now get up…"

Finn immediately stood onto his feet.

"And sit down," Damian expressed. "I have something to discuss with you…"

Finn turned around and came to the lounge where he cleared some of the garbage to make room for Damian who sat down and then raised a leg up to place his ankle over his knee. Finn sat down a few feet away from him. He continued to rub his neck.

"While you've been spoiling yourself at my own expense, my son, I've been busy at work," Damian stated. "I'm set to travel to East Asia as I close in on the location of the last stone that I need – this one gives the user the power to manipulate the flow of time, and when I have it in my hands, I will again be champion of both space and time, capable to create the world we envision."

"That's good news then…"

"Yes," Damian affirmed, "because the days of this world will be numbered. I still have much work to do, some of it will have to be spared. I suggest to you to do whatever you need to do, and do it now. I also hope you've been doing the exercises I gave you…"

"Of course, I've been training with the stone you gave me… but I'm going to be honest with you, I don't know what I'm supposed to do to unlock this 'potential' you say I have within me," Finn expressed. "I've been doing the meditations… I've been doing the rigorous training… I've even let your scientists strap me to that machine, but it's not doing anything…"

"Of course it's not," Damian barked, "look at you. You're not suffering enough to let it awaken with you. You're too soft, Finn. Enough with the girls, and enough with the binge drinking. You lack discipline – you remind me of me when I was your age, pursuing the worldly things… misguided and naïve. Do you know what the Zionist pigs did to me when they captured me? They did not torture me – do you know why? Because instead, they let me have anything I wanted – especially the carnal pleasures of the body; food, drink, sex, all of it was mine whenever I wanted, and rather than attempt to coerce me to give in to them, they manipulated me. They brainwashed me. They had me see as I saw – they told me I was King David reborn, with a heart of gold and soul of silver. They treated me well because I was royalty, and after a while, I believed them.

"After a while, the chief rabbi approached me and asked me to pledge my loyalty not to him, but to their god – a god they called Beliyal, the very essence of evil and malice, of hatred and gloom. An essence as it were of tremendous power that extends through all of the earth and which they said would make its rise, especially if I served it. Though, they did not introduce Beliyal to me in that sense – all I was told that it was an entity of immense power that would aid me in our mutual goals. At the ritual, they gave me a knife – they told me that all I had to do was pledge my loyalty to Beliyal through the offering of my own blood as a sacrifice, and in return, I would be able to command his legions and rule this world. In exchange, I would receive all that I desired through my kingship, because through these human-pigs, I was of course learning that what I already had and indulged myself with was not enough – it's never enough with them."

Damian parted his hands and then showed the palm of his left hand where there was a lengthy scar that ran from the top of the index finger down diagonally down to the wrist bone. The scar was white and plainly visible.

"I swore a blood pact with Beliyal, unknown to me that this entity was what is also known as a great demon, a true unholy spirit," Damian stated. "In the name of Beliyal, I consecrated my life... those bastards tricked me. Of course, after a while, I caught on to their Talmudic ways to realize what Christianity calls the Devil, they call their god. I was skeptical, very skeptical, and also felt betrayed as I began to hate them. Eventually, I caught on to their Talmudic ways that I conspired against them. I pushed away from the hedonism to gain some discipline of myself lest I become too like them, and I began to think for myself and make my own rules. There is no God. There is no Devil, although there certainly are demons on Earth, and they were some of them – though they are no threat. No, when I was older, I realized that a fallen human being can be more sinister than the Devil or any other demon – it's the same I expect from you if you're to take up that mantle as my son. We will be the rulers of this Earth, Finn. You and me."

"Who are these demons?" Finn questioned. "I remember in Berwick-Northumbria, you briefly spoke about them, but who are these guys? Is it the Jews?"

"No, and I thought I told you to abandon this primitive conception that all Jews are evil. These demons that walk the earth are the ones behind all the malice and chaos," Damian expressed. "The true worshippers of Beliyal. I suppose they do come in two classes, those of which walk this earth and are among us, and those that belong to the sky. My mother had an encounter with the demons of the sky when she was young – the angels, she said, though I'm convinced they are all just evil, ugly beings. The story goes that thousands of years ago, the demons came from an advanced civilization with superior technology to our own. However, for reasons that are unclear to me, a portion were banished to Earth where they made contact with human beings, assimilating into human society as half-breeds and hybrids, some of whom retained their distinct powers in different forms. Like their fathers, they were wicked beings, but their power saw them rise to become the rulers of early civilizations. The fate of the hybrids is unclear, but from what I understand, according to the history of western civilization, a majority exist within the Chosen, specifically though, the Children of Moloch, although I'm sure there are handful of docile ones that do not foray with the elite. For the past almost two thousand years, Christianity has ruled Western Civilization, and civilization has abided by Christian theological and moral principles, which, as Nietzsche describes, is a philosophy for slaves, to humble oneself. To exist in such a world would be difficult, but not impossible as they assimilated with the Jewish people that opposed Christianity and integrated into the early leadership and people of the Jewish people. Over time, some of them have themselves rebelled and gone off to start their own movements and kingships, especially among the still-pagan cultures, particularly in India, but through it all they remained close to Zionists who they used as their own proxy. The most powerful of the descendants of these demons exist today in Israel, in the Zionists, and their allies abroad in all sorts of institutes of power.

The Second World War saw an implosion of these descendants to positions of power. Their goal is to tear down all that is good and create a world in servitude to them where they can rule forever.

"On the other hand, you have the demons of the sky, or 'elders' as the Children refer to them as. The Children continue to commune with the Elders, seeking their wisdom and guidance, almost acting on their behalf on this Earth. In general terms, both the Children and Elders worship Beliyal, who exists not in a physical form as he is an essence, or great evil spirit, in cooperation with the other evil spirits that do not exist in physical form. In my own words, I believe the Elders to be a miserable breed of ugly creatures that lack emotion and have around them the greatest accomplishments of ingenuity and technology, but nothing to aspire to other than to be non-physical beings rather than the physical creatures they roam the world as. I've heard it expressed to me that the aliens want to create better bodies for themselves, more beautiful bodies, which ties in with the conspiracy theories you may hear of human abductions – an attempt to replicate the beauty of human flesh, because there is a wonder – the wonder of the human physical form, of human physical beauty... an aspect of our existence that I admire so much...

"The Elders exist in a near immortal state, but I've been told they're envious of us which is why they loathe us. They wish to have what we have and destroy us. They want to remain immortal but be like us. On the flipside, the Children exist in a mortal state, but through years of inter-breeding, have been able to look like us, though many are still ugly, but with a bit of plastic surgery, can correct the errors of their flawed genetics. The Children are envious too; they want to destroy the true inheritors of the Earth, us human beings, and rule a world of their own as immortal creatures. This philosophy is expressed among the transhumanists, which in a way can compare to the Elders' desire to ascend and be immortal too. It is a wonder on its own how their aims all unite, and to that extent they are not so different from each other. The ones on Earth want to ascend to the skies, while the ones in the skies want to either become immortal and beautiful, or ascend further to the aether realm."

"And what do we think of them?" Finn questioned.

"I'm not even sure if these Elders really exist," Damian stated, "while I know for certain that the Children exist. The Children are some of the most proud and arrogant creatures I have ever met. Their leaders talk down at me as if I'm subservient to them, but I will destroy them. I will kill every last one of them, and that is our mission, Finn – we will create a new world that is free from the Children of Moloch, free from the dreads of humanity as well, and it will be a new world."

"What's the difference between us and them?" Finn asked.

"What's the difference?" Damian repeated as though offended.

"Yeah, I mean, sure we're not the same breed as them, and the very fact that we aren't the same breed makes me disgusted in them, but aren't we a little transhumanist too? We've been looking into both technological means to extend our lifespan, and on a level I never knew existed, also attempting to unlock the potential of the human mind to integrate it with psionic capabilities. We want to create a new world free from them and other human scum, but what if we become desolate too? Is ascension from the physical to the non-physical possible?"

"Absolutely not," Damian rejected. "The non-physical doesn't exist, Finn. It is all physical. There is no Beliyal, and likewise his legions do not exist. The Elders aspire for the impossible based on a fable of their own creation – they are insane. We have our eyes set on realistic objectives, a new world that is purged from the worst of humanity and is centered upon the wonder of humanity instead. Do not set your eyes away from our goal – it will be a new world for the most beautiful humans, free from humanity, and you will rule it with me as a prince and I will give you dominion over all of the natural world, which you yourself take so much awe in – not just the entirety of the British Isles to return to its former glory, but all of Europe and beyond. I will manipulate the atmosphere so that there is no more storms and no more destruction that ruins the natural world – no winds to knock down trees and no capability for lightning to strike and start fires. You will be not just a prince over this dominion, but if you keep your eyesight forward upon your training, can very well be a god as we were born to become as per our birthright. Enough with the carnal pleasures – the physical form is beautiful, but the wonder of its beauty is tarnished in lustful deeds, and in this new world, you will be able to gaze upon that beauty and without guilt."

"Yes, master," Finn simply stated. "I'm sorry, master."

"Don't be sorry – do better," Damian remarked, standing up. "I will hopefully see you in a few weeks with good news. I hope to see you do better than you have been..."

"Yes, master," Finn expressed, standing up as well.

Damian stepped forward and placed a hand on Finn's cheek. He said, "You are a beautiful boy, Finn." He looked intently at him. "Your mind too... an above average human being. I would not have saved you from that forest otherwise if I did not see potential in you for greatness." He gently slid his hand down and moved his eyes away as he walked to the door.

Finn stood in place with a plain expression on his face. His eyes then looked over to Damian as he was about to leave. He asked, "Master, what if you don't return from Asia? What do I do then?"

Damian paused in place and then turned around with a frown, "Do you doubt my abilities?"

"No, but I just thought – being your contingent and everything... I should ask what to do if you don't return..."

"You know what you ought to do, Finn," Damian expressed, "so do it. We'll see each other again, I'm sure."

Finn did not respond as he watched Damian leave. The door slammed shut behind him. He held a continued plain expression, but one that almost switched to hatred, if not resentment, as he looked at the back of the door.

Act 4, Scene 1

Finn and Moira sat in the cabin of his small aircraft. Finn wore his aviator jacket and sunglasses as they rode through the sky from Alaska. The skies were clear and the land below them showed the snowy prairies that belonged to Alberta. Finn's backpack, the rifles, and the exoskeleton and optic camouflage suit were stored behind them. Moira typed into her laptop as she examined some of the data files she transferred from the Global Defense Project headquarters. Her backpack sat between her legs in front of her. The ride from Alaska back into Canada was silent, and the ride through Canada into the continental United States would be all the more silent as Finn concentrated ahead of him and Moira concentrated ahead of her.

"No way…" Moira remarked, closing her laptop. She then sat up straight as she looked ahead of her, frightened at what she had seen.

"What is it?" Finn questioned.

"It's all real… everything that you and Dr. Lambert told me…"

"You still had doubts?" Finn asked. "You think we've been lying to you at the cost of our own lives and homes?"

"No, that's not it, I just… Finn, it's all too much. It's a lot to process, between aliens that are angels and demons, a secret society that function in the same way as the Men in Black, and robots that been killing us for reasons that I'm still not sure of."

"You didn't find those reasons in the files you plundered, did you?"

"No, unfortunately I could not find anything about what you told me about these 'Chosen' or 'Children' or whatever," Moira answered. "I also couldn't find any answers about why the GDP may have been attacked. I've listened to the recording left behind by that soldier over and over again, and it still puzzles me."

"I'm puzzled by whether they won or not," Finn stated, "surely if they had lost, the world would have been in for a bleak 2023, and surely if they had won, they would have returned to their Alaskan headquarters. At the same time, robots came to hunt us down in both Allabrese and now those headquarters, and the one that hunted us down in Alaska was the same one that hunted them down, but it was acting odd… it almost felt as if it had been trapped down there all this time and never left… as if itself was a guardian, or as if it were still following orders… I don't believe that robot and the robots that attacked us in Allabrese were on the same side. I think the one that we met in Alaska was rogue, because if it had been on the same side as the other ones, we would have been attacked by more, and that's what I feared through the night…

"What about the Children or Chosen?"

"The Chosen definitely seem likely to be the ones that controlled the robots that attacked us in Allabrese," Finn stated, "but I've been thinking about another aspect of it all. Autonomous robotic soldiers like these have their history in the Second World War – a German scientist perfected the prototype of that fighting force, and my father discovered them in Greenland on his research ship. According to my dad, the concept was stolen by Soviets and taken to Russia where it was made into its own program and variation, and then that idea was stolen by Zimmerman who himself made his own program and variation – if you've ever looked into conspiracies about what happened in January 2021 during that systematic glitch, you'll have seen pictures of Zimmerman's robotic soldiers, and yet these themselves feel like variations of that robotic soldier to an added degree. Zimmerman had ties to the Children, and it's very much possible that they stole his idea and developed it on their own."

"I still don't quite understand who these people are…" Moira stated. "Are they like… the United Nations or something?"

"No, although they do have power and influence in those New World Order type organizations. They practically have a hand in all global organizations, from the World Bank, International Monetary Fund, United Nations, European Union, and especially the World Economic Forum and the United States government, without a doubt. The most concentrated bit of their power though is in… and this may be a tough pill to swallow, but is in Israel, in the Zionist regime out that way, expanded too in their interests in Ukraine to be honest, but that's besides the point. The Children want nothing more than to subvert humanity – they hate humanity, so perhaps too it would make sense why the GDP could have been replaced by an autonomous fighting force. When your instructing robots, there is no treachery or under the table deals to be made against your wishes…"

"Okay…"

"Look, I know it all may seem like a lot, but trust me, it's the truth," Finn stated. "And to clarify, the Children all operate within a network of people called the Chosen, which itself was adapted through the assimilation and subversion of some outdated secret societies, namely freemasons."

"I know them… my grandmother really, really didn't like them," Moira stated. "She tried to convince me any my brother that the entire liberal-democratic world was built by freemasons."

"Sorry to say, but she wasn't wrong…"

Moira sighed and then opened her laptop again. She replied, "I'm starting to wish I never inquired about dad's death. Everybody was right in the end – he died a hero."

"If there wasn't such a large price to pay for knowing the truth, I would have told you," Finn asserted. "I hope you can appreciate what I was trying to protect you from."

"Yeah… well, maybe you guys should have just kept me locked up in that jail cell."

"You guys? As if I had any part in you skipping out on jail time," Finn stated. "And don't go blaming this on Dr. Lambert either. He did you a favor – typical women, refusing to take blame for her own actions."

"You don't have a girlfriend, or any woman in your life other than your mom, do you?" Moira asserted. "Who could ever love a misogynist like you."

"Plenty of women have loved me just fine," Finn grumbled before realizing as he cleared his throat. "What I mean to say is that there's more women in my life than just my mom who I respect and love me. Take for example, my aunt... or my adoptive mother in England... and Diana..."

"All woman with family ties..." Moira mumbled.

"Yeah, well, it's not like you've got many men loving you... from what I heard, your brother told you to get out of his life, and not like you have a dad since he's... oh right..."

Moira suddenly raised a fist and hit Finn in the shoulder twice.

"Ay, take it easy, will you!" Finn remarked. "Don't bother the pilot..." The plane swerved as Finn temporarily lost control.

Moira growled and then sat straight. She replied, "I hate you – I hate all of this. I hate your dad just as much as I hate you because the pair of you get people into dangerous situations like this without any regard for others. I'm glad he's dead. How many people would be alive if Zimmerman or whoever didn't pick our town to torment?"

"A lot more would be dead if Zimmerman was just let loose without anyone to stop him..." Finn pointed out. "But please, tell me about how your pain is more special. You know, you don't have to join me on this quest. You can go about living your life while I take care of the hard work."

"And go where? I have nowhere to go right now," Moira stated. "Until I'm certain that those things won't come after me or the people I love, I'm not going anywhere else."

Finn didn't respond as they continued to fly. A dark grey cloud could be seen ahead. He suddenly turned his head and asked, "I don't suppose there is any other male in your life though, right? No boyfriend?"

Moira glared over to Finn and then looked forward as she replied, "No... not in a while..."

Finn nodded as he continued to approach the dark grey clouds on the horizon. He brought down the microphone in his headset and began to turn some knobs in the cabin.

"And you?" Moira asked.

Finn shook his head and then turned to Moira with a smile, "None in close to four years... and nowadays... well, my heart is taken. No dating for ole' Finn no more."

Moira raised an eyebrow as she replied with the question, "Why?"

"Not something you'd understand, my dear," Finn replied, waving a finger at her. "Now don't interrupt, we're crossing the border again."

Moira allowed Finn to chat over the radio as he talked to U.S. customs and got permission to land at an airstrip in northern Montana. As he did so, Moira looked down and could see some low mountains and forest that they passed over. The entire land below was snowy and a winter wonderland. Finn turned the plane westward slightly as he approached the storm ahead and began to fly over it.

"What are you doing?" Moira questioned. "Isn't that dangerous?"

"It'd be more dangerous if I flew through it or under it," Finn stated. "Besides, our destination may be either around it or in the eye of the storm. I hardly doubt our destination is going to be in another storm."

Finn flew over the storm as he looked at his GPS system to get an idea of where he could land. He kept his eyes close and continued to communicate with air traffic control.

"How do you know where you're going?" Moira questioned. "You haven't been here already as well, have you?"

"Of course I have," Finn answered. "Another one of my such adventures – Diana and Tristan visited this place a month after the quarantine in Allabrese and a year after the near-miss with the alien invasion. We're set to visit an irregular sorority of religious nuns – they're quite lovely folk, though I haven't been since around the time I was in Alaska. Let's just hope that they didn't expect..."

An alarm began to set off in the cabin. Finn looked at the radar and then in the rear-view mirror.

"What the hell..."

"What's going on?" Moira asked.

Finn didn't answer as he immediately turned the plane to tip it down and over. He spoke over the radio in a panicked state as he communicated the situation, stating, "May Day! May Day! May Day! Salt Lake Center, Charlie-November-Delta-Juliet-Hotel is buddy spiked. I repeat, Charlie-November-Delta-Juliet-Hotel is buddy spiked one-eight miles of Kalispel approach. Flight level ten, track southwest! Taking evasive maneuvers!" Finn immediately turned the plane over again as they flew into the storm clouds below and began to go through the turbulence to come through. Luckily, as Moira saw them enter the storm, she noticed there was no precipitation. The cabin continued to shake as Finn dipped the plane down. "Hold on..." Finn stated to Moira as he looked into the rear-view mirror. Immediately, the plane began to spin and do a barrel roll. "Hello? Can anybody read me?! May Day! May Day! May Day! Salt Lake Center, Charlie-November-Delta-Juliet-Hotel is buddy spiked. Cease fire! I repeat, cease fire! Friendlies at one-eight miles of Kalispel approach!" Finn continued to take evasive maneuvers as he brough the plane to a lower altitude and flew close to the mountain range.

Moira looked behind her and saw a missile track them, but as Finn dipped down behind a mountain, the missile flew into the peak and set off a large explosion that resulted in an avalanche.

"Bloody hell!" Finn remarked, flying upwards as the cabin continued to shake. The alarm on the radio quieted down. "Salt Lake Center, Charlie-November-Delta-Juliet-Hotel, does anyone copy?!" he questioned over the radio. "What the hell is going on...?" he muttered to himself.

Suddenly, the alarm began to set off again, prompting Finn to look and see two missiles on approach. He flew up and began to do a barrel roll as the missiles approached, flying through the clouds as Moira held on for her life. The plane shook as it came through the clouds, but then she let out a relief as they flew out of the clouds and into the skies above and an explosion trailed from behind.

"I can't do this all day..." Finn remarked. "We've got to land but we're miles off from the airstrip... and these buggers are putting me off trail."

Finn turned the plane and began to fly through the clouds to return into the storm. Moira looked around them as she suddenly saw something trail from behind at a far distance. It looked like another missile, but it did not come for them. The alarms also quieted down as Finn flew and kept a close eye out.

"Oh no..." Finn remarked as he heard the alarms set off again. He saw the missile on approach and immediately dipped the plane down towards the earth as they passed the mountains and came to the forests below.

"Charlie-November-Delta-Juliet-Hotel transmitting in the blind and buddy spiked! If you copy this transmission, abort fire! I repeat, abort! Abort! Abort!"

Finn flew towards a lake below and quickly maneuvered the plane to fly over it as the missile crashed into the ice and the plane then continued upwards, flying in tune with the wind as they travelled northeast instead.

"Where are you?!" Finn questioned, looking around the plane in all directions.

"Finn – what's going on?" Moira asked.

"What the hell does it look like is going on?!" Finn replied. "We're under attack again! Worse off, nobody is responding to me on the bloody radio!"

The aircraft began to gain elevation again, even as the travelled the wrong direction.

"Salt Lake Center, transmitting into the blind, Charlie-November-Delta-Juliet-Hotel, do you copy?!" Finn pleaded. "Salt Lake Center – do you copy?! Oh, this is useless!" He removed his headset and then looked out the rear as he saw another object approach. He quickly put his headset back on and began to transmit. "Charlie-November-Delta-Juliet-Hotel transmitting in the blind – we are buddy spiked at six o'clock. Position is two-zero miles of Kalispel approach. Flight level is eight. Cease fire, we are friendly. I repeat, cease fire on friendlies!"

The alarm set off as the object made its approach. Finn turned out of the way and began to go back west. He was about to take evasive action, but before he did so, he noticed that this object was not a missile.

"What is that…?" Finn questioned.

Moira looked behind her and saw the object on approach was fast like a missile, but had two wings at either side like mechanical bird wings. The object shot past them and let out a loud screech, causing Moira to bring his hands to his ears for a moment. Finn did the same as he brought his hands to the headset. Finn caught sight of the object that passed them and then fly upwards. He looked around for it, but then his eyes turned to his right as he saw it fly beside them.

"Charlie-November-Delta-Juliet-Hotel transmitting into the blind. I have a hostile aircraft on my niner. Taking evasive maneuvers…"

Finn flew the aircraft the opposite way, tipping it over and changing directions. The hostile entity continued to follow them.

"What is that supposed to be?" Finn questioned, squinting.

Finn flew the plane into the opposite direction of the wind, causing turbulence in the cabin, while the hostile entity flew without any issue. He looked at the entity again as he attempted to concentrate on flying the plane, and as he did so, he noticed that beneath the wings or glider mechanism of the entity, was a rider – a robot just like the one that they had encountered in Alaska, but this one had a pearly dark grey surface, blue eyes and a grenade launcher with a drum magazine in its hand. Finn flew the plane into the beast, prompting it to evade and then disappear above them.

Suddenly, the plane began to shake as the beast landed atop. The pair then felt the beast punch into the roof as it attempted to smash its way inside. Finn immediately flew the plane upwards and then began to spin around, causing it to fall off but not get left behind. He stabilized the plane and saw it fly up from behind as it triggered the radar alarm again. The plane then began to shake violently as an explosion detonated from behind, prompting Finn to keep the plane steady.

"May Day! May Day! May Day!" Finn shouted. "Charlie-November-Delta-Juliet-Hotel is hit! Hostile on my six o'clock! May Day! May Day! May Day! Losing control! Going down!" He then removed his headset and turned to Moira. "Grab the parachute under your seat!"

Moira rummaged under her set and found the parachute.

"Hurry, put it on! We're going to jump!" Finn stated.

"What?!"

"No time to argue! Put that damn parachute on!"

Finn did the same as he let the plane fly with the wind. He put one arm through the backpack, placed a hand at the door beside him and watched Moira slowly put on the parachute before he opened the door. He took Moira's hand and pulled her out of the plane with him, the two tumbling out into the skies together as the plane trailed smoke and was set to crash.

Act 4, Scene 2

Finn fell forward from the parachute with his hands and feet spread apart. He looked down upon the taiga forest that stretched beneath them and which there was no sight of civilization, but an extensive white bliss of snow that stretched upon this land he now fell towards. On his right, Finn saw the small aircraft hurl towards the earth as smoke trailed behind it, and passing him from above he saw Moira with her arms and legs tightening around her as she refused to look at the wonderland around and instead froze in terror at this peculiar situation. Finn looked above and saw the robotic entity fly above them like a vulture, making circles around as they continued to descend. He then looked towards Moira as she hurled towards the ground at a faster pace, prompting him to bring his hands and arms to his side, and feet and legs together as he shot down after her. Finn flew down and came to an even level with Moira.

"Put your arms out!" Finn shouted. "You're going too fast – you need to slow down!"

Moira refused to put her arms out, prompting Finn to grab her arm. She immediately retracted her arm and looked to him.

"Arms out! Look at me! Give me your hand!" Finn shouted.

Moira gave Finn her hand.

"Stretch your feet apart," Finn said, doing the same as he held on to her. She slowly complied and the two began to descend towards the earth together. "Keep your eyes on me!" He then looked down and then quickly back up to her. "On my signal, I'm going to let go. Pull the chord to trigger your chute! I'll be right behind you! Ready?! Go!"

Finn released his grip, and Moira closed her eyes and pulled the chord as hard as she could. The parachute immediately launched outwards from the backpack, pulling Moira along the stream of the wind and away from Finn, but at a graceful pace as she made a careful descent. However, as Moira flew away from Finn, he heard a loud noise approach as well as the terrible screech of the robotic entity. The robotic beast made its pass and snapped the chords of Moira's parachute, causing her to descend to the earth at a rapid pace.

"No!" Finn shouted. He immediately tipped his body and pursued her as she was nearly set to touchdown upon the earth. He quickly grabbed hold of her and placed his arm around her torso. He then used his other hand to pull his own parachute before reinforcing his grip around Moira's body so that he could hold on to her. "Don't worry – I've got you!"

"Oh my God! Finn – I'm going to die!"

"No, you won't," Finn denied. "I've got you – just keep still." He looked around to see if he could see the beast coming for them, but it had left. The wind continued to guide them northeast, closer towards a plume of smoke from where the aircraft had crashed landed. The pair hovered over the forest without the capability to guide it as Finn's arms held Moira. "Moira – I need you to grab hold of the chute for me. I'll keep my grip on you, but you need to hold on to something too…"

Moira opened her eyes as she looked over the horizon of the forest. She looked at the two handles and raised her arms. Finn kept her body close to his. Her hair was partially in his face.

"Alright," Finn said, "you see that clearing of snow. I need you to guide us to it – won't be any fun if we get caught in a snag of them tall trees."

"Okay…" Moira remarked, bringing them over.

"Atta girl…" Finn commended. "Just like that… okay… You're not going to like this next part, but I need to let you down in that snow. It's a thick pile of snow and at this height, you'll do just fine, but I need you to roll into it when I do drop you. Can you do that for me?"

"Now?!"

"Not now – when we've got less height between us… but before we head back into the forest… On my mark… Go!"

Moira fell and tilted her body into the snow, crashing into and the depth of the snow embracing her like a mattress. Finn continued to descend at his own pace. He took hold of the chute to guide him around and away from the forest, and then when he saw his chance, he removed the backpack and fell into the snow himself. Finn kept his legs and knees together as he descended, and upon touching the snow he turned his body and rolled into it and was thrown a fair distance. His eyes looked up towards the dark grey skies as he lay in a pile of snow around. He then slowly began to climb himself out and look around.

"Moira! Where are you! Are you alright!" Finn shouted.

"I'm over here!" Moira called out, waving her hand from the pile of snow she was in. "I'm a little stuck!"

Finn began to wade through the snow as he went to her direction. He then found her in a deeper pile of snow and stretched his arm out to pull her out.

"Looks like you got lucky with where you landed – I wasn't quite sure how deep the snow was to catch you…" Finn expressed. "I'm glad you're alright…"

Moira immediately embraced Finn as they came together. She held on tight to him and he held a stunned look on his face. She shuddered in place, prompting him to slowly place a hand on her back.

"Easy there… you're alright…" Finn stated. "We're going to be alright. We better go salvage what we can from the air wreck, including the GPS. We'll then have to hike our way to the monastery. We shouldn't have much trouble with that thing from here on."

Moira sniffled and parted from Finn. She held an ashamed look on her face and kept her head down. She put a hand at her forearm. "Thank you… you saved my life back there…"

"I wasn't just going to let you fall to your death…" Finn replied. "Now come on, before it gets late."

Moira raised her head up and then followed him through the snow as they made their exit out and found firmer ground underneath the trees of the forest. The pair caught sight of the robotic entity fly above the sky.

"That thing is just like the one we saw in Alaska, but it can fly rather than swim…" Finn stated. "We should keep our heads down – as soon as I get my hands on the energy rifle, that thing is dead… Bad enough I lost me home, but me airplane too…?"

Finn and Moira began to go through the forest in the approximate direction of the crashed airplane. The streaks of the smoke in the sky were still fresh and provided an approximate direction. The pair walked through the snowy forest at a normal pace. Their breaths from exertion was readily visible. The snow came up to their ankles. The trees around them were similar to the ones in Alaska, close to twelve feet in height and thin. Unlike Alaska though, there was less shrubbery and no ferns. The only flora that could be found was around trees and the odd bush that stood apart. Finn and Moira ventured through the forest and came out to a lone road that stretched through and went the direction they needed to go in.

The road continued through the forest at a lower depth than the land around them. The road curved around and then continued along a stretch that cleared out with less trees at either side. However, eventually the road ceased to continue in the same direction of the plume of smoke, so they ventured back into the forest and came closer and closer to the wreckage. The small aircraft had crashed propeller first into a tree in a small clearing. The tail was completely pulled off from the rear of the aircraft, but the rest of the body was more or less intact despite the fierce blow. Finn and Moira approached the cabin, where Moira went around to fetch her backpack and check her belongings, and Finn opened the rear cabin and pulled out their backpacks. He quickly removed his aviator jacket and opened the rear hatch to pull out the exoskeleton suit. He put it on and then put his coat back on. He put the poncho over top as well as a pair of gloves. Moira pulled out the optic camouflage suit and exchanged it for a warmer winter coat from her backpack, and then also put the poncho over her body. She put on a warm toque, pair of gloves, and then picked up the rifle. Finn looked above the sky as he attempted to see if he could spot the entity that pursued them, but it was gone.

"Keep your eyes peeled," Finn remarked. "As soon as you see that thing, blow it out from the sky..."

"You don't have to tell me twice..." Moira replied.

Finn put the energy fuses into his backpack, as well as the propeller add-ons to his exosuit, and then picked it up and put it around his shoulder. Meanwhile, Moira picked up the GPS and then passed it to Finn. He looked at the waypoint he had set and then said, "A little bit of a ways from us. We won't make it in one day..." He returned the GPS and then looked around. "Alright, this way..."

The pair went in the opposite direction from where they had come from and began to continue along through the forest. Every so often, the wind would pick up, but there was no snowfall although the skies remained a dirty grey color. Finn looked up at the sky every so often, but there was no sight of the robot that attacked them. Every so often, a gust of wind would push through, picking up a thin powder of snow that would cause them to cover their head. Eventually, they stopped in the midst of the forest to have some lunch.

"I think I'm more worried about it to start snowing than for that thing to show its ugly face again," Finn stated. "Last thing we want is to get caught in a blizzard."

Moira warmed herself near the fire while Finn checked their location on the GPS. He then put it away and continued to drink his coffee. The pair stayed quiet as they enjoyed the warmth of the fire, but after a few minutes break, they continued on their way along as they followed a thin trail through the forest. The foreground ahead of them showed off two tall triangle peaked mountains that loomed over them and were close by. Each of them appeared taller than a high rise, at least five of them stacked upon each other. Towards the left side, there was a tall cliff wall half a mile ahead which was as tall as a high rise. The skies above became harder to see as though the clouds descended upon them, or they ascended towards the clouds as their elevation grew. On approach of the tall cliff wall which extended a fair distance in either direction were some smooth hills covered in snow with the far side consisting of an outline of a few pine trees. There were also a few pine trees to their right. As the trail began to curve leftward, they both caught sight of the base of the right mountain and its steep slope upwards. A large density of trees covered around, but the tall peak continued to stare down at them. The base also had a fair share of boulders around. They continued along the path that came around the base of the mountain, and by the time they were little more than half past the peak, they began to ascend up a low slope that caught sight towards a large crevasse in front of the tall cliff wall. This crevasse appeared to be at least fifty feet wide and an unknown depth as fog covered the mouth of it though some trees could be seen poking out through the cloud. After a few more hundred yards, the slope became more intense as they walked slowly up the side of the mountain. At a bend that continued leftward, there were some large boulders besides the cliff walls of the mountain to their right. The adjacent mountain stood beside them as they both trekked, Finn stopped to look further to their left around the way they were going to notice an even larger mountain further ahead in the direction they needed to go. This mountain was triangular but taller and wider than the ones they stood beside. The pair continued along and eventually passed the rightward mountain to find a canyon pass between them that ventured a different direction, but they continued on the path they were on as it began to narrow, and they were met with a tall cliffside to their right and boulders on their left before the drop into the crevasse. Around this point, the path stabilized and wrapped around the end of the crevasse to bring them to the other side of the canyon. By the time they were on the other side, they also passed the base of the mountain and found themselves at the start of a wide snowy plateau. Additionally, it also began to snow lightly, which with the wind that came every so often, cut at the cheeks. The fog was thick in these parts, and they could barely see more than fifty feet in front of them as they reached a pass between two boulders. On their right, the ground hilled up a fair distance, creating a tall hill that disappeared in that direction, while ahead there was another tall boulder with some trees on the left. They began to ascend upwards along the slope to this boulder where some trees could be seen above it. At the top, they found a frozen pond to their left and then a few more trees before a smoother set of snowy plains on the stretch ahead. The density of trees began to pick up again as they looked ahead, but so did the darkness around as the sun began to set on this shortened day. Moira warmed herself around a fire they had set up at the base of the forest while Finn pitched the tents.

After a moment, Finn removed the exoskeleton and began to tinker around with the propulsion system again. Moira simply stayed near the fire as night set upon them. Eventually, Finn put the propulsion pieces back into his backpack and left the exoskeleton alone. He threw it into his tent and then joined Moira by the fire.

"Say... what sort of wildlife are in these parts? Mountain lions?"

"Definitely some of them around," Finn stated. "Shouldn't have to worry about wolves though. The Americans seem to have purged most of them from their borders. I believe they're only found in Washington, Idaho, and western reaches of Montana. No, I'd say that thing still hunting for us would be a worse foe to come across..."

Finn began to fiddle with his bow. The two sat quietly around the fire. Every so often, Moira would jerk her neck and look out towards the darkness around them, especially as she heard noises from abroad.

"Finn…" Moira stated, "can you tell me a story?"

"A story…" Finn repeated, looking towards the fire.

"Tell me a bit more about you…" Moira asked. "You said you lived with Audric Zimmerman – what was that like?"

Finn sighed and replied, "I didn't have much of a life with Audric – or Damian, as he was really called. He was able to squeeze me into the American taxpayer system, a full-blown American citizen with voting rights and all (not that you need to be a citizen to vote in some of those parts). He let me live in Manhattan, at his apartment suite at the Equinox Hotel, and it was… some of the most loneliest days of my life. I only saw him about four times before I… didn't see him again for close to a year. Listen, I've had a lot of regrets in my life, but these days… they were particularly regrettable. I didn't know who I was, but I saw this man, as powerful as he appeared to me, and I was in awe. He had a vision – a deadly vision, based on a beautiful idea. We both shared in the wonder of the natural world juxtaposed to the industrialized, artificial world, and Damian convinced me to believe that humans, our own existence, is a wonder too – not in a theistic sense, but in a purely nihilistic sense. We were both nihilists… which in case you don't know is a belief of disbelief – that God does not exist and therefore nothing matters, including our own existence, but Audric told me that it was up to us to create meaning in our lives, which was in this vision we shared. 'What are human beings to be so beautiful, so deadly, and yet have so much potential…' is what he would often say to me. He lamented that some humans spoiled the gifts of their own existence and convinced me that we had an obligation to be better creations, to be the best, which captivated my formerly extremist, former fascist heart. I suppose to that extent, Audric captivated me because he was a strongman. He was charismatic. He was intelligent. He promised better for me… He told me I was his son, when we both knew I wasn't, because he wanted to adopt me even though I was already nineteen or so years old. Still, even as I felt motivated to be with him, I felt out of place.

"After Zimmerman didn't return from Asia, eventually the company began to foreclose on his property, and that meant that little ole' me had to fly the coop. I had a part to play in his plans, but I was still curious at what I had heard about Charlemagne Cabernet potentially being my father. I also wanted to meet Tristan again, so I plotted to come to Harlech, and with Zimmerman gone, didn't have to pretend like it was somehow apart of that plan. I went to the University of Harlech and became Tristan's roommate, and that's where we re-united. After Zimmerman left, I fled from that plan he had, the script he had written, but unknown to me it was all part of his plan. I hesitated to approach my biological father, having idolized him a bit since I learned more about the eccentric man he was in contrast to my deadbeat of a father. I also began to feel resentment though – at what was lost upon me." Finn sighed and then said, "Have you ever read *Paradise Lost* by John Milton?"

"No…"

"It's a beautiful book, even if it empathizes the Devil," Finn stated. "I also understand and acknowledge it is a work of fiction adapted from scripture, but the character resonated with me so much, especially in these years that I felt so fallen – so lonely that I didn't even feel like my place was within my dad's home. In that book, there is an ongoing theme that the Devil stares upon God's work, humans for example, and their goodness, and the wonder of all his creations, and he sees the 'what if' he had not rebelled and the potential to stop his wickedness, to repent, and take his place… but he doesn't do it because his heart is so overtaken by evil. He believes he is not worth it. He believes that he deserves more. He believes he was betrayed, and all sorts of lies. Lucifer was a proud being for certain, because that is what pride is more than anything; it's a deceitful heart that refuses to acknowledge truth and the realities of the world, and in him it was refusal to acknowledge God's mercy and the part he had to play which was a beautiful one, but rather, he wanted to play his own part that fit his vision, and worst of all, he believed he could do it – this little fallen angel and his followers against the extent of goodness and God..." He sighed and then said, "I was the same... I looked at what Diana and Tristan had, and I looked at my father, and I could not believe that I had a part in that home. I believed... the lies that Zimmerman told me, out of his own proud heart, and I was a divided man. Eventually, I did approach my dad, of course, in the New Year, and we began to talk and spend quite a bit of time together, and it made me happy. And then the day came that he brought my mother to meet me, and I broke down... I questioned their actions; I judged them when I had yet to judge my own heart, and... well, to make a long story short, eventually I got over my emotions as I understand that they loved me just the same way, even if I was a horrible, wicked person – I was humbled, and in the context of this story, in opposition to Pride, to be humble means to see things as they really are, to see yourself as you really are, to be in touch with the reality of the world, and I saw myself as... a loved child with a depth of brokenness that let evil seep out and cause them so much harm, and yet they still loved me because they were my parents; Diana and Tristan, my sister and brother who too loved me. I realized that I had hurt them in my emotion, and it was then that I became meek too, not just humble, but meek..."

Moira did not respond as she finished listening to Finn's tale. He looked into the fire while she stared at him.

"Anyways," Finn interrupted, standing up and pouring water over the fire. "We best get some sleep. Early rise, and we'll be at that convent by lunchtime, I suppose."

Finn left to his tent, while Moira left to her own. They each slept through the night and then in the morning, Finn lit another fire, and they had some breakfast. The morning was silent, and the snow had stopped although the wind hadn't. If anything, the wind grew worse, especially as the gusts came from the direction they had to go. The pair left the campground to venture into the forest as soon as they finished packing, and Finn wore the exoskeleton suit again as well while Moira held the high-energy rifle.

The pair continued along the path ahead of them, which was a natural path through the forest from where they had camped. They passed a wide stone in the midst of the earth and then carried on for little more than a mile until the earth began to slope upwards again. The skies were less foggy this morning and Finn could see the large mountain that he saw yesterday loom over them. He could also see a cliff wall to the right at the base of this mountain. They continued along the sloped increase, and it began to narrow out, especially as boulders and rocks lay the track beside them towards a drop down not into the crevasse, but a clearing below. The cliff walls came closer towards them and the path narrowed out at a pass through a tall mound on their left. On the other side of this pass, they were flanked by tall pine trees again and the slope decreased, and path widened out. From this height, Finn and Moira could see a horizon of pine trees covered in snow like frosting. The pair continued along this path until it smoothed, and they found themselves back on a straight path that went away from the crevasse and into the depths of the forest ahead.

By midmorning, Finn and Moira continued to walk along this path until which point they found themselves surrounded by man-made wooden structures, first a post, and then a collapsed wall. They walked a few more yards ahead to reach a clearing where there were numerous collapsed wooden structures, an abandoned village of sort in the midst of the woods.

"Ah, here it is…" Finn remarked. "The commune…"

"Commune…?"

"Diana and Tristan said there was an anarchist commune in the midst of the forest near the convent, but it burnt down thanks to Zimmerman," Finn explained. "Seeing this must mean that we're close…"

The pair looked around the ruins where sure enough, singe marks could be found around the overgrown ruins of this former village. Finn stopped to stare towards a barn, or the ruins of a barn, and then they continued along as he checked the GPS.

"Just a few more miles to go," Finn stated, putting it away. "Flock of loons got what they deserved…"

"How can you say that?" Moira questioned, insulted.

"Because I know them more than you did," Finn barked. "Don't be so presumptuous to a complete set of strangers – they were cannibals, and a cult engaged in pederasty and incest."

Moira did not respond. They continued through the forest for another few miles where eventually the path began to lead along a descent with a cliff wall on their right and boulders on the left that almost formed another broken cliff wall. As they travelled, Finn suddenly stopped as he heard a familiar howl. Moira looked around while Finn simply froze in terror and grabbed his bow.

"Watch out!" Finn shouted.

A trio of three large wolves appeared from overtop of the boulders, one of which stood at the very top and barked while the other two came towards them. Moira shrieked and opened fire at one of the dogs as it lunged at her. She then held the dog back with the rifle body, while Finn swatted at one of the dogs as it bit into his arm. The dog flew off and Finn pulled the bow with an arrow at it, but not before the other dog came at him. He kicked the dog, knocking it over while the other came at him and he shot the bow and pierced the neck of the dog. The other dog barked at him, and he reloaded his bow, but the dog quickly lunged forward to him, knocking him over too. Moira continued to scream as the dog attempted to bite at her and she continued to hold it back with the rifle body. Finn used both hands to keep the jaws of the dog away from him, instead grabbing it hold by the neck with one hand and the jaw with the other. He hugged the wolf as he subdued it and then took a hand and punched it in the side. The dog squirmed and he thew it over and went to pick up his bow. He picked it up and looked over to Moira, shot the arrow and killed the dog as it pierced the skull. He then turned to the other dog and aimed the bow at it as it barked at him, and then ran off. He retracted the arrow and then looked over to help Moira off the ground.

"No wolves in this part, huh?!" Moira remarked.

"Rather fight three wolves then one cougar," Finn replied. "Come on, we're lucky to be alive..."

"Look at your arm..."

Finn looked as blood dripped through from under his jacket. "Ah dammit..." he said. "Let's take a moment break here... we're almost at the convent. Best have some lunch first..."

Act 4, Scene 3

Finn wrapped bandage around his right forearm. He brought the roll of gauze around and around, tying it around his hand and then cutting a piece off. Moira observed as Finn finished applying first aid to himself.

"What are those numbers here?" Moira questioned. "At your wrist…"

Finn turned his hand over at the cuff of the exoskeleton suit where sure enough there were some numbers. He looked at them closely to notice that one displayed his heartrate, the other his oxygen levels, and the last his body temperature.

"I didn't even notice that…" Finn remarked. "Good eyes…"

"Thanks," Moira replied. "Are you going to be okay?"

"Well, if around midnight, I start to howl, you'll know something is up…" Finn responded in a plain tone. "I've had worse licks – a pack of oversized dogs don't scare me. Stupid beasts…"

"You don't like wolves or wild animals?"

"Just wolves," Finn stated. "They're a vicious, self-centered lot – the very definition of a beast, and it pains me more that people look up to them or even behave like them."

"I've never seen a person act just like that…" Moira replied. "Ganging up, ambushing two people, taking a bite out of one man's arms."

"Sounds to me like you haven't lived much…" Finn responded, standing up and putting his first aid kit away. "Come on, break's over. We don't have much left to the monastery."

Finn walked over to one of the two wolf carcasses. He stepped over them and continued on his way.

"I hope we can get a warm meal over at this monastery," Moira stated. "I don't know about you, but I'm sick of rations."

"I hope we can get a warm meal so I don't feel so bad about leaving those two wolves behind without harvesting them for some meat," Finn responded. "I suppose we aren't very similar."

Moira gave an estranged look at Finn. They continued on their way as they continued to descend. The path ahead was less defined as trees scattered around everywhere. The walked along on a curved bend, keeping up with the cliffside wall on their right which soon became a cliffside wall on their left too. After a while, Finn caught sight of a structure ahead and stopped to get a better look.

The convent of Our Lady of Maidens was a large stone-built compound, at least two stories above ground level with a bell tower at the center. The structure had a squared W-shape to it, and the face they approached from was one of two sides. The building was constructed in neo-gothic architecture with pointed arches, greyish-beige exterior, flying buttresses, ribbed vaults, and large stained-glass windows, and spires. The surrounding perimeter had a tall iron gate fence with plenty of perimeter room from where there was a visible garden at the corners and rear. At the sides, there were plazas. At the center, on all three sides was courtyard, as at the entrance too.

"I'm guessing you've gone inside and visited this place, right?" Moira asked. "You know the people here?"

"I know of the people here, but I can't say I've been inside," Finn responded. "From what I understand, they don't let men inside – but today must be an exception, especially when our plane was shot down not too far from them."

"No men allowed?" Moira questioned. "Sounds like my type of place, especially with the week I've been having."

"You're more than free to stay," Finn replied. "In fact, I encourage it – could do you a whole lot of a good."

"What's that supposed to mean?" Moira asked as though offended.

Finn did not respond and instead continued to descend down towards the convent. He soon noticed on the opposite side of the convent from where they approached, the large mountain could be seen past the forest ahead. He looked at the mountain as it was much closer than before and caught sight of an immobile wind turbine along a perch. The mountain was incredibly tall, but still quite a distance away from them. He continued along the path as they came around to the front gates and placed their hands on the bars. They each looked around the plaza as the wind sent snowflakes into their faces.

"Isn't there a main entrance?" Moira questioned. "Come on, let's not be rude…"

Moira led Finn around to the front entrance of the convent where they approached two halves of a wide black gate connected to a stone pillar either end. Finn approached the intercom on the right pillar and then pressed the call button. No sound came through, but Finn stepped forward anyway.

"Hello? Hello? This is Finn Cabernet, friend of Diana and Tristan Merrick, son of Sister Witeveens…" He then released his finger from the button to wait for a response, but none came. "That's strange…"

Finn came around to the front gate and placed his hands on the bars as he looked inside. The snow was piled up around the main entrance courtyard, including the inside of the small fountain in the middle. The snow layered the entire rooftop of the convent, front steps, and around.

"What time is it?" Finn asked.

"Almost one o'clock…" Moira replied, looking at her watch. "Why?"

"Hello?!" Finn cried out. "Is anyone home?!" He waited for a response but then turned to Moira and said, "I don't like it… I think we may have a case of the GDP."

"You think… you think they got them too?"

"It's possible, but we won't know just standing out here. What time is it now?"

"One minute to… What did you make an appointment?"

"Shh," Finn hushed. "Let me know when it's one o'clock."

Moira watched the time while they stood in the cold, and at the strike of one o'clock, she said, "It's one o'clock now."

Finn stayed put as they listened to the sound of the chilled air and howl of the wind.

"No bells," Finn stated. "I'm going to need to do a wellness check and make sure all of these nuns haven't died of carbon monoxide poisoning. Come on."

Finn grabbed hold of the two sides of the gate and with the strength of the exosuit, pulled them apart and pushed the gate open. The pair walked into the courtyard and approached the front entrance. The front door was a tall arched mahogany door. Finn knocked a brutish knock, nearly breaking the door, and with impatience, just resorted to kicking the door down. He entered into the main foyer where he looked around as it was dark and silent. He took in a deep breath and then turned to Moira. She looked back at him and the continued inside.

The main entrance of the convent was a fair-sized room with two sets of stairs on the left and the right, and two sets of rectangular wooden doors beside them. Likewise, above them was another set of two doors, but these arched though the same height. On the left was a tall arched wooden spruce door, shorter than the main entrance, and likewise on the right. A set of smaller arched wooden doors could also be found on the left and right from the respective staircases. Between the two rectangular doors besides the stairs was a statue of the Virgin Mary with her arms stretched forward as though to embrace. The foyer floor consisted of greyish stone tiles, while the walls carried the same exterior texture.

"Hello!" Finn cried out.

"Anybody home!" Moira called out. "Jeez, did everyone go on vacation…" She began to look around the place as she held her hands in her pocket. "Never been in a monastery before… At the same time, haven't really been in a church in a long time…"

Finn didn't respond as he looked about. He held a worried look on his face. "I'm starting to get a little annoyed at people not being where I expect them to be." He approached the arched doors to his right and pushed them open, stepping into the great hall.

The great hall was a long room with three fireplaces on the left, tall and narrow stained-glass windows on the right, and long wooden tables that stretched up to a platform where another table was before a wider fireplace. Each of the four fireplaces were unlit and the room was also dim. He turned around and came over to the opposite door which he pushed open to find the library was also dim and empty. He turned around and went towards one of the two rectangular doors besides the staircases, pushed them open to enter a corridor with another set of two double doors ahead, pushed those in, and came to the chapel. He stepped forward and stayed beside an empty metal font before the pews. The chapel was dim. He looked forward towards the tabernacle behind the altar. The chapel was fair-sized, shorter than the great hall, but with tall arched windows at the end, and many other beautifully designed stained glass windows on the sides of the pews. The altar was made of chiseled stone, and likewise the tabernacle sat upon a chiseled stone mantle on top and itself was a gold-colored cabinet mixed with white. Finn quietly mumbled to himself from where he stood.

"Are you alright?" Moira interrupted, causing Finn to jump.

"They're gone…" Finn remarked, leaving the chapel. "We need to find out where they've gone. They're the only ones that could have helped us in this situation – the only ones that know about the Chosen like I do, and care enough about it too… at least, I haven't been able to locate sister convents, or their brother order."

"I have no idea what you're talking about, but I'm sure there must be some sort of explanation. I mean, it doesn't look like there was a fight here like there was at the GDP place."

"We haven't exactly started to search the entire building. Come on..." Finn said, going left from the chapel. He approached another set of double doors, pushed through them, and came into an exterior corridor that came around a courtyard.

The courtyard was a rectangular space that looked out towards the gardens. There was a bench near the exit from the chapel, and a water pump in another corner. The corridor they entered was L-shaped. Finn walked down to the corner and entered into an interior corridor where he began to search the various rooms. These rooms were workshops, study rooms, and other hobbyist places. They exited out from this corridor and went to a room at the other end that was a long storage room with lots of furniture, and other crates and boxes. They left this side of the convent and returned to the corridor in front of the chapel to go the other way. The other side of the convent mirrored each side with another courtyard, L-shaped exterior corridor, and more options between two sets of double set doors, one at each corner. The courtyard also had a bench besides the exit from the chapel, but instead of a water pump had a statue of the Virgin Mary holding a baby Jesus. Finn entered the first one and came into a corridor like the other side, with a set of double doors at each end on the parallel wall. He pushed through the doors in front of him and found himself in a wide garage-like room with white square-bodied Armstrong SUVs. There were two of these cars at least, one that was in the midst of maintenance with the tires missing and another at the other side. At one side of the garage were some lockers, while at the backside next to the rectangular double doors were some workshop benches. On the immediate left from the entrance were some crates and cupboards.

"Looks like my twelfth-grade auto body class in here..." Moira stated. "I guess even nuns have their hobbies..."

They walked down to the end of the garage and exited out the other door. They came into the interior corridor and pushed through a set of doors directly ahead to come out into the exterior corridor as well. They then turned to the perpendicular wall and entered into a similar room to the one above, but appeared like a barn. There were stables on the left for animals, though no animals in the pens, and on the right were kennels. On the wall directly beside the entrance there were cages. At the end of the aisle between the kennel and the pens there was a tall door that led outside. They walked back outside where Finn saw a door directly ahead that led into the library.

The pair looked around the library; it was the same height as the great hall, two stories with vaulted ceilings, and it consisted of tall bookshelves along the walls not facing the windows. The library had wooden floorboard floors. Finn saw a door on the right that led into a room behind, similar to the great hall, and so he entered through and came into a wide room with stained glass windows on the opposite and left side. There were tables around the room with maps, and on the right side there were computers and some rectangular machines that sat beside them. In the corner beside the windows was a tall rack with computers lined up and many wires connecting them together. The pair looked around the room as they found more bookshelves on the walls to the left.

"Interesting..." Moira called out, going to the computer. "I didn't expect to see one of these here... You see that, it's a server." She pointed at the tall rack with computers.

"They're nuns, not the Amish," Finn replied. "Besides, even if that computer looks old enough to hack into, what good will it do? There's no power..."

"I trust that all we have to do is find the fuse box," Moira said.

"I'm not looking to turn the lights on," Finn responded. "I'm looking for answers, and we're not going to find them on the computer."

Finn and Moara left the computer room and returned to the foyer where they climbed upstairs and went to the right. They walked down an L-shaped corridor with several doors. This corridor had wooden floorboard floors and paneled walls, but the windows were shorter and diamond-patterned. There were no rooms in the first half of the corridor, but on the other half only. There were six dormitories in total, some of which had two beds. Finn stood in the second room which only had one bed and looked over to a workbench where there normally was another. He stepped forward and opened the drawers in this room, but there was nothing. He then left this room to search through the others, but they were likewise empty. As they walked down the corridor, they stopped to notice the wind pick up outside. They then entered a room at the end, above the storage room, which was a gymnasium with old weightlifting equipment and some new exercise machines spread around. Finn and Moira left this room to go to the other side where the dormitories were similar, except for one room that had one bed at the very end.

The pair entered through the door at the end, which led into a squared parlor, or common room. There was a fireplace at one end and some sofas. Another set of double doors were on the other side, and this led into an office space with a large desk in front of a tall arched window. Finn looked through this room, but could not find anything, especially in the filing cabinets.

"I think it's safe to say they fled," Finn remarked, "unlike the GDP, and took all their secrets with them…"

"I'm telling you; we should look at their computer – who knows what could be inside…"

"We'd need to find a way to turn the power on," Finn replied. "I may have missed something…"

Finn and Moira left the abbot office and came downstairs again. They returned to the garage where Finn examined the cabinets and found a portable generator at the end. He looked at it and saw that thick wires led into the walls. He pressed the button on the side of the generator, but nothing happened.

"Out of fuel…" Finn stated. "I'll have to siphon some from one of the jeeps, which is a shame because I really wanted to use one of them as our ticket out of here…"

Finn picked up a jerry can. He found a tube in one of the workshop benches and went to the SUV without the tire to siphon fuel and fill the jerry can. He then took the cannister to the portable generator, filled it, and then turned it on.

"I wonder where those wires go…" Finn remarked. "There must be some sort of fuse box somewhere. I also suppose there must be another one or two generators. I'll siphon some more fuel and then we go to find the fuse box."

Finn extracted more fuel from the SUV and then went to search for another generator. He found one in the storage room, directly next to the entrance, poured the fuel and then switched it on. He followed the wire into the wall again, and then left to fetch more fuel. Moira picked up two radios from a workbench and examined them.

"Look at this…" Moira remarked. "Two-way communication radios. They look similar to the ones that the Nattau County use." She turned the nob and they both turned on. "Catch…"

Finn caught the radio while Moira hit a button, causing them to screech at each other.

"I'm going to go look around," Moira said. "We'll split up and hopefully find any other portable generators together."

"Sure thing."

Finn began to extract some more fuel from the SUV. Meanwhile, Moira looked around the computer room and saw that many cables disappeared into the wall as well. She left the room to go into the library, and then passed it to enter into the great hall. She went down to the end and entered into one of the narrow doors at either side of the end where she found herself in the kitchen. The room was not perfectly rectangular as there was a rectangular space with a door at the end on the opposite side. She approached this door and found a set of stairs that went down. Finn began to make his way to join her as she called him on the radio.

Finn shined his spotlight flashlight down the stairs and then began to go down with the fuel can in the other hand. Moira joined with her own spotlight, and they entered into a tall basement with some machines kept under cover. At the corner of the room, going towards the great hall, they found a doorway, but it was locked. Finn bashed his body into it, but it wouldn't budge.

"Something blocking the other side..." Finn stated. "No way through..."

"No need," Moira replied, pointing her spotlight at the fuse box. "Found what we're looking for."

Finn went over and began to flip the switches. The lights turned in the room for a brief moment before they powered down.

"Need more juice," Finn remarked. "Stay here, I'm going go look for another generator."

Moira stayed put by the fuse box while Finn went upstairs. He looked around the building and found a generator in the chapel. He poured the fuel, and then returned to siphon some more, but there was very little left. He hesitantly looked over to the jeep parked and ready to go, but instead returned to the basement to turn the power on. He flipped the switch and again the lights turned on, staying on for a while longer before they went out.

"Okay... I'll go find the last one..." Finn stated. He returned to the garage, siphoned fuel from the parked jeep, which had very little to barely fill the can. He then took the can with him and thought for a moment. "These stupid things really will generate carbon monoxide and kill... You're supposed to install them outside, not inside. Although..."

Finn left the garage and walked into the stables. He walked down the aisle and found the last generator inside one of the pens. He poured the gasoline and then hit the switch. He then picked up his radio to communicate with Moira.

"Hit it," Finn said.

Moira hit the switch, and the power turned on, and this time stayed on. Finn went to test the light switch, and the room illuminated. He then returned to the library where he met with Moira. Moira came around to the computer and immediately began to connect in. Finn sat down at a table with a map of the region while Moira set off to do her work. As he did so, he noticed his exosuit had a flashing light on his wrist, indicating low power. He proceeded to switch fuses while Moira hacked into the convent computer network. Moira searched through the files.

"What the..." Moira remarked. "What's with all this hardware if there's hardly anything here but research data..."

"I don't' suppose you didn't notice the lack of many computers upstairs, did you," Finn remarked as he put his suit back on. "This convent and its nuns were eccentric, researchers mainly, seeking answers about the natural world. They basically function as a research center of their own, at their own resources..."

"A lot of this data has to do with the weather... according to the last set of metrics, there was a powerful windstorm in the region," Moira stated. "Unbelievable... terabytes of space, and all I find is a few gigabytes of useless scientific data. Hm... what's R-Talk?" Moira opened the program and looked over at the hardware besides the computer. "Oh… I see… it's a dispatch software. These machines besides the computer, they're transceivers for telecommunications. Amazing, it's like a little battle station here. They were analyzing weather patterns, atmospheric conditions… Why?"

"Do they have a jammer?" Finn immediately questioned. "No, I don't suppose that would make sense if there was no power…"

"Hm…" Moira remarked. "Looks like there was a sound file that was set to play over the radio system on loop. It's named 'SOS' which means it must be important." She clicked to open the file. "I can't play it… this is a format I'm not familiar with. Let me try and convert it…"

"Is it playing right now?" Finn questioned. "I could scan for it…" He began to adjust his radio to change frequencies. He scanned the airwaves and picked up a few radio stations, especially static channels. "I'm not getting anything…"

"Give me some time," Moira requested. "I'm going to see if I can decrypt this sound file."

"Sure, take all the time you need," Finn responded. "I'm going to use some of the tools here to install the propulsion jets to this exosuit."

Act 4, Scene 4

Finn used one of the workbenches in the garage to lay down the exosuit and begin to install the propulsion system into the nodules of the lower legs of his suit. He had opened the garage doors to let in some air as the generators chugged away to power the convent. He carefully removed the propulsion system from the pieces of the elite soldier's exoskeleton suit that he had hacked off, and then applied them to his own. He then carefully tested them as he hit the two sensors together to cause them to activate and de-activate. As he did so, he took the opportunity to examine the suit in greater detail. He looked at the right wrist where it had displayed his biometrics, and then he looked at the left wrist to find some notches. He came back around to the right forearm to see scratch marks from the wolf that attacked him. He also looked at his wounded forearm, the bandage of which was covered in dry blood. He unravelled the bandage where his flesh was pierced and peeled skin still hung loose. His arm was smothered in dry blood as well. The jaws of the beast imprinted into his arm, and as Finn stared at it, he closed his eyes and then looked up towards the ceiling. He opened his eyes and stared, and then he sat down at a bench nearby to clean the blood with some bottled water, using the bandage to scrape at what remained and used a small pair of scissors to cut off the loose pieces of skin. He then began to re-apply a fresh bandage over his forearm. When Finn had finished, he sat down and put his hands together, legs spread apart. He then stood up, picked up the radio on the workbench and left the garage.

Finn walked into the north courtyard and began to go around the ambulatory aisle, coming around to the center to stare towards the statue of the Virgin Mary. He raised and placed his left forearm on one of the pillars as he looked outward, closing his eyes, and then stepping forth to walk back into the center wing. He walked into the corridor before the chapel, and made his way inside. He stopped in front of the door and looked outward towards the tabernacle. He then approached the metal font, hourglass-shaped and like an oversized goblet. He placed a hand inside as though there was water, touched the bottom, and then looked down the aisle again. He placed his hands in the pocket of his aviator jacket and then began to go down to the very end of the aisle, before the sanctuary and two yards away from the altar. The sanctuary was a small raised wooden platform with two doors at either side of the altar that led into small rooms within this room at either side. They did not detract from the shape of the chapel building, but did make the sanctuary a smaller space. In front of each of these rooms were metal racks with candles, on one side a depiction of Jesus with detail around his heart as a fire burned around, and thorns wrapped around it. On the left side was a depiction of Mary with a child Jesus in her arms. The sanctuary was separated from the rest of the church by altar rails and lightly cushioned steps before them. The rails did not extend from each of the two rooms as there were small gaps for others to enter inside besides the shrines. A wooden cross hung over the altar that had a crucified Jesus nailed to it and looking down upon Finn. The representation of Jesus was carved out of wood and was detailed to show even blood upon his body, pouring forth from the nails, torso, and head. Finn looked closely at the five wounds of Jesus, closed his eyes and then brought his right hand to his heart. He knelt down before the altar and tabernacle, but before he could do anything, his radio set off.

"Finn – I've got it…" Moira spoke over the radio.

Finn quietly growled as he continued to hold his eyes closed.

"Finn, do you read me?" Moira questioned. "Come back to the comms room."

Finn opened his eyes and stood up. He turned around and left the chapel to return to the library, going through and reaching the computer room where Moira was.

"Don't you know how to use your radio?" Moira questioned. "You're beginning to make me think that it's a you problem we can't find this transmission."

"What did you find?" Finn instead asked. "Did you decrypt the sound file?"

"Not in the slightest," Moira responded. "I did convert it to a readable sound file, but it's just static which tells me that it's encrypted and can only be heard over broadcast."

"Does the static match any of the channels we pick up?"

"No," Moira replied, "and here's the other part. I ran R-Talk to troubleshoot the problem, and it came back with an error – the sound file isn't even being broadcasted right now. I went through the manual, set up the file to be broadcasted out, but came back with an error – there's no transmitter connected. If the convent had this file playing before they evacuated, then it may tell us why they had to leave and where they went."

"Of course," Finn responded, putting his hands into his jacket. "So I suppose then we ought to get the radio transmitter to work, wherever that may be."

"I'd guess it to be on the roof somewhere," Moira stated. "With all this wind, it probably was knocked off. Can you fix it?"

"Of course I can fix it," Finn replied. "I'll scout around the perimeter to see if I can find it anywhere… doesn't seem like we'll be able to follow the cables in the wall… Stay here."

"Where else am I going to go?" Moira responded. "I'll monitor R-Talk to see if we can broadcast, and wdhen we do, I should have the frequency to tune in and listen on my radio."

"Got it."

"And Finn," Moira interrupted before he could leave, "be careful out there. I was able to run some of the other equipment here, and the winds are starting to pick up. I also noticed that… thing flying about not too far from here. If it sees you…"

"If it sees me, it'll wish it hadn't," Finn replied, picking up the high-energy rifle. "I'll be fine – keep eyes on the scanners if you can in case it does show up."

"Of course," Moira affirmed.

Finn left the communications room and went through the library to go outside, enter into the garage and then retrieved his belongings. He placed the rifle down and began to equip the exoskeleton suit. He set his radio down and began to look at his suit in detail again, placing his hand over the notches in his left wrist. He picked up the radio, removed the battery, and then placed a chip inside. He turned a dial and saw that the left wrist worked to pick up and transmit broadcasts just the same. He pressed a button to talk into his wrist.

"Moira, do you read me?" Finn asked.

"Loud and clear – what's up?"

"Just testing comms before I head out," Finn replied. "You're loud and clear too."

"Ten-Four."

"Ten-Four... what the hell does that mean?" Finn questioned to himself. He picked up the rifle and also the bow and some arrows. He used the holster around his thigh to carry the arrows again, closing the pouch to stop them from falling out. He then began to step out into the cold outdoors as he looked around. He looked up to the rooftop and then down to the propulsion modules he installed. "Alright, let's see how this works..."

Finn hit his legs together to activate the propulsion system. The jets began to emit a haze of hot air that warmed his legs. He then jumped, launching himself up a distance of close to six feet higher than the original distance he had jumped. He slammed into the side of the building, falling, but as he was about to land onto the ground, the boots gave off a weak pulse to break his fall, although he still landed on his bottom.

"Brilliant..." Finn remarked. "Obviously I'm still in need of some practice..."

Finn stood up, de-activated the boosters, and then walked over to a compost bin beside the garage. He re-activated the propulsion system and jumped up, giving a weaker jump that mimicked his efforts. He was given a soft boost that helped him onto the bins. He then looked up towards the roof, seeing to be more than ten feet high. He turned around to the balcony behind him and instead jumped towards that with greater exertion, and the boosters aided to reach the target. From here, he jumped even higher as he crouched down, and the propulsion boosters responded and helped him onto the roof.

"Alright... progress..." Finn told himself.

Finn began to look around the rooftop above the north wing, but could not find any identifiable antennas. He turned off the boosters as he climbed around, going to the other side of the library and likewise not seeing any attachments from the communications room except for a radar dish. He came around to the radar dish and examined the cables that protruded out and into the walls, going into the roof.

"Perhaps there's a cut connection," Finn remarked. "I need to get into the roof."

Finn continued to look around the rooftop as he walked towards the central partition at the base of the bell tower, looked up the tower, but could not see much. He then went around to the other side where he began to look around sheepishly. However, before Finn could make a move, his radio set off.

"Finn! I've got bird-brain homing in on you from the east!" Moira cried out.

"East..." Finn remarked. He instantly turned towards the front of the chapel, away from the main entrance where sure enough, he could see a black figure on its way to him. Finn knelt down and aimed the rifle. "Come on... you son of a bitch..."

The aerial robot flew towards him like a missile, and as Finn saw it point the grenade launcher, he shouted out in anger.

"Die!" Finn cried out, opening fire. He opened fire towards the entity and in return it shot off some rounds from its grenade launcher. The rounds hit the front of the chapel and surrounding courtyards, but did not harm Finn. He continued to open fire as it made its pass and flew off, unsure of whether a single shot hit it. He then turned around to assess the damage to the building, and he found the grenade blasts had destroyed a portion of the roof and the side of the building. "Where are you!?"

The robotic entity circled around, but seemed to have disappeared around the forest, if not around the perimeter of the building as it flew low. Finn circled around as he thought he heard the thrusters of its glider around him. He then jumped as the beast appeared from the front of the chapel as it launched itself upward, landing in front of Finn. Finn stared towards the beast as it loomed over him. This entity had taller legs than the one in Alaska, and for good reason as it almost had a third attachment to it– a third appendage, an even lower leg with raised feet as though it stood upon its toes. The feet of the beast had pincer like appendages that could separate out to stabilize its footing. The body of the beast was much like its predecessor, though dark grey, and its head likewise with the piercing blue eyes that looked upon Finn. He watched though as like its predecessor, its neck and head jerked as though possessed. The wings were lengthy, at least twelve feet in total size with missiles underneath, yet to be fired. The robot made a terrible screeching sound that caused Finn to cover his eyes before it took off and flew off. He watched it fly off and immediately raised his rifle towards it as he opened fire, but missed the shot as it twirled around and then went south. As the beast came back towards Finn, he saw it point the grenade launcher, prompting him to hide this time. He jumped into the hole in the chapel and found himself inside. The building shook as the grenades detonated, but they did not hit the chapel this time.

"Moira, be careful," Finn communicated, "that thing is locked and loaded with some explosives, and it seems like it will bring this building down. If you can, get yourself and your laptop to the basement."

"Copy," Moira replied. "What are you going to do?"

"I'm going to hunt down this bird..."

Finn turned on the propulsion jets, walked down the aisle and boosted himself up onto the balcony above the entrance into the chapel. He found a doorway in the side and walked into it. He found a staircase that went up to a third floor, a square room that looked up towards a staircase going all the way up to the belfry. He looked ahead and beside him as he saw two doors into the attic. He walked towards the north wing again as he entered the roof, continuing to hear the enhanced robot outside as it flew around. He came towards the end where he saw the cables enter through from the radar dish, joining together with some other ones that went down. He did not see any tears or issues with the cables, so he followed the other set that came towards the bell tower. He re-entered the bell tower and walked towards where the cables would have entered through. He moved some boxes stacked in the corner and saw the cables climb upwards, so he began to go up the stairs. However, as he did so, he saw the shadow of the beast as though it were circling the bell tower and stopped. He looked out the window and saw it pass again. Finn smashed the window with the butt of the rifle and then began to open fire at it as it was about to pass again, this time hitting the torso and causing it to swirl away as it let out a glitched noise. However, that was not the end of it – the beast quickly rose up and began to fly off. Finn then felt detonations set off across the rooftop and even blow a part of the upper bell tower. He covered his head as he ran towards the corner, and debris fell downwards. The beast then appeared in the hole in the wall and looked towards Finn, pointing the grenade launcher at him. He likewise pointed the rifle and took a shot at the robot, piercing its body and causing it to fly off. Finn stayed put and then continued up the stairs, eventually reaching the portion that was blown out. He turned on the propulsion system and jumped across, landing on the other side, and then continuing upwards as he checked every lap of the northwest corner that the cables were intact

As Finn was about to approach the top of the bell tower, he stopped as the beast screeched a violent sound that caused him to bring both hands to his ears again. He then climbed up towards the top of the belltower, reaching the belfry. The belfry consisted of an open square gap in the center from where bells hung down and could be rung, and around the belfry were shutters that could be raised and brought out. As the wind currently blew into the belltower, the bells gently sounded every so often, but it was quiet. He came around to where the cables joined up, and saw them come out towards the outer balcony. As Finn examined the cables to see they were intact, he felt the breeze of the robotic entity flying around.

"Finn – what's your update. Are you okay?" Moira questioned.

"Yeah, I'm alright," Finn whispered. "Currently in the belfry of the belltower. I haven't been able to find any issues with the radio connections, so I'm still investigating what's wrong."

"Forget about that – what about that thing flying around us?" Moira asked.

"Currently on my position – if something is wrong with the antennae, I can't fix it with this thing flying about. I'm going to have to neutralize it…"

Finn readied his rifle as he reloaded and then began to open the blinds to allow light into the dim belfry. He looked out and could occasionally see the robot pass as it flew around. He ducked down and moved to the other side, looking out and seeing that there was an antenna, but it lay on the floor and was disconnected. He closed the blinds and opened the other ones at the other side, catching sight of the robotic entity as it flew around. He watched for it to pass again, but it did not. Suddenly, an explosion erupted at the perpendicular south face, prompting Finn to cover his face as debris flew towards him. The robot then approached and landed on the balcony, looking towards Finn as it pointed the grenade launcher. He turned and opened fire at it, hitting the body again, and causing it to fall off. The jets from the glider system ignited and singed everything around it, prompting Finn to cover his face again from the radiating heat. He hurried over to the other corner and looked out as the beast flew off. The exhaust and fire from the jets left behind some small fires that burned around the belfry. The wind that entered through from the south face began to chime the bells. As Finn looked out through the hole it had made, he knelt down. He readied his rifle and waited for the beast to fly past so that he could open fire at it.

The shots that passed missed the beast as it twirled around and evaded the fire. It then passed him, but did not return. He quickly stepped out onto the balcony where the wind was fierce. He hid behind the wall and listened for the sound of the glider. Suddenly, the beast blew out the east face of the belfry and immediately landed. Finn opened fire at it and pierced the body again, but did not cause it to fall off or fly off. He continued to fire at it as it let out a horrible screech, hitting the neck and causing it to quickly retreat. The beast flew off from the perch of the east balcony and then fell down before flying off. He quickly ran down towards the east corner of the tower and continued to fire at it, even as his ears were ringing. The beast flew off and then came back around, prompting Finn to retreat back inside as it volleyed explosives towards the base of the bell tower, causing the structure to shake. The beast then glided past the tower on the south face and went around the north. Finn entered the inside of the belfry to reload and waited with abated breath to see where it came from. The beast just circled about, going around and around the tower as the wind howled and continued to pick up. He stayed put as seemingly the beast stayed put outside, but eventually, Finn decided it was time to move and began to crawl around as he attempted to get into position. He moved towards the east face and stayed in the corner. He occasionally peaked out to get a look of the enhanced robot as it flew around. After a while, Finn began to open fire towards the entity as it flew past, missing the first time and hitting it the second time it passed. He then stayed in position as he hoped for it to pass a third time, but didn't come. He listened to the glider and quickly moved outside to take position towards the north and west face. However, rather than repeat the same move three times in a row, Finn saw the beast fly over head and bomb the rooftop, causing the bells to ring and collapse as the entire ceiling collapsed and caved in. The west face was also destroyed. Finn attempted to open fire at the beast as it flew past and circled around before launching upwards. It began to approach for another pass, and Finn stayed put as he opened fire at the beast. The beast evaded and swerved right to go northward. It made another circle around and began to approach from the north. Finn immediately took steps back as he stayed put where he was and opened fire. He hit the beast and caused it to crash below. He then stood up and looked down the side of the collapsed railing where the bells were piled up. The beast shot through the other side of the belfry and then flew up. It stared down upon Finn with the grenade launcher in hand, and Finn immediately shot at its arm, causing it to drop the grenade launcher as he tore through its wrist. The robot let out of a sore noise, causing Finn to bring a hand to his ear. It then flew off and passed over head, proceeding to fly around Finn as there was no roof to cover his head. The winds picked up, but there were no bells to ring and instead only Finn as he looked at the beast circle above him and began to open fire at it. The shots passed the beast like anti-air flak, and after a moment of dancing above him, it tipped down and disappeared out of sight.

Finn took another chance to reload before it reappeared through the center of the tower and pointed its arm towards Finn. The left hand began to glow as Finn anticipated it to let out a cannon shot. He immediately switched on the propulsion system and jumped out of the way as it fired out in one burst, and then a second burst, and finally a third burst as Finn hopped around the top of the belfry. The high energy shots tore stone off from the ruined walls. At the third jump, Finn span around and opened fire directly at the front chest of the beast, hitting the wings as well. He hit the cannon arm, sending smoke and sparks out as it was blown backwards as it hovered in place. Finally, the beast screeched again and this time, the noise up close was too much for Finn that he dropped his own rifle to cover his ears. The beast then took the opportunity to fly up and grab Finn by the shoulders through its pincers.

"No!" Finn shouted.

The beast took hold of Finn and lifted him up from the belfry. He brought his hands towards the limbs of the robot and grabbed hold, and as the beast flew over the air, it released his shoulders and tried to drop him, but Finn held on. The beast flew around helplessly as it began to fly away from the convent and towards the tall mountain ahead. It flew in a way as though it attempted to inefficiently shake Finn off, but failed to do so. They flew further away from the convent as they approached the base of the mountain a few miles away. Finn saw where it was taking him as he noticed the wind turbine. The wind turbine was large, a three-winged propeller with a balcony around the three-quarters point and a wide stalk. As the beast flew to this perch, he noticed a bunch of machine parts around the circular balcony, like a nest. The beast began to attempt to shake off Finn around the nest, and he fell off and landed on the balcony. The enhanced robot then began to circle around the nest as Finn recomposed himself. He looked at all the metal pieces that lingered and saw that it was just about all trash. He picked up a flat piece of metal and held it in his left hand like a shield. The beast stopped and aimed its cannon at him, and he quickly raised the shield up and caused the cannon fire to deflect in a random direction. He held on as he felt another shot come towards him, followed by another until it became too hot to hold the piece of metal that he dropped it and took cover behind the tower. The beast screeched out and he stayed in place where there was a door into the tower itself. He stood up as the enhanced robot began to fly around again, looking at the door and seeing a latch to open it. The wind continued to howl, and it was more violent from above as it brought snow with it. The area around was also foggier. Finn took his bow and prepared an arrow as he watched the beast fly around him.

"Finn – I'm back in the comms room. Did you do it? I couldn't hear the robot, and I don't see it around the monastery," Moira reported. "Did you find the antenna?"

Finn lowered his arrow and brought his hand to his wrist. He pressed the talk button and replied, "A little preoccupied still with 'birdbrain' – I'll talk to you in a bit."

"What? Where are you? I can barely hear you…" Moira replied. "It looks like that thing is far from here and over by the mountain…"

Finn did not reply as he prepared an arrow and saw the beast come towards him. He shot the arrow at the beast, and it pierced the side of its body, but did not do anything else.

"Would be nice to have some better arrows…" Finn muttered to himself. He then looked up towards the propellers of the turbine. "Hm…"

The beast flew past and so Finn knelt down and talked into his mic.

"Moira – I'm at the wind turbine up the mountain. I'm still fighting this thing. What do you know about wind turbines?"

"Wind turbines?" Moira questioned. "I don't know – what do you want to know?"

"How do I turn one on?"

"Uh… let me see if I can find the answer to that question. B-R-B."

Finn stood up and began to confront the enhanced aerial robot again. It stopped in place and was about to let out a screech, but Finn pointed an arrow at it and hit it int the eye. He quickly aimed for another one, but as he did so, it shot towards him and so he hid behind the stalk of the tower and stayed put. The robot flew directly past him, and he stuck close to the base of the tower as it began to circle him about.

"Come on, Moira…"

The beast hovered in place and pointed its cannon arm at him again. It began to glow, and so Finn hid behind the tower. A first volley shot hit the tower, but then the beast thrusted to the side to get a better sight of Finn, but Finn switched on his boosters and dodged the second shot. It then thrusted around the opposite side, so Finn dodged the other end as well with light jumps. At the third shot, Finn pulled an arrow and aimed for the head, but missed. He then picked up the piece of metal he used as a shield as it cooled down and began to carry it as the beast circled around him again. The beast hovered in place and pointed its cannon arm at him again, and it began to glow once more and so Finn stayed in place as he readied himself. A shot fired towards him, and he refracted it away. He dodged the second one and then held on tight for the third one as he swung his arm and parried the shot to cause it to hit the cannon, blowing off its arm.

"Alright! I got it – in technical terms, a wind turbine is never shut down. It has a brake system that keeps the turbines from moving when it needs to be slowed down or stopped…."

"Brakes, of course! Got it!" Finn replied, dropping the shield and going around to the door. He placed his hands around the latch, but the door was frozen shut. He tugged at it and with the strength of the exosuit was able to yank it open. He then stepped inside and found himself in an interior balcony with a ladder down the side. Various machines were set up around, and thick cables came down from the turbine itself above to the ground. He looked around at the various machines until he found a box that said 'Emergency' on it, tore it open, and then pulled a switch that said 'Brakes'. He then heard a ringing noise and heard the turbine come to life. The beast continued to hover around. "Alright, we've got power…" he muttered to himself.

Finn exited out as he began to see the turbines move at a gentle, very slow pace. He saw the beast evade the turbines as it continued to fly around. He readied an arrow and began to prepare for the attack. The beast flew around and attempted to latch onto Finn again, but he evaded as he jumped around the balcony and waited for the opportune moment. That moment came as the beast hovered in place, but without a cannon or a grenade launcher, it instead aimed one of its last missiles as it tilted forward. Finn quickly aimed the arrow and shot at it. He missed. The missile flew past, and Finn evaded it at the last second, and it flew off and went towards the side of the mountain where it detonated and caused an avalanche of snow. He came around and saw the beast aim a second missile, dodging it too, and at the third missile, Finn shot his arrow and hit it in the eye. The beast tipped even further down, and the missile fired at the ground below. He then put his bow aside and raised his hands to his ears as it cried out.

"What are you going to do now?" Finn questioned. The wind turbine began to pick up in speed as the robot hovered around. It narrowly dodged the blades of the turbine, and Finn looked and felt the wind pick up too, causing the turbine to pick up in speed. Finn looked around as he waited for the propellers to hit the robot by chance, but then he positioned himself near the propellers and called out. "I'm over here!"

The robot flew towards Finn, and as it did so, the propellers hit the side of the beast and launched it backwards, slicing its feet. Finn ran to the other side and then called out to the beast again, and doing so caused it to pursue him once more, only for the increased speed of the turbine to finish it off as it slammed it into the ground below. Finn came to the railing and looked down below, seeing where the enhanced robot had crashed and noticing that it did not move anymore. He took a deep breath and raised his wrist to his mouth to report back to Moira.

"It's over…"

Finn hopped down the ladder inside the turbine and came to the ground floor. He opened the door and then jumped down the base of the tower. He came around to where the robot lay, in two pieces. The wings were bent, and it twitched in the ground before silently shutting down.

"I don't imagine you'll be anymore of a problem…"

Finn hopped down from the pile of snow he was on and began to look around from where he was. He could see the convent a fair distance below. However, as Finn looked around, he noticed a collapsed shelter besides the turbine. He looked over to it and found a set of smaller glider wings inside similar to the one that the robot wore, but attached to a black suit masked with a jet pilot helmet and tube that come out from the mouth. He quickly came around and looked down at the corpse of yet another elite soldier. The glider was attached to an exoskeleton suit. He removed the mask and found the skeletal remains on the other side. He looked at a light on the wrist and pressed it to play the departure message.

"The date of March 21st, 2023," a deep voice spoke in a Russian accent, "the time is approximately 13:00 hours. Under orders from Director Black, I, Valery Kartygov, or as I am referred to among the Organization – Yelata, have been instructed to defend these sacred grounds of the Order of St. Agnes as they too come under threat.

"We arrived as soon as we could, a company of our finest soldiers that we could spare to aid in the defense of these people for reasons that the director saw fit. I have patrolled the skies and not seen our enemy approach, but I am told to expect them. We have evacuated all of the women and sent them on their own way, and now it is quiet… the silence reminds me of my native lands in Siberia, and so does the chill and the wind – a beautiful wind that comes and goes, but will surely aid me in this battle that is to come.

"At this moment, the director is devising a plan, a counter-attack, and if I am successful I am to join her, but my priority lies to hold the ground against all foes that come. Herself and the others travelled south – if I am unsuccessful, it could be detrimental to her own success. I cannot fail. We do not know what it is that attacks us, except that it seeks to destroy all that stands opposed to it. Who am I to question what the enemy is, or where it comes from? We are always told to brace for the unknown, and that is what the enemy is to us, an enemy unknown…"

The transmission ended. Finn stood up and began to climb down the mountain. He returned to the convent after dark, meeting with Moira at the base of the belltower where he set off to climb it and collect the antennae. He then hopped down and attached it closer to the roof. Moira picked up the grenade launcher that the enhanced robot had used, but it was nearly out of shells.

"What? You thinking we'll need to blow up some stuff to get going?" Finn questioned as they stood at the base of the tower. "Come on, let's listen to this broadcast…"

"You… you defeated that thing just like the other thing…"

"Yup…"

"That's amazing…" Moira replied in awe. "How did you learn to fight like that…"

"It's less knowledge and more instinct," Finn remarked, "but I suppose some due credit is to Zimmerman to an extent. I'm not much of a fighter otherwise…"

Moira did not respond. They came back to the communications room, and Moira proceeded to transmit the message. She gave Finn the frequency, and they listened.

"Hello, hello – if anybody can hear this message, *Columbia* has fallen. I repeat, *Columbia* has fallen. It has become apparent to us that our Enemy has finally led and been successful in the collapse of both the Order of St. Athanasius and St. Agnes. For the past several decades, our numbers dwindled, and our abbeys shut down, one after another, but today this job is now complete. We cannot continue our work in this environment, so we have no choice but to go into hiding. If you hear this message, come and find those of us that survive with a spirit that they cannot extinguish. We will be in the land of gems… at the place of fire."

"Land of gems… place of fire…" Finn repeated. "Very cryptic – at least cryptic enough for some stupid AI to not figure out."

"If they left so long ago, why did that thing continue to linger around here like the other thing that lingered around in Alaska."

"I don't' know," Finn replied, "but I'm eager to get the hell out of here and find this land of gems… We should be able to easily figure it out. Not many places for a dozen or so nuns to go and hide in."

Act 5, Prologue

"Set it down right here," a regal English accented voice stated.

Finn carried stacks of lumber on his shoulder and placed it down atop of a table. The sun was bright, and its rays exerted tremendous heat upon the earth and all its creations. The skies were a dreamy light blue and there was not a cloud in sight. Still though, despite the weather, Finn wore a pair of cargo shorts, a wifebeater sleeveless white shirt, and a blue-beige-tan flannel shirt overtop. He still appeared young in these days, clean-shaven, though stockier than in past times; fit in both legs, torso, and arms. His skin was warm, fair, and his hair likewise dirty blonde and medium length covered in a University of Harlech Harriers ballcap. He lifted stacks of lumber from one pile and brought them to another, squatting down and picking them up from one place to another. With him, the regal English-accented man that stood with him was his father, Charlemagne Cabernet, who in these days appeared poorly. His skin was pale despite the weather, his hair short and white, and a likewise colorless moustache above his lips. He was slim, his cheeks bony and his hands shriveled, one hand dark at a bluish-black color. Charlemagne wore khaki cargo trousers and a likewise collared shirt. He held a blueprint in his hands as he looked around the area. The pair stood behind the south wing of the manor, atop of a section of land that extended from the gardens but was now a concrete platform with the early imprints of an outer perimeter. Finn carried more lumber from pickup trucks parked behind the gardens, requiring him to make trips from the construction zone, through the gardens, and to these trucks where workers were laying them out on the ground.

The heat struck down on the manor harder and harder as the sun made its rise across the sky. Finn wiped the sweat from his forehead and continued to work. After the lumber was brought over and into the construction zone, he sat down and picked up a water bottle to douse himself. The water fell onto his face as most of it fell into his mouth, the rest of it fell across his cheeks, down the side of his body and dripped all the way down to the side of his legs. He wiped at the side of his legs and then tilted his head down. Charlemagne picked up his brimmed hat from a project bench and placed it over his head. He continued to examine the schematics with careful eyes. After Finn had finished resting, he stood up and joined his father as he looked at the schematics. He picked up a belt besides the bench and placed it around his hips. The belt had numerous pouches for tools and other items. Charlemagne wore a similar leather belt around his waist.

"All done?" Charlemagne questioned in his East Anglian accent

"All done," Finn affirmed in his own Londoner accent. "What now?"

"Well, the lower walls are finished, but we'll need to be careful with the upper walls," Charlemagne stated. "We stuck to a simple design, but even with the curve of the roof, it's not so simple. The tricky part is connecting this annex to the old building; that building was never built with intent that it be more than what it is. The last time it had an appendix added was the stables, and that was a project between my father and Salmar."

Finn turned around to look at the current state of the construction site. "Not bad though for a month of work? We should be finished before the end of the summer…"

"Yes, that we should," Charlemagne replied, walking over to a workbench. "The tough bit of the job was in clearing the roses and dismantling the patio that was here. It is now time to construct a place more fitting for matrimony."

The pair divided the labor, where Finn cut the lumber and helped lift, Charlemagne stuck to planning and using the nail gun to put pieces together. He also measured and made sure that everything was the right size that it had to be, stopping every so often and discussing with Finn before they continued onwards along in the project. Finn cut two-by-four inch pieces of lumber into small lengths, which Charlemagne then took to put together with longer two-by-four inch pieces of lumber arranged in a rectangular. He reinforced the shapes with these studs, and once they were finished, began to tie rope around the ends of it.

"Right… here's the next step," Charlemagne remarked. "We need to be very careful – I'll raise the wall section with the crane, and I need you on the ladder to gently ensure that it lands atop perfectly so, nailing it together at both ends."

"Understood," Finn replied. He walked with his father out and around to the corner of the property where there was a small crane. The side of the crane read 'Medici Construction' and it was orange.

Charlemagne approached the control panel atop of a small platform and began to extend the arm of the crane. "Yes, this takes me back to my days in university – when we foolishly built our own crane out of scrap metal and hoisted a vehicle up the side of the Harlech office building."

"I heard of that…" Finn replied. "It's one of those tales they tell engineering students to this date at the uni. It's been replicated so many times in other ways since then… of course, none as grand since they don't use a full car anymore but a chassis."

"Bah, you could lift a chassis with ease," Charlemagne responded, "but a full-sized car? No, it takes a different sort of *willpower* to do something so bold, but at the same time, it was foolish of us. What were we after but… vainglory. At any rate, I'm bringing the hook down now, make sure it's connected for me…"

"Yes, pa."

Finn came around to the other side of the construction site as the chained hook gently lowered and he took it and secured it around the rope tied to the wall section.

"Alright, you're good!" Finn shouted.

Charlemagne began to raise the wall section up gently, causing Finn to back off as he supervised its ascent. The wall section swung as it was lifted upwards, requiring Finn to intervene as he grabbed hold of it and caused it to calm down. He then watched as Charlemagne brought it around to the section it was to rest upon. Charlemagne lowered it and Finn picked up the ladder and placed it beside the far end to his father. He climbed the ladder with the nail gun in one hand, and used his other hand to stabilize the wall. He placed the nail gun atop of the ladder so he could use both hands to adjust it. He looked at both ends, shifted the wall down slightly, and then judged to see if it was exact.

"How is it?!" Charlemagne shouted out.

"It… looks good!" Finn replied. He quickly began to shoot nails, bringing the ladder down as he fastened it along the length of the lower section. He came around to the end and adjusted the wall slightly so that it was parallel to the lower section, and then stood up on the ladder to look over to his father. "All done!"

"Excellent, Finn," Charlemagne replied, releasing the grip of the crane. "Very good."

Charlemagne moved the crane away from the construction site and then came around to help Finn as he hopped atop of a taller ladder to remove the lengths of rope.

"How about that? Now we just need to do that seven more times, and we'll be a two-thirds done," Charlemagne said, pointing around the site. The lower section of walls were set up in seven sections, two facing the rear of the manor, two perpendicular to these walls, two diagonal at forty-five degrees, and then one section joining the two diagonal sections together.

Once they finished securing the upper section, they proceeded to repeat the same work as they constructed an entirely new wall section through the use of two-by-four wooden studs. They precisely measured each stud so they were equal in length. Finn sawed the pieces through use of a sawblade, and Charlemagne put them together.

"Not quite the same, eh?" Charlemagne remarked. "As putting together machines, or circuitry, but it is simple work… and it is exhaustive work. I'm only doing what I can – I can't imagine how you must be right now…"

"Mr. Cabernet," an English-accented voice cried out from the garden, "lunch is ready."

"Ah, there we go," Charlemagne expressed, standing up. "Thank you, Ms. Quinn!"

Charlemagne picked up a towel from the project bench and wiped his forehead. He then placed a hand on Finn's shoulder while Finn removed his ballcap to wipe the sweat off his forehead. The pair left the construction site to come upstairs to the patio. Ms. Quinn, an elderly lady at this time, wearing a black dress with a white apron, set the table with two silver trays at either side and a pitcher of water. She then left as Finn approached, entering through the trophy room doors to go into the north wing and disappear into the kitchen. She returned with two glasses.

"Thank you, my dear," Charlemagne expressed as he pulled a chair out. "Much appreciated.

"Cheers," Finn quietly remarked.

Charlemagne raised the domed cover of his tray and looked at the sandwich on sourdough sliced bread.

"Let me know if there's anything else I can do for you both…" Ms. Quinn stated before she left. "Enjoy."

"I'm going to wash my hands…" Charlemagne expressed. "Be right back."

Finn watched his father leave. He then left the opposite way and entered into the kitchen where Mavis was cleaning up. She sprayed bleach-laced cleaner onto the granite counter tops and wiped with a dish towel. Finn came around to the sink to wash his hands while he listened to her hum. He then turned to face her, and she smiled at him. He gave a nervous smile back at her and then left to come to the patio as he looked around. A mild breeze came through. He looked down to the pool and over to the hot tub in the corner. He took in a deep breath and then pulled his seat out.

"Is everything alright, Master Louis?" Ms. Quinn questioned. "Something I can do for you?"

"No, ma'am. All is well," Finn politely responded.

Ms. Quinn smiled at him as she looked at him. "You're the spitting image of your father, and your grandfather, and your great-grandfather. I've served all three of them, and it's a pleasure to have met in my old age the fourth son of the Cabernet name. You've also made your father quite happy young man. The happiest I've seen him in a long time…"

"Thank you, Ms. Quinn," Finn responded. She left back inside. He looked up to the sky as the sun pierced directly down and sat down in the sunlight despite the parasol above, but it only protected Charlemagne's side of the table. Rather than change sides, he removed his flannel and threw it onto an adjacent seat. Finn removed the cover and placed it on his right. He then picked up the sandwich and began to eat. He heard the sound of the toilet flush through the window, and then after a minute or two was rejoined by his father who pulled his seat out.

"Awfully convenient having Ms. Quinn around, isn't it? No need to cook, no need to clean…"

"Yes, it is an immense privilege," Charlemagne remarked, sitting down and placing a hand over his food cover again. "Oh, before I forget…" He brought the two damaged fingers of his hand, the middle finger and index finger together, and also likewise brought the thumb together so they pointed out. He took these fingers and touched his forehead, and then he touched his chest bone followed by his left shoulder and his right shoulder. "In the name of the Father, the Son and the Holy Spirit," he said as he did so. Finn stopped eating as he watched. "Bless us o'Lord, for these thy gifts, for which we are about to receive, from thy bounty through Christ our Lord. Amen." After Charlemagne finished saying grace, he opened the cover and began to eat. He picked up the fork and poked into the salad. Finn continued to eat. "All of this feels just right, doesn't it... My father built this house with my grandfather, my father and my brother added onto it, and now here I have the privilege to do the same with my own son... God has blessed me, Finn. He truly has, and what better addition to build than that which was missing and long overdue – a chapel."

"A place of private prayer should be nice – it's always nice and quiet around here, but like a library, it helps set the mood, I suppose."

"Oh, it will be more than just a shrine, my boy," Charlemagne replied. "You see, I've received permission from the archbishop regarding our little project, and this chapel will not just be any chapel, but a chapel that houses a tabernacle with our Lord in it. Perhaps the sizeable donations we make to the parish and archdiocese has something to do with it, but the pastor at our parish has also agreed to the project as he would need to say Mass every so often here. The archbishop and Fr. Wilfred will attend a ceremony, we'll invite some folk – hopefully Diana and Tristan will be able to attend, but it will be a very good thing, especially as I grow weaker everyday because of the cancer."

Finn stopped eating and responded, "Have you felt weaker?"

"No, on the contrary, I've felt more alive than ever before," Charlemagne encouraged. "I could hardly tell I even had cancer to begin with. The treatments have gone well, but I won't say much else as I have an appointment with Dr. Moore in a week from now." He looked at Finn with a smile, but then his eyes looked at his broad upper arms, particularly at the burn scars.

Finn noticed and looked down. He finished his sandwich and began to eat his salad.

"Don't take shame in your scars, Finn," Charlemagne stated. "We should never take shame in them, but let them remind us of what we have survived. I said the same to Tristan – of course, the disfigurements upon his body are worse than the ones on yours, but the same applies."

"Yes, sir."

The pair continued to eat in silence. Finn finished his lunch, while Charlemagne ate only his salad and half the sandwich. Once they were finished, Ms. Quinn moved the plates indoors and they finished their refreshments before they continued outside.

Charlemagne sat down in front of the project bench while Finn cleaned off some sawdust from his workbench. Charlemagne picked up some steel rods from the pile of materials and brough them to another workbench, one that was not made of wood but had a steel panel atop. Beside the panel were tanks with tubes that led to some tools. There was also a welder mask nearby.

"Come over here," Charlemagne said as he put the mask on. "I've forgot to do some welding that I was going to do last night. These rods are anchors for the columns. I need to weld them together to the brackets. Have you welded much before?"

"Not particularly," Finn replied.

"Ah, then put on a mask," Charlemagne responded. "Come and watch me do it. You must have smoldered before. It's the same…"

Finn put on a mask. Charlemagne turned on the valve and then placed the bits before him. He brought the torch close to the metal rod as he placed it along a bracket and began to attach the two. He carefully moved the torch around the rod as he fastened the two pieces together. As he did so, sparks flew outwards towards them.

"Columns are trickier than walls," Charlemagne remarked. "I was advised to stick these rods into the concrete, fasten the brackets to the concrete, and fasten the brackets to the pillars, and we should have a pretty sturdy pillar."

"Quite a bit of confidence to a foot long rod," Finn replied.

"Yes…" Charlemagne replied, finishing the first one. "Here, give it a try…"

"What?"

"Go on," Charlemagne encouraged. "It's safe – it's efficient, and it gets the job done. It's quite strong, believe me."

Finn took hold of the torch and began to takeover for him.

"Atta boy, just like that," Charlemagne encouraged. "Just take it slow any easy. If you go too fast, then you'll do a shoddy job for sure. Better we do a good job than rely on some brackets welded quickly by the Chinese."

Finn smiled and continued to finish the job. He fastened the second rod and then began to do the third.

"Yes, thanks be to God for modern engineering… of course, this technology existed when my grandfather and father built the house, but these techniques in constructing were lesser known," Charlemagne stated. "I suppose overall though, God bless fire which made this steel and steel fabrication possible."

Finn finished the job as Charlemagne supervised, and when they were finished, he turned the valve to shut off the tanks. They then removed their masks to reveal the finished product.

"Alright, now that goes in the holes left in concrete. They should just slide in," Charlemagne remarked, standing up. They dropped the bracket into the holes, kicking it down where it stayed nice and tight. "Excellent. Now to repeat that three more times… Of course, that's not all we'll do – otherwise the column may be too loose. We really want it tight enough so that it cannot even move a nanometer."

Charlemagne and Finn returned to the bench where they continued to work. Charlemagne held a smile on his face as Finn concentrated on the work ahead of him, and Finn held a focused look as he worked on the bracket.

"Well done, my boy. You're doing brilliantly," Charlemagne commended. He took in a deep breath and smiled at his son.

Finn's expression did not change as he remained focused on the work ahead of him, ensuring that the weld was done perfectly and completely well. Once he was finished, they repeated the process. Finn returned as Charlemagne looked at him admirably.

"What's the matter?" Finn questioned.

"I was just in thought of it all," Charlemagne expressed. "As you know, I've held my grandfather, who raised me, with much esteem through my life. I wanted to be just like him, though I ignored for much of it that which was most important – both God and neighbor. Only in my old age do I feel truly connected to him. I can only imagine how he must look upon us from above and smile. He was truly a great man, and he would have loved you very much, Finn."

Finn looked at Charlemagne and nodded. Charlemagne placed his hands on Finn's shoulders.

"Never forget the power that we have, my boy," Charlemagne expressed, "especially to do good."

Finn drove one of the white SUVs left behind at the Convent of Our Lady of Maidens down an arid highway. The road they passed along was flanked by two tall hills, and the ground around them was a mixture of dry grass and coarse dirt. There was not much snow in these parts as most of it was melted and lay in piles. The sun shined down, although the skies were partly cloudy. Finn brought the sun visor down as he continued to drive along the road. Behind them, their backpacks, the exoskeleton suit, as well as the glider removed from the elite soldier's exosuit, lay upon each other with the back seats pulled down to create a partially flat bed. Moira typed away at her computer as she sat in the front passenger seat. Finn drove over sixty miles per hour on the road as they sped past other cars and ranches in the U.S. countryside.

"We seem to be in the right direction," Moira expressed. "The State of Idaho seems to be known as the Gem State, but there's about sixty or so Catholic churches in the state. Just glancing at the list on the diocese website, I don't see any that match the words they used as a 'place of fire' and such."

"I didn't think you'd find an exact match…" Finn replied. "The use of 'fire' in the name of a parish is an awkward one, but thinking about it, I'd imagine that anything close to what fire may refer to could substitute in – in Catholicism, 'fire' as something sacred could refer to the Sacred Heart of Jesus, the Sacred Heart of Mary, or on another hand, the fire of the Holy Spirit, so anything to do with the Holy Spirit, the Holy Paraclete, or something like that."

"I have two – no, three parishes named Sacred Heart," Moira replied. "Do you want their addresses?"

"Where are they?"

"Just about at three opposite points of the state – we passed one on our way here..." Moira said. "Do you think that could fit?"

"No... I doubt they'd use that one if there were multiple locations," Finn responded. "No, these nuns and their Order... they're a little weird. They're eccentric. They wouldn't stand out like a sore thumb – what about monasteries. How many of them in Idaho?"

"Uh..." Moira typed into her computer and replied, "four: Saint Gertrude, Our Lady of Ephesus, Sacred Mountain, and Ascension."

"Hm... Ephesus... no. Ascension... not really..." Finn thought aloud. "Well, isn't this disappointing. Here I thought they were giving their position away to anyone with a human brain, but I'm stumped..."

"Maybe gems refers to something else," Moira suggested.

"Idaho as the Gem State fits too well for the fact that it's a neighboring state."

Moira typed into her computer and then sighed. "There really aren't many search results for the Order of St. Agnes on the Internet," she said. "You're right, they do seem like a bunch of 'nobodies,' to use your words."

"I didn't say nobodies, I said nobody knows much about them," Finn replied. "You won't find much about the Order of St. Agnes on the Internet other than what is written on Wikipedia, and what you will find about the Order of St. Athanasius is the same, and the rest segregated to fringe image boards, conspiracy theory websites, white supremacist forums, and trad groups on social media."

"What the hell is a trad?" Moira questioned.

"It's best not to ask," Finn responded. "Although... search this: Society of Pius X, and let me know how many of their churches you find."

"Okay…" Moira replied, typing away. "Let's see… in the District of the United States, there are five associated churches: Immaculate Conception, Our Lady of Guadalupe, Saint Dominic, Saint Joseph and Saint Isaac Jogues."

"Hm… not likely…" Finn said with a sigh of disbelief. "Let's broaden our scopes again – sorry, I don't know much about this order as much as I thought I did. There's not much circulating public knowledge because they died out in the seventies or so, and what I do know about them comes from my father and my great-grandfather. Let's see… they're a traditionalist bunch, where out here they seem to be on similar wavelengths to the trads while in Egypt for example, they were Coptic. In the Levant, my great-granddad had a run in with some Melkites and Chaldeans. Let's see if some Eastern Catholic rite could be our ticket in. Search for Eastern, or Byzantine, Catholic churches and see what can found in Idaho."

"Eastern Catholic…?" Moira questioned. "I don't know what that is, but sure…" She typed away. "Let's see…"

"Most people understand 'Roman' Catholic, but within the Catholic Church there are subsections distinct from the Latin Church, but in communion with the Pope. These are referred to as the 'Eastern' and/or 'Oriental' Catholic Churches, not the same as the Orthodox Churches because those are not in communion with the Pope. The Eastern Catholics are a small minority who hold to their own traditions and liturgical rites, for example the Byzantine Catholics or Syro-Malabars."

"Alright," Moira replied, "according to this website, there are three: the Exaltation of the Holy Cross, which is a Byzantine monastery; something called the Ruthenian Outreach of Boise – oh, but both of these are also listed as 'suppressed,' which doesn't sound good. The last one is called – oh, this is definitely it – Miracle of the Holy Fire, a Byzantine monastery and parish community in Jefferson, Idaho."

"Jefferson? Are we anywhere near that?"

"We've definitely not passed it," Moira answered. "Keep driving south and eventually you'll want to go west into the mountains again. They should be just outside of the town."

"Okay..."

Finn continued to drive along the highway as they went through the state countryside. The terrain remained the same; dry grass, rolling hills to flat plains with low mountains on the horizon. The skies remained the same, light blue and sun shining through. The heaters in the SUV continued to run, and the glass stayed cold to touch as Moira rested her head.

"You know an awful lot about the Catholic Church for somebody who doesn't strike me as religious..." Moira stated.

"You know more than me, and I was semi-raised Catholic."

"Semi-raised?"

"My grandparents more than anything; neither of my actual parents seemed to care," Moira replied. She then paused for a moment before she asked, "What about you?"

"I was raised Anglican (protestant) – standard procedure for a British-born aristocrat. I went through all the hoops," Finn stated, "mostly to please my grandparents too, but otherwise we never really went to church on Sundays, or were active in the community. My adoptive-father was a godless man, but my mother held her own private sentiments that she kept to herself. Me – I was a mix of both. I could not *not* believe in something..."

Moira did not immediately respond as she looked at Finn. She then looked ahead and replied, "It almost feels like too much of a burdensome question – whether to believe in the existence of God or not. I've seldom thought about it, but even for me, dealing with programming and computers, it all seems more complex than all that. I would rather not think about it..."

Finn did not reply. They continued to drive along the single lane freeway until they began to diverge westward. They proceeded across some flat plains with wired fence on either side with pasture lands otherwise. A few deciduous (leaved) trees and bushes could be found on occasion, but the majority of the trip through the lands they went through consisted of tall and dry grass. The pair stopped in a small town for lunch, and then continued onwards as the skies became covered in a greyish-yellow haze. The air had a smoky smell. There were more deciduous trees along the road they continued on, but less farmland as they passed a few pastures, ranches, and mostly homes to roadside protestant churches and casinos. It was almost impossible for the entire car ride to not see a flagpole bearing the American star-spangled banner waving in the wind every five minutes or so. As they travelled deeper inland, the sight of residents dwindled significantly and could only be found in the next town over. By midnoon, the pair found themselves in the small town of Jefferson amidst a small valley. Finn drove through the town, and Moira guided him onto a dirt road that led up one of the mountains. They passed a few skinny and barren trees on the road as they went around some farms and then began to approach and pass a signpost that read 'Miracle of the Holy Fire Monastery' and below 'St. Elias Parish Ukrainian Greek Catholic Church' with Mass times. A flagpole besides the entrance also bore the American flag, which they passed as they drove down a short driveway that led around to a two-story farmhouse. The land was surrounded by deciduous trees that encompassed a surrounding forest. Either side of the driveway was flanked with pastureland with horses and other animals grazing. Before approaching the farmhouse, the road curved to the left and entered into a parking lot with several dozen spots in front of a large rectangular white structure, and besides this structure on the left was an attached annex or church hall. The road continued along the right as a small lane that curved around the right field and from where amidst the trees one could see cabins. There were a few cars in the parking lot, so Finn came around and parked near the church itself. A gate prevented further travel along the lane and towards the cabins. From where Finn had parked, he could not see movement ahead or around the cabins.

"Is this it?" Moira questioned. "Not what I expected."

"What? No pictures on the Internet?"

"Nope."

"Let's see if anyone is inside," Finn suggested.

They both exited out from the car and began to approach the white structure and its double doors. The façade of the building was simple, and the white was an off-white crème color. There were two turrets at either corner of the building, and then a central partition both with peaked roofs. There were small arched windows in front of the turrets, and then two above the main entrance. The main entrance steps had a small shelter, itself with a turret. Above the central partition there was a small bell tower with a domed roof. At the right side of the landing above the steps was a wheelchair access ramp, and on the left was a sign that said, 'St. Elias Ukrainian Catholic Church' with a small, squared icon of a bearded male, and beside it the Mass times. Underneath the words were repeated in Cyrillic. Finn stepped up the doors and attempted to enter the church, but it was locked.

"No dice," Finn stated, stepping down and looking around. "There's got to be a side entrance or something. Come on."

Finn began to go around the right side where he saw a side entrance into the church. He attempted to open it, but was unsuccessful. He then came around and approached the annex, but likewise was unsuccessful.

"Alright, last-ditch effort, we bother the parish priest," Finn stated. "Come on."

Finn began to walk across the parking lot and approach the rectory. He stepped up the front porch. Like the church, the rectory had a plain appearance to it, peaked rooftops and white walls. Finn knocked on the front door, and waited. He then knocked again and finally the door opened. A grey bearded older male with fairish-tanned skin, wearing a black robe looked back at them.

"Hi," Finn greeted with an awkward smile, "sorry to bother you, Father, but we're two travellers looking for nuns belonging to the Order of St. Agnes. I understand they re-located from their convent in Montana here..."

The man looked at Finn suspiciously.

"Are you perhaps a member of the Order of St. Athanasius?" Finn questioned, lowering his smile as he continued to stare back at him.

"I am not," the pastor answered. "What business do you have with the sisters of St. Agnes?"

"We just had some questions for them," Finn answered. "My name is Louis Cabernet, and this is my friend, Moira Macmillan. We were just at their abbey in Montana, and I heard they may have come down here – are they still here?"

"The abbey does not accept visitors at this time or day," the pastor answered, "but I will call the abbot and let her know you are here to visit."

The pastor closed the door, prompting Moira and Finn to step aside and sit down at a bench.

"What are the chances they're even here and haven't moved on," Moira stated. "2023 was two years ago..."

"I don't know where else they would go other than disperse, which is what I really fear..."

After a few minutes, Finn saw a woman in a black gown approach them as they continued to sit. She came from the gate and walked across the parking lot. Finn noticed that she was an African female with dark skin. The habit that she wore came down to her ankles and her hair was covered with a headdress that only left her face visible. She approached the pair as they came down from the porch and met with her at the entrance of the parking lot.

"I am Mother Josephine. You are here to see the Agnesian sisters?" the abbess questioned.

"I suppose so," Finn stated. "Are you with the Order of St. Agnes?"

"Absolutely not," the abbess answered. She spoke in a southern accent, "but as the Lord would have it, they are still here under our refugee. What business do you have with them?"

"We have some questions," Finn remarked. "Can we speak with the mother superior – if she is still with them."

"Ah, Mother Doherty, yes," the abbess replied. "Come with me – perhaps you can help them find a new home… this community was not built to sustain two sisterhoods, you know."

"Oh, I believe it… Mother."

Finn and Moira walked with Mother Josephine as she took them across the parking lot, to the gate, and then down the lane as they came around to the cabins. They stopped at one of the cabins and Mother Josephine walked up and slammed her fists into the door as she called, "Mother Doherty, a boy and a girl are here to see you." As they waited, Finn looked around, the lanes diverged into two lanes that circled around. There were only five cabins in total, but they were small duplexes. At the end of the land was a paved clearing with a barn and another structure. Finn turned his head as the door opened and he saw a nun with a different habit, a black one with a white cover around the head, but black hood. She wore a large crucifix around her neck and looked at Finn and Moira questioningly with a hand to her chest.

"Yes…" Mother Doherty spoke.

"Good evening, Mother," Finn greeted. "My name is Louis Cabernet, son of Charlemagne Cabernet, and brother and sister to Tristan and Diana Merrick. May we come in?"

Mother Doherty let out a soft sigh and looked over to Mother Josephine, as though annoyed, and then said, "Very well… come inside…"

Moira and Finn entered into the cabin, where on the right was a staircase that went upstairs, while on the left was a small living space. They followed Mother Doherty down a narrow corridor besides the staircase which brought them into a kitchen. On their left in the living room were two sisters that looked towards them. Mother Doherty sat down at a kitchen table and offered a seat to Moira and Finn, while Mother Josephine closed the door behind her as the other sisters peered in to look.

"What can I do for you, Mr. Cabernet?" Mother Doherty asked, opening a pack of cigarettes. She brought one to her lips and began to light it, and then offered the pack to Finn and Moira.

"No thank you…" Moira quietly said.

Mother Josephine took a cigarette and began to light it up while Finn waved the smoke from his face and then leaned forward.

"Listen, we were just at your convent in Montana – we listened to the broadcast and found you here. We need your help…"

"Oh, is that it?" Mother Doherty questioned, raising an eyebrow. "You need help from me, but what can I do to be of service to you? I am a little short on resources that I used to have, but the sisters and I can say a prayer for you for certain."

Finn sighed and began to explain from the beginning – he told her about Moira's curiosity, the attack from the robots and governmental forces, their escape and trip to Alaska, the state of the GDP headquarters, an encounter with an enhanced robot, and then their visit to the convent in Montana and the enhanced robot at that location.

"I just want to know what happened to Director Black and the rest of the GDP under her, and who controls these robots and what can we do to get them off our backs," Finn asked.

Mother Doherty flicked ashes into an ash tray and then replied, "There is nothing you can do – the powers behind those robots are a terrible force that is not be trifled with. The best you can do is hide… like we have been."

"What happened on March 20th, 2023?"

"On March 20th, the sisters and I were visited by the GDP who told us that we were in grave danger because the Enemy was coming to strike us down," Mother Doherty explained. "Ms. Black informed us about what happened. She told us that they were attacked by an army of robots, as you detailed, and that they came to warn us and assist in our evacuation because we would be a target for extermination."

"Why you of all people?"

"As Ms. Black put it, Operation Upheaval had been activated," Mother Doherty stated. "A plan that detailed the destruction of the Global Defense Project, their allies, and all those considered enemies to her boss, where we fell into the latter part. The Order of St. Athanasius and St. Agnes have long been enemies to her bosses…"

"The Chosen."

"Yes," Mother Doherty answered, flicking her cigarette again, "and it came at little surprise to Ms. Black because she long suspected a power move from the Chosen to do just as that. Since what happened at the start of the year in 2021, the Chosen had taken aims to consolidate the technologies in those robots, or in other words what was referred to as 'Zimmerman's Legacy' and harness their powers for their own purposes. She suspected that it was the aim of the Chosen to replace the Global Defense Project with these pets that could be easily controlled…"

"The Global Defense Project was not supposed to survive," Finn recounted. "In an alternate world, one not too different from our own, they're absorbed into the Chosen's direct control and cease to exist…" he said. "I suppose I should have seen something coming, but this… it's too soon and too different. So that's it then – the Chosen launched those robots to eliminate the GDP and you lot – I didn't realize you were so much of a threat."

"We've always known more than we should have," Mother Doherty confessed, "and a part of that knowledge has been passed on to us from the Order of St. Athanasius, who no longer exist in the North America. We're all that is left, and even what remains of the Order of St. Agnes is little... a convent or two across the world, so I hear."

"Good riddance," Finn remarked.

"Excuse me?"

"You heard me," Finn replied. "I know all about both religious orders. Tristan and my father told me all about you all. You're all sick – all of you proud and misguided. Your aims are no different to those of the Chosen. Look at Tristan, a product of *in vitro* fertilization, which is expressly condemned by the Catholic Church, in a eugenics campaign to create 'better' and 'holier' humans, when all those efforts did was make him suffer more than the average person. If he didn't have the people he had in his life, he would have surely been an awful person to say the least. I know because I've met someone in the same circumstances who was the worst person I had ever met, and his name was Damian Cambridge, or as you may know him, Audric Zimmerman. And don't even get me started on the metahumans Bishop Tristan Williamson pioneered. All of you are like the Catholic version of the *Schutzstaffel*, playing god yourself and denying what is already before you and which God has offered us through the Church.

"When did all our calamities begin but in the Fall of Man, when God had created us in *his image* to be physical beings in this world he had created – to share in his creation. We rebelled and he respected our free will and choice to live in this world at our own volition, but God did not abandon us. He did as much as he could from afar to love us, and he promised us that he would open the path to us for salvation. He chose countless persons through salvation history to prepare the way. He prepared the way for Christ to come and lead us back home – to open the way in which we could oppose evil through love, to realize that there is hope in this world for us that are hurt and forgotten by all this evil, and to fill us with faith in God who could deliver us to our salvation. All that you seek in science is in vain, because long before the Order of St. Athanasius was founded, Christ already paved the way for us to become a better person through charity, the rejection of sin, and sanctification. Shame on both you and the Children, to pursue by human means what only Christ can provide – a new and better body after the resurrection, a means to replace our stone hearts with hearts of flesh, and the capability to strive to become better people. You forget that after Christ came to Earth, he left us with a Church, a New Israel, and that through this Church we can strive for what we long for – to emancipate ourselves from our animality and become gods by grace, as we were born and predestined to become at Creation. Only through Christ is that possible."

Mother Doherty flicked her cigarette and replied, "You are very opinionated, Mr. Cabernet. We have never denied the resurrection, nor the powers of Christ to give us what we strive for in our scientific efforts. We have only wished to correct the errors of our ways, the errors of the Fall, but don't suppose because we are Catholic that we are perfect. We did what we thought was right, and perhaps we had become lost in our vision. I certainly have no other way to explain why it is that we are in exile, while the Children and the Chosen run rampant – how demonic powers and influence rise to unprecedented levels not seen since before the Christianization of the world. We are indeed, as some would put it, in end times…" She then put out her cigarette. "At any rate, you are here for a reason, so let me finish my story. After the Global Defense Project came, we left and came here. Ms. Black, who stayed with us for several months, told us that her elite forces would defend key areas she believed the Chosen would strike in Operation Upheaval – the Global Defense Project headquarters in Alaska, our convent in

Montana, and then a Blackmore extraction mine not too far from here, and a power plant in Wyoming providing power to the robot manufacturing facility in Colorado. All of them set off, while Ms. Black awaited either their return, or our destruction. We waited, and we waited... but no news came – Ms. Black believed that all of her fighters had been defeated. She was devastated, but found solace here, particularly in the story of St. Joan of Arc. We attempted to convince Ms. Black to stay, and she certainly felt the pull of our faith community, but ultimately, she followed her calling when she left and did not return. In her letter, she mentioned that she went to Colorado to sabotage the production facility, and all that I know is that she never returned and the robots never came back ever since."

"I don't think Ms. Black won," Finn replied, "and I don't know who won, but I do know that we were attacked by robots like the ones that attacked the GDP, and they were supporting government agents. Some sort of successor agency exists..."

"The Chosen obviously won," Mother Doherty replied, "but as to why they have not come for us, or why they have not finished you off, I do not have those answers. You are both lucky to have survived yet."

"Finn destroyed both of the enhanced robots in Alaska and Montana," Moira interrupted. "We're more than capable."

"Very impressive, but what do you aim to do?" Mother Doherty questioned. "Both of those locations were abandoned for a reason, and I'm surprised both of those automatons remained at those sites, but do you intend to go now to the extraction mine? To the power facility? To the research labs?"

"We might," Finn prompted.

"Ha, you'd be wishing death upon yourself," Mother Doherty replied. "These three locations are the most precious sites to do with the production of these robots that you'd surely find more of them – an entire army of enhanced robots. You are wishing death upon yourself."

"So we'll be more covert."

"You will only get yourself and this young girl killed in the process."

"What other choice do we have – we're marked and they're out to get us anyways."

"Unless you actively oppose the Chosen, like us, they will not hold grudges upon you. Even we have been a target they have not been hellbent to find, no less I suppose because they already have all of our secrets."

"You mean the diary of Bishop Williamson?" Finn asked. "The one Sister Witeveens programmed into Tristan's blood and Zimmerman extracted?"

"Yes, that one… but at the same time, we do have our other secrets and knowledge."

"I'm sure losing Sister Witeveens put a hamper on your eugenics project."

"As I tell all those who question our methods, including Mother Josephine, we seek to pool together the best of a gene pool together and remove defects and negative traits. Would you not want your own children to inherit the best of what the two of you have to offer?"

"I don't intend to have children," Finn quicky responded, "and secondly, Moira and I aren't dating. As a matter of fact, I'm set to join the seminary next September…"

"So that is where is all lies…" Mother Doherty remarked. "If only the Order of St. Athanasius still existed – it could benefit from another brilliant mind."

"I would rather become a Jesuit," Finn replied. "I would never want to become what you, or Sister Witeveens (God rest her soul) became."

"Why do you say that?" Mother Josephine responded. "Why does he speak as though Sister Witeveens has perished?"

"What? Because Sister Witeveens is dead, Mother," Finn replied, turning around to face her. "Unless…" he turned and faced Mother Doherty with a frown. "What is she talking about?"

Mother Doherty held her hands together as she looked at Finn and then over to Mother Josephine. "Just couldn't keep your mouth shut, could you?" she snarled.

"Is... Is Tristan's mother alive?"

"Hush now," Mother Doherty remarked, "the walls are thin, and the other nuns would be scandalized to know about Sister Witeveen's son."

"She is, isn't she? She's alive – why did I have so much as a hunch..." Finn remarked. "You liars! You lied to that poor boy!"

"He was not supposed to come and find us – yes, as a matter of fact, Sister Witeveens did survive, and you keep that to yourself."

"Absolutely not," Finn responded. "I will do no such thing... Tristan is my best friend, and I won't lie to him that his mother is not alive."

"He does not need to come here again... If you truly understood what happened the last time, you would not, no less with the Chosen looking for us."

"Zimmerman is dead, Mother. All his accomplices are dead too. Tristan has a right to know that his biological mother, who he wept for, is alive, especially so that she can know that she has a daughter-in-law and grandchildren..."

"We are aware of all these details... before we left the convent, Diana used to write to us."

"Does Diana know?"

"Of course not," Mother Doherty stated. "Listen, you do not understand, but what happened with Tristan seeking his mother last time was psychologically dangerous and unnecessary. For a start, although his biological mother, Sister Witeveens did not raise him – her sister did, and in already having lost his adoptive mother, he did not need to meet his biological mother too because it opened unclosed wounds that turned that fledgling young man into a boy again. I saw the pain in Diana's heart, to have become cast aside when she had done all that she could to help him. Yes, I do understand that Tristan and Diana are married, have a child..."

"Two children now."

"And that they are happy together, and it is best that they continue on their lives in such a manner without Sister Witeveens who wants to be left alone. If it was her own volition, she would have gone, left us, and informed her son, but it could not be. Now, if you, as his friend, wish to open Pandora's Box, go ahead."

Finn looked at Mother Doherty. He took in a deep breath and then said, "Where is she? I want to talk to Sister Witeveens."

Mother Doherty looked at him and then over to Mother Josephine who left. After a few minutes, Mother Josephine returned with another nun. Finn looked at her and saw the feminine face similar to his best friend.

"Oh my... you *are* alive," Finn remarked.

"Sister Sophia," Mother Doherty spoke, "this is Louis Cabernet, son of Charlemagne Cabernet, and his friend..."

"Moira Macmillan," she groaned.

"Nice to meet you both," Sister Witeveens remarked, putting her hands into her habit pocket. "I didn't realize Mr. Cabernet had a son."

"I guess he liked to keep his secrets too," Finn responded, shaking his head. "How could you just go on with your life and let your son believe you were dead?"

Sister Witeveens sighed and then replied, "For about seventeen years beforehand, Tristan did not even know I existed. I had no qualm with that life, so no less did I feel objection to let him believe I was now dead."

"You're lying to him though – you're actively lying to him in pretending to be dead. How are you going to answer that when you pass on to the next life? Provided of course you don't repent and damn yourself!"

"I am hopeful that he will have grown old and full of wisdom by then that he would understand what I had to do for him."

"You have two grandsons by the way," Finn stated, "likely another on the way. Damian and Maximillian."

"I was only aware of Damian... thank you for telling me about the other... Maximillian..."

"I'm sure they would have loved to have had a grandmother in their life," Finn responded. "They're both quite busy these days, between family life and work."

"I'm sure they are..." Sister Witeveens responded, looking to the others in the room. "Could you leave us for a moment, please?"

"Certainly," Mother Doherty said, standing up and leaving with Mother Josephine.

Sister Witeveens took in a deep breath and then asked, "What are you doing here?"

Finn briefly told her. He then said, "We can't return to Allabrese, and I suppose I can't negotiate with the Chosen, so I in the least intend to take it to them. I want to go see this mining facility."

"I see... well, it is not far from here... but it is well protected and in somewhat inhospitable and dangerous lands..."

"What? Like a military zone?"

"Not quite... it's in a preserve, hidden in caves beneath lava fields around a low volcano. You see, this mine was established to extract rare metals used in the production of these humanoid death robots, specifically their circuitry. From my understanding, the contents are airlifted out and delivered to a production and research facility."

"Mother Doherty told us about that part, yeah..."

"Did Mother Margaret tell you where in particular this location is...?"

r take a look
dy it. I also
n fields here
ay here with
 row."

an to follow
d fight from

: the others
no life here
to be.,."
erty, even if
an out here.
s like you'd

 death trap
g in a deep

leadweight,
 share some
own…"

atever defense lies within?"
robots," Finn remarked. "I'm

n believed robots to be reliable
ed, walking around the room.
because they believed them to
ie same time, they would be
here, she and her team brought
sisters who better understands
a look at it."
"Do you still have it?"

that… We could exploit their

at it?"
e though," Sister Witeveens
icr Josephine, but I'm sure you
you so need to (although Louis
ier Charon). We would also
Mass tomorrow morning."

hat you do not go to Tristan and
" Sister Witeveens requested.
: need to know that I am alive.
ove him as you say you do, do

d replied, "You need to do it —
come out of this convent, leave
n. I won't — not unless he asks
because I won't lie to him."
ediately respond. She began to
u." She then left.

Finn sighed again and looked at Moira, "We bett‹
at that robot tonight. I won't to look at it too – st·
want to install the wings onto my exosuit – the ope
should make adequate testing grounds. You'd best s
Tristan's mom and the others than join me on deat·

"I'm not staying here."

"Hmph, this place would serve you more good t·
me," Finn rebuked. "You heard them – it's an uphi·
here on out. I'm going to war with the Chosen…"

"And do what? See that you don't return lik·
didn't? To be like Ms. Black and go anyways? I hav·
– I'm not religious. I'm certainly not going to star·

"A life with Sister Witeveens and Mother Doh·
under their schismatic order, would do you better t·
This is your ticket out of this mess. Besides, sounc
make a friend with one of them."

"No way. I would rather join you in whateve·
you're about to walk into," Moira responded takir·
breath. "You may need my help."

"You can remote in."

"It's not the same," Moira replied. "I'm not a·
Finn. My dad was a former cop, and he made sure t·
of that experience with his little girl. I can hold m·

Finn simply looked at her.

"I'm not going anywhere," she repeated.

Act 5, Scene 2

The next day, Moira and Finn joined the nuns, pastor, and few Eastern Catholics for Divine Liturgy (Mass) inside of the church. The church interior was small, but organized and clean with pews on red carpet. The side of the church had small arched overhang windows besides the pews with icons below. In front of the final row of pews, there was an open space with a shrine on the left and right, one of the Virgin Mary and the other of Jesus Christ holding an open book with the Greek letters for alpha and omega. The sanctuary in this church was raised above a set of steps, but the altar on the other side was hidden by a wooden fence that had four arched icons, two smaller icons between them, and then a gate door in the middle with two icons of angels. The icons were depictions of saintly figures with gold backgrounds, halos around their heads, beautifully painted. The fence was ornated in gold-colored or painted wood designs. At either side of the gate were lit candles, and at the start of the liturgy, the gates were opened to reveal the altar and at the end they were closed. The sanctuary was an arched space and the wall behind the altar showed a depiction of the Prophet Elijah on a flame chariot rising to heaven where there was a depiction of the Father, Son, and Holy Spirit.

At the insistence of Mother Doherty and Sister Witeveens, Moira and Finn stayed at the monastery through Sunday, which gave Finn time to equip and test the function of his exoskeleton suit with the wing attachment, but he was unable to get the flight function to work although he did manage to get the wings to allow him to hover in place above a few inches off the ground and glide from place to place. Although, by the end of his tests, he ran through the last of his fuel cell, at which point he gave in and retired for the day. As promised, Sister Witeveens provided them with access to the droid that was recovered from the GDP headquarters, which was in pieces. Moira began to attempt to hack into the robot, while Finn examined the armor. By the end of the day, Moira and Finn split up again only to reconvene at breakfast.

Father Charon blessed both Moira and Finn in the early morning before their departure, and they said farewell to both Mother Doherty, Mother Josephine, and Sister Witeveens. The SUV travelled eastward along the same route that brought them to Jefferson, and when they returned to the interstate highway, they continued south where they then took an alternative route that took them southwest. By late morning, Finn looked ahead as they arrived at the outskirts of the nature preserve. The road to the preserve took them to a flatland with mountains and hills in the distance around them, while in the immediate surroundings was nothing more than grassland that stretched for miles at either direction.

"I don't even know where to find this volcano," Finn remarked, looking ahead at the many mountains. "Are we going the right way?"

"Yeah, just keep going along the road. You'll want to take us off-road at some point. We looked over the maps to find the most ideal entry point into the facility, and this will save us almost an entire day's hike."

As they continued to drive along, Finn began to see some snowcapped mountains on the horizon directly ahead. The grass around them became drier too and came in patches of dry dirt. After a few more miles, the pair began to notice patches of dark brown land on the left as well as the presence of a wide mound in the distance.

"Is that it?" Finn questioned, unimpressed. "I was expecting a ginormous mountain that we'd have to scale. I think I could climb that in twenty minutes tops."

"We're not going to climb the volcano, *Louis*," Moira replied, annoyed. "Why would we want to do that? The sisters told us to find the crevasse down that'll take us to the entrance into the mine."

"All that I remember from the briefing last night is to watch out for lava pools," Finn responded. "I'm more worried about our clothes setting ablaze from afar. I didn't anticipate we'd be climbing any mountains, *Isadore*. No less a volcano – least of us have the equipment to do that."

"Even if we were climbing the volcano, it would be more than possible. What you're seeing ahead, the pioneers and indigenous people used to use as a waypoint. It's a young volcanic dome, barely even a few hundred thousand of years old."

"Aw, is that all?" Finn sarcastically replied.

"Ugh… turn left ahead…"

Finn turned the vehicle onto a dirt road that began to take them into the nature preserve. They began to travel down and around a hill on their left. There were a few lanky trees around their position, and the shrubs on the ground varied from dry to green. There were a few boulders positioned about, but they were broken and fragmented. They were also colored dark brown to black. As they travelled deeper into the lands, the sand-like dirt became replaced with plain brown dirt like that of commercial soil, and the number of shrubs, bushes, trees, and patches of grass dwindled. They drove around the hills and occasionally met signs that said, 'Warning: Lava Field' to others that said 'Warning: Lava – Hot' to others that just said 'Watch your step'. After a few minutes, the land became flat and stony at the sides, and they approached a hill ahead of them with a fork in the dirt road. After approximately fifteen minutes driving along a dirt road, they came out to a flat enclosure with boulders surrounding them and a rugged terrain ahead.

"Suppose this be the end of the line," Finn muttered. He parked at the very end, turned off the SUV, and then began to step out. The pair looked around – the air was tame and temperature mild. There was a burning smell in the distance, but no smoke in sight. The ground at their feet was smooth and tender. Finn equipped the high-energy rifle and exosuit with a new fuel cell, sporting the propulsion upgrade and the glider wings, while Moira equipped the grenade launcher, and the modified optic camouflage tailored to her body size. She closed the SUV door and then joined Finn as he climbed up a boulder and looked ahead. "Blimey... I can see for miles on end. You were right, this place is as big as Berwick-Northumbria."

Finn climbed down and began to proceed forward into the nature preserve. They took their first steps and immediately found themselves in a sea of broken brown rocks in varying shapes and sizes. In small patches in and around there was a greyish-brown thick dirt.

"Ugh, it's like being at one of them awful beaches in Harlech... when the tide is out," Finn complained, carefully stepping around. "I really hope this isn't the brunt of it."

"Barely a few minutes in, and you're already complaining," Moira responded. "If it's so much of a burden, why don't you fly over it."

Finn did not respond. He instead continued to step over the rocks. As they continued to traverse over, Finn looked up to smoky and hazy skies as the sun shined down through. The haze was thick, and the heat was intense, though not from the sun but the air. The path ahead of them went up and down, up and down, as there was no consistency in the landscape though it remained smooth to the sights as they could see ahead for miles and yet still exhausted themselves with upwards ascents for a minute to a descent the next minute. Eventually, the rocks became greyer and more clumped together, which was easier to traverse. The ground then smoothed out some more as the rocks became entrenched in the ground and could easily be stepped over from clump to clump. The ground then smoothed out once again as it was just a flat rocky plateau. The pair passed a fissure in the ground, at which point Finn stopped and looked over to Moira.

"Reckon we stop now for lunch, or continue on? I don't want to trek in the dark," Finn stated. "How much more?"

"How much more? We've barely broken in a kilometer," Moira remarked, looking at the GPS. "We've got at least a lot more than that to go."

Regardless, they stopped for a quick meal as they sat down at a rock and started a quick fire. They each ate some rations, newer rations that they had bought from an army surplus store.

"Hiking in the states isn't what I had on my bingo card for this month," Finn remarked. "Still though, it's nice to be out from the cold… it's quite nice around here. Could almost take my jacket off."

"I was worried it might be a little warm around here," Moira remarked, looking around. "When do you think they do their transport?"

"Probably at night when nobody can see," Finn responded. "Wouldn't want anyone to know their little secret…" He looked around himself as he sipped his coffee. "What do you reckon made the land around this place like this?"

"I don't know. I don't remember what I learned in earth science class…"

"In keeping with what I said about the beaches, it's really as though this entire place once was underwater…" Finn expressed. "Now it's all land…"

Both Moira and Finn jerked their heads over to the fissure as they heard a hiss of air protrude outwards. Finn shielded his face from the radiation of warm air that towards them.

"Bloody hell…" Finn expressed, "wouldn't want to have been standing there. It'd be one hell of a bidet."

Moira laughed and looked at him. He held a plain face as he rubbed his neck, noticed her smile and then raised his own smile.

"Right, enough sitting around," Finn remarked, pouring his coffee onto the fire. "Let's get on with it…"

The pair stood up and proceeded forward along the path ahead. The terrain shifted between totally rugged, to partially rugged, to smooth, to then clumps of rock again. The texture shifted between rough and coarse rocks, to stony surfaces, to coarse dirt to a mixture of sand and dirt. The vegetation continued to range from small plants growing out cracks between the rocks, to small coniferous trees growing in solitude, and a few patches of moss on the sides of boulders. The wildlife was non-existent, at least to the naked eye. Neither Finn nor Moira saw any birds in the air, or little critters around the crags, or at worse a predator or its prey. The pair walked along the ground at their feet with caution at every step. No wind came through the land, and even as the sun beat down upon them, its stare was often blocked by the clouds every so often that brought light and took light away from them. As they continued to travel along, they eventually found some natural distinctions in the landscape as they found a very narrow and low-level cave entrance in the ground. The entrance into the cave was through a steep drop in the ground into the unknown beneath where the ground consisted of piles of stones. The pair traversed around the cave, meeting holes in the ground that dropped down into the same cavern. They carefully navigated around these collapsed sections. Eventually, they reached a boulder where Finn, using his exosuit, hopped onto and looked ahead. Finn stood from above and looked out ahead with his binoculars, but the landscape was more or less the same.

Finn ran off the end of the boulder and the wings allowed him to glide down and onto the ground. A few feet from above the ground, the propulsion system kicked in to break his fall, and he dropped down onto the craggy ground.

"Aren't you having a fun time," Moira remarked as she joined him.

"I don't suppose the ability to glide will bode well in a cave system," Finn replied. "I may as well make the most of it."

The pair continued along the same terrain as they walked side by side with each other. They caught up in silence as they enjoyed the scenery around them with Finn looking often towards the volcano ahead.

"Say, *Louis...*" Moira remarked. "Can I ask you a question?"

"At this point I should say no," Finn replied, "but seeing as how we've got to travel together for the foreseeable future, I'll say yes."

Moira smirked and then said, "Okay – it's just a small question because I don't know, but what's a seminary?"

"Ah, yes," Finn replied, pausing for a moment as he walked along. "Well, you know how doctors prepare to be doctors by going to medical school, and lawyers prepare to be lawyers by going to law school? Well, priests become priests by going to the seminary..."

"Oh," Moira responded, lowering her smile, "that... explains a lot actually..."

"What do you mean?"

"No, it's just – that explains why you brought it up to the nuns at the convent."

"Truthbetold, I was attempting to flex on them to get some leverage. I thought they may have well respected me if I told them about it – seems to not have worked as much as promising to not tell Tristan about his mother being alive... which saying it aloud doesn't seem like the kindest act of charity."

"So that nun, Sophia, is Tristan's biological mom?"

"Yeah..."

"I thought his parents died."

"Yeah... it's complicated. You see, when Tristan was young, his mother created him in a tube – which for Catholics is kind of an ethical problem – taking the seed of a man she loved as a teenager – again, another ethic problem, and she, through her own hubris and sin, had a virgin birth, but as you well know now, those nuns aren't likeable people and have plenty of people who want them dead, so to keep Tristan safe and not have him be raised by a bunch of nuns, was sent to live with his aunt and uncle when he was close to a year old or so. Tristan didn't know he was adopted, so he assumed his aunt and uncle were his biological mother and father, especially after they died, and later found out they were his aunt and uncle. I believe I mentioned him, but that supersoldier, Maximillian Bauer, he was Tristan's biological father – that nun's lover, the one that saved the town."

"Oh... right..."

"Anyways, Tristan was under the impression that Audric Zimmerman had killed his mum a few days after they met on their own trip to the convent, but I suppose that's not true. I don't know – I'm stumped on whether to tell the poor lad, but they made some good points. I don't want it to affect his marriage to Diana, or cause Diana to suffer, but at the same time, Tristan's a hardened man now. He's dealt with his past and moved past it, so I don't see there being the extent of harm that they expressed. I don't think they know my good friend the way I do, but I don't want to cause any storms in their life so I trust that Sister Sophia will do what is right..."

"You really think so?"

"I hope so," Finn remarked. "The least she can do now is correct her ways. I swear, that entire religious order needs to cease to exist. They're so much fewer than the Chosen and yet they're just as dangerous if not more. I'm often reminded that the sinful actions of a Catholic priest are so much more deadlier and sinister than those of a layman or woman because of the scandal it can lead to – a priest represents not just the Church on Earth, but is meant to be like another Christ. The most sinister man in my mind is one that is a priest that acts in contrary to Christ's words and actions -a true anti-Christ. To an extent, the same is true with the Order of St. Athanasius, but that's just so typical for Church history to talk about awful religious orders. The Franciscans, Jesuits... they were all rotten to the core at some point or another, and to an extent still are. Evil festers in no better place than religious orders and institutes not because the Catholic Church is evil, but precisely because it is good and there is no more vulnerable place than to attack the imperfect and easily targeted humans within to spread chaos and malice. The corruption within the institutional Church, the clergy, and the Vatican drive me nuts…"

"So why do you want to be a priest?"

"Because… it's so much more than the Church itself," Finn replied, looking up to the sky. "I'm not going it for the people within… I have my personal reasons…"

"Alright," Moira replied, "I can respect that…"

"I was supposed to attend the seminary in Edmonton this September," Finn remarked, looking back down. "I worked myself up to this moment… it was a hard decision to make to go through the application process, and I was accepted last month. And now… I may not even get to ever return home now…"

"Sorry…"

"Not your fault," Finn replied, shaking his head. "I don't blame you even if you've dragged me into a fight with the Chosen. I'm where I need to be."

Moira didn't respond as they continued to roam over the craggy earth.

"What about you?" Finn questioned. "What do you want to do? You say you went to school for programming, but what's that going to get you? What's your aspirations?"

"Aspirations? I'd like to pay off the debt I accumulated – that'd be nice. Right now, being able to return home to Allabrese, or even Edmonton doesn't sound half bad. A stable paying job would be nice that allows me to put my skills to practical use too…"

"Suppose there's not much of a market for hackers," Finn replied.

"I'm more than just a hacker, *Louis*," Moira remarked. "I'm a software engineer – I create strings of programming, put them together, sell them, do small jobs, do big jobs."

"Oh yeah, and is staring at a computer screen what you want to do with your life?"

"Hey, I didn't judge you when you wanted to be a Catholic priest," Moira replied. "I could have made at least a few dozen jokes, some of them inappropriate, but I didn't."

"I certainly wouldn't have found them very amusing…" Finn responded. "You can also stop calling me by my middle name."

"Not how you introduced yourself back there…"

"I was known as Finn Louis Cunningham for most of my life," Finn remarked. "My mother, when I was born, named me Louis, but that's not the name that my adoptive folks wanted me to have, so they called me Finn and let Louis be my middle name. I always wondered growing up why it was spelt Louis and not Lewis, as it's supposed to be spelt in British English, and I suppose I know the reason why now. When I migrated to the United States and Canada, I changed my name around to Louis Finn Cabernet – thought it'd also help avoid any alarm bells."

"You really wanted in the United Kingdom?"

"Absolutely," Finn replied, "but I suppose that's what I get for sticking my neck out for childish reasons. I was not a very nice person, though I suppose to an extent I can still sympathize with my past beliefs. I hold firm on the importance of conservation and stewardship towards the planet, but all the rest – the violence, that was unnecessary, and I see the errors of my ways. At any rate, most people who know me call me Finn, while those just meeting me typically learn me as Louis, if I don't insist they call me Finn that is."

"You prefer Finn?"

Finn shrugged his shoulders and said, "I prefer to be called what I'm familiar with. Sometimes Louis can be less intimate and more formal. I let others decide how they would like to call me..."

"I think Louis is a nice name," Moira confessed, "but to be honest, I'm going to stick to calling you Finn."

"As you please."

The pair continued to roam the nature preserve as they stepped down from the craggy surface and entered into a smoother and softer land. The ground at their feet was smooth, but fine. Finn knelt down to put his hand through the terrain, lifting up a pile of dark grey sand-like material. He let the grains fall from his fingers before he let it all down. He looked ahead of him as the terrain continued further along. There were a few patches of coarse dirt, especially around where bushes and other vegetation grew together, but otherwise, the land continued in this same manner for the foreseeable distance.

"The ground is like ashes..." Finn stated, seeing some smoldered tree remains. "We should be careful – there's likely fires activating at random through here."

The pair proceeded and reached a barbed wire fence that was approximately five feet tall. A sign post a few yards down on the left stated 'Warning – No Trespassing' and another sign below it said, 'Danger – Lava Pools & Volcanic Activity' with a caricature of a figure caught on fire. Finn looked around the fence and found a collapsed section further along that they travelled through. They entered inside and continued their hike along as they followed the GPS to reach their waypoint. They noticed that they were not entirely free from the stretches of rock as they came in piles, especially large boulders entombed in the earth or wide sections of just a rock-hard surface. The fissures became more common, but they did not see them vent vapors upwards though they nonetheless steered away from them. They were closer to the base of the volcano as it now loomed ahead of them. After a few more minutes of wandering around the plains, Moira and Finn found a large crater-like ditch. The sides of the ditch were marked with a few stones, but also streaks of orangish-brown dirt around otherwise plain brown dirt. They travelled around the crater with a diameter of close to fifty feet, The pair proceeded along and passed a few rock formations on approach to an ascent that brought them to a clearing with ponds of water surrounded by steam.

"What are these…?" Moira questioned as they passed along. "Are these safe?"

"It's certainly safer than lava," Finn responded, approaching a pond. He raised a hand over the hot spring before he took out his water bottle and scooped some out. He then placed his hand inside and closed his eyes. "Quite warm… perhaps a few degrees over fifty C. I would still disinfect the water though…"

Moira picked up some water while Finn continued to wash his face before he stood up. He turned to Moira and the pair continued to trek through.

"Bloody shame I'm not here on vacation… would be nice to take a dip – if I make it out of this fight to the death with the Chosen, I may just take a vacation to the hot springs near Jasper or Banff."

"Oh, those are nice," Moira replied. "I was around for a bachelorette party when I was younger. I highly recommend."

From the hot springs, the pair continued to travel forward where Finn took out the GPS to examine their location.

"We're getting to be close… there's a drop further ahead – not sure how steep."

The pair walked another mile south as came around to the center of the preserve. They continued to roam the ash-covered grounds when they reached the waypoint. They came to the edge of a cliff with a steep drop downwards of close to a hundred feet with another hundred feet gap to the other side. The canyon tore through the land and went along as they found themselves at a gulch.

"Alright," Finn expressed, activating the wings. "Just like we talked about…"

"Yeah…" Moira remarked, putting her arms around Finn to embrace him.

Finn kicked himself off with the propulsion system, and then began to glide down precariously to the bottom with the aid of the gliders. He found himself at the bottom as he landed upon the gravel surface. Moira let go as soon as they made foothold, and they began to carry on foot. They passed a few more hot spring pools and then began to reach an ascent along what was none other than the base of the volcano proper. The ascent kept them in the canyon though, which wrapped around the side, taking them underneath natural arches until they reached a cave that curved about. The cave exited out and they continued their ascent, reaching a cliff wall that they had to physically climb. Finn made use of the propulsion jets to ascend the steeper bits and then extended his hand over to Moira to help her up. They continued up nearly twenty-feet before they looked ahead at what lay ahead as the skies began to darken. The canyon continued to stretch forward as it became more difficult to see as the sun set, so the pair decided to stop at a small hot spring pool.

"I hope the nights won't be so cold out here," Finn remarked. "This hot spring should keep us warm. Let's rest up and continue tomorrow – there's still a fair distance to go."

Act 5, Scene 3

Finn quickly jerked his body forward from his sleeping bag as he heard a patter of movement from outside. He picked up the high-energy rifle in his tent and quickly opened his tent flap to look out, but he could not see anything as it was too dark. He knelt down and looked around the immediate area for a few minutes, only seeing the starry night sky up above. The campfire had burned out and he wore his aviator jacket with a wifebeater underneath. He slowly closed his tent flap and went back to lie down in his sleeping bag, placing the rifle beside him. He looked at the rifle as he kept his eyes open, slowly closing them to drift back to sleep again. Suddenly, the noise came again, and he immediately grabbed the rifle. He stayed put in his sleeping bag as he heard the patter of mechanic limbs cross from behind. He brought himself onto his knee, and then crouched forward towards the tent flap. He opened the tent flap and then looked around again. An hour or two had passed, and it was now dawn. Finn looked about, standing up and examining his surroundings before he went back into his tent. He put his cargo pants and boots on and then proceeded to examine the surroundings in greater detail as they remained in the canyon trench. As he returned, he began to light a fire and cook some oatmeal in some water from the hot spring. He sat down on the opposite side from his tent and looked about. He then stood up to put on his exosuit as it lay outside, the wing attachment being too large to bring into his tent now. Moira woke up and joined Finn by the campfire and she quietly ate her breakfast. She took advantage of the pool of water nearby to brush her teeth and wash her face, while Finn packed up the tents and put out the fire. Once they were ready, they proceed along the canyon.

The ground at their feet was pure grey stone. The camp was set up atop of a ledge, so they went down and continued forward as the path brough them down a few mild slopes as they began to descend again. They reached another ledge which looked down, and sure enough on either side of the path they saw pools of molten lava that glowed upwards and provided minimal light. They began to descend down the slopes where the heat from either pool radiated strongly. They began to cautiously walk down the middle as they passed the lava and continued on the path ahead. Some rocks that stuck out had reddish-orange veins as though lava was infused within them like blood to the earth. Once they passed the pools, they came up a slope that became steep towards the end, prompting Finn to jump up and then lower his hand down to help Moira up. They then turned around and looked at a few boulders and a smooth gulley of hardened basalt that stood out from the rest of the stone. The smooth basalt continued along the right-side like a cascade. They went down and began to reach some pointed rocks as the canyon narrowed. They met with a large boulder between two of the pointed rocks, prompting them to go around the side and shimmy around as they walked on gravel ground and then came around to a hot spring pool on the other side. They continued down along a mixture of gravel and hardened stone, passing shallow pools of hot water and a bit of steam that rose up as they came around this section of the canyon. The path began to narrow out again as they reached a ledge that looked down to another descent downwards.

The canyon below was very narrow at the top, but widened out towards the bottom significantly. The drop below was another forty to fifty feet. Like yesterday, Moira took hold of Finn before they glided down to the bottom and then continued along the path ahead. They passed a few more gulleys, these smaller, which had smooth basalt stone run down like a stream and stretch up on the inner walls. They continued along the narrow path, eventually reaching another canyon ledge on the left hand side with metal poles installed into the stone. As they continued around the curved canyon, they found some rail lines that proceeded along. They followed the rail lines as it took them along the same path as the canyon, going around at a descent. They reached a wider space with equipment and metal crates set about, but there was no sight of any supervision. Above them was a bridge that passed through one crack to another, and ahead was a slope that went upwards. They followed up the slope, Finn requiring to boost himself up and then pull Moira up from a boulder. They came around to a continuation of the canyon where they then found some more hot springs. There were also some fissures. They passed along and began to continue down where they looked below to see another canyon below them, but it was too dark to see the bottom. They instead continued down this path where they came across a bridge and cave walls at the end.

"I think for all intents and purposes, this cave should be the entrance into the mine," Finn concluded, looking at the GPS. "If not one of the entrances…"

The pair began to step inside the cave. The ground at their feet was made of gravel and the air inside was hot. In the midst of the path was the end of a rail line. Against the right wall were lamps connected and installed within the stone wall. They continued down the pathway as it began to wrap around and curve to the left, bringing them into a large cavern. The rail line continued across, curving and sloping downwards to reach another cave tunnel. Nearby, there were some mine carts. The descent down from the cliff side took them to a pool of lava below.

"It's quiet…" Finn expressed looking around.

"So what? You think they're expecting us to raid their mining operation?"

"I would have expected a bit more defense," Finn replied. "Instead, we just waltzed in here unopposed. I don't like it…"

"Do you think they abandoned this mine?"

"No," Finn replied, looking at the lamps that provided light. "I just think… nevermind. Let's get going."

Finn walked over to one of the mine carts, picked it up, and placed it on the rail line. He then helped Moira inside before he began to give them a slow boost and then hopped in himself. The cart slowly rolled forward, reaching the slope at the end and then going forward. The cart went down and streamed through the tunnel at the end, rolling down and then continuing straight. The cart took them to a larger cavern space where there were some more rail lines below, coming around to a stop as they lost momentum. Both Moira and Finn hopped out and continued down the side of the rail line on foot, eventually reaching a collapsed cave in. Finn walked over to examine the boulders, attempting to push the top ones, but they were too large.

"I'm going to get the mine cart and push it over here," Finn expressed, pausing for a moment as he wiped some sweat from his forehead. "You may want to get that grenade launcher of yours ready."

Moira raised an eyebrow and did just that. Finn returned with the mine cart, tilted it over and then left it on his side. They used the mine cart as a shield while Moira prepared the grenade launcher with some rounds they purchased at an army surplus store. She fired two rounds, and the detonation was large enough to blow the rocks in a way that Finn could push through. They then continued forward with the mine cart, eventually reaching another slope. Moira and Finn hopped aboard and were carried down the line as they were brought out to a larger cavern with a tall cliff wall at the other side.

"I've never seen anything like this…" Finn expressed, looking about all the lava beneath them at a beachhead of gravel. "What could they possibly have been mining here?"

Finn helped Moira climb the side of the cliff as he used his propulsion jets to boost himself up, and then lowered his hand to help her up. They eventually reached the top of the cliff where the rail lines ended that went down and over the cliff. There were more mine carts lying about, but most of them appeared broken. There were also some crates that held some rocks, and a few machines lying about including excavation drills. The pair walked forward and passed under a concrete frame in the stone walls with metal doors either side that were partially open. Ahead of them was a corridor with a metal caged catwalk raised above a lava pool. There were also some pipes raised above, some of which hissed steam. A rail line was parallel to the catwalk. The pair approached the cage and began to walk down to the other side where there was another set of blast doors.

On the other side of the blast doors, they found themselves in a square canyon with a tall ceiling. The entire canyon had metal platforms around it that allowed one to navigate within as there were no rocky surfaces to walk on. From the platform they arrived on, there were a set of stairs and ramp that led up to a circular platform with an 'H' on it. The rail line crossed over with a perpendicular rail line that went left and right and continued forward at the approach of another set of blast doors, but these were shut. This area connected with a set of stairs to the left that went up to a crane with a long boom, or arm, that dangled over the helipad. To the right was a shelter with a set of metal windows that looked out and a metal door. A sign on the door read 'Security'. Besides this shelter was a set of stairs that went up to a catwalk that continued around the perimeter of the cavern. Beneath the platforms, at a drop of around fifty feet, there was a lava pool across the entire ground floor. To the left and right of the helipad were platforms that approached additional blast doors, one of which was partially open and the other one closed.

Finn approached the security station, kicking the door open and then finding a control panel with levers that opened specific doors. A map of the space labeled which doors were open and closed, including the set of blast doors above. He pulled the lever for the blast doors above, causing an alarm sound to ring and sirens to the flash. Suddenly, blast doors from above began to open, exposing them to the sky and natural light from the sun.

"What are you doing?" Moira questioned. "You're going to let them get us. What if they send robots after us?"

"Relax, I know what I'm doing," Finn remarked. "I want them to come… if they dare. Look around you – do you see any robots defending their most valuable mining operation?"

"You're going to get us killed."

"No, I'm not… I…"

The pair stopped as they heard mechanical patter against the stone walls. The pattering echoed around them. They both looked out the door but could not see anything, so Finn looked at Moira and took point. She withdrew her holster blaster, and the pair looked about, but saw nothing.

"What do you think that was…?"

"I don't know…" Finn replied, checking the area.

Moira took her laptop out and placed it on the table. She began to attempt to hook it into the computer system.

"A lot of stuff here looks pretty old," Moira stated. "I don't think there's a computer security network to breach, but I'll take a look and see if there's anything else of use."

Finn approached the control panel again and pulled a lever for the doors ahead of them which went into an area labeled 'smelting chamber.' The doors did not open. The map listed all areas accessible to them, where they had just come from the south mine, but there was still an east and west mine. As Moira began to boot up the computer systems, a monitor turned on above the control panel which showed low quality closed-circuit camera footage from the other areas. Finn stepped forward to take a look, but did not see anything of note other than motion – machinery at work. He did find another map on the control panel though which showed steam pressure levels in all areas, as well as room temperatures. Some of these rooms were over fifty degrees in temperature.

"I'm going to get a heat stroke being down here," Finn groaned. He looked up to see some vents above them. "Can you see if there's some sort of aircon...?"

"You mean air conditioning? Yeah..."

"This place is powered through geothermal energy – if it was abandoned, who knows for how long the power has just run and run..." Finn stated. "The pressure system seems to be okay... I think if we're to bring this place down, it'll be through the boilers. It looks like each mine has a boiler and generator of its own, but the one for this central chamber is in the smelting chamber."

"Well, I still have about four grenade rounds – one for each quadrant," Moira stated as the air conditioning began to turn on.

"I don't think that'd be such a good idea," Finn remarked. "I don't know if you noticed, but it's quite hot around here and the risk for a spontaneous explosion are pretty high. No, if we're going to do this, it can easily be done by overloading the boilers and causing them to explode. If you take out the boiler, you take out the generator and probably do some bad damage in the process to each mine as well."

"Holy crap..." Moira remarked. "There's quite a lot of data here... it doesn't seem like any controls are connected to the computer system here, but there is a bank of information. I'm going to siphon through some of this crap while you get to work."

"I'll need to also find a way through these blast doors," Finn remarked. "There should be excavators around – maybe I could drill through the doors. Ugh... it's so hot out there and it's grown so cool in here." He removed his backpack and dropped it down. He also set the high-energy rifle down. Finn removed his jacket, took off his exosuit and removed his flannel shirt. He then put the exosuit back on, prompting Moira to look at the remains of burn scars on his arms. She looked back down at her computer as she attempted to avoid eye contact. "Okay… you still have your radio?" he asked.

"Of course."

"I'll be in touch in case I need anything."

Finn left the room and began to go up the ramp that came around to the helipad. He then went down and approached the partially open blast doors. The blast doors were held open by a lodged mine cart on the other side. He stopped as he was about to climb over, hearing the echoes of some movement from afar. He looked behind him but saw nothing. He then climbed up the mine cart and went over, entering a rectangular wide corridor. He reached a ledge and saw there was a caged platform that went down to the other side. There was also a rail line that went to the other side too. He entered the caged bridge and crossed over the lava pool in the room, reaching a set of blast doors that were open. He then stepped through and found himself in a large, tall cave reinforced with steel pillars at either corner.

The east mine consisted of this tall cavern going upwards thirty feet with a grated platform above that formed an interstitial space approximately twenty feet tall. Likewise, Finn arrived and stood atop of a platform that was raised above a sublevel at least another five feet tall below him where there were some machines and conveyor belts. Both ahead and on the right were tall rectangular tunnel corridors from pillar to pillar, also ten feet tall, but around twenty-five feet wide. On the immediate left was a shelter with a single sloped roof, and beside the shelter was a caged stairwell and an elevator system within the stone wall that went either up or down. Approximately twenty feet at the start of each tunnel were some large metal trap doors to the left that led to conveyor belts underneath and took either rocks or ores to the interstitial space below, transporting them to an unknown location. On the right were some large heavy-duty machines that were connected to tall power banks, noticeable by large heavy-duty power cables that ran up to the interstitial space above. Finn also took note of pipes that ran around the space above. A mine cart rail connected along the main floor platform and went into the elevator. Lying about the main floor were some machines with thick wheels, and others were mine carts, both the standard ones already seen and also some others that had motors on the front. As Finn examined these machines, he noticed that in the cabin of one of them was a robot similar to the one that he had examined the other day, but without any sort of weaponry. The robot was simply an anthropoid-like automaton, but hunched over the wheel. Some other machines in the room had robotic arms. The ends of the arms had drills, saws, and other tools to cut through and chip away at rock. These arms could be connected to the mine carts or on these separate four-wheel self-propelled machines. There were other machines parked in the large room, some of which had different tools unlike the arms.

"Anybody home...?" Finn muttered to himself, looking around. He examined some of the machines that were lying around. He then walked towards one of the dark tunnels from where he could hear some sort of machines ahead. He caught a glance at a machine make a pass through a perpendicular tunnel, and continue along as the machines mined and mined. "So, this is automated mining then, huh?"

Finn entered the shelter where he found a similar control panel to the one in the central chamber, but this one had controls to the blast doors out of the mine as well as a monitor of steam levels within this section. He found a map that detailed the boiler to be above. There were no controls to stop the automated mining operation, or even interfere with the boiler or generator, so he left the shelter and climbed the stairs to go up. He looked over at the pipes and saw them connect to some water tanks. He followed the pathway and saw they went leftwards, behind the elevators, so he followed through a concrete corridor that took him to a large room where there was a pool of hot water. The pipes connected out from the other end of the elevator, and then went upwards past an upper ledge. This room was less warm than the others, but ahead was a pool of hot water. A caged platform and staircase was collapsed, prompting Finn to jump up using his propulsion jets and reach the top. He pushed through a set of metal doors and found himself in a maintenance room where there was a boiler and generator that hummed. He approached the valve, but before he began to turn, he stepped back and returned to the mine.

Finn looked at the machines around and found one that had an excavation drill head. He hopped up and found another robot inside, pulling it out and turning the ignition as he held on to the side of the cart, but the machine did not start. He stepped out and found the battery pack to be missing, so he took one out from the other machines and installed it, and then he sat back down to turn it on. The machine roared to life, and he precariously drove it over to the mine rail, unable to sit down in the cabin due to his exosuit, guiding and causing the wheels to connect and then driving it forward as he left the mine. He brought the excavation drill towards the blast doors with the lodged mine cart, pushing the cart forward to dislodge the cart, blocking the doors. Finn backed up and then began to take the drill towards the doors, busting through them with ease and then continuing forward at which point he stopped. Finn looked behind and retracted his steps to return to the boiler room where he turned the valve and overloaded the boiler.

The pipes in the room began to burst, prompting him to escape outwards as the boiler exploded behind him, setting the generator off and causing the room to cave in. The lights flickered and turned off as he returned to the mine chamber, but he turned on his headset lamp and then returned back to the central chamber.

"Alright, I've taken out the east side," Finn remarked over the radio. "Can you check and see if there are controls to move the central platform? I found an excavator to drill through the west mine blast doors."

"I'll see what I can do."

Finn drove the excavator towards the blast doors, but this time he was met with some resistance, sending sparks flying. The excavator punched forward and eventually broke through, creating a hole in the rusted metal doors. Finn backed up the cart and brought it towards the helicopter landing pad. He then continued forward down a similar corridor as those behind, but with water below instead of lava. He then found himself in a rectangular chamber similar to the one behind, and with two tunnels ahead, and one on the right again. The catwalk platforms above were caged and went into separate tunnels. The tunnel on the left sloped downwards – activity in this room was noisier than in the other room. Finn looked around for any sight of pipes, but couldn't find it. He entered a shelter on the right and then began to climb up to the platforms above where he followed through a tunnel that came out behind the elevators again. This led into a large room with another pool of water. The pipes extracted water and stored them in tanks in this room, but the rest of the pipes led into a side room where the generator could be found. The room was divided by a cage from where the boiler could be found on the other side. One of the tunnels on the other end led into the boiler room. Finn backtracked and returned to the catwalks, stepping towards one of the many tunnels, but the connection of tunnels created a labyrinth. He returned to the main room and began to look around. He then approached the middle tunnel and came around to a cave in. He pushed against one of the rocks to cause them to fall backwards, and then climbed over to continue down the path. He found himself in a large room with another pool at the bottom, pipes that pumped water and stored them, and also pumps that took that water up and away. All the catwalks and stairs were destroyed, so Finn jumped atop of the caged platform and then began to walk around to the stairwell. He climbed up and then jumped towards a ledge. From the ledge, Finn jumped up and glided across to the other side where he then continued down to find the boiler room. He found a door in the cage that separated the generator portion, opened it, and then went over to the boiler to release the valve and make his escape. By the time Finn returned to the central chamber, Moira had figured out how to turn the helipad platform rails. Finn drove the excavator onto the platform, and then Moira began to turn it around.

Once the excavator faced the blast doors, he let the machine drive on its own while he exited out and watched from behind. The sparks flew and it pierced through the metal, eventually continuing on its own. Finn caught up from behind and watched the machine slowly drive forward. The machine reached another set of blast doors that it began to cut into, but as it attempted to pierce through another time, the machine died out.

"Dammit…" Finn remarked, opening the rear hatch with his gloved hands. Smoke poured out as the battery caught on fire. He removed the battery and tossed it aside. "I'm going to need to find a new battery… I've still got to clear the south mine out seeing as we can escape from the central chamber elevator shaft. I'll be right back again…"

"Roger dodger," Moira replied. "When you're finished, swing by the security office. I've made a breakthrough in this data."

"Copy."

Finn rushed forward and returned to the central chamber. He walked over and then returned to the south mine. However, as he did so, he noticed the caged bridge was collapsed.

"What the…"

Finn looked around, but saw nothing around. He jumped off the ledge and then glided towards the top of the caged bridge, climbing up the ceiling and reaching the other side. He then returned into the south mine where he looked around more carefully. There were numerous older mine carts around, and the rail paths ahead appeared sporadic. Numerous crates full of rocks were on the left, while a concrete corridor on the left led into a wide tunnel. Finn followed this tunnel and reached an elevator shaft. The shaft took him up a level, opening doors on the opposite end, and presenting a room similar to the others with a main tunnel on the left that led down a slope, and other tunnels on the same plane ahead and to the right. There was an interstitial space below, but no platforms above. Finn looked down and could see pipes along the walls, so he climbed down the stairs and entered the lower level. He crouched down as he moved around, following the pipes as they disappeared into tight gaps and then reappeared elsewhere. He carefully followed along before seeing them go towards the rightward tunnel. He exited out and followed the rightward tunnel, seeing the pipes in the grates at the entrance. He then saw a tunnel side door and followed through as he found the generator and boiler room. Finn looked around, and then began to turn the valve and set the space to destruct.

As Finn exited out, he pulled a battery out from one of the machines and took it with him. However, as he arrived in the elevator shaft, the lights turned off. He looked around and sighed.

"Great..." he remarked, setting the battery aside. He began to examine the elevator shaft, and used the rifle to shoot at the brakes at either end. The shaft then slid down and collapsed at the bottom, prompting him to come around and pick up the battery. He then carried both the rifle and battery, and fell over. Both the wings and the propulsion jets kicked in as he was about to hit the platform, breaking his fall significantly and allowing him to land. He then carried on forward and exited out the south mine. "Let's see what Moira found..."

Act 5, Scene 4

Finn returned to the security station where he shuddered as the cool air hit him as he stepped in.

"It's like a refrigerator in here," Finn expressed. "Alright, so what did you find out."

"It's strange..." Moira expressed, holding her laptop at her side. "I didn't find anything useful in the data, but I did think it was interesting to see that all the data was being exported out to a specific IP address. The only problem is that there's no external network connection in the entire facility. I tried to troubleshoot the problem, but there's just no capability to connect to the outside world from here. Just like the GDP headquarters and convent, we're in a dead-zone, and even with my laptop's own SIM card we bought, I can't get a signal. I wrote down the IP address to investigate later, and then I went in deeper to the network around here.

"The network is a simple one and runs a program that keeps the lights on and everything running in a very precise way. However, as I was digging through, I got a warning that there was some sort of virus that had corrupted the system. I was able to isolate the virus and take a look at its code, and when I did, I found this same word repeated over and over again. Beliyal..."

"Beliyal..?" Finn questioned.

"Yeah, spelt B-E-L-I-Y-A-L," Moira clarified. "Am I saying that right?"

"I think you are..." Finn replied, suspicious. "How many times did you find that word written?"

"It's the only written word," Moira replied. "I saw it more than a hundred times at least... perhaps a thousand times. It's not a command I'm familiar with, which tells me that it's just a name, but I don't know why it's repeated so many times other than to believe that it's just a corruptive agent. Sometimes hackers will throw in something nonsensical as an identifier, so I can only suspect that's what this is…"

"Maybe…" Finn said, "we can talk about it later. I have the battery and I'm going to hook it up. The other one overheated – those excavator drills are tough, but it takes a lot of power to cut through so much metal. Come on, we're almost done here."

Finn left the security station with Moira. Like her, Finn equipped his backpack again and began to come around to the excavator drill to equip the battery.

"Alright, let it rip…" Finn said, coming to the cabin to switch it on. He then stepped back and let it cut through the metal. Sparks flew back and Moira covered her eyes as it did so.

Eventually, the excavator tore through the metal doors and continued forward at a slow pace, but before Finn could step forward, the pair were met with the sudden halt of the drill.

"What the heck…" Finn remarked.

The cart began to tip up and before long it was pushed forward as something crouched through the hole and then spread its arms out. One of these arms held a drill that was brought down and into the motor of the excavator cart, causing sparks to fly out and a small fireball to exhaust upwards. The cart was then thrown towards Finn, who jumped out of the way and landed atop of it. The drill continued to run as the robot gave off a terrible screech.

The enhanced robot that stood before them had a reinforced body size compared to the others they had met so far. It appeared larger and it also had four limbs, two at each side, the two of which had human-like hands with four fingers and a thumb at each one. The other two limbs, the one on its right had an immense drill, while the one on the left had a cannon-like end though with some sort of device pointed forward and sideways at the forearm. One of these gadgets was a shield device that could extend outwards and retract inwards. The creature did just that as it hid the shield and stared towards the pair. The enhanced robot had blue eyes like the others that looked around the room.

Finn immediately aimed and fired the assault rifle, but as he did so the shield popped out immediately as well to cover his left side. Moira on the other hand aimed the grenade launcher and popped a round off at it, sending both her and the robot backwards as it exploded. She shot another one at the creature, prompting it to make a retreat inside. Finn shielded himself with his arms crossed together and then look over at the smoke. He jumped down and ran over to Moira, helping her up onto her feet.

"Are you okay?"

"Yeah…"

"I should have known that thing was around here," Finn remarked. "I've been hearing something running around and spying on us."

"Forget about me – just kill that thing!"

Finn rushed in through the cloud of smoke as he entered into a tall, wide and long corridor with two catwalk platforms at either side of the concrete room, and another two down the middle. The ceiling was arched. The smelting chambers was a hot room with machines that poured liquid metal from casts into vats on either end. There were also sparks that flew further along. The initial half of the room only had the raised platforms and a few casts that were raised above the ground, while the rest of the machinery was two-thirds behind. The rail line continued down the middle where there was an empty cart further ahead. Finn looked around for the enhanced robot but could not find it. He walked with careful step forward and made sure he could not see the creature lingering around. Moira joined him from behind as she walked with a limp.

"Be careful with those," Finn warned. "We may not be in the mines, but we're still in an extreme environment. You could trigger a sudden combustion with that in your hands."

"I know what I'm doing, just go!" Moira shouted at him.

Finn looked at her and then looked ahead. He looked around the smelting chamber and began to climb up a set of stairs to go up a floor while Moira lingered back. She took position behind a mine cart and sat down. She activated the optic camouflage as Finn looked towards her, and then he turned around and continued to look around the environment. He eyed the walls where he caught sight of pipes, but they continued in sporadic directions. As he looked around, he took in the rest of the environment. At the sides of each middle and upper catwalk platforms there was the occasional small tunnel entrance that extended outwards from the smelting chamber, though they were blocked off with metal bars. He looked at two entrances at either side from the section of the mill he was in, and looked further down to see if he could find more, but as he searched around, he heard a heavy object slam down behind him. He immediately turned around and opened fire at the enhanced robot as it approached him with heavy steps. Finn looked and saw the robot loom over him as it span up the drill in its arm and attempted to bring it down onto him. He jumped back and away from the robot, at which point he took a few shots, but the robot quickly activated its shield.

The enhanced robot huddled behind the shield, prompting Finn to jump off and hover above the ground beside the catwalk as it approached him. Finn landed on the platform at the other side and continued to aim his weapon. Suddenly, a grenade launched from the end of the platform and hit the enhanced robot in the back, sending it forward. Finn jumped up to get a boost off the platform and hover in place, and he opened fire at the robot as it lay on the ground. The high-energy rounds made dents into the armor, making a tough impact as it had difficulties in standing up until the two upper arms grabbed the grate and lifted the robot up, pushing off and causing it to do a flip to land on its feet. It then fled forward, jumping off onto the side of the wall and crawling away like a salamander or lizard.

Finn watched it run off and then took in a deep breath. He continued down the platform where the platform into the rest of the mill only continued on the right side, so he stepped down and proceeded to continue through the lower half. He walked with careful steps as he listened to sounds of machines and robots processing metal. He heard the patter of the creature running across the walls again, prompting him to look around to see if he could find it, but it was nowhere to be seen. He then continued forward as he kept himself below the catwalk platform and passed around a large heavy machine. He then heard the sudden thud of the enhanced robot drop down behind him again, prompting him to pivot and open fire. The enhanced robot stomped towards him with its shield raised up and then brought the drill down towards Finn. Finn backed off and the drill broke into the concrete with ease. He looked in horror at the damage and then returned fire at which point he was required to step back. The robot pointed the drill and began to march towards him, which prompted Finn to run away as he climbed up a set of stairs and came above it. The creature lowered its shield and pointed its cannon. Finn stared at the cannon when he noticed a small fire at the end of it, which told him enough to quickly run away before a burst of flames poured out and towards him. He pushed himself forward and then landed on his side. His rifle thrusted ahead, and he crawled towards it, picking it up and running off as the flamethrower continued to spue fire through the catwalk and up towards him. He climbed a ladder nearby, jumping up and taking in a boost from the propulsion jets to get away from the tall column of fire faster as he could feel its heat radiate below him. He climbed up at the top and looked down at the mess of machines, but could not see the robot as it disappeared. Finn watched from above as he attempted to locate the beast, but it was nowhere to be seen.

"Moira, be careful, that thing has a flamethrower," Finn reported in. "As if we had enough troubles as it is…" he muttered to himself.

No response came.

"Moira, do you read me…" Finn repeated.

"I read you, numb-nut," Moira complained. "I'm trying to lay low here…"

"We need to work together if we're going to take this thing out…" Finn remarked. "We've got to use the most of that grenade launcher you have."

"Yeah, well, I got three rounds left with its name on it."

"Come up above," Finn requested. "We can ambush it…"

Finn waited as he looked around. He crossed to the other side of the room at a bridge between the two platforms and kept close eyes around. The noise in the room was loud below, and the clash of metal and the sound of drilling and sawing from further ahead made it difficult to concentrate as any sudden noise caused Finn to turn around as though paranoid. He began to hear the pattering from one side, prompting him to turn and be ready, but the ambush never came. Suddenly, the pattering came again, and he saw the creature crawl up along the wall and come across the ceiling before going down to the other side. Finn attempted to take some shots off at it, but missed and instead hit the concrete. He stopped and knelt down to reload, and as he did so he began to hear the sound of the drill. He looked down to get a look at where it may be but could not see it. After a moment of uncertainty, Finn kicked off the ground and hovered above, at which point he began to wait in midair. He looked about and looked around while he saw Moira on the opposite end as he could see the slight image of distortion from the optic camouflage. He then looked about and began to hear movement from below. Finn waited as he looked about, moving to the other side and it became quiet again.

The enhanced robot climbed up the side of the wall near him after another minute wait, landed on the catwalk and immediately began to come towards Finn with the drill in hand. He pushed himself backwards as it came. The drill tore into the catwalk instead, creating a rift between them as the catwalk collapsed on Finn's side. He pushed himself backwards again as he took some shots off, and the gunfire hit the torso of the robot which rather than defend itself pointed the flamethrower at him and let out a tall flame.

"Hey, asshole!" Moira shouted, standing up and launching a grenade towards it. The grenade impacted directly on the robot and blew it against the concrete wall. The catwalk collapsed at that side and the robot disappeared below.

Finn touched down and then began to look below to see if he could catch sight of the robot, but it was nowhere to be seen. He did catch sight at one of the arms, none with any of the weapons, but still one of the arms nonetheless had blown off. He dropped down and landed atop of the platform, and then jumped off to touch the concrete ground to get a closer look. The hand twitched from where it lay and Finn picked it up with one hand, causing it to twitch and freak out. He quickly threw it into a pool of magma where it sank in. He then turned around as he could hear some sort of maniacal robot laughter in the distance. He began to walk down and go back towards the rest of the smelting chamber, but stopped before he entered through.

"I'm going in!" Finn shouted. "I've got to find this boiler – set the place to blow… I'll make this part of the mine its tomb!"

Finn entered and began to climb up to one of the catwalks that went through this part of the smelting chamber. Moira watched from above and kept a close eye, swapping angles as she walked down the bridge to the other side. He looked about cautiously when he suddenly saw below the beast ram into the pillar beneath Finn's feet. The creature used what remained of the drill and the other arm to knock the pillar off, going to the next one as well as Finn jumped off and attempted to hold his bearings. At the end of the catwalk, Finn turned around and saw it point the flamethrower. He quickly made a side thrust and dodged the flames, lightly grazing his right arm as he felt his arm hairs singe. He flew off into the depths of the smelting chamber as Moira's sights were obscured and she saw it go after him. She went down the catwalk from above, while Finn slid down a ladder staircase and began to hide in the bottom level. He turned around and aimed his rifle the way he came, but the beast did not come after him this way. However, as he stayed put, he heard the drill start up from behind, prompting him to jump out of fright and turn his rifle over to point it at the head of the creature. He shot the head clean off as the high energy rounds hit the neck, causing it to do a flip and land on the ground nearby. The drill missed Finn and hit the concrete beside, locking it in. Finn yelled out in anger as he pointed the rifle close to the body of the beast and shot several rounds inside as it loomed directly over him and struggled to release itself from the concrete. Finally, the other hand grabbed Finn by the shoulder and pulled him out. He kicked off the beast's own shoulder and launched himself out through a hole above, landing on the catwalk above. He pointed his rifle down and took some shots, but the creature quickly reacted and opened its shield. The drill also span up and came for the pillars beneath him, but was swung in a sporadic and blind manner. Despite its blindness, the droid continued to protect itself with its shield from any direction that Finn shot from, prompting him to simply retreat as sparks flew and machines were drilled into. He ran down the catwalk and came to the end where he stepped down and found himself in a clearing with conveyor belts at either side, press machines, and robotic arms that worked. At the very end of the room he could see a control room on raised pillars. He looked around him from behind as he knelt down, breathing quickly before he stood up and turned around. Finn entered the control room and immediately began to look around.

The control room had a long panel with various controls, and behind him were some electrical boxes, but there were no valves or other objects like that. In fact, as Finn looked outside, he could not see any pipes come towards this room and instead they diverted into a tunnel at the side. He growled, especially as he saw the robot wander towards him as it continued to maintain its shield out.

"Did you find it?" Moira questioned from behind.

Finn jumped as he looked over to her. "Don't just appear out of nowhere!" he complained. "No – it's not here. I just noticed the pipes go into the side tunnels, which is the least of all places I want to go right now. Ugh… look at that thing… with that shield up, I can't do much."

"I'll climb up onto the roof again," Moira said. "Engage it in a fight and we'll finish it off…"

Finn nodded. He reloaded the rifle and then walked towards a door onto a side catwalk. He kicked it open and then stepped out, engaging his boosters and wings. He whistled towards the robot and pointed his rifle.

"Over here!"

The enhanced robot pointed its flamethrower towards him, but as he began to fire, it flexed its arm and caused the shield to come out. It then began to spin up the drill in the other hand, while Finn stopped firing at the shield. As soon as Finn stopped firing at the robot, it began to point its arm forward with the flamethrower. He kicked himself off to the side and then flew away from the flames. He hid behind a pillar as the wave of flames made its pass. He then turned the corner and jumped off the catwalk to land below. He opened fire at the robot, and it stuck its shield out. He then jumped off the ground, hovering above and continued to do the same as it approached him. He came up towards the platform across from where he was, kicking himself up and then touched down on the other side. He stopped firing and began to run down the platform as the flamethrower came up. He then ducked down though and entered into the control room again. The flamethrower spat fire into the control room and caused some of the items to catch ablaze as it sprayed while Finn kept his head down. After a moment, Finn looked up as the room was more or less on fire, and he ran down to the other side and saw the creature about to climb up the staircase. He took a shot off and the robot shielded its body. He then made a side thrust again as the flamethrower spat flames towards him again, this time continuing as it climbed up and made it to the top of the platform. He flew off and glided down to the ground, jumping up to the platform, and then kicking off to drop down on the other side. Before Finn could get another round off at it, it continued to point the flamethrower which reached across the room and caused Finn to hide behind the pillar instead. The robot began to step towards the side as it launched another shot of flames, prompting Finn to quickly dodge out of the way as he went towards the machines on his left rather than the control room, but as he did so, the flames singed his right arm causing Finn to yell out in pain. Finn released control of his rifle, letting it dangle on its strap as he brought his left hand to his arm. His right arm was badly burned, the skin a deep red. Finn panted quickly as he grit his teeth to hold in the pain. He seemed as though he was about to cry as he remained knelt down and shuddered. He closed his eyes for a moment and then opened them to look at his arm. His arm remained severely reddened, almost unable to move as the muscles seized.

Finn looked up as he heard the robot approach. He used his left arm to abandon his rifle and then ran off into the depths of the machine room.

"Hey, up here!" Moira shouted.

Finn turned around before he peeled around the corner and saw Moira appear in her distortion.

"Moira!" Finn yelled back.

Moira pointed the blaster pistol and began to take shots off at the robot, hitting once in the back before it turned around. It raised its shield towards her, which prompted her to use the grenade launcher to take a shot off and hit the shield point blank. The robot was blown back, and Finn quickly hid himself around the corner and ducked down. He then stood up and turned around as he saw the robot seize in place. The shield was torn off and fell down the side of the catwalk, but the flamethrower and drills remained as they were. The robot used its third arm to push itself off, and then began to charge forward as it wound up the flamethrower to spit fire at Moira.

"Moira! Run!" Finn shouted.

Moira ducked down and ran away as the creature spat fire towards the control room again. Finn's right arm continued to remain limp so he used his left arm to propel himself forward. He kicked off his backpack and picked up a metal rod laying beside him with his left arm, swinging it towards the back of the robot and hitting it. The third arm quickly snatched the rod, prompting Finn to jump back and run into the tunnels.

Finn turned on his lamp and began to look around the tunnels as they criss-crossed in numerous directions. He lost sight of the pipes and continued in a random way before he stopped to catch his breath. He attempted to move his right arm, but cringed as he did so. He took his left hand touched the exoskeleton appendage on his right arm, but immediately retracted his hand as it was too hot to touch. He instead hit the eject button and shed his suit. He sat down and tilted his head back as tears came down the side of his face. He breathed heavily and continued to grind his teeth to hold back his growls and shouts of pain. His arm was mutilated by the exosuit poking into his hot damaged skin, or what remained of his dermis, while at the same time the cuff marks left circular markings of what his skin used to look like, fair rather than deep red.

"Finn… do you read me. Finn…" Moira communicated over the radio.

Finn opened his eyes and leaned forward. He crawled to his suit and hit the microphone button.

"I'm here…" Finn spoke in a fragile voice.

"That thing went after you in the tunnel… be careful…"

Finn dropped the cuff as tears fell down his face. "I've… I've kippered me arm…" he muttered. "I… I can't do this…"

Finn stopped as he heard the robot began to approach him from around. He stood up and began to hide again.

"Destroy the boiler!" Moira shouted over the radio. "Destroy it, Finn!"

Finn came into an intersection where he could see the robot at the end of it. The robot immediately turned to him and began to spew fire from the flamethrower again. He dodged the fire but heard the robot run towards him with the drill. He quickly turned the corner and went in a random direction as he escaped the beast and slowed down his steps as he continued forward. His eyes soon caught on to some pipes in the ceiling. He began to follow them, but stopped as he turned the corner and could see the robot in an intersection, almost as though it was listening for movement before it trudged off. He then continued to follow the pipe down, stopping at the intersection where he saw it look around for him as it sensed its location and then went off again. He continued to follow the pipes, but as he turned around the corner, noticed that the pipes were leading him back to the smelting chamber rather than anywhere else, so he turned around and went the opposite direction, but as he stopped to cross an intersection, the enhanced robot roared at him and immediately charged at him with the drill. He jumped out of the way and ran off as he drill was brought into the concrete. The flamethrower then lit up and he turned the corner. Finn followed the pipe and then diverted to come around a corner as the creature finally caught up to him and looked around an intersection. Finn was less than a few feet from the beast as it looked for him, so he took in a deep breath and held it. The creature sensed around before it began to go off in a random direction, prompting Finn to come out and continue to follow the pipes. He went down and then went around a corner, and stopped again as the creature was ahead. He waited for it to disappear before he followed the pipes the rest of the way and came into a large room. He looked ahead and could see a line up of many water tanks on one side, and two boilers and a generator at the perpendicular side. Finn came to the valve of the first boiler and brought his left hand around it, but then crashed his body against it and brought his head down as he held in tears.

"How the hell am I supposed to move this thing if I... I can't even feel my bloody arm..."

Finn's tears began to fall down in front of him. As he leaned forward, a necklace around his neck dangled before him and he looked at the gold medallion.

"Where are you...?" Finn jumped as the beast found him and it let out a terrible shriek. He turned around and looked at it. The drill began to spin up and stared towards it. He grinded his teeth as he began to growl and yelled. "Come at me then you bastard!" He jumped out of the way as the robot was about to hit him with the drill. He landed in the prone position and immediately stood up to run off as the drill hit into the side of the boiler, immediately causing hot water to spray out.

The enhanced robot attempted to retract its drill, and the boiler tank imploded, causing the generator to explode and the adjacent tank to erupt as well. Finn evaded the explosion and eruption of the water tanks as he fled back into the tank, but felt water at his feet as however much water was stored began to flush through. He knelt down towards the end of the tunnel as he made his escape and ran his left hand through the hot water. He then gently placed some of it on his right arm, but it only caused him to cringe. He stood up and looked ahead and came out into the smelting chamber as the power was now out. He looked about to get a sense of his direction as bells rang and he could see the glow of some magma ahead as well as some continued fires in the control room. He then turned around and jumped as he was met with the sudden appearance of the robot behind him. The drill had been blown off from the robot's grip, but the flamethrower continued to remain, though as the creature pointed it, it struggle to light a blaze. Instead, it pointed its other arm from where the drill was as it began to light up.

"Oh no…" Finn muttered.

Finn quickly vaulted down as beams shot off and hit the wall on the other end. He then ran down and into the many machines as he escaped the beast. The beast spew fire behind him, but it was too far to reach. He escaped the other end and ran towards the exit.

"Moira!" Finn shouted. "Moira! It's time to go! It's still after me but we can go!"

Finn returned to the central chamber and climbed up onto the helipad. He looked around for Moira.

"Moira?!" Finn yelled as he stood above and looked about. His right arm continued to hang limp at his side. "Moira!"

Finn caught sight of Moria besides the crane. She waved over to him and caught sight of his arm, but before there could be any communication, the enhanced robot appeared and began to slowly step towards Finn. Moira got into the crane and began to bring it around. The crane had a metallic plate, and she left it above the stairs the robot was about to approach. Finn took a step back as the flamethrower spewed out fire, but before it could do much else, it began to float upwards to the magnet and stick towards it. It continued to point the flamethrower, prompting Moira to bring it around and dangle over the lava pool. She then released the magnetic pull and the robot fell downwards, into the lava pool where it began to let off a terrible screech as it melted into the magma. Finn caught sight of the robot from above and then took a sigh of relief.

Moira came around as Finn went down the steps and joined her.

"Oh my God, Finn..." Moira remarked. "Look at your arm..."

"Tsh, you don't say," Finn sarcastically remarked. "How bad does it look?"

"Bad..."

Finn looked over and then moved his eyes away. "Looks nearly like third degree burns..."

"Where's your suit?"

"Left it behind – it was causing too much discomfort..." Finn stated. "I'll have to go and get it before we leave..."

"I'll come with you..."

The pair walked back into the smelting chamber, both using their headlamps to guide the way. They entered into the tunnel and began to walk around, coming around to find the exosuit, but not too far from it at a dead end did Moira see something else.

"Oh no..."

Finn looked up and caught sight of human remains propped up against the wall. The sight was similar to the other GDP elite forces at this point, but they had an additional set of limbs that extended out from the back of the exosuit. Rather than have a drill though, they had a minigun as a main weapon. Finn looked at the remains and the broken helmet spoke for itself with the charred remains underneath.

"Looks like mate was cooked alive like a warm meal in the oven in some aluminum foil."

"Finn..." Moira scolded.

Finn approached the right wrist, and they listened to the recorded message. The voice that spoke was deep and had a slight Sub-Saharan African accent of some sort. "... Attention to anyone who is able to listen – this is Sergeant…. Sergeant Njami Nkosi." The background noise was loud, and a lot of shouting could be heard. "Director Black, if you can hear me… we are overwhelmed. There are too many of them, and only a few of us left. To make matters worse, I am challenged by one of them who mirrors my abilities. I cannot battle them and this one… I will take as many of them as I can with me to the grave, but I…" a loud shout could be heard in the background. "I am unable to secure the mines… I only hope that you and the others are more successful…" There was some inaudible noises that followed. "They are killing everyone and everything here… I do not know why! Are these not…" The recording then cut out for a bit as gunfire could be heard as well as the screech that was similar to the robots. A woman called out the word 'Shaka' at which point Nkosi could be heard. A deep voice could be heard shouting out in a foreign language, followed with heavy gunfire and loud explosions. The recording then cut out completely…

"What a lad…" Finn remarked, "all of them fought hard and well…"

Finn brought his left hand over to the left forearm of the exosuit. "He had one of them flamethrowers. I'll try and get it off him. Anything you want?"

"I would rather not pillage the dead…"

"Take a look at those hands… there's something about them that allow them to climb onto walls as though they were adhesive… I'll nick them off for you."

"What? You don't want an extra set of hands? You need them after what happened to you…"

"Awf, that's too soon, isn't it? My arm is still warm for you to be making jokes about it…." Finn remarked, cringing in pain for a moment. "All joke aside, I am in quite a bit of pain. I'm going to need to go and sit down in that aircon for a bit and cool off… have a sip of water and maybe pass out… I'm exhausted."

Without another word, Finn sat down and fell over as just like that, he passed out.

Act 6, Prologue

Finn stared down at a gravestone in front of him as it bore the name, 'Charlemagne Phillipe Cabernet' with the date of birth from 'July 22nd, 1961' to his death 'October 21st, 2021.' The tombstone was a moderate sized one with a depiction of the late Charlemagne imprinted upon it. Below was an excerpt from the Book of Job that said:

I know that you are all-powerful: what you conceive, you can perform. I am the man who obscured your designs with my empty-headed words. I have been holding forth on matters I cannot understand, on wonders beyond me and my knowledge. I knew you then only by hearsay; but now, having seen you with my own eyes, I retract all I have said, and in dust and ashes I repent.

Finn looked at the engravings as he knelt before the tombstone. Beside it, not too far was another tombstone that had the name 'Wien Edelweiß Cabernet,' and likewise on the opposite side was the joint tombstone of Derby Martel Cabernet and Ophelia Victoria Cabernet. The arrangement of the tombstones placed Charlemagne on the left with extra space on his right, Vienna to the right in the center with extra space on her left, and Derby and Ophelia to the right with no extra space between them. There was additional space to the left of the cemetery as these tombstones lined the cliff walls. Finn placed flowers before his father's gravestone and then stood up. A few years lined down the side of his face. The cemetery on this particular day was snowy but the clouds gone and skies light blue. The ambience in the surroundings was of a crisp coldness in St. Allan's Cemetery. Finn looked down from where his father lay and wiped the tears off his face.

Nobody stood around Finn as he looked down at his father's grave, and there was nobody else in the cemetery on this particular day. He stepped back from the tomb and opened a small book that he took out from his pocket and then began to point his middle and index finger together with his thumb. He brought them up to his head and touched his forehead, and then down to his chest bone, and across to his left shoulder and then right shoulder. He then opened the book and looked at the thin pages inside and the Times New Roman font. He cleared his throat before his lips opened and his mouth sang.

"*Re-qui-em ae-tér-nam don-na e- is Dómin-ne: et lux perpétu-a lú-ce- at e- is,*" Finn chanted. His voice echoed around the rest of the cemetery, flawless in tune. "*Te de-cet hymnus De-us in Si-on, et ti-bi reddétur votum in Ierúsalem: exáudi orati-ónem me-am, ad te omnis caro-véni-et. Re-qui-em ae-tér-nam don-na e- is Dómin-ne: et lux perpétu-a lú-ce- at e- is. Requiescat-ant in pace. Aa-aa-men.*"

At the end of the chant, Finn closed the book and then made the same gesture with his hand to his forehead, chest, and shoulders. At this time, Finn appeared the same as he did when he was last with his father, clean-shaven and hair at medium length. His face appeared colder and paler in the cold weather, and his eyes were sunken and red. He otherwise appeared young and healthy as he wore a suit in the cold. After a moment of silence, Finn put his book into his blazer and then placed his hands into his pocket. He turned around and stopped as he noticed the sight of a lone figure sitting at a stone chiseled bench on the main pathway in the cemetery. The figure appeared to be elderly and holding a cane in his hands.

The elderly man had pinkish warm fair skin that was wrinkled, especially around the forehead. At either side of his eyes, which glared forward as they could barely be kept open, were crow's feet that stretched outwards. The irises that poked through were a faint blue. The sclera white of his eyes were tired, bloodshot and old. He was a bald man with a greyish-white beard, no hair over his head, though a stocky man despite his age. He had a mild hunch to his posture, holding himself firm as both hands rested upon the wooden cane. He wore a blouson jacket overtop a collared plaid shirt. He also wore a pair of greyish trousers and hiking boots.

Finn approached the man as he looked at him from where he sat. He looked down at him as the two stared at each other. Finally, Finn said to him, "You're late, for your own son's funeral. Two weeks late to be exact…"

"You unmistakenly must be his son," the man said, pushing himself up to stand before him. "Everest Cabernet – I suppose I'm your grandfather. Apologies on the delay, but travel can be difficult for me. I don't move as fast as I used to…"

"Allodia said you weren't really eager to leave South Asia to come here," Finn expressed. "She said you'd turn up about now though. I'm not sure why seeing as that everybody already left to go their separate ways and continue on with their lives. Just about all of them are back in Harlech… your son, Salmar, of course is still in the slammer, he didn't make it for obvious reasons, but here I am – someone you don't even know."

"Is that a reason enough to come around?" Everest questioned. "Charles told me about you – Louis, isn't it?"

"Some prefer to call me Finn…"

"What do you prefer?"

"I don't have any preference," Finn expressed, looking around. "How did you get here all on your own?"

"A car brought me down," Everest remarked, stepping forward and looking towards the graves. "It's been about a year since I was last around when Charles, your father, put the love of my life to rest in these parts too. Quite a bit of work it was for him to exhume her body from the Caribbean just so that she could come to rest here. You know, I'm not one to believe where it is that we die has any impact in where we end up…" His eyes then looked towards the tombstone of Derby and Ophelia. "However, I can understand the gesture to wish to have the family all together, and for wishes of the dead to be honored. She would have wanted to have been here for certain…

We all die, Finn, every single one of us have that reminder that we must not forget. At some point, we too come here," he said, looking at the space besides Vienna's grave. "However, I'm a stubborn old bastard as I'm told, and I could not come to rest if I had not let the work of my hands be completed. We only get one life, and it is a different life for many of us… We can go our entire lives in whichever way we so choose, but what is the point of our existence if not to bring love to this world? What is it that is lacking in this world and which the world needs more of but a helping hand – a world in which there is so much evil?" He took in a deep breath and then turned around to Finn. "Walk with me, for a moment – I've been sitting on a plane for many hours… let's go around the path here…"

Finn walked with Everest as they came around the cemetery.

"You know, your father and I did not see eye to eye much," Everest expressed. "He was, of course, born when your grandmother, my Vienna, and I were both sixteen years old. We were young lovers, and her adolescent pregnancy put her at odds with her family. My father took her in – for many years I thought he did it to punish me. 'Be responsible,' he barked at me. I never believed he cared about Vienna. He hated Germans, but her… he made a change in him, and he made a change in her. I was not ready to be a father though… not at my age. I psychologically denied for many years that Charlemagne was ever my boy. I told myself that he was my father's son more than he was mine, because that's what a boy needs… he needs a man to be his father. Perhaps for that reason too, it was always difficult to see Charles as anything but my son. I loved him not as my son – but as though he was my younger brother.

"Vienna was not the same. She loved him for the pain it took her to birth him – the pain of losing her family and the pain of childbirth. She loved him greatly. I was jealous of that love. I took her from him as we left Charles with my parents, and we travelled the world for selfish gain. When my grandfather died, Vienna and I had no choice, especially since she had become pregnant again. At this moment though, at the age of twenty-three, I felt a little bit more ready. I loved Allodia and Salmar as if they were my own children, and Charles saw the difference. He loved my father as though he was his father too. He resented me for being neither father nor friend to him. We were at constant odds with each other, and it was my punishment that in being unable to love my own father for our differences that I now had a younger version of him lambasting me at times in which he would have too.

"Make no mistake, to love Allodia and Salmar and be there at moments in which other fathers are not, was a tremendous joy, but it was not meant to last. By the time Salmar was eighteen, I found myself interested in the workings of Cabernet Industries, thinking I could make a difference in reshaping this aged empire that reeked of men of the past, especially the fathers of the past, and turn it into a force of good in the world. Never did I realize just how wicked men could be than my short time at Cabernet Industries, and how impossible my dreamed seemed to be...

"In my short time at Cabernet Industries, I realized that you cannot expect others to be good for you. I realized that in order to do any good in the world, you have to act in that capacity yourself. I also learned what it means to love, to really love another, and in doing so my eyes were opened to the wonders of the world and our existence – that people of such honest and kind hearts exist, and how much more powerful those hearts were in comparison to the rotten ones I had been exposed to.

"In realizing that Cabernet Industries could not be converted as I hoped it could, I aimed to decentralize power from the corrupt men that earned and gained from the misery of other people. Make no mistake, Cabernet Industries, at least in those days, was an awful corporation. The operations it ran in the third-world were exploitative, destructive to nature and the lives of its workers and other peoples, and it only added to the pockets of the investors. Even in the first-world, it was no better, but I tried to make it better. I founded the Cabernet Foundation, but it wasn't enough – they turned my charitable foundation into a public relations department rather than a charity. When that didn't work, I aimed to reform the company and take away power from the board of directors in a two-tier system, but they told me it would destroy the company. I didn't care, but in their desperation and treachery they aimed to have me step down. I would have rather seen the company torn to shreds.

"My wife, my dear beautiful city known as Vienna, supported me through and through. She told me she would stick by me in whatever decision I would make, and that she would be with me to the end. How much more of a promise can be asked from one's spouse? I could not be so impulsive in my final decision-making, so I stepped down from Cabernet Industries and forfeited control to my children… though unbeknownst to me that Charlemagne already had a sizeable investment in the company. I suspected that he would have taken some form of leadership between his siblings, but none like he did in the end. It was not my intention to have Charlemagne make the rise he did, but it was his life, and I made the choice to live mine in a certain way. I don't ask from anyone to do what I have done, not even my wife, but she followed me because she wanted to as well. I remember that we immediately left for Africa with whatever we had in our bank account, and we disappeared from civilization to serve the poor. Just as we had done when we had left high school, we travelled the world again, going anywhere and everywhere that would receive us with open hands – not on behalf of Cabernet Industries, or the Cabernet Foundation, but just as ourselves. My wife and I had an aspiration to visit every country on Earth… and we had just about done it…

"We had travelled for little more than thirty years by the time that my wife – your grandmother, passed away. We had met *marvelous* people in that time, of all sorts of languages, cultures, and races. Certainly, I can say that we had met a lot of good people, but also a lot of bad people of all sorts. Despite all our efforts, it was only a matter of time before the worst of them caught up to us. My dear Vienna's life was cut short when a man just like those that I had escaped from at Cabernet Industries, in his pride and greed, kidnapped us to make a stance. We were in Isla Paraiso at the time, a small island territory in the Caribbean, helping the indigenous population adjust to resettlement as we helped construct houses because the U.S. government sold land to allow for the construction of homes in lands they had occupied. At the same time, young children were being kidnapped by the same forces for the purposes of human trafficking. Your grandmother and I were also kidnapped, but in an effort to silence us and our assistance to the indigenous people as they attempted to scare and control them through fear. Your father and his adoptive-children saved me, but they could not save my dear beautiful city… my Vienna lost her life when she was poisoned during her rescue and she passed away. Her death devastated us all… I did not know what I would do, or how I would live without her, but live… I had to.

"It's a terrible feeling to have the woman that you've spent so much of your life with never be seen again. So much so, that I could hardly say that we even said goodbye to her when her death was so spontaneous to us all. The only one who was as devastated as me was Charlemagne, and that is when I realized this competition we had for her all our lifetime and yet now she was gone. I realized too the guilt I had to have deprived her from him – eighteen years of her life, when I had gotten more than triple that. I had been unfair to him, as his biological father, and even at this point I had grown tired of the conflict between us. Take for consideration, I had last seen my son in 1989 shortly before I had left to travel the world with Vienna, and this moment at Isla Paraiso was the first time in which I had physically seen him since. I wanted no more trouble, but Charlemagne... unfortunately, he was still hurt. Only when Vienna was now gone could we develop a human connection, and I believe that experience was made possible too in himself, having realized he was a father to you. I only learned about you from Allodia at first, and then Charles, this year, but I was happy to have learned that my eldest son had a son of his own, but I hoped, as any good father could hope, that he would not make the same mistakes I did. On a deeper level, I hoped that the mistakes I had made would not impact and bleed through.

"I understand that it is called generational trauma," Everest expressed. "When the mistakes and errors of one generation, continue on for generations to come. In understanding our family, you need to understand this legacy that we have from father to father, son to son, and that is that each of us were not perfect beings who made mistakes. My grandfather was not a good father to my father. My father was not a good father to me. I was not a good father to Charlemagne. Understanding that Charlemagne was not present in your life, I can say in general terms that he was not a good father to you either. However, these words are not to say that each father did not love their son... We Cabernet, we are born rich with silver spoons, but how true it is that we are poor in love. We only have so much as we can give to our sons, reaching the end of our lives and wishing we could have given more. I remember when my father had reached his age of regret... I can say that I too am there, and so was Charlemagne.

"Finn, my interest in sharing these words to you are not to dismay you, but I have this one ask of you – break free, and do not blame your father. Do not let any pain that may be within you punish your children the same way, but put an end to this

Cabernet legacy once and for all, and be a good father to your sons – create your own legacy and re-shape the Cabernet one."

Finn looked back at Everest as he put a hand on his shoulder. He looked at his hand and then back to the loving glance of his grandfather.

"I don't intend to continue the legacy of old," Finn replied.

"Good."

"I don't intend to, because I don't intend to have children," Finn expressed. "I'm sorry, but I'm not going to get married. I'm... I'm going to become a priest – a Catholic priest and devote my life to celibacy. You don't have to worry about generational trauma anymore, because there won't be a Cabernet family anymore."

Everest looked at Finn with a plain expression and then nodded. "Very well," he said. "If that is what is set to come to the Cabernet family, then it is better than to let anymore children suffer. Allow me to just say this... I hope your intentions are pure. When I was your age, I did not want anything to do with the Cabernet legacy and all that brought forth, and in me that expressed itself in dissatisfaction and indifference to the company name. Like my father, when he was your age, he too wanted nothing to do with Cabernet Corporation, as it was called in those days, and even Charlemagne shared in that burden and sorrow. My father was not supposed to have inherited the company from his father – it was supposed to have gone all to the eldest, my aunt Alcmene, but she emancipated herself from the family. He attempted to refuse what his father offered him, but going through the war changed him to rethink his mind. In all my efforts, I attempted to run from the company name too especially as they told me my decisions would sink the company, but it was not the corrupt men that motivated me to go full steam ahead, but the legacy. Your father, in case you did not know, was the same at some point in his life too. He intended to liquidate the company and throw it all away, but by some grace did those two come into his life, his adoptive children – I suppose your adoptive siblings, and he relented… he also changed too. Those two, Diana and Tristan, transformed his life immensely, and being a father to them helped him mature and find joy. All our actions came from disdain to our family name, and our disdain for our family name came from our disdain in our fathers. I hope that you do not carry disdain in our family name, and I hope that you do not carry disdain or regret in your father. I hope that your intentions are pure in your actions, and that this choice spell goodness rather than contempt."

"I assure you, I'm not making this choice to be petty," Finn remarked. "I've forgiven my father in having more or less abandoned me. I loved him, even if I did not know him for very long, the same way he loved me even if he did not know me for very long. He was… definitely the father I never had, and I wished we could have spent more time together, but such as it is… I can't let what had happened in the past drag me down because I've already been down that path…"

"Good," Everest replied as they continued to walk through the cemetery. They came around to the exit.

"Where are you going to stay?" Finn asked. "Will you come back to the manor with me?"

"I would be happy to return to the manor, but I have a flight to catch to go to Harlech and see your aunt," Everest expressed. "Since Vienna passed away, I've continued to travel for the purposes that I took on that quest – not for our sake, but for the sake of others. Although it has been difficult adjusting, I continue to mourn the loss but must prevail. I wish to travel to Central America to partake in some charitable missions with the Cabernet Foundation."

Finn looked at Everest and then said, "Take me with you. I want to join you on these missions and be a helping hand."

"Finn, these missions are not for the faint of heart, I assure you. If you are truly serious, I must know your conviction."

"I am convicted," Finn expressed. "I'm no stranger to poverty – I practically lived on the streets as an adolescent, and I want to help others. I... I have to help others, and to love others as you say – is it not a marvel of our existence to love others in a world that has so much evil?"

Everest did not respond. Suddenly, a bolt of lightning lit up the sky in many branches, like veins in the sky. The boom of thunder then echoed around the valley.

"Ah, that's unfortunate," Everest expressed. "A storm would surely cancel my plans to travel to Harlech."

"Stay with me in the manor then," Finn requested. "We have the extra space of course, and I would love to talk to you more."

Everest looked at Finn and replied, "Sure, I would appreciate that offer."

"Thank God for the lightning then," Finn responded. "You won't regret it."

Act 6, Scene 1

Finn sat at the back of the SUV as they were parked on the side of the freeway. The freeway was in the midst of a grainy desert region, the ground of which was a mixture of dry grass and thick sand. He wore the same cargo pants, boots, and sleeveless shirt as the one he had been wearing in the mine. Both his cargo pants and shirt were dirty, the right side of his sleeveless shirt was singed and in some spaces had small holes and tears. His right arm was covered with a white gauze from around his palm up to his shoulder. Only his fingers were visible, and the skin there appeared scraped and torn. The outlines of his shoulder also appeared reddish pink. Finn removed his sleeveless shirt, exposing his chest and the side of his torso where there were a few burn marks. He slowly unwrapped the bandages around his right arm and exposed his wounded and damaged skin to the fresh air. His burnt skin was deeply red to brown colored. The texture of the burns was rough too, and at some points there were blisters that had formed or white gaps where there used to be skin altogether. The only untouched parts of his arm were outlines from where the exosuit sections had covered in a straight line by close to two inches across the length of his arm. Likewise, around a cuff at his wrist, though these outlines were deeply mutilated at the edges. Finn looked at his arm with a horrified glance and then looked over to his left where he had his first aid kit. He began to gently clean his arm with a small wet towel, patting it as he did so. He then left it to dry as he brought his hands together and leaned over in silence. The sound of cars passing them on the freeway, Moira typing at her computer in the front passenger seat, and ambience of the desert around them caught in his ear. After an unspecified amount of time, Finn sat up and began to wrap the wound with gauze again, hiding every single inch of his disfigured arm. When he finished, Finn brought a clean white sleeveless shirt down and then put on his flannel. He then stood up and began to clean up and put items back into his backpack with his left hand, at which point Moira opened the front passenger seat door, got out, and came around to the back of the SUV.

"How's it doing?" Moira asked, putting her hands at her hips.

"The good news is that it doesn't hurt as much…" Finn expressed, looking over to her. "The bad news is that I think it doesn't hurt as much because there was some nerve damage. I've lost some sense of feeling in some places."

"Oh, Finn… why don't you go and see a doctor about it?"

"Why? So they can tell me what I already know?" Finn questioned. "Unless they're a plastic surgeon, not much they can do to help me with…"

"Okay, but your skin will grow back though. Right?" Moira questioned. "I mean…" she looked at Finn's left arm and noticed the second and first degree burn scars on that arm.

"As far as I'm aware, most of it will grow back. The nerves… that's hit or miss. Will it ever look as it used to? Not likely."

Moira did not reply.

"What's important though is that I survived, we made it out of that place without much trouble, I got a neat little upgrade to install on the exosuit, and we destroyed that mine which'll put a hamper on the Chosen's capabilities to produce more robots," Finn stated. "On the flipside, we've now hit at them and made our move, which could put us at odds with them in a clearer way – although, I don't think they'd suspect us to be the ones behind the attack. However, regardless of who they think we are, as soon as they realize what's happened, they'll raise defenses at the power station and elsewhere, which means we got to move. We need to infiltrate the power station in order to find where their secret base of operations is, so that's got to be our next destination. Did you find its approximate location?"

"Yeah…" Moira responded, looking at Finn's arm and then down to the ground, "I mean, I found the desert that the nuns were talking about, but bad news is that it's quite a large area and satellite imagery doesn't give us much to go on."

"I can't imagine wherever this place is that it's too far from where we need to be going..." Finn stated. "I also can't imagine that either of these places are very far from each other. That desert... do you have a map?"

"Yeah, let me get my laptop," Moira said, going around to the front passenger seat. She picked up her laptop and then came back around. She logged in and showed Finn the satellite images. "You see, it's a quad-state area with a little bit more surface area than the preserve we were just in. The interstate freeways go around it at every corner, but the depths of the park appear to be remote. The majority of the desert is just as they said it would be – in Wyoming."

"Wyoming, Wyoming..." Finn remarked. "I've never been to Wyoming, though I believe that Yellowstone is in that state. Not too far from where we just were..."

"We're actually in Wyoming right now," Moira pointed.

"Ah..." Finn remarked, looking about. In the distance was the sight of some mountains, while the rest of the surroundings composed of rugged sand with patches of dry plants, and low hills. "Well, that certainly explains it..." He stood up and looked closer at Moira's computer screen as the SUV rear provided a bit of shade. "Looks like we've got to come down here, but that'll be quite a drive. We'll have to lodge somewhere nearby..."

"Sleep in the car again?"

"Or pitch our tents in the wilderness..."

"Can we not?" Moira questioned. "Come on, you're Finn Cabernet. Aren't you one of the riches men on Earth?"

"I don't own anything," Finn objected. "Not in the least now that my aeroplane is scrap metal in the middle of Montana. I only brought emergency funds, American dollars to pay for food and supplies."

"Didn't you tell me you had your wallet with you?"

"Yeah, but do you think I'm going to use any of my bank cards out here?" Finn questioned. "The Chosen own nearly every bank in the world, and not a chance will I tip them off on our location because you wanted to stay at the Windsor hotel."

"I hardly think we'd find a Windsor out here..." Moira grumbled. "I just want to sleep in a bed and have a hot shower. Besides, doesn't it get insanely cold at night in the deserts?"

"Yeah..."

"And it's still technically winter for another couple days..."

"Yeah, and? We've got sleeping bags with insulated linings. Your body will keep you as warm as you need to be. Just keep the rubber bottle filled with hot water and keep that close to yah. It'll feel like all the love in the world you need for a cold night out. Besides, how cold can it get to be – it's almost twenty out here now."

"I want to sleep in a bed, Finn," Moira begged. "I want to put my head down on a pillow."

"You slept in a bed at the monastery a few days ago."

"It's not the same..."

"Not the same?" Finn questioned. "You're one to talk... look, let's just get to the nearest town at the brink of that desert and then we'll talk."

"I've already marked one out. We'll want to keep taking this route south. It's about four hours or so away."

"Fantastic," Finn remarked, closing the rear of the SUV. "We're just about at the end of this little adventure that I didn't ask for, so let's get on with it..."

Moira went around to the passenger seat while Finn came and sat down at the driver's seat. He turned the ignition key with his right hand and then gently took the steering wheel with his left and right hands. He looked into the rear-view mirror to let an approaching car pass and then pulled out and began to speed up so he could carry along on the arid desert road. The only object in their vicinity other than the cars they passed were telephone poles on the opposite side of the road. There was also the odd fence from time to time, the odd offshoot onto a sand-dirt road, and the odd unexplained anomaly in the distance. Moira went onto the Internet again as they continued to drive on the country road, typing into the search engine 'Beliyal' and returning some obscure articles to do with the Devil and demons, prompting her to widen her search to 'Beliyal program' and 'Beliyal virus' which returned some obscure information that was of no use to her. Eventually, Moira lost connection to the rest of the wider world as the signal died out and they entered into the true depths of the Wyoming desert plains for the next hour or so. She closed her laptop and kept it on her lap, but raised an elbow beside the window, and for the next hour plus, the pair remained quiet.

"Well, this takes me back to doing road trips with my dad," Moira suddenly expressed. "Although, it's certainly a lot quieter. Can we at least turn on the radio? We should pick up something…" She turned on the radio and there were numerous static channels. "I can't find anything nice… this sucks…"

"Certainly is a tough life to hide from the authorities that be," Finn replied. "Who knows if this level of sabotage will be enough to get them to stand down and leave us alone. I already have my Plan B if this fails, you should figure out yours."

"Plan B?"

"If the Chosen decide to continue to hunt us down for the rest of our lives," Finn stated. "I'm going to have to change my name again – no idea what I'll call myself now. I'd probably just take the name Gabriel…"

"Gabriel? What kind of name is that to call yourself? Why not just take the name John – it's common enough."

"Alright, Moira, what would you call yourself then?"

"I don't know… I always liked the name Barbara for some reason."

"Ah, like St. Barbara – that's a fair name."

"Is there a St. Gabriel?"

"Of course," Finn replied, taking his left hand to his gold medallion and showing it to her. "Patron Saint of the Cabernet name, or at least one of few. There's three to be sure: Saint Gabriel, the Messenger; Benjamin, the twelfth son of Jacob; and St. Paul, the Apostle of the Gentiles (himself a Benjaminite)."

"What about a St. Finn or a St. Louis?"

"There's St. Finn Bar of Cork, Ireland, and St. Louis the Ninth, king of France."

"You're just an encyclopedia of religious knowledge, aren't you."

"To add to that further, there's not a St. Moira, but there is a St. Maura, as well as a St. Isidore of Seville (though a male)."

"I don't understand this fascination with saints..." Moira replied.

"I don't understand the world's fascination with heroes without virtue. In ancient times, there used to be men of legends, people you couldn't know for certain whether or not they existed or lived their life in such a way, but were virtuous: Perseus, Odysseus, Achilles, Arminius... Roland, Richard the Lionheart, King Arthur, Siegfried... By the time of the Renaissance, heroes were just political and military leaders we knew to exist... George Washington, Napoleon, Oliver Cromwell, Frederick the Great... most of these having led revolutions that changed the way people lived. The trend continues in the same way – they're just politicians and activists, John F. Kennedy, Franklin Delano Roosevelt, or Ronald Reagan and George H.W. Bush – who are they to be called heroes? What about Rosa Parks, Martin Luther King Jr., Mahatma Ghandi or Malala what-ever-her-name-is – what did they do but stand up for the liberal social order? To empower and direct the political landscape in a particular way? To standout in those capacities and make something out of their lives in contrast to the average person? Since the pandemic there's been this attempt to make the status of heroism a more attainable virtue, which is good if it wasn't a propaganda campaign to label every healthcare worker, police officer, and first responder a triumphant figure, while in reality there were nurses twerking on TikTok in front of patients, cops beating the crap out of minorities and shooting innocent people's dogs, and all those folk just being what is true for every average person – being capable of evil and selfish desire. The world does not understand what it means to be a hero because it does not understand morality and virtue. Even in the fictional realm, superheroes aim to create variations of this question that the secular world struggles with, in what does it mean to be a hero. From what I can reckon, only two heroes come even close to that ideal – Batman and Captain America, though the whole pantheon attempts to re-create and revitalize this desire in humans for heroes like the ones of ancient and medieval times.

"The Catholic Church venerates Saints because these are real-life men and women who have virtue and who have lived their lives selflessly for love of God and neighbor. The only hero that the secular world seems to understand for who she was seems to be Saint Mother Theresa because of her commitment to the poor – although there was so much more that was beautiful about her, such as her wisdom and faith. According to the Catholic Church, canonized saints, which means to be added to a list, are figures who with confidence of the Church believes to be in Heaven. To be a saint, is to be a hero – there is a difference between capital S saint and lower-case S saint. The capital S are the ones that are canonized, while a lower case S is anyone who is in Heaven, whether the Church knows it or not. The Catholic Church teaches that we are all called to be saints, because we are all called to come into Heaven, but the idea of sainthood and being a hero according to the Catholic Church is not as grandiose and can be truly done by just about anyone else. In short, the Catholic Church is the church of heroes, the calling for heroism in the world, and that comes from the greatest hero of them all, our Lord and Savior Jesus Christ who was blameless because he was sinless, and yet humanity killed him. I have no other way to explain what a hero truly is than to say that a hero is one that loves in a godly way, like Christ, to give oneself up for another in deed and action through sacrificial love that repels and fights the evil of the world. If Christendom is coming to an end, it is because there is less love in the world, which is true..."

"I... I never realized there was such a depth to what Catholics believe," Moira expressed. "None of this was ever shared with me, even from my grandparents."

"It sounds like you weren't catechized very well."

"What does that mean?"

"Instructed, or taught, in what the Church believes."

"No."

"Which is a shame, because the Catholic Church is more than just a religion – it is a nation, a kingdom, and a community of believers. It is a New Israel, just as how there was an old nation, kingdom, and community of believers of the God of Israel, that is made new in the Church which continues to worship the same God of those ancestors. Every Catholic is a New Israelite and provided a legacy passed down from the Old Israelites, and every baptized Christian is a Children of God predestined for salvation from this fallen world."

"It seems like a lot still though, to believe or not believe – I suppose that's what gets me the most, having family who don't necessarily believe like my grandparents do. What happens to them at the end of their lives?"

"I... I can't say for certain," Finn expressed, "but assuming they were baptized Christians, probably more than the unbaptized. You know, it really comes back to this important point about the world – this world was made in a particular way, and is very beautiful, and it is ultimately the world of man. I said it in the monastery to Mother Margaret, but in the beginning this entire world was predestined to be paradise, but humanity in their freewill chose to live their own way and such it became a corrupted world in which evil exists because God removed himself from our lives as our ancestors desired. God has little to nothing to do with this world other than the interventions he has already made and the Church he has established as his kingdom on Earth. He respects the freewill of all people to live in the way they so choose, even if that be a life of suffering and misery. For thousands of years, most of humanity lived without hope to the questions of suffering and misery, except the Israelites who had a promise from God that if they stayed faithful to him, they will be saved from the misery of the world in death at some point, but they had to stay faithful to God, hopeful in God, and continue to love God, and by extension of their love in God, love each other as well. Jesus Christ was the fulfillment of that promise, because he was God who walked on Earth, and he instructed and taught the people exactly what they need to do, how to live their lives, in a way that was faithful to God, hopeful in his promise, and loving him and neighbor. He lived and died the way he taught, and for that reason he remains the most inspirational human being because he was God in the flesh – a God that does not subjugate nor destroy, but serves, and liberated us from the darkness of the world. His death was at the hands of us humans, us evil ones who saw him and did not recognize him as the savior of the world, and the same evil that overcame the Romans and the Jews to condemn him to death, we all share in our humanity which is why we all share in the blood shed of Christ. Furthermore, if it was not because humanity had rebelled, Christ would never have had to suffer and die for us. Christ taught us what we need to do to be better persons, to be the person we were meant to be created before we rebelled, and in doing so and remaining faithful to him, hopeful in his promise of salvation, and loving him and neighbor, we can become the creations we were meant to always be. He has offered us an undoing of our rebellion, and that is what the Church provides on Earth, but access to the lives that we can; were meant to live, instead of the ones that we do live, together. I'll say it again, hopefully for the last time here, but the world is a miserable and horrible place – you know that, so here is the path away from all that. To clarify though, becoming a Christian is not a solution to your suffering nor will it alleviate you from the sufferings of the world, but it will give your sufferings a meaning and understanding that is worth enduring and persevering through in a worthwhile way, and we live that way together rather than alone, because we journey together to our final destination that all humans are predestined to, but only few are willing to say yes to.

"The rest of humanity is free to make their choice about the way they live their lives; it's their lives and their choices. I hazard though that most of humanity does so because they do not know how much better and freer the life they can live is than the life they currently live with empty promises, false hopes, and superficial love. I know I've lived that life, so has my father, my father's father, and so on… My grandfather, Everest Cabernet, was a man who stood out from the rest and defeated the expectations of his father and son – a man who presented to them as a selfish brat who lived for himself, abandoned his son and travelled the world with his lover, became a somewhat of a saint himself and perhaps the greatest of the Cabernets. My grandfather committed himself to serve the poor and the marginalized. For more than thirty years, he travelled the world with my grandmother, helping every sort of community in every corner of the world. When my grandmother died, he felt at loss for what he was really doing all this charitable work for, believing it to have been his own adventure for the sake of adventuring with his life and to an extent losing heart at their intentions to serve the poor rather than find adventure. Losing his wife made him realize the true purpose of their charitable work – to serve others. When his son (my dad), died, he felt at a greater sense of loss, but then I offered to travel with him. He taught me so much in that short time I was with him – a year and a half or so. We went to so many different places, saw so many different people, and it was an eye-opening experience to say the least because it made me fall in love with people. I felt moved at the experience of other persons, in how they live their lives, and I also saw a lot of goodness in others that I did not recognize in the developed world. I had lived my life in such a different way, always in self-pity and self-loathing until I saw how others lived and were grateful for the lives they had. The most bizarre part of it all was that these people did not know who I was, but they loved me too. Though don't get me wrong, there were some pretty awful people in these parts too – absolutely awful people, but a lot of good people who deserved so much more, but were content with what they had. The entire experience... it changed me for the better, and it was a shame when my grandfather died when he did come around, but he knew that when he did come around, he wanted to be with the woman he loved, so he made he received his final rites and went quietly. There was a man though he did not necessarily believe in God, he certainly loved in a way as if he did. He was virtuous... he was manly too. I loved him a lot, and he loved me too."

Moira sniffled as he brought the upside of her hand to her eyes. Finn quickly turned to her as she cried.

"What's wrong with you?" Finn questioned.

"That was... just really beautiful..." Moira remarked as tears fell from her eyes. "Don't mind me..."

Finn didn't respond as Moira took a tissue and blew her nose. They continued to drive down the road until they came around to a small town at the end of the freeway.

"Well, here we are..." Finn stated. "The middle of nowhere..."

Finn drove slowly through the town, passing a few buildings before they began to leave eastbound and could see a discount motel. He took in a deep breath, changed lanes, and then turn signaled to turn left and come into the large parking lot. The hotel sign read 'Far Far Away Motel' and below it was a green light sign that read 'Vacancy' with another black and white sign that read 'Pool Closed'. He parked the car in front of the motel where in the corner was a restaurant pub.

"I thought we didn't have any money for this…"

"Hardly anyways," Finn replied, "but you seem to want to stay in a cockroach infested motel room for the night just so you can have a hot shower."

"Cockroach?"

Finn exited the car and went to the motel lobby, which was a small room besides the restaurant with a coffee machine and check-in desk. Meanwhile, Moira began to prepare the backpacks and put her laptop away, while Finn returned with a pair of key cards.

"All yours, princess," Finn remarked, tossing them to her. "I'm going to scope the desert and get a sense of where we need to go."

"Wait, what?" Moira questioned. "How can I trust you? What if you don't come back? You can't just leave me here…"

"Oh, now you want company as well? Aren't you just full of wants and needs," Finn replied. "Sorry, but it's just one room and you're the only one who wanted to stay here. I'd rather sleep in the cockroach infested outdoors, or in the least in the car than stick around."

"That's not my point – you're going to leave me here, aren't you."

"I never said that…" Finn replied. "Besides, I got to do some reconnaissance and also make some time to install the shield attachment to the exosuit."

Finn picked up Moira's backpack and passed it to her.

"You wouldn't dare to go into that desert without me because you don't know where the power plant even is," Moira threatened. "You need me, Finn…"

"I'm sure I could figure it out eventually, but sure. Whatever you say." Finn's eyes looked over to the road as he saw a black van drive down. "Ah damn," he remarked, dodging around the side of the car. "Get down…"

The van passed the road and continued along. Finn gradually stood up and then looked over to Moira.

"How common is it to see a heavy-duty black van in the middle of nowhere?" Finn questioned. "They look just like the ones that my father saw the GDP use. Go ahead and make yourself at home… I'll be right back. If you don't see our car out here at night, worry all you'll like but I promise you I'll be back."

Finn came around to the driver's seat and then left the parking lot. He came onto the road and began to drive out, following the GPS waypoint and then turning off-road and going into the desert. The landscape around this town was much the same for most of the car ride over, though the sand became a little finer although there was still many dry plants and grasses that poked out. Finn stopped the car a fair distance from the road and then came out to the rear. He pulled the exosuit out and began to equip it, but as he brought the right arm attachments around, he hissed. "Ugh…" he growled. He brought his hand to the power button, and as the suit tightened. His growling got louder, and he stood up visibly uncomfortable. He began to look at the two attachments he retrieved, the flamethrower and the shield, but as he looked at the flamethrower, he instead picked up the shield attachment. He began to install it and when he was finished, began to try it out. At a flick of his left hand, the shield extended outwards and gave him a sizeable area of cover. The shield was oval shaped and also tall at close to a yard and a half. He grabbed the assault rifle and held it with both hands as he also had the shield out. He knelt down and the shield continued to cover him. He activated the propulsion jets and glider, and began to test all the items in combination as he ran forward and hopped onto a large boulder. He began to move along the desert as he jumped onto some buttes and got into position. Finn came forward and looked above. The sky was cloudy and sand-colored, and there was a partial thickness of fog as though the clouds covered the desert ahead and made it difficult to see. There was no wind though, and the air was stale though a bit polluted with sand. He took his binoculars out, but it was practically impossible to see too far ahead. He instead continued to traverse forward as he came into the desert itself and began to grow disoriented. Finn came around with careful steps as he tried to light the way with his headlamp, but it did little to provide clarity.

Eventually, Finn stopped as he found something poking out from the sand in front of him. He approached it and began to uncover the sand around it, seeing that whatever was buried was smooth and shiny. He grabbed hold of a portion of it and began to use the propulsion jets to pull it out as he yanked up, causing some of it to come out and reveal a robot buried in the sand. The robot was similar to the one seen in the monastery. Finn stopped his jets and simply looked at the robot with curiosity until its eyes suddenly shot open like two small light blue irises and a hand went for Finn's neck. He immediately began to struggle with the robot as it choked him, eventually using the rifle to shoot the robot in the chest and destroy it. The arm also fell off and without any power, the grip loosened, and it fell off though leaving a mark around his neck. He gasped for breath and then looked at the robot closely as it surely was the same robot as the one autopsied in the monastery.

Without hesitation, Finn immediately began to leave the desert as he followed the GPS to return to the SUV, and he was able to return without issue although the GPS lagged and showed inaccurate location details from time to time. He removed the exosuit and immediately pushed it inside the SUV as the sun began to set, and then he came around to sit down and drive back to the motel. He came around to the parking lot and pulled up in front of Moira's room. He then came around to the room and knocked on the door. Moira opened the door and Finn stepped inside.

"Ah, this looks lovely," Finn remarked. "A little better than I expected to be honest..."

"How did the reconnaissance go?"

"Visibility in the desert is low, but it should hopefully die down by tomorrow," Finn stated. "It's also a little chillier outside."

"What happened to your neck? Did the exosuit do that?"

"Hm? Uh, not exactly..." He explained to her what happened with the robot. "I'm not sure what I encountered, but we should be careful when moving in. Seems like we'll actually have to put up a fight."

"I can't wait then."

"I'm going to go for a drink in the pub," Finn noted. "Care to join me for a meal?"

"Sure..." Moira replied, "just let me shower and get ready."

"I'm hungry now," Finn noted. "You girls and your showers and getting ready takes up to an hour to do."

"I'll be twenty minutes tops," Moira complained. "Not like I have any other clothes to get changed into..."

Finn rolled his eyes and sat down in front of the mattress. Moira disappeared into the bathroom, while he looked out the crack in the blinds and then knelt down in front of the window. He looked out towards traffic on the street nearby, eyes going towards the gas station beside the motel, and then back to the traffic. He saw another one of the black vans, prompting him to stand up and close the blinds fully. He then sat down again and turned on the television set, changing channels to find the news. He watched some national coverage, but the news was typical and there was little out of the ordinary. He then switched to local county news and attempted to distract himself from looking out the window. After more than twenty minutes had passed, Finn stood up and looked out the window by which time Moira came out in the same set of clothes.

"Alright, I'm ready!" Moira remarked. "What are you looking at?"

"Nothing…" Finn replied, standing up straight. "About time – I'm starving."

The pair left the motel room and began to walk down the aisle that came around to the restaurant pub. The pub was rustic and there were only a few seats and a few windows that looked out around them. They came around to sit down at a table in the middle of the area where they ordered some drinks. There were a few people around the pub, mostly at the bar. Finn's eyes glanced everywhere from the people to the television sets to the windows. He appeared distracted; more distracted than usual.

Finally, a waitress came around with their drinks. Moira picked hers up and brought it to Finn's drink. "Here's to defeating yet another one of those horrible robots." Finn picked up his glass but did not move it towards hers. She moved hers and they clinked. She then took a sip while Finn downed a bit more. He then continued to look about.

"Do you reckon anyone here in this town may know about the power station?" Finn questioned. "The construction of something like that can't go a secret among so few people. People talk, it's just typical human behavior."

"I don't think people give up secrets that easily," Moira responded. "Life isn't a roleplaying game like Oblivion or Morrowind."

"I have no idea what you just said, but I beg to differ," Finn remarked. "I bet you I can approach anyone of these strangers and they'll tell me something wildly fascinating about this place. Just watch…" He stood up and approached the bar. He sat down besides a rugged male who looked at him. Finn raised a smile and said, "Hello there."

"Hello there yourself," the man responded in a bored tone.

"What rumors have you heard about this county?" Finn asked.

The man paused for a moment as though to think, and then turned to Finn and said, "Well, a while back they say there was a hiker who went missing looking for some ruins," the stranger stated. "Nobody ever found them, that's for sure."

"Ruins?"

"Yup, some ancient American ruins in the desert down south. Never found them either…"

"Interesting… thank you for your time…" Finn returned to his seat and sat down. "Told you," he said to Moira. "Ruins… ancient Americans, surely he means Native Americans."

"What does that mean?"

"I don't know, but it's proven my point – the term used for such behavior is similar to what is used in video games: non-playable characters, or NPCs, and refers to average everyday folk who babble on like that."

"That's so dehumanizing to say…"

"I'm not saying it's true. It's just a point of view," Finn scolded. "It's of course a generalization of how the average person thinks and acts, but to certain extents true nonetheless, especially when people fail or become submissive to their animal nature. I've seen it all too often in the UK and Canada."

Finn and Moira ate and drank, and people came and went through the restaurant pub. After a while of relaxation, Finn paid for the meal, and they left to return to the motel room. Moira laughed as she and Finn continued to chat and banter. However, as they came around to the motel room and Finn stopped in front, Moira smiled as she looked at Finn.

"Wasn't this nicer than being out in the cold right now? I know it's better than holding on to a rubber bottle filled with hot water," Moira expressed. "You know, if you want to not spend the night in the car or camped somewhere, there's another bed in the room."

"Ah, thanks, but I've been thinking about the hot bottle for a while now. I'm looking forward to it," Finn said with a smile. His eyes then looked towards the parking lot as he saw something move. He looked over and caught sight of an someone hunched over, dragging their feet as they traversed the parking lot. The pair turned and observed, eventually realizing that the someone was an object, and that object was another robot. "Oh no..."

The robot slowly approached them as it was hunched over, one arm dislocated from the others and wires pulled out from its chest.

"Is that the same one I met in the desert... Did it follow me here?" Finn questioned. "That's quite the determination, for a robot." He stepped forward and looked over at the robot as he squinted at it.

"Finn, be careful..." Moira cautioned as she stood back.

Finn looked at the robot and then turned his head over to the street as he saw half a dozen more. He stepped back as Moira realized too.

"Oh my gosh..." Moira quickly ran back and opened the motel room. She quickly pulled out the blaster and came around while Finn stepped back as they homed in towards them.

"Don't..." Finn warned, "as soon as you shoot, you'll raise eyebrows towards us for carrying experimental weapons. Let's just... perhaps, call the local police... They don't seem to be that much of a threat..."

The robot nearest immediately projectiled towards Finn, knocking him back and grabbing hold of his neck. Moira instantly shot its head off, and shot at its torso to knock it off him. The rest of the robots began to fasten their pace as they came to him. Finn opened the car door and picked up the rifle, stepping back as he saw them quickly come around.

"Come on!" Moira yelled to him.

Finn closed the door and retreated into the motel room. She closed the door behind him. Finn came around to the sofa and pushed it in front of the door. He also brought one of them beds over, tipped it up, and covered the hotel room window with it. Moira helped him move more furniture before he picked up the telephone to call 911.

"Hello, we need immediate police assistance at the Far Far Away motel!" Finn shouted. "We're being attacked by a bunch of robots! Please send the police to help..." The dial tone came through and Finn looked over at Moira. "Hello? I think they hung up on me..."

"Maybe you shouldn't have made it sound like a prank call."

"Ugh..." Finn remarked, dialing 911 again, "dammit!" He stopped the phone and shot at a robot that smashed through the window and attempted to crawl through a crack left in the barricade. Moira shot at the robot too. "There's only a couple of them... they're no threat..." He picked up the phone and listened to the dial tone again. He dialed 911 one last time, but it instantly went to dial tone. "I think they blocked this number...!"

Another robot attempted to insert into the motel room, while another also pushed through and the bed was pushed back. The pair instantly moved to the back of the motel room as they shot back at them, but after another minute the wave of robots began to pour through in larger numbers. They retreated into the bathroom where they could hear some voices speaking out from outside. The robots began to thump against the door while Finn went towards the window, shattered it, and then began to help Moira crawl through. Finn tossed his weapon up and then pulled himself through too, coming down to the other side where Moira passed him the rifle. The pair came down to the corner of the building where they could hear screams as robots infiltrated the restaurant. Some sirens could be heard not too far, but worse than seeing a police car, a black van zoomed in and came around in front of the parking lot. Some figures came out of the vehicles, but it was unclear what they looked like as Finn moved out of the way and began to lead Moira around to the other side. Finn saw that the horde of robots had disappeared from their bedroom, prompting him to take Moira's hand and make a dash towards the vehicle. He hopped over the hood of the SUV and looked towards the bedroom as most of the robots had vacated. He opened his car door and used it for cover as he took position.

"Ugh, wait!" Moira complained. "My stuff!"

"Forget about your stuff!" Finn replied. "Let's go!"

Moira left him and went back into the bedroom, going through the window and seeing remains of robots inside. Meanwhile, Finn looked over to the black van as he could hear some screams coming from the restaurant. The van was parked right in front of the entrance and made it unclear to see, but he could see some people running for their lives. A few robots lingered around, but they did not target Finn who continued to hold his place until he looked up towards the sky and saw a streak of fire shoot down and land in the parking lot – this robot, intact and with a fist pointed forward began to scan the area with its red eyes.

"You bastards!" Finn shouted, opening fire at it. The high energy rifle immediately incapacitated the robot and caused it to fall over. Some more of these robots began to land in the area, prompting Finn to let loose and open fire at them all. Moira came back and threw her backpack into the car, and then joined him as she opened fire. The gunshot hit the side of the van, causing the engine to erupt into a fireball, as well as some other vehicles parked in the parking lot until he ran out of ammunition. By the time the gunfire had settled, the parking lot was quiet and in the background was the flash of blue and red from police sirens. Finn looked about as his body trembled. Moira looked over to him. Some police officers from nearby also looked over, prompting Finn to step into the car and pass his rifle to Moira. The officers stood up and pointed their pistols at them, but Moira shot with her blaster and kept them down while Finn started the car, and she continued to take shots with the door open as she sat down until it shut on its own. The car then raced out of the motel, and they made their exit towards the desert. "I think it's safe to say that the Chosen know where we are…"

"You think?"

Act 6, Scene 2

Finn drove the SUV into the desert after a few minutes driving eastbound. He went along as the car bumped up and down, while Moira kept an eye behind them as the flash of sirens and screams of chaos were left behind them. After the town was no longer visible behind them, Finn drove slightly into the midst of the sand cloud that ravaged the desert lands, hitting a cactus, prompting him to drive more carefully as he came around and hid behind a butte.

"Alright…" Finn remarked, taking in a deep breath, "I think that'll do."

"So much for my pillow and beauty sleep," Moira mumbled.

"Hello water bottle and sleeping bag," Finn replied. "I'll start a fire…"

The pair began to set up behind the large butte, although it was difficult even to see in the storm cloud they were in. The lights of the SUV were kept on to give them some light, but even with that light they could barely manage to set up the tents and a campfire. They both sat down around the fire, weapons at their side, and began to set in as some water was boiled.

"I didn't get a chance to pick up much water, so we'll have to use this for both comfort and survival."

"It's so cold right now…" Moira remarked. "It's got to be ten degrees below freezing… How did you want to sleep in this?"

"No better than it was in Alaska or Montana," Finn replied. "You just got used to how warm it was in Idaho…"

"Do you think they're looking for us?"

"Most likely, but they won't be looking in here," Finn responded. "Both the police and the Chosen have no idea what we're capable of, or that they're dealing with a certified survivalist. We'll have to lodge here for the rest of the night, but at daybreak start to drive in a bit more with the car, if we can and this cloud passes. Otherwise, we'll travel on foot."

"I barely got a chance to charge my laptop…"

"What do you need your laptop for in these parts?" Finn questioned. "You'll barely be able to get a signal, I reckon."

"If it weren't for my laptop, I doubt we'd be able to have made this amount of progress," Moira replied.

"Dammit, now that we've made some noise out at that motel, the Chosen may put two and two together…" Finn noted aloud, ignoring Moira's remark. "We'll definitely need to act fast these next twenty-four hours as they mobilize."

"Do you think they see us as much of a threat?"

"I would say so," Finn responded. "Come on, let's get some sleep." He finished boiling the rest of the water, pouring it into a hot water bottle, and then the two went to their respective tents for the night. Before Finn went to bed, he came around to the SUV and turned off the lights.

The next day, Finn woke up and immediately opened his tent cover to see that it was still foggy and difficult to see. He sighed and went over to the fire pit to begin to light it again and restart the fire. He re-used the water from the hot water bottle and began to make them some breakfast, and by the time Moira was out, they were huddled around the fire as sunlight attempted to poke through the cloud barrier before them.

"I could have sworn I heard thunder last night," Moira stated. "I could also see flashes of lightning."

"You're losing it," Finn remarked. "How and where?"

"Somewhere nearby. It happened a few times. I almost woke you up but then it went away."

"Could have been an explosion…"

"No, it was definitely thunder and lightning," Moira responded. I saw the flash out that way," she said, pointing down south. "It sounded just like thunder too."

"I'm no expert, but I doubt that's possible in a cloud like this… I seem to recall lightning comes about when two different weather fronts meet together, or something like that."

"I'm just telling you what I heard and saw. If you want to believe me or not is your problem."

Finn didn't respond and instead continued to finish his breakfast. When the two were finished, he poured out the rest of the water from his coffee into the fire and then they began to come around to the car.

"So, are we going to drive the rest of the way?" Moira questioned.

"I'm going to see how far we can go before it's impractical," Finn replied. "Come on."

The pair got into the car, and Finn took the keys and began to attempt to turn them. The car attempted to start up and a few lights and such turned on, but then they died out.

"What the hell..."

"Oh my God..." Moira muttered.

"Watch your mouth," Finn replied. "The battery is dead..."

"Did you leave it to charge your exosuit or something? How can it be dead?"

"I don't know – I didn't leave any lights on, did I?" Finn questioned, looking around. "Alright, there's no need to panic. We'll just take what we need and set off on foot. Did you set up the waypoints for us on the GPS?"

"I looked at the satellite images I saved and marked some places for us to investigate."

Finn looked at the waypoints on the GPS. "Great," he replied, "as if we'd be able to even tell where we're going in this storm..."

"You don't think that... the storm could be related to any of it?"

"What?"

"It's just that, in Alaska, there was a rainstorm that disappeared after we destroyed the robot guardian there, and in Montana, a windstorm, and in Idaho a heat storm of some sort... and this... a sandstorm..."

"… that apparently spews thunder and lightning?"

"So you believe me?"

"No, I think you're being absolutely ridiculous. You're practically suggesting the Chosen are able to control the weather."

"Not them, but the robots must be doing something…"

"It's just a coincidence, now come on."

Finn opened the rear of the SUV, took out the exosuit, and equipped it. Meanwhile, Moira put on the optic camouflage suit. She also picked up the grenade launcher and put her blaster in the holster, tightened it to her right thigh, and then picked up her backpack.

"Not so fast," Finn remarked, "put these on, the gloves from the elite soldier. They should give you an enhanced ability to climb on most surfaces."

"How kind…" Moira replied. "What happened to my shield?"

"Sorry, the flamethrower didn't quite suit me," Finn said, showing his forearm. "Besides, I'd rather protect what's left of my left side lest it become like the right."

Moira took the gloves and put them on. She attempted to climb up the side of the SUV, which she was able to do with ease. "Not bad…" she replied, "thanks." She hopped down.

Finn closed the back of the SUV and then locked it. "Okay… we'll aim to rendezvous back here if we get lost or split up. Let's do this…" He put on his sunglasses and then approached the dust cloud.

Finn took the first steps forward as he came into the desert with Moira. They were able to see close to a few yards around them as they traversed forward with careful steps. The ground at their feet was similar to the rest of the desert thus far, grains of sand with bits of dry vegetation. There were a few cacti and other signs of life as they wandered into the desert, but for the most part they moved slowly and as a result made slow progress travelling to the first waypoint several miles away. After a few minutes, the pair came along a sand-colored rocky surface and began to go up slope and past two cliff sides. They came up to a small plateau with other pointed rocks around them, and continued forward as they began to climb the side of a dune. The ground at their feet also turned to a finer and lighter sand than the coarse sand from before. This dune took them above and along a plain surface that sloped up and down at yard length intervals. Eventually, Finn noticed an edge in the land ahead of them, prompting him to walk carefully and find a large cliffside descent downwards into a crevasse. They walked carefully around the edge of the crevasse and bypassed it to travel forward. The sand in this part of the desert became even finer, at a nearly light blonde color with grooves in the texture of the landscape. The area at their feet continued to be flat with ups and downs at regular intervals, and the sandstorm cloud began to thin out as they approached a set of rocks in the distance. Finn took a step towards the rocks as he noticed one of them tall and arched as they approached.

The pair passed underneath the rock and stayed put under the shade of the arch for a moment as they caught their breath and rested.

"It's a little hot out there," Finn admitted, drinking some water. "The dust storm is not making it easier... we might run into a water problem soon."

"A water problem?" Moira questioned. "Oh great... more problems..."

The pair continued down and began to pass a few large boulders before coming around to a stony plateau in the midst of them. They continued along where there was a steep slope downward in the middle of their path, burrowing into a cave in the ground. They went around and came around to a few more large, pointed rocks in the earth. They then reached a tall ledge that looked down and across a sizeable section of land. The dust cloud was thinner in this part and the ledge a couple yards above gave them a view of the area around them. There were a few dunes that rolled up and down like hills in the foreseeable distance, and tall cliffs at the side of plateaus and mesas around the sides, but otherwise the desert stretched on for miles upon miles. Moira lowered herself with her gloves, while Finn gently glided down, and the pair then proceeded to continue forward towards the first of many checkpoints. They went up the side of a dune ahead and then continued along the top of the ridge as they continued in the direction they needed to go. As they continued, they passed a few cacti and then made their descent downwards and continued as the sand became a lot coarser again. The ground at their feet also became mixed with dry grass again as they continued along, passing a few clean-cut stone rocks in the way. The vegetation was spread out in bunches, and they were about a foot tall. They were not alone as there was an odd shrub or two spread out amidst the entire field of land ahead of them. The sun continued to pierce down through the dust cloud as they ventured forward. They began to climb up the side of a cliff and then continued along its ledge, where on the right was a sporadic displacement of rocks with gaps between them in a particular set up. They then continued past this space as they found themselves in a more consistent grassland, still mixed with sand at their feet but this time with more cacti spread out in bunches that were hard to see. The grassland came up to another low sloped rise that went upwards to another cliff edge with a tree atop. The pair stopped for lunch near the tree where they were shunned from the dust cloud for a moment to catch their breath.

"Ugh, it's all over my skin," Moira complained, looking at her arms and hands. "It's only been a few hours…"

"Should've kept yourself clothed better," Finn replied, removing his sunglasses. "We're a few miles away… I've set my suit to detect electromagnetic signals. I think we're going to have to triangulate the position of this power station."

"You just think of that?"

"I've had a lot of time to think," Finn responded, having another drink. "We'll use our waypoints as sample locations and then that'll hopefully point us in an appropriate way."

After the break, the two continued along the desert as they came across another smoother section, but this time the sand taking on a redder color. By the time they reached the waypoint, the pair slowly began to approach a slim metal tower that was propped up.

"Alright, let me get a reading…" Finn looked at his wrist and then waited for a moment. He then read the reading out to Moira who wrote it down. They then proceeded to climb down the side of the cliff to continue in an adjacent direction when Moira nearly tripped on something in the ground. The pair turned around, especially as the object in the ground shook. Moira gave a brief screech as she saw the robot climb out of the sand, prompting her to quickly pull out her pistol and shoot it. Meanwhile, the rest of the ground began to shake, and other robots began to surface. "Oh no…" Finn complained. "What is this?"

The robots began to rise from the ground like zombies, but these robots were similar to the ones that they had encountered at the motel. They were misshapen, badly beaten, and sometimes had missing limbs and hangings wire. Their eyes were light blue, and they also twitched like the enhanced robots they had encountered, but they had no weapons though some of them attempted to point their fists outwards, but no projectile came forward. Finn shot at the robots around him with Moira until it became quiet again. Moira put her pistol away and Finn looked over at her.

"I don't understand... how are they doing this?" Finn questioned. "Is it some sort of end-of-life survival mechanism? A last wind?"

"Seems like it..." Moira remarked. "If we weren't in a hurry, I'd see what sort of code is running through their system right now. How far is the next way point?"

"A bit of a ways away," Finn remarked. "If we encounter anymore before sundown, we can take a look, but right now I want to just triangulate an approximate location."

The pair left the scene and then continued to go along the desert way as they began to pass through a thick storm cloud.

"Argh, the GPS is malfunctioning..." Finn remarked. "There's some sort of interference..."

The pair stopped as the saw a crack of lightning ahead. They were then met with a loud boom around them.

"Now do you believe me?!" Moira questioned.

Finn looked ahead, stunned at what had just occurred.

"I don't know about you, but whatever did that can't be good news..." Finn remarked. "Let's not go in that direction."

The pair continued to stroll through the desert cloud as another crack of lightning could be seen in the corner of their eyes, followed with the roll of thunder.

"You don't think that could be the enhanced robot that's waiting for us in the power plant, do you?" Moira asked.

"A robot with the capability to summon lightning strikes would be just as bizarre as the capability of the Chosen to control the weather," Finn rebuked. "I only know one being that's capable of summoning lightning, and that is not our worry right now."

The pair kept their heads down as the storm intensified. They continued to proceed along the path as they found themselves within an hour at the foot of the second waypoint. This waypoint was placed at a bizarre looking butte in the midst of the desert storm.

"Is this it?" Finn questioned. "It's just a weird looking rock?" He attempted to jump up to get a better look, but his propulsion jets could not take him the entire length upwards. He attempted to kick off the side of the rock to get a double jump, but it was impractical. Finn's glider broke his fall, and he looked over to Moira. "Can you see if you see anything up there?"

"Uh… I could, but how am I going to get down from there?"

"The same way you got up," Finn replied. "Just think of it as though you were climbing a ladder."

"Okay…" Moira replied, stepping forward. She began to climb up while Finn steered around the side of the rock to keep an eye on her. He then stepped on top of a metal object in the ground.

"Dammit…" Finn remarked, shooting into the sand.

Moira turned around to look, and as she did, she noticed three more rise up from the sand. Finn turned to them and began to point his rifle at them.

"Oh my… Finn!" Moira shouted.

"Nevermind them – I'll take care of them. You just keep climbing…!"

Moira turned to the rock wall and continued to climb up the side. He continued to shoot back at robots as the emerged from the sand, but for every one robot he shot and destroyed, three more arose to replace it. He began to back up as they continued to emerge, while Moira continued to climb. The robots came up and up, and Moira climbed up and up too. Eventually, she reached the top of the rock and found another pole with subpoles attached perpendicular to the main section. She then turned around as she saw the robots continuing to swarm around, prompting Finn to evacuate with his glider and hover away. She knelt down and loaded her grenade launcher with a round, and then shot towards the horde causing a majority of them to be destroyed. Finn shot at the rest while another horde appeared from nearby and began to go towards Finn. She shot another round towards them and blew them into pieces while Finn cleaned up the rest.

"Good grief…" Finn muttered, looking up and over to Moira. "Alright, what do you see?!"

"It's just another pole…" Moira replied. "What do you want me to do?"

"Hm…" Finn thought for a moment. "Destroy it!"

"Okay…" Moira replied. She took one of her rounds, placed it at the base of the pole. She then climbed down the ledge and took a shot at it with her blaster before she hopped down, covering her head and then climbing down the side of the rock. The blast destroyed the base of the pole and caused it to crash down. "Not sure what that was supposed to achieve…"

"It's supposed to deter any potential signal interruptions," Finn replied. "Take note of this."

Moira took note of the signal and then the pair continued along the desert as they crossed from one point to another. This journey through the desert took more time than the other, and it involved going through the thickened cloud again for approximately two hours. The pair found the last anomaly to be atop of a low mesa. They were both able to climb up the side of the formation and found another pole, which they destroyed with ease. The pole came crashing down and Finn took another reading. Moira noted it and then they began to do some calculations.

"Alright… I've marked the GPS with the next waypoint," Finn remarked. "Let's hope that this is it… These are some pretty powerful electromagnetic signals I'm picking up…"

"Uh, Finn?" Moira questioned, pointing over the mesa. "Look below…"

Finn looked over and could see a dozen or so robots submerged in the sand on the other side. They began to twitch and move, rising up from the ground like the dead alive once more.

"Oh, come on!" Finn complained. "We didn't even do anything to trigger them!"

"I don't think it's about that..."

Moira and Finn began to take shots at the robots from above, but as they did the robots in the surrounding area began to pick up their speed and fasten their crawl towards the top of the rock. Finn activated his glider to hover mode as they got close.

"Let's go!" Finn remarked.

Moira shot a grenade towards them, causing a lot of them to be destroyed. They were then able to clean up the rest.

"I'm sorry? You were saying?"

"Nothing."

"Before we go to this next waypoint, I want to return to the original and see if we can destroy it and get another reading. I'm afraid they may be interfering with what we're doing here."

"Lead the way."

Moira and Finn began to retrace their steps to return to the initial pole they had encountered. As they came around to the pole, they both noticed robots lingering around the base of it. Moira shot two grenades at them, clearing the area, while Finn picked off stragglers. The force of the blast caused the pole to collapse, and once it was clear they took a moment to rest.

"I think we have an hour or two before the sun sets," Finn remarked. "I would rather set up camp somewhere indoors than outdoors, so let's..." He paused as he began to hear a noise in the distance.

"What is it? Thunder?"

"Ssh..." Finn hushed. He looked up and then suddenly, surrounding them at four corners they were met with the same variant of robots that attacked them in Allabrese. "Ambush!"

"Cease and destroy!" the robots chimed in a deep voice.

"I'll cease and destroy your ass," Moira replied, firing a grenade at one of them. She then pulled her pistol and shot at another, while Finn took two at the same time as well. The robots did not stand a chance at their weapons, but they were not over yet. Another two showed up near Moira, and then another two showed up near Finn. "You've got to be kidding me..."

Finn exposed his shield and then began to back up as the robots wound up their cannons and began to open fire. The robots fired high-energy shots as well, but the shield did its work. Moira shot another grenade at one of them and then backed up towards Finn and took cover behind a rock. She readied another grenade and then shot at the robot that approached her, destroying it completely. Meanwhile, Finn was able to take care of the two on him as he protected himself with his shield. The pair paused for a moment, freezing at the sound of thunder in the distance. Finn lowered the shield and then turned to Moira.

"I'm going to get another reading," Finn remarked, looking at his wrist. "Just as I thought – it's different now."

"Is it different because of what we've done here, or because whatever is being tracked is moving?"

"What could be moving that emits this much energy?" Finn questioned. "We should have a new waypoint. Let's see what it is..." He and Moira made some calculations and then punched the coordinates into the GPS. "A lot farther away from the initial... let's go."

The pair went down and began to travel in a straightforward direction as they continued through the desert. They eventually began to go into another sand shroud where they covered their eyes and kept their heads down. Some more thunder and lightning could be heard and seen, but none that was near them. Additionally, Finn often stopped as he thought he heard the sound of missiles from further combat robots flying in to the desert, but they were from a distance. As they ventured, they stopped as they found some palm trees and shrubs near a small oasis besides a cliffside wall.

"Thanks be to God," Finn remarked, coming around to the water. He dipped his hands into the water to douse his face, and then began to wash it too.

"Gross, don't put your germs into the water. I want to be able to drink that…"

Finn stood up as he looked at her and then around as it became darker and darker. He saw a crack in the cliff wall that created a small cavern and walked towards it.

"We have a few options here…" Finn remarked. "We can continue forward and hope we find the power facility at the waypoint, which I'm not entirely confident of, or we can go back to the SUV where it's possibly nice and safe, or we camp here for the night and risk a nightly encounter with the Chosen-bots."

"You think they'd find us here?"

"We'll have to pitch our sleeping bags in here and cover the entranceway," Finn stated. "That should be enough to keep us safe and obscure. Obviously, we'll have to destroy whatever fire we create now to boil the water."

Moira looked at her watch and then around her. She turned to Finn and replied, "Let's rest up. We can continue on in the morning. I feel like we'll need to save our breathes here after we've been walking around almost aimlessly all day now. Who knows what more is left for us to face."

Act 6, Scene 3

The next morning, Finn woke up a foot or two away from Moira within the small cavern in the cliff wall. He stepped out of the cavern where the tents were pitched in front of to block view of the crack, and then stepped down to re-ignite the fire. The surroundings around the oasis were clear. The skies and general atmosphere had also cleared out somewhat which allowed him to assess the scene and realize that the oasis in itself was somewhat secluded as cliff walls surrounded it on two sides, and passageways out from this grotto on the other sides. After Finn had started the fire, he equipped the exosuit and began to investigate the surroundings in greater detail. The area around the oasis appeared much as it felt to have walked on, seeing rolling dunes in either direction. He came back down as he assessed there to be no hostiles in the nearby area, and began to prepare breakfast, at which point Moira woke up and joined him.

"Good morning to you," Finn greeted. "We've got a few miles to the waypoint, and hopefully we'll be a little closer to this power facility. I checked the scene, and it seems like we're in the clear – none of those death robots nor zombie robots in sight."

"Lovely..." Moira replied. "Always nice to assess the chances in which we may die today..."

"I'll take it that you didn't sleep very well," Finn responded. "Something obviously rubbed you the wrong way."

Moira didn't reply. They ate breakfast, wrapped up their belongings, and then began to continue the journey into the desert.

Finn followed the GPS carefully as they began to walk into a thick dust shroud. They heard a few rumbles of thunder, and the GPS began to lag again as they went forward. The sands in this area were fine and blonde colored. Eventually, they came across a barbed wire fence with signs that read 'RESTRICTED AREA' in large font followed by 'No Trespassing Beyond This Point' while another sign read 'Private Property' and another said 'Warning!' in large letters with a threat of imprisonment and a hefty $10,000 fine. Finn jumped over the fence and then used the exosuit to bring a pole down and create a space for Moira to climb through. They continued along without much issue, reaching a cliff wall and then finding an entrance into a canyon. They followed the canyon path forward as it brought them around a set of pointed rocks and then they reached a cave-in in the path. Finn boosted himself up to begin to climb, stopping to give Moira a helping hand as she climbed up on her own. They traversed over the rocks and then looked down as the path winded around. They followed forward as they went along before reaching a clearing with a slope around the sides for them to follow upwards. They began to ascend the side of the cliff and reach a plateau above where the shroud was thick, and it was difficult to see in front of them. As they walked, Finn stopped as he could hear the sound of something crawling in the sand. He also heard the sound of rotors as they moved, but he could not see anything around him. He continued to look around until Moira pointed out.

"Look!" Moira shouted.

A robot began to approach them with a hunch, followed by few more. They took a step back as a few of them came out and Moira fired a grenade at them. They both covered their heads as scraps of metal fell down around them. A few more came around, so Finn shot at them with the assault rifle while Moira used the blaster pistol. They moved forward, shooting at stragglers and maimed remnants around them before they began to see ahead where against a cliff wall was a short Mesoamerican pyramid, partially covered by a dune of sand. Finn quickly looked at his GPS and then back over to the pyramid.

"This can't be our waypoint..." Finn remarked. "It's a pyramid... Where's the fusion reactor?"

Moira didn't respond as she looked ahead towards an entrance below the top of the pyramid. She looked at the sigil as there was an object emboldened outwards from the emblem. The object of which was like that of a spider. She began to raise the grenade launcher towards the sigil, to which Finn noticed.

"What is it?" Finn questioned.

Without hesitation, Moira fired the grenade launcher and caused the spider-like object to drop from the emblem. The object dropped beneath the entrance, and immediately jumped forward onto its feet before hunching over and then crawling forward at a quick speed as they opened fire at it. The creature jumped forward and launched itself, flipping through the air and then landing in front of them. It then began to crawl forward as its clawed feet split apart, giving it two sets of legs that allowed it to propel forward, raising a fist as it came towards Finn. Finn quickly activated his shield as the creature propelled a fist towards Finn. The blow was absorbed by the shield, but it pushed him back at least two feet in the sand. Moira shot at the creature's head, causing it to aim its left arm as it held a rifle of some sort and shoot a bright beam of light forward, but Moira was gone. She disappeared and was nowhere to be seen. Finn pointed the rifle towards the torso of the creature and was about to fire when it used one of its legs to disarm him, tossing the weapon aside. It then attempted to punch him again, creating a dent in the shield before Moira re-appeared and took a shot at its side. Finn used his shield to bash the creature, prompting it to push itself off from the shield and then scatter away. It did a flip forward and then propelled itself up towards the side of the pyramid. Finn quickly re-armed himself with his rifle while Moira disappeared again. He then brought his shield out as it began to fire this beam towards him. He took cover behind a rock and stayed put as the plasma hit the side of the rock. Moira fired another grenade at it as she took cover behind another boulder opposite from Finn, causing the ledge it was on to collapse and for it to fall down.

The creature let out a horrible and high-pitched screech, causing the sand around them to shake as robots appeared from beneath the sand and began to approach both of them. Moira shot a grenade in the midst of them, while Finn began to open fire at a few of them and then she did the same. The creature meanwhile scrambled to get itself off the ground and then began to crawl away from the debris, climbing up the side of the pyramid as it contorted and flipped its body to reach the top of the pyramid again. As the others cleaned up the robots that appeared from amidst the sand, others began to appear from around them and the enhanced robot began to shoot its beam towards each of them, forcing them to stay huddled behind the rock. Moira shot a grenade at a crowd of robots that approached her, and then she turned and shot towards a crowd that approached Finn. The robots were blown up in large portions and left stragglers for them to clean up. As they did so, Finn noticed the plasma beam stop and so he turned his head to check on the enhanced robot, which had jumped down and began to go towards him. He instantly turned and shot towards it, but it pivoted upwards and did a side flip in a quick reaction to his gunfire. The enhanced robot then crawled up the rock and pivoted its body around to take hold of Finn by the shoulders, bringing its body around to entrap him. Finn struggled to move and saw the robot point its cannon towards his body, but Moira quickly shot at its head and torso, shooting at the claws that kept Finn trapped to knock it off. He quickly shot at it too as it disappeared, turning around to watch it go back towards the pyramid. Moira prepared another grenade as it came to the top of the pyramid and pointed its arm out towards them. She launched the grenade and hit the stone beneath the robot, causing it to collapse inward. She quickly reloaded and fired another one, causing the entrance to collapse in and send dust upwards. The creature let out a horrible screech that summoned a few more robots from within the sand around them, but before Finn re-acted to them, he shot towards where the creature was as it began to crawl up and disappear into a slim crack atop of the pyramid.

Moira and Finn stepped out of their cover as they began to approach the base of the pyramid and cleaned up the few robots that appeared and began to home in on them. Once they were finished, they knelt down and reloaded their weapons.

"That thing is here, so perhaps that's a promising sign," Finn noted, checking his left wrist. The signal is also strong here – there seems to be some powerful electromagnetic presence within this pyramid."

"What do we do?" Moira questioned. "We're not here to go tomb raiding…"

"I know," Finn noted, "but these things… they act like guardians to their surroundings, so I say we follow it into its nest," he said, equipping the flamethrower to his forearm. "Who knows where this pyramid could lead or take us… All these robots laying around – something happened here, and I'd hazard that our fallen GDP elite soldier fought in these parts."

"A hiker went missing going into this pyramid," Moira pointed out. "Who knows what traps could be inside…"

"I'm more worried about the creature inside," Finn stated. "Any hiker that comes across one of those is done for…"

The pair stood up and looked up towards the pyramid behind them. This Mesoamerican pyramid was tall even though an unspecified amount of it was submersed underneath the sand. The side of the pyramid were smooth, though cracked and somewhat overgrown with dried vines. The front of the pyramid had a set of steps that went up the entrance, and above that entrance was another layer from which the enhanced robot disappeared through. The corners of the pyramid had small turret-like towers with statues at either corner. The base of the pyramid was close to one hundred or so yards in length. The pyramid was backed into the cliff wall on the other side from where they stood in a round and large canyon.

Moira and Finn went up the steps of the pyramid to come up towards the entrance, which was caved in, but tall. The entrance was also triangle shaped and led into a wide rectangular corridor with three pillars on either side. There were piles of sand that had collected in either corner of the entrance. At the end of the corridor was a tall metal door within a nook that prevented them from carrying forward.

"Should we find another way?" Moira questioned.

Finn placed a hand on the door as he examined it, "I didn't realize Native Americans were skilled in metallurgy to be able to construct such a heavy door." He looked down at the ground and then began to take a step back as he looked at the walls. He approached a crack in the wall and placed his hands over it. "A sophisticated door means sophisticated interior wiring..." He raised his right leg up and kicked at the crack, causing it to crumble. He kicked it several times and then knelt down. He turned on his head lamp and looked inside. "Do you think you can get in here and take a look?"

"Do I have a choice?" Moira questioned, kneeling down and then crawling inside. "What am I looking for?"

"Anything that could get us through to the other side," Finn shouted. "Tell me what you see..."

"Not much space in here... I can't turn my body. I see some wires and some... pistons? I also see... a vent cover..."

Finn listened as Moira moved around in the interstitial space. She opened the vent cover and then stepped inside to the other side.

"Okay, I'm in!"

"How about getting me through?!" Finn questioned. "Any switches? Levers?"

"There's no power!" Moira cried out. "Nothing does anything..."

"No power…" Finn muttered. "Hm… See if you can find any release inside somewhere…"

Finn listened as Moira began to shuffle around. She climbed up the wall and found a switch. She pulled it down and then came around to the other side and pulled another switch. The doors immediately fell open and collapsed. Finn came around to the door and looked around. He found a panel besides the door that was turned off. Moira came out through the vent cover and joined Finn who passed her backpack to him. The space they were in was squared and tall room. The wall ahead of them consisted of tall five by eight feet bricks with a small square gap in the middle. Finn listened as he could hear a faint moan down the steps.

The pair began to descend down the steps together, going approximately fifty feet downwards and coming out to a corridor with a metal catwalk over a gap. There were two catwalks separated by a space in between. The gap beneath the catwalks was approximately ten feet by ten feet, squared, and dropped down close to twenty feet below. Finn attempted to look down, but could not see the bottom of the pit. The pair crossed over and came to the other side, bringing them into a square room. A pair of steps on the left brought them into another squared room, which led into a corridor with reinforced steel walls. A set of nodules were set up in a vertical straight line in three pairs across the corridor on either side, prompting Finn to examine them.

"What are they?"

"Look like some sort of laser pointer," Finn stated, "but they're dead." He stepped through and nothing happened. He walked down to the other side of the corridor and then came to a corner. The corridor doubled down around in a near squared shape before they reached a corridor that went down again. This corridor was sloped like a ramp, and a covering was placed overtop to increase grip. The ramp led into a large rectangular room with a drop in the middle. At the opposite side of the room was a small corridor that led out. The surroundings of the dropped space had a catwalk, and around the sides of the room were crates and machinery for moving crates. Within the dropped space were some more crates. The drop was accessible via a ramp at the side that went up. "I think it's safe to say this isn't looking much like a tomb than it did on the outside."

At the end of the room was another ramp that led down into another rectangular room, which stored all sorts of equipment and machinery. To the left of this room was another, larger ramp, which led into an incredibly tall room with light pouring out from above.

"Looks like we've found the heart of the pyramid," Finn noted, looking above, "which means that creature thing could be anywhere."

"Is this it? Is this the power plant?"

"I don't know," Finn replied, "but I'd hazard a guess to say no." He stepped forward into the room and noticed that the surrounding was covered with a raised floor made of see-through grate pieces with thick wires underneath. They all came together towards the center of the room which had a solid squared platform. The squared platform had a set of lamps at either corner and there were many more lamps set up throughout the chamber. Finn walked up onto the platform and found a lever aboard. He then went down to the other side where he found a set of doors that continued through to the other end. These doors were thick and grated and the wiring beneath them continued into this other room. Moira looked around the rest of the chamber and noticed that there were a set of stairs that came around, going up the chamber at intervals. These stopped at four intervals each, going down corridors that went in each compass direction. "Wherever we are, it must be some sort of preparation area for the reactor."

"What makes you think that?" Moira replied.

"Because there is no power," Finn responded, annoyed. "How can it make sense that this is a power facility if there is no power. What's providing power to the production line of robots otherwise?"

"Alright, keep your pants on."

"Besides, this space is too small and crowded. It's all makeshift," Finn asserted. He pointed towards the cables that ran up along the side of the wall. "Let's restore power to this place and see where this lift takes us." He approached the doors ahead of him. "Come over here, see if you can fit underneath."

Finn squatted down, grabbed the end of the doors, and then began to lift them up. The exosuit helped him push up and pull the heavy doors open. Moira quickly crawled through and began to look around. She went down a squared corridor and came out to a large room where there were servers and other equipment set up with monitors, dashboards, and sloped control panels with levers and gauges. She also found some batteries and power vaults.

"I found some sort of control room," Moira reported over the radio. "There's a couple of robots in here that look destroyed, but otherwise I don't see anything else."

"Okay, you should find an emergency generator, maybe," Finn replied. "Let me know if you see it."

"Yeah, I see something like the one at the GPD headquarters," Moira responded, approaching it. "I'm going to turn it on." She began to pump the switch, and then pressed the button. She then flipped a switch, and the generator began to hum. Some lights in the room began to turn on, and a monitor also flipped on. She walked over to the monitor and pressed enter on the keyboard, and then she lowered her backpack as the computer turned on. "Alright, I've got power..." prompting Finn to step through as the doors opened. He joined her in the control room as they both looked at the console read 'No Power' and display four progress bars. "Or at least I thought I did..."

"Looks like we're need to activate some generators set up around the pyramid," Finn stated. "I'll get to it…"

Finn left and began to climb up the stairs, coming around to a landing that led down a corridor. He came around to a room with a tall and long corridor set up, and the wires went underneath a pair of turbines that slowly turned. He began to carefully navigate through the turbines to reach a tunnel that went around both directions, but was grated on one of them. He approached a ladder that went up to a small room within. In this room, he found several generators set up in each corner with platforms around them. The wires travelled underneath the turbine structures set up and connected to each generator. Some consoles were set up along a side of the room, so Finn went to them.

"I'm in a generator room," Finn stated. "I've got access to a console, but it's asking for a password."

"Hold on," Moira responded. "Do you have the PC number?"

"Yeah, one second…" Finn replied, reading a serial number on a label besides the console. He then waited.

"Okay, I've got the password…" She then read out another serial number, which Finn typed in. He then pressed enter.

"It worked," Finn reported. He then began to go through several options as he worked to get the generator to run. The machines soon began to hum and the lights in the room flickered on. The turbines began to fasten their speed. "Not good…" He then turned to face the console again as he read some instructions on the screen. "Wait a minute… Fusion reactor status, off-line?"

"I found some instructions," Moira added. "Each of these generators power up the facility independently, and seems to me like this place is as you say it is – some sort of preparation area to provide plasma to the fusion reactor. "I'm looking at schematics. You're going to need to activate the plasma generator at the end of those tunnels. There should be another control room on the other side of that room you're in."

"I'll take a look," Finn replied. He glided down and began to walk down the circular tunnels as the fans spun. He came around to the opposite side where he found himself in a squared room with a circular ditch in the middle. The ditch was covered by protective glass. He climbed up a ladder to a catwalk above it, and approached a console. Like at the other console, he provided a PC number and she provided him a password. "Alright, I'm in..." The computer began to run its own code and self-automate, while sparks began to present in the vat while a turbine spun underneath. Soon, a cloud formed within the vat and after long, a long streak of plasma developed. Finn followed a set of tubes from which the plasma travelled down as he returned to the main chamber and saw them go down into the grate below. "Alright, I've cleared the first floor. I'm moving up to the second."

Finn exited out and began to climb up the stairs to come around to the second floor. He found a corridor that led into a small square room which had similar generators and consoles than the room before. He approached the console and began to repeat the PC number to Moira, and in return received a password. He typed the password and then began to set the generators to run, creating light in this level of the pyramid and also providing guidance towards a catwalk that went around to the opposite end. He travelled to the opposite end of the main chamber on the second floor and went down a corridor that took the power cables through. He found himself in a medium sized room with a plasma vat underneath a control room above. A corner of the room was broken into, and natural light poured in, but with it came lots of sand. As Finn looked around, he also found a pole similar to the ones that he and Moira found throughout the desert. He stepped forward and began to see robots buried in the sand around, and as he took a single step in, they began to move and rise up. Finn equipped the flamethrower and began to spew fire out towards them, causing their wires to catch ablaze. He then opened fire with the assault rifle, jumping out of the way as they came close to him. He cleaned up a few of them, but the rest awoke one by one until he found himself with the same initial amount. He shot at them and then began to concentrate fire on the pole, causing sparks to fly out and for it to tip over and collapse. Finn launched himself up onto the console platform and then approached the computer. He read out the PC number, got the password, and then typed it and watched the computer self-automate and create plasma within the vat as two turbines span up at either side. The plasma was conducted along tubes that disappeared downwards. Finn exited out the room and began to go up the stairs to the third floor to repeat the task.

On the third floor, Finn found a corridor that came around to a medium sized room with a raised platform above. He hopped up and then came around to a smaller room with generators, as well as some robots that began to liven up. He quickly began to open fire at the robots before they could even wake up, allowing him to take care of them sooner rather than later. He then approached the console in the generator room, read the PC number, got the password, and then activated the generators. He followed the cables as they went out, came around another catwalk, and then led down another corridor. He followed the corridor as he could see crystal tubes that led out and went down to the bottom of the main chamber. These tubes likewise went down a drop point, a square vertical tunnel. He looked down and could see several lasers that pointed in sporadic directions. He could see a lit room at the bottom, prompting him to activate the glider and tip over. He gently lowered himself down, passing the lasers and avoiding contact with them. He landed at the bottom of the room and found himself with a generator room on one side and vat at the other. The room was protected with a tall metal wall with reinforced windows. In the middle of the wall was a set of blast doors. He came around to the console, read the PC number, got the password, and then typed it in to cause the machines to self-automate and generate plasma. He was also able to open the doors and walk out, coming out onto the first floor.

"I'm almost done," Finn reported. "After I get this last one, ready yourself. Who knows when and where that thing will come out from. I'm surprised we haven't seen it again..."

"Maybe you under-estimate how much damage a grenade launcher can really do..."

"Oh, you don't have to remind me..."

Finn climbed up the stairs to reach the top floor where he came around to a small room. The room had the generators and then divided in two directions down corridors. He approached the console and read the PC number. He then got the password and activated the generators. Once those were activated, he looked around but could not see any tubes that conducted plasma. He followed the tunnel around and reached a room on the opposite side. He found a vat and the consoles in this room, and began to turn it on. The plasma began to come out and conduct along tubes that exited the room through a small crack in the wall. Finn went out the other side and came around to the exit. He then slowly lowered himself to reach the bottom. Finn walked down the corridor and made his way into the main control room to rejoin Moira before he went to confront the enhanced soldier and enter into the lower depths.

Act 6, Scene 4

Finn joined Moira as she typed away at her computer. The monitor in the room displayed completed progress bars for all of the generators. She looked over to Finn as he joined her.

"Looks like we've got full power," Moira remarked. She hit enter on the computer, prompting it to self-automate and display lines of code. The vaults in the room began to hum while the monitor showed positive indicators on the flow of plasma to the reaction chamber. "I haven't been able to find anything about where power is being routed to other than the fusion reactor. All I've been able to find are schematics to the fusion reactor, and instructions on how to turn it on. We seem to have done all the right steps, and now we just need to journey to the reaction chamber and begin the process to turn it on."

"Let's hope its as easy as it was to get the plasma production started," Finn replied. "I was hoping we'd get to pick up some fuel cells because I'm on my second-last one."

"I'm sure there must be something like that…" Moira responded, closing her laptop. She put her laptop away and then put her backpack around her. "I'm going to guess that there are more computers in the fusion reactor chamber, so we'll see where the power goes from that room."

"Let's not keep bug-face waiting then," Finn replied. He then led Moira out of the control room and into the main chamber. They stepped up onto the platform and he hit the switch. The elevator began to emit a loud beep, while railings propped up and trapped them in a low pen. The elevator then began to descend downwards. The elevator went down and down, travelling along a sloped angle at a slow pace. Above their heads, Moira and Finn could see the thick cables and four distinct plasma conductors shooting hot plasma along. "We should be careful down there – no more explosions…"

"I only a have a few left, and I would rather save them for the robot factory."

"I'm serious," Finn remarked. "We don't know what kind of setup this reactor has. I've seen a few of these over the years and they're all different. From what I can hazard a guess on, this one would be similar to the ones that Zimmerman Corporation built."

"Okay, no explosions, I get it," Moira replied. "You don't have to tell me twice."

Finn looked at her, and then looked up at the end of the tunnel above as he began to see some creatures looking down towards them.

"Oh no…" Finn remarked. He pointed his rifle upwards and began to open fire. The creatures began to attempt to crawl towards them, instead sliding down as they were shot and incapacitated. The speed in which the robots began to approach them doubled, prompting Finn to launch himself off with the propulsion jets and activate the glider. He pointed his wrist forward and began to emit some flames. He then shot the weakened robots as he held them back, causing the remainder to slide down. Once they were taken care of, he too slid down and rejoined Moira. He broke his landing with the propulsion jets, and then began to reload the rifle. "I'm running low on ammo. Should be a bit more at the SUV if we make it that way. I don't suppose this 'robot factory' can be too far from this location, but we'll see."

The elevator began to reach the bottom of the tunnel where it landed in a circular and large tunnel space. The space curved around on the left and right, while the pipes continued forward and went down a gap in the wall ahead. A set of doors below had a security console. The room they were in was not made of stone, but concrete with large metal rings around, and platforms at the side. Additionally, large tubes span across the side of the tunnel with even larger and thicker cables doing the same. The reinforced door ahead of them read, 'Reactor Room.'

Finn examined their surroundings as the room they were in was lit by dim lights. He looked both ways and then approached the main doors into the room.

"Do you want me to climb up and get through to the other side?" Moira questioned.

"I don't want us to get separated," Finn replied.

"I'll put on the optic camo," Moira propositioned. "If that thing is inside, it won't be able to see me. I'll sneak in and see if I can hack into the system." She stepped forward, and activated her camouflage as she set her backpack and grenade launcher to the side. Finn looked at the blur in front of him. She began to climb up the wall and enter through the gap of space.

Moira crawled down a lengthy gap to reach the end, but there was no surface to climb down from the other side other than the grate above her. She looked around and then began to grab hold of the grate ceiling. She then began to climb out where she saw the gap behind her curve down to the ground. She repositioned herself and began to climb down the curved segment, reaching the door and finding the same security console. She turned around and got a better looked at the reactor chamber. The chamber was large and domed, and in the middle of the room was the fusion chamber, but it was off. The tubes and wires above her connected with the chamber, while larger cables and tubes connected with the chamber on the left and right at the base of the reactor system. About two-thirds above the reactor was a circular catwalk, and above those were receptables pointed outwards. The reactor chamber was large, and its glass was thick. In front of the reactor was a port to insert and remove capsules. She examined it carefully, removing a capsule out and looking at it. The capsules were as big as her head. She put it back and then began to climb up a set of stairs that went over the tubes to find a raised platform with curved windows that looked down at the rest of the room. At the corners of the reactor chamber were metal bulbs that pointed outwards and towards circular platforms in all four corners. She observed them, especially as cables ran towards them from all four corners. She then began to approach the stairs that went up to the control room. She entered and saw a monitor with a string of code across the string. Moira came around and sat down at the computer, typing enter and then seeing strings of code pass through. The room lit up and other monitors began to turn on with more code as the system automated.

"What kind of fusion reactor is this?" Finn questioned, looking around. "How much power does this place need to generate to fuel a production facility?"

Finn stopped looking around as he could hear the reactor hum, and he observed as he began to see a beam of light circle around in the large glass tubes.

"What's Moira doing?" Finn asked himself. He raised up his wrist and asked the same question, "What are you doing?" but no response came. "Moira? What's going on?"

Moira sat at the computer as her radio at her belt went off, but it was static. "Finn?" she questioned. "Finn?!"

Finn began to bang at the door to let him in, but as he did so, he looked up as he heard something crawl above his head.

"Oh no…"

The shadow of some entity passed over head and entered into the gap of space that she herself went through.

"Moira!" Finn shouted. "You've got company! Let me in!" He began to bang his fists on the front of the door.

Moira turned to her radio as she placed it atop of the console. She continued to hear static through the other side until by chance she heard the shouts of Finn say, 'Open the door!'

"Jeez," Moira remarked, "he's so impatient." She looked at the console and found a switch to release the doors and opened it. Just as she unlocked the doors, a metallic fist smashed through the glass of the control room and grabbed hold of Moira by her shoulders. She was dragged out and left to dangle over the ground as the enhanced robot held on to her, even as she was camouflaged. Finn quickly bolt through the doors and could hear the screams of Moira. She attempted to reach for the blaster pistol in her holster, but could not reach. She instead de-activated her camouflage. The creature began to carry her down the ceiling with it while Finn ran around and climbed up to the top of the platform. "Finn!"

Finn knelt down and began to open fire at the creature, causing it to drop down. Moira quickly took hold of the ceiling and held on tight. The robot crashed onto the floor while Finn continued to fire at it. It quickly launched its feet upwards to regain its footing. The creature shouted out towards him, before its head began to glitch. This enhanced creature was slimmer than the other ones, its body more skeletal though apparent at its movement was a lot more flexible and agile. The enhanced robot held not objects in its hands, though its feet were split apart, three digits each as it stood its ground with four limbs in an X-shaped. Its right fist appeared larger than its left. Its head was similar to the other robots, and it had light blue eyes that looked forward, but for whatever reason twitched and its limbs jerked randomly more than the other robots. The creature re-adjusted its footing as it brought its legs together, and while doing so, it detached the plasma cannon it kept attached to its back. Finn released his shield and stood his ground as it fired at him. Moira dangled in place as she looked down and over to Finn. She began to climb down the ceiling and then gently lowered herself down into the control room. She then stood on top of the panels and knelt down. She took out her pistol and opened fire at the robot. The robot immediately span its head around to look at her, and the sockets of his arms twisted around to point the cannon at her. She quickly hid back and disappeared into a blur as the optic camouflage re-activated, and she made her escape out of the control room. Finn noticed the fire stopped at him, prompting him to lower his shield and picked up his rifle to continue to open fire at the creature. The creature span its head around, but rather than point its cannon, it ducked down and began to evade the fire as it jumped into random positions. It then ran towards Finn and tackled him onto the ground. He pointed his rifle towards its torso, but it pushed back and took hold of his neck. Finn struggled with the creature as he used the strength of his exosuit to support him, at which point a light burst out from the creature and Finn lost all his strength. His suit began to beep, and the wrist modules flashed before they died out.

"No...!" Finn cried out. The creature began to crush him, but as it did so, a shot from Moira's blaster hit it in the back of the head as she re-appeared.

The creature did a flip and then ran off as she continued to shoot at it, eventually disappearing back into the tunnels. The creature ran at an above average human speed. Moira came over to Finn and helped him off the ground.

"My suit...!" Finn complained. "Whatever that thing did, it shut down all the power to my suit."

"Do you have a spare fuse?" Moira asked.

"It's in my backpack," Finn reported, raising a foot up. "Ugh... this thing is so heavy without any power on."

The pair ran off and began to climb up the stairs to the control room. Moira removed the fuel cell and sure enough it was dark colored. She rummaged through Finn's backpack, taking out all his belongings and then opened the lead-lined case where the fuel cells were kept. She placed the fuel cell inside and then took the last bright one. She inserted it into Finn's suit, and then hit the power activate button for him. The suit began to reboot.

"Whatever that thing did, it has the power to cancel out all power around it..." Finn remarked. "It's like an electromagnetic pulse burst of some sort..."

"Just take it easy..." Moira replied, going over to the computer. "I need my laptop to hack into the system. Can you go and get it for me?" She typed into the computer. "The startup process was stalled. I need to get the password..."

"Sure..." Finn replied, placing the lead-lined case with the fuel cells on the panel. "I'll be right back."

Finn left the room and then glided down to the bottom. He kept his assault rifle raised as he examined the nearby scene. He then went up and over the staircase, and around towards the front of the fusion reactor. He examined the plasma capsules and placed a hand over it. He removed one and then turned a knob to see it have five spots for fuel cells. He then put it back and went over to Moira's backpack. He picked it up, but stopped as he could hear echoes of the creature crawling along the corridor. He looked around and noticed the red beam along the tubes that continued to glow in preparation. He then backed up as the creature gave a maniacal cackle, coming around to the control room again. He climbed up and hopped up to the platform, and passed Moira's her backpack.

"The receptacle at the fusion reactor can charge my fuel cells," Finn stated. "I'm going to go and get them charged."

Finn left while Moira opened her laptop, connected it to the console, and began to generate a password to enter into the older computer system. She then typed that password and began to activate the fusion reactor. The reactor hummed in changing frequencies, from high pitched to low pitched, as energy span the entire length of the tunnels outside, speeding up and going faster and faster. Finn came around to the receptacle, removed the capsule, and then began to insert the fuel cells inside. He then locked it and put the capsule back in, locking it in place and causing a green light to turn red. Finn stepped back and began to turn around as he listened to the machine work. He stayed in position while he kept an eye out, standing up to patrol around the generator room as he noticed the spherical balls that hung from the ceiling by outstretched arms began to develop thunderbolts. He came up to the platform above and watched as the thunderbolts intensified in unison. He stayed put as he watched all the entry points into the room. There were four in total, the main entrance, an exit beneath the control room, and then two tall gaps on the left and right from the entrance. The creature cackled from a distance as it roamed the corridors until suddenly, as the thunderbolts became brighter, it appeared from the left and quickly crawled along the ceiling grate to dangle nearby – spreading an arm outward towards the top right tesla coil. Suddenly, bolts of thick lightning extended outwards from all four coils, three of which connected with the fusion reactor while the other connected with the enhanced robot, causing its eyes to glow as it received the charge. The creature laughed as it received the charge and then the coils grew dim as the process began to repeat itself.

Finn raised his rifle up to open fire at the creature, prompting it to point its fist towards him and shoot a strong beam of plasma. He quickly jumped out of the way and activated his shield. He then withheld as the plasma beam hit the shield at full force.

"No…" Moira complained over the radio, "Finn, something went wrong with the fusion reactor. I got an error message…"

"Yeah, the power was intercepted," Finn replied. "Reset the process – we'll try again."

Moira typed away as she began to reset the power up sequence. The fusion reactor began to sound an alarm, and a timer presented on the console as the system went into cooldown. She then noticed the creature firing a plasma beam towards Finn as he held on, prompting her to take her pistol out and shoot its arms. The creature fell down, releasing the pressure on Finn's shield, and allowing him to open fire at it. The creature again evaded the shots, but Moira took shots as well. The creature flipped around in place, and then began to ran up the stairs to find Moira, but as it did so, she quickly disappeared and moved away from the console. She hid behind a table and crawled underneath. The creature stepped forward and slowly began to examine the area while Finn jumped up the stairs and then opened fire at it. The creature quickly flipped its head over to him and opened fire at its own cannon. He blocked the shot and began to step towards it. The creature relented as he got close and instead threw a punch with its right fist. Finn absorbed the punch and then another one. He then hit back as he pushed himself towards the creature and bashed it with the shield. He went for another strike, triggering the creature to take hold of the shield at either side with both hands and fling Finn towards the wall. He broke his fall as the propulsion jets kicked in with the motion. He then kicked off the wall and bashed his shield into the robot, knocking it back slightly. He then hit it again, but as he did so, the creature grabbed the shield once more and this time swung Finn out of the control room. It then hopped up onto the control panel and then began to climb up onto the ceiling grates above. Finn landed on his feet and began to open fire at the creature as it dangled above him, but then the enhanced robot dropped down from above. He quickly dodged it, but it moved quickly to take hold of the rifle. The pair struggled for control of the rifle. Finn pushed the creature backwards, prompting it to split its legs to prop it up. Moira looked down as she attempted to see what was going on, but the struggle took them underneath the control room. Eventually, the creature was able to remove the assault rifle from Finn's hands. It then used the rifle to bludgeon him at the side of the face. It then retreated backwards and pointed the rifle at him, but Finn opened his shield again as it pointed his rifle towards him, taking shots at him as he held his ground. However, after a while, the rifle began to waver. Finn lowered his shield and watched as the creature destroyed the assault rifle with both hands. He growled as he saw it happen and pointed the flamethrower to launch a spray of flames. The creature was unaffected by the spray of flames and threw another punch towards him. He absorbed the punch with the shield once again. Finn pivoted himself around the robot as it continued to punch at him until he launched himself backwards, seeing the creature draw its own cannon out. He quickly equipped the bow and took out the eyes. The arrow connected with the eyes, followed by the other as the sensors were destroyed. The creature screamed as it continued to point its cannon and opened fire. Finn pivoted out of the way and took another shot at the cannon, causing it to backfire and stun the creature. He then equipped the shield and went in for a boosted shield bash, knocking the creature backwards. The robot cried out and in a flash, it let out a burst of energy and rendered Finn's suit useless again. The shield retracted and the creature looked towards Finn. He stepped back as it attempted to punch at him, hitting the ground instead and creating a dent in the metal floor. The creature then ran off and disappeared again.

Finn panted and knelt down. He equipped another arrow and looked around, waiting for it to reappear, but instead he heard its maniacal laugh in the distance. The spheres began to charge as the fusion reactor reset, prompting Finn to come up and over the set of stairs to the base of the reactor. He looked at the capsule receptacle and saw that it still had a red light on it. He growled and then left, going back around and coming into the control room. She looked over to him as he took weighted steps, releasing the exosuit from his body and letting it fall backwards. He then kept his bow on him and joined Moira.

"What happened to you?"

"EMP," Finn replied. "Also, that son of a bitch destroyed my gun."

"Where'd it go?"

"It retreated like the coward it is," Finn stated, looking out. "Seems like releasing an EMP costs it a lot of energy, which is why it'll come for the reactor now. I was also able to blind it.

I'm going to be honest; I don't know how we're going to destroy that thing now."

"We still have my blaster," Moira replied, reloading it. As the pair stood in the control room, a high-pitched screech could be heard in the distance.

"Oh no…" Finn remarked, "don't' tell me."

"Sounds like we've got company…" Moira remarked. "On second thought, I'm keeping this… Make use of that bow…"

"We got to keep that thing away from the fusion reactor," Finn complained. "I need to get those fuel cells charged so I can use my suit."

"What good is your suit if you don't even have a weapon?" Moira questioned as he left.

Finn positioned himself above the catwalk as he saw robots begin to swarm into the room through the many entrances. He kept note of those below him as he began to fire arrows at them. Usually one or two arrows was enough to render the robots useless to fall over again. Moira covered the other side and used her pistol to open fire. As they held off the wave of broken robots, the coils charged up as thunderbolts developed around them. Finn continued to fire what arrows he had at the robots as they attempted to climb up the stairs. In a split second, the enhanced robot reappeared and attempted to position itself near the fusion reactor. Finn noticed and pointed an arrow at it, shooting its arm and causing it to fall off and hit the ground. The coils spewed lightning towards the fusion reactor from all four angles, and the plasma went into the vat. Finn shot another arrow at the creature as it pushed past robots to make its escape and disappeared. He cleaned up the rest of the worn-out robots while Moira came around to the console. The monitor showed an error message. Moira began to reset the machine as it entered into a cooldown, while Finn came down the steps and destroyed the remainder of the robots. He then ran over to the fuel cells and saw there was a green light. He began to extract the fuel cells and place them in the lead container, and then he took them with him to the control room where he removed the dud cell and placed in a new one. He then equipped the exoskeleton suit and came out of the control room as another screech called more robots and activated those thought to have been fully decommissioned. Finn positioned himself at the opposite side while Moira took the other one.

Moira and Finn shot at the robots that began to flood into the room. He made use of the flamethrower as they began to climb up the stairs, and then shot at the rest as they began to make their entrance into the room. As the pair engaged in combat with the robots, Finn noticed a random bolt of lighting come out from the tesla coil and electrocute a robot as it moved quickly towards them. The excess electricity caused the robot to seize and then explode. He thought for a moment and then continued to shoot the others. The coils charged up and thunderbolts began to develop. The robots began to thin out and Finn moved around to hit the last few with the last few arrows he had.

"Finn! It's here!"

Finn quickly moved back into the control room as he saw the creature position itself to receive the charge from one of the coils. He pointed an arrow at it, but he was too late. The robot received the charge and began to light up. He shot the arrow and it flicked away as a bolt of lightning parried it. He readied and shot another one, but the same affect occurred, and the robot instead turned to point its arm towards him. He saw the brightness of light began to charge up, prompting him to run out of the control room and smash what glass was left in the windows. He rolled in the air and then landed on the floor. The robot fired a shot towards him and hit the ground nearby instead. Finn jumped out of the way as another volley came, and then another one. He then pulled an arrow out and shot at the robot, causing it to fall to the floor. He then quickly ran towards it as he brought his shield out and hit it with brute force.

Meanwhile, Moira came back to the computer as the broken robots were taken care of, and she began to reset the fusion reactor system.

"Fourth time better be the charm…" Moira cursed under her breath. She then picked up her blaster and came around to look down as she saw the robot engage with Finn in close quarters combat. It kept attempting to punch at him with its right arm, but missed. Finn used his propulsion jets to hit the robot back, but it did little damage. Moira reloaded her blaster and continued to watch. As they fought, a few more robots began to appear to keep her preoccupied, especially as she kept them from coming near Finn to interfere with his fight with the enhanced robot. "Watch out!"

Finn continued to concentrate on his fight with the robot to notice the others attempting to tackle and intercept him. He used his shield to push back at the robot. He was eventually able to push it towards the base of the reactor, but before he could take another swing with the shield, the robots came in towards him and forced him to unleash the flamethrower. He sprayed fire towards those around him, including the enhanced robot as it was stunned. He then switched to the shield and parried another punch. He pushed himself towards the robot with the propulsion jets as he jumped, and then smashed the robot against the base of the reactor. He then swung the edge of the shield into the right arm and caused the forearm to snap off from the joint. The creature shouted out towards Finn and took a swing with the weaker left arm. He bashed towards the creature and sent it back towards the base of the reactor, but it then jumped up, grabbed the catwalk above, and took control of the cannon as it began to fire indiscriminately. Finn jumped out of the way and then retreated behind a pillar. He took an arrow and shot towards the creature. Finn continued to fire arrows at it as he aimed to get it to drop down, and once it was down, it continued to fire outwards with one arm at anything that moved.

Unfortunately, in its random fire, it took a few of the other robots with it. The coils began to charge up. Finn came out towards the stairwell and went up to the top to join Moira. Moira looked at him. The creature stepped forward and began to shoot towards them, prompting Moira to retreat to the other side. The enhanced robot let out a screech and called in more reinforcements. Finn took cover within the control room and took a moment to catch his breath. Moira shot at the robots as they began to re-activate while others reappeared. In the corner of her eye, she saw the enhanced robot began to climb up and reach the top of the ceiling where it stayed put and began to point its cannon towards her. She quickly hid around the side of the control room as the beam fired. Finn looked out and saw the coils flash with lightning. A bolt of lightning hit a robot at random as they continued to fire up.

"Moira!" Finn shouted. "Whatever you do, do not hit that bastard!"

"What?"

"Do not hit the advanced robot!"

Finn came out from around the corner and quickly backed away. Moira did the same as she retreated into the control room. She continued to fire shots at robots as they went up the stairs, while Finn opened fire with the flamethrower and used his own foot to kick them out of the way and over the edge of the staircase. The enhanced robot alternated between both sides to lay coverage with its cannon. Finn looked over and saw that the robot was facing one of the coils only. He then looked up towards the roof of the fusion reactor and took in a deep breath. As the robot alternated to Moira's side, he jumped up onto the roof of the control room and began to come around to the ceiling grate. He ran down the length of it to come around to the top of the fusion reactor, prompting the robot to redirect its cannon at him, but he dodged it as he jumped forward and landed on the roof of the fusion reactor. The robot swung itself onto the roof and then began to run towards him. He activated his shield and intercepted the weaker arm as it swung at him. The coils continued to charge as they engaged in combat on the roof of the fusion reactor. Moira noticed as she came into the center of the control room and the robots thinned out. The monitor displayed close to full percent charge as it crossed the ninety-percent threshold.

"Oh my God," Moira remarked, "he's going to kill himself! Finn!"

Finn bashed the creature onto the roof. It grabbed a hold of the grate and then used all four legs to spin. He dodged with his shield as all four limbs hit and he absorbed the blow. The coils showed visible signs of near full charge, and the room was loud with the crackle of lightning. The robot attempted to make an exit, but Finn grabbed hold of it with the shield and held it close to him. He then slammed it into the ground, smashed it with the shield several times around the wrist.

"Finn!" Moira shouted again.

Finn quickly backflipped off the side of the roof, falling over as the creature struggled to stand up, but finally did. The bolts of lightning hit it at all four points, causing it to seize as lightning flashed out and caused Moira to close her eyes. Finn's landing was botched as the glider glitched and he made a rough landing on the ground, but as he looked up, he could see the bolts of lightning take its target. The enhanced robot continued to seize until its interior components exploded outwards and plasma shot out of its body before it exploded into several pieces. Finn quickly covered his head with the shield as shrapnel rained down from above.

Moira opened her eyes and could not see Finn above the fusion reactor. An error message flashed on the monitor screen, but she ignored it.

"Bloody hell…" Finn complained as he lay on the ground.

Moira looked down but could not see Finn. She scrambled out and came around the staircase, going down to the bottom and rushing towards him as he sat up. She embraced him by the side and tucked her head close in to him.

"Oh my God, Finn, I thought you were toast," Moira acclaimed.

"Toast?" Finn questioned. "That's my left arm you're talking about..."

Moira laughed as she continued to hold him in. She soon let go and smiled at him. Finn looked at her with confusion and then raised a mild smile at her. He raised himself up and then took a deep breath.

"Well, now that's taken care of, I suppose we can see about this fusion reactor," Finn remarked. "Let's see if it'll tell us where we need to go."

The pair climbed up and Moira reset the process. The machine cooled down while the pair rested, and then it began to charge up again and activate according to protocol. The central chamber lit up in a bright yellow glow, and the monitors showed green lights. After the fusion reactor was confirmed to be back on-line, the lights in the chamber brightened. Moira typed into her computer and began to pull maps and schematics out.

"Looks like the power is diverted in a horizontal line out of here," Moira remarked. "Less than a hundred kilometers south, going into... Colorado..."

"Another state?" Finn questioned. "I thought it'd be nearer than that..."

"We're already near the Colorado state border," Moira replied, "but looks like there should be some power lines we can follow. I'm putting it into the GPS now. Hm... looks like this base is deep within a mountain range..."

"Great... nothing like a hike up a mountain to end it all off..."

"I'm looking at the schematics of the power plant," Moira said. "Looks like there's an emergency exit behind us."

Once the pair were finished, they collected their belongings and began to exit down underneath the control room. They came into the corridor where ahead of them was an exit point, and around them were tubes filled with bright yellow plasma. They began to climb up a set of stairs that marched upwards. At the end of the stairway, Moira punched in a code at the security console and the doors opened to reveal the orange skies as evening came down on them. They stepped forward onto the cliff edge as they exited out from a cave and found themselves next to a corpse leaned up against the wall half buried in some sand.

Finn knelt down the soldier, helped him off his feet, and then placed him down. He played the message, and they listened, "Captain Ramiel Barak, of the Global Defense Project elite unit…" a voice spoke in a deep foreign Middle Eastern accent. "I've taken the rest of the survivors from the attack at our base and we've come to this desert where a storm rages for days without end, making it difficult to see. We are at the mercy of our enemy without end, and the more we kill, the more they come. Still though, we have a mission to see through. Before I left, Director Black spoke to me personally about the mission ahead. She told me about our enemies, where they came from, and who they served. She asked me a few questions, the last of which being if I was willing to die; to lead this undeniably suicidal mission. I told her it would not be the first nor the last time I would say yes.

"I left the Israeli Defense Force when my country had told me that I could serve in something as important to them as the defense of our nation – the defense of the world. I reluctantly accepted, and in my years with the Global Defense Project, I've had my differences with the team and the leadership, especially as my country has become the subject of hostile remarks and our people have seen hatred like none other. I've been suspicious of the others as though they should turn on me as I suspect that the sentiments that I am an enemy rise, but Ms. Black did not ask me if I remained loyal to the cause of the Global Defense Project, or if I intended to betray them, or even that I was placed under arrest – to clarify, she did not exactly ask me if I would die for the defense of the world, but instead she asked me if I would lead this important mission, to destroy the experimental power facility, and should I survive and be capable, to march to the military base and destroy every last one of these robots that defy us. I reluctantly accepted – I'm told that an enemy awaits me within the pyramid ruins. I only hope that it knows that *Iyyov* is coming for it, ready to deal a terrible punishment." The recording then cut out.

"Honorable lad," Finn remarked. "I only wish I could have done something more for him, or the others…"

"You avenged their deaths," Moira pointed out. "I don't think they'd want anything more than that than to see the mission through."

"You're right…" Finn replied. He picked up the weapon at the soldiers side and saw that it connected with the suit. "Hm, a plasma rifle just like the one the robot had – an endless supply of ammo if it draws power from my suit."

"Finn has got to plunder, doesn't he…" Moira responded.

"Look at his wrist console… I'm sure there's something here you can appreciate…" Finn pointed out. I'll remove the suit and we'll give this lad a proper burial as well before we set off for the night. I don't think we'll be able to return to the SUV. We're reaching the end of this journey, and I can't wait."

Act 7, Prologue

"Believe me, you have nothing to be worried about," a feminine voice stated.

Finn sat in the driver's seat of a black Dolores-Ganß sedan as he drove through downtown Allabrese on a dim and cloudy night. The cabin of the SUV was dark though warm as the buttons of the dashboard lit in his face, and the touchscreen monitor played soft piano-based classical music. He held both hands around the steering wheel as he drove through the snowy town and went into the eastern suburbs. He wore an Italian wool sweater, dress shirt and beige trousers. Over his clothes he also wore a black raincoat. Around his face was a thin blonde beard and his hair was lengthy around the sides and back. Though less than two years had passed, Finn also appeared a little stockier than a few years ago, his chest firmer, limbs broader. Beside him in the front passenger seat sat a blonde-haired woman in a wool coat. She had fair skin, fairer than Finn with rouged cheeks and neatly maintained eyebrows. Her hair was luscious and a bright shade of blonde, though in the cabin of the vehicle was difficult to notice. Her coat came down to her knees where she wore brown stockings towards a pair of designer boots. As Finn drove, this woman looked at the sun visor mirror as she finished applying lipstick and began to apply mascara. Her small purse sat at her laps for convenience as she swapped make-up items through a smaller pouch within. Still though, despite her best efforts to gussy up, she could not hide the wrinkles underneath and around the sides of her eyes, nor the wrinkles that formed across her hands.

"I've visited him a few times, checked in with him, and he seems to be doing alright," Allodia stated. "Even before he was released from hospital, he was doing alright. He's a changed man. After losing daddy not too long ago, and Charlie a few years ago as well, it's nice to have some positive change around here. Between you and him living out here in Allabrese, I may think of buying some property and moving here – the city is driving me nuts."

"I highly recommend it," Finn replied, "though the town is not too far from the city."

"Tell me about it…" Allodia decried, "but it's a start. I'm not the only one that wants out – you wouldn't believe how often it gets brought up by human resources. There's almost little reason to expand business in the city, but that's besides the point. I'm not here to talk about the company – we are here for you to be able to meet your uncle, Salmar. Again, you have nothing to worry about."

"I wasn't worried," Finn said as they began to come out of town and into Champion Plains. "You keep bringing it up though, and it makes me think that I should be worried. Look, I know why he was thrown into prison and such. My dad told me all about it – he tried to kill him and Diana and Tristan seven years ago because my dad wanted to sell the company. He also told me that Salmar was not well mentally at that moment, though it took him a while to realize it. As soon as he did though, he did everything he could to have Salmar's condition re-examined. Luckily, before he died, he was able to push through enough to have some psychiatrics testify that Salmar had lost his mind – admittedly for different reasons than actually were, though the quacks didn't know. Still though, it was enough to have the case tossed out and Salmar admitted to forensic psychiatric care so he could be rehabilitated."

"I knew there was something up with him," Allodia remarked. "From the moment that Charlie told me that Salmar was arrested, I knew something was amiss. He was always considered the angel in the family – a saint. He never sought to harm anyone, and he always did what was right. For Pete's sake, that's why he became a lawyer, because he's a rule follower. Always having to follow the rules… Sal wouldn't hurt a fly unless he had a permit to do so. Little did I know that losing his wife in that accident did him so much pain…"

"I heard he had a wife," Finn replied, "but dad didn't tell me much about it."

"He did… Gloria," Allodia explained. "They were high school sweethearts, though she was a year younger than him. He took a gap year for the sole purpose that he could stay in Allabrese and be with her. When she graduated, they both went to Harlech together. They were inseparable. She meant the world to him. They both became lawyers at the same time, and then… She got into a car accident… died in hospital a few hours later while he was away. He missed the chance to say goodbye because he was on a business trip, even though he told me his last words to her were as such."

"Jeez…" Finn reacted. "How long ago was that?"

"I was with Cabernet Foundation for a while then when I got the news, but before I became 'top fundraiserer' as he jokingly called me. It must have been in the early 2000s," Allodia answered. "At any rate, I suppose I should have seen the signs – Salmar worked, worked, worked after she died. He did not take care of his mental health at all – adopting Tristan must have just pushed him into a spiral, and here we are now after he finally got some goddamn therapy."

"I guess you don't know either…" Finn muttered under his breath.

"What was that?" Allodia questioned as she applied some blush to her cheeks.

"I'm sure it played a part," Finn instead said. "I'm looking forward to getting to meet him. No offense, but this family doesn't many members left."

Allodia sighed as she lowered the blush and said, "You're right – we've had a rough few years since mom died. It's been one after the other… I don't think any of us are quite over losing Charlie- Charlemagne. Your dad…" She put her makeup away as the car diverted off the freeway. "Still though, such is life – you lose some, you win some. "

"The Lord gives and the Lord takes away; may the name of the Lord be praised…" Finn silently muttered.

"We've had our losses, but also our gains in you, your mom, Diana and Tristan, their baby boy Damian," Allodia remarked. "Oh, and Diana texted me a few days ago saying that she's pregnant again with number two on the way – here's hoping for a girl in the family."

"The way those two are at it, you're more than likely to get a few of them."

"Honesty, I'm so happy for them," Allodia remarked as she closed her purse. "As a middle-aged woman who never got the chance to have kids, I live with the regret that I never got to settle down," she said with a sigh. "I never even dated much – mom told me I was always too mean-spirited with boys, and bossy, but I know that I was just very picky. Of course, the one chance I did have, the guy turns out being some sort of Russian spy."

"Oh, what could have been…" Finn replied as he pulled up to a two-story home in the midst of some farmland. "Here we are…"

"Honestly, Salmar was not doing himself any favors in staying in the same house he and Gloria bought and lived in together," Allodia complained, looking at the house ahead. She shook her head. "Imagine if I lived in a place that constantly reminded me of the dead."

The car shut off and he pair opened their respective doors. Allodia carried a wine bottle in her hands with a bow around it, and then came around to the front door eagerly as she walked up the steps of the porch. Meanwhile, Finn put his hands in his pocket and silently followed her. She knocked on the front door and then hit the sound of the doorbell.

"Oh, Sally!" Allodia cried out.

Finn stood behind her towards her right side as he waited for the door to open. After a minute, the door began to unlock and door open to reveal the face of his uncle, Salmar Cabernet. In this time, Salmar was the same height as he was in the present, six feet and two inches tall, and his blonde hair was medium length. He was a stockier person than his brother, Charlemagne, but had lost body mass since his incarceration and was average sized, though a little stockier than Finn, albeit Finn was more muscular than him.

"Helloo…" Allodia greeted, presenting the bottle.

"Allodia!" Salmar replied. "So nice to see you! Thanks for making it – I know you are always so busy nowadays." She moved in for an embrace and wrapped her arms around her brother with a tight grip. He extended his arms out both sides and then relaxed them as she squeezed his torso. "Not so rough, buttercup."

Allodia released her grip and then backed away as Finn's eyes met his uncle's. Salmar looked at him and held a plain face while Finn's appeared tired and mildly grim.

"So, after much hype and many words said," Salmar expressed, "I finally get the privilege to meet the face of my older brother's only son."

Finn did not reply. He looked at Salmar and raised his expression to a plain one. Salmar stepped forward and extended a hand towards him as he looked at him with a respectful glance.

"A pleasure to meet you, Finn," Salmar greeted.

"Louis," Allodia interrupted. "He prefers Louis."

"Louis?" Salmar questioned, turning to Allodia.

"Finn is fine," Finn replied, extending his hand. "Nice to meet you, Salmar."

"Sal is fine," Salmar responded, shaking hands. He looked at him intently as they shook hands. "Wow, I can really see him within you. It's uncanny…"

"People say the same about you and daddy," Allodia replied, "more than they did about Charlie and daddy anyways."

"It's a shame he's not with us," Salmar said, releasing his grip. "I mean that for all of them, but hey, here we are – the three of us, the survivors; what's left of the Cabernet legacy." He turned to Finn and then waved him in. "Don't just stand there in the cold like a stranger. Come on inside and let me close that door – you two get comfortable, dinner is at least half an hour away."

Finn stepped inside and Salmar closed the door. He then turned to them as he examined the bottle.

"A speciality – Finn found it in the basement of the manor," Allodia stated. "Apparently Charlie had an entire collection of stored goods."

"From the vineyards," Salmar noted, "yes, Charles had lots of these laying around. They all came from the original Cabernet mansion, so I'm told."

"Original mansion?" Finn questioned.

"Yup," Salmar affirmed, "out in Walham Valley to the south of Harlech where it all began. In the mid-1800s, our forefather Sennett Cabernet founded Cabernet Vineyards and established what later became the many industries of Cabernet Industries (or Cabernet Corporation as they were previously called). His son Lycidas built a mansion in those same lands, surrounded by the vineyards, and that structure was our family home, at least until it burned to the ground. Dad was just around six or seven years old when that happened… He wrote about it to me in some of the letters he sent me… Are you interested much in our family's history, Finn?"

"It's a little interesting," Finn noted. "My mum and dad told me a little bit about the history of the Cabernet's: the split of the family between the French and Germans after the Franco-Prussian War, their exile to London and then emigration to Canada… Just some basic information…"

"Since I've come home, it's been one of my hobbies to take a closer look at the genealogy of the family," Salmar remarked, "especially since I found out that Charles had a son, but even then, Diana and Tristan – speaking of them, did you extend my invitation? Are they coming? I never heard back from them."

"Uh... yes, I did, but no they won't be coming," Allodia answered. "I think they still need some time to, uh... prepare themselves..."

"Right..." Salmar replied, "at any rate – how about I get some glasses, and we can break open this bottle?"

Salmar led the two into the living room to the right of the foyer entrance. The living room was one-third of the room, otherwise split up between the dining room and kitchen.

"Can I take your coat, Allodia?" Salmar offered, placing the bottle on the counter.

Allodia took off her coat and left it on a sofa.

"I suppose that works as well," Salmar replied. "Take a seat, Finn. You too, Allodia."

Salmar fetched three glasses and then brought it over to the coffee table. He poured the wine and then placed the bottle down. Finn sheepishly took his glass while Allodia whiffed the aroma of the wine.

"You'd think that after all the parties and fundraisers I've been to, I'd know how to distinguish a fine glass of wine," Allodia expressed. "Truthbetold, I don't."

Salmar whiffed the wine and then taste-tested it. He swished the wine in his mouth and then swallowed.

"I can attest that this is some damn good wine," Salmar expressed, looking to the others. "How about a toast? To the Cabernet name – may the souls of our mother, father, and dear brother – grandmother, grandfather and father to Finn – rest in peace." The three brought each other's wine glasses together. "Cheers." Salmar sat down next to Allodia, each at opposite sides of the sofa, while Finn sat on his own at a loveseat in front of a wide window. Salmar placed his ankle upon his knee and stretched out his arm as he looked to the others with a smile. "So, how's work, Allodia?"

"Miserable," Allodia confessed. "I don't know why I ever agreed to be chairwoman – it started off as a favor for Charlie, and somehow became my primary focus. I've had to take a backseat to the charity's business, but having a wider vision of both sides lets me steer the company a certain way. We're hopping aboard this 'green' technology-drive, especially since government subsidies and incentives have helped off-set costs to a booming business, but we want to do everything properly and not exploit taxpayers. We're looking at cost-efficient electrical vehicles, efficient power methods, and all sorts of innovative ideas to not just sell that image but also reform the company in that direction too. We've also got this artificial intelligence initiative, looking to transform how data and information is transferred between the organization – Charlie left that one up to Cabernet Technologies to formalize. We've also made headway with Cabernet Rockets, which I'm going to be honest, didn't even know existed until I took this role. Apparently we make lots of money from launching satellites into space."

"I can't imagine too much of your time is taken up in just being chairwoman," Salmar responded. "Charles always found time for his pastimes – being chairperson was like a part-time job."

"Yes, but with what spare time I do have, it's cleaning up office politics in human resources, or jumping aboard a meeting with the Cabernet Foundation – meetings, meetings, meetings… no more travel for me – well, there is travel, but not to the places I want to go to. I wish I could have travelled with daddy more before he passed away since that was my plan, but then Charlie got sick and needed me in Harlech. Luckily, Finn here got to travel and keep him company."

"Oh, you got to travel with the old man – how was it?" Salmar asked.

"It was… eye-opening," Finn remarked. "By no means was it easy. He lived a hard life doing what he loved to do for others. I felt like I was punishing myself, especially my body, in doing what he's been freely doing for more than thirty years, but never did it seem like a punishment to him."

"I guess it would have been thirty-five years this year…" Allodia noted.

"Yup, those two really gave it their entire lives in the end," Salmar expressed. "God Bless the two of them, really. What about you, Finn? What do you do now? Do you have any sort of role in the family business?"

"No," Finn answered, "I dropped out of university when my dad's cancer got worse, took an extended leave to travel with Everest until he died last year, and for the past year since I've just been living out here at Cabernet Manor on my own."

"You've got to have something you do with all your time though, right?"

"I have my own hobbies," Finn expressed. "Right now I've primarily been helping Diana and Tristan with a project, sometimes visiting them in Harlech, or they come to Allabrese."

"What project?"

"Well, Tristan had a series of journals that he'd write into. He told me that when his folks died, he was told to write in a journal his thoughts and frustrations. I've been translating those journals into a cohesive narrative to tell the tale of his life since meeting Diana and Charlemagne. It's becoming a bit of a book series, sixteen novels in total. We've called it The Fourth Level series because of how much Charlemagne expressed to them to pursue the higher happiness in life, or what the Greeks call the fourth level of happiness."

"Fascinating…" Salmar responded. "Very fascinating…" he repeated with a smile as he brought a hand to his chin. "Would you believe me if I said that I was the one that told Tristan to start a journal?"

"Did you?" Finn questioned.

"I did," Salmar affirmed, "because you're right, I saw how hurt he was after his parents had died. I sent him to therapy, and it seldom did much for him and he didn't like it, so we made a deal that instead of going to a therapist I'd get him a journal and he'd write in it. I'm happy to hear he kept that promise all these years..."

"Yup, he filled to the brim about four of them with all his crazy thoughts and reflections, and it's been my pleasure and also his confidence in me to get to read them. When I'm done writing, I'm going to send it to Diana who's going to read through it all. If it meets her approval, we're going to publish through Cabernet Industries."

"Aw, that's so cool," Allodia expressed. "I want to read about their little adventures... I will do all that I can to make sure those get published."

"So, I suppose that makes you a writer then," Salmar replied. "A very good writer at that if you're going through this entire process to craft together a narrative. I foresee this being a very good series... I have a proposition though. I have journals and letters, and e-mails and other documents that I've collected over the years from my grandfather to my brother, talking about all sorts of moments and experiences from their life. Now, I don't know what worth they may have to anyone else other than us Cabernets, but I think if you put your creative power to it, Finn, you may just be able to make something of it all."

"I think that'd be an interesting premise to dwell on," Finn agreed.

"You don't have to right about their life story, per say, but something to honor them, especially dad and Charles who've recently died," Salmar suggested. "I'm sure that you can find some overarching theme to it all. Anything to talk about this legacy they leave behind and we all share in – the Cabernet Legacy."

Finn nodded and then looked down to the ground. His ears drowned out the noise of Allodia continuing and steering the conversation. He contemplated on those words, and they stayed with him.

Act 7, Scene 1

"Do you ever think about what you'll leave behind?" Finn questioned to Moira.

"Not particularly," Moira replied as they hiked through the outskirts of a dry grassland. The pair had left the desert and came around to a region of short grass in sandy dirt with a few deciduous trees barren and ahead of them.

"You don't ever think about what you might contribute to the world before you die?" Finn asked. "How about your own existence? The breadth of it all and who you are in this world? Have you ever thought about the wonder and awe in our own existence? The existence of humanity, and what it all is supposed to mean?"

Moira sighed and replied saying, "No, Finn, I haven't. I exist. I'm a person. I've got a crippling debt and not much to show for it. I don't have time to contemplate these ancient wonders. I'm not a philosopher."

"You don't have to be Aristotle to think about your own mortality," Finn responded, "and how we all share in an inevitability in our deaths. The Chosen fear death, and so do the Children – that's why they've sought means to transcend from their mortal state of life so they can be eternal, but I know that there is no possibility to become immortal through technological endeavors. If I was any other person, I would be right there – certainly Audric Zimmerman was there too. For as powerful as he was, he was not immortal.

"I wonder though about our existence, and how feeble we were to have failed to meet that goal in our own efforts. The Order of St. Athanasius preached upon this need for humans to evolve biologically, and they too sought those answers. They saw the continuation of humanity, of generations onto generations, as an ongoing effort of a family to attempt to transcend – if not one generation, then the next will be successful, and so on, and when that generation succeeds it will mean victory for all the people of that past generation – a capability of a descendent to uplift and save their ancestors, but also bring honor to them. I often contemplate that philosophy and how it relates to the so-called great men of past generations like Alexander the Great to Napoleon Bonaparte, and how these great men share in being somewhat childless, or at least for both of them, to have not had surviving offspring and direct descendants. Either these great men were so great that they achieved immortality in legend, or they failed to win at this truest struggle of mortal men to become immortal beings, almost as if it was our lost birthright. And then I think about the Saints and how they lived, and sure some of them had children, but for the most part, others did not or there was no record of their prodigy. I also think about clergy and the discipline of celibacy as it relates to legacy, and sure some of them have spiritual or adoptive children, but others do not. What is it about greatness that involves being childless? Is the Order of St. Athanasius true in what they preach? I know in part they are, but are they also true of the evolutionary principle that it is a natural principle and not just a theological one?

"Just about everyone that I love knows that I want to become a priest. All of them know and see me differently, and all of them have had different reactions to that intent and desire. My uncle, Salmar, when he found out, had a different reaction than the others. He asked me if my intent was to throw away the Cabernet legacy. He wanted to assure himself that I was not acting in a self-destructive way, so to assure him, I gave him an honest answer. I firmly believe that all goods things must come to an end eventually on this Earth, and maybe the same is true about the Cabernet name. Salmar does not intend to re-marry and have children, and Allodia is too old to bare children. The most either of them can do is adopt, but is an adopted child really a Cabernet? I mean no offense to Diana and Tristan who are surely a part of the family, but neither of them have accepted nor believe they have a part in our family's legacy knowing they are their own family in blood and principle, even if we share a closeness. I told Salmar that I may very well be the end of the Cabernet lineage, the last generation, but I told him what I believed in – I told him that I intended to rise up and uplift the family name, especially than let it rot and corrupt itself. After I shared those words, he seemed to somewhat understand that I was not acting under nefarious intent, even if he did not quite understand my intentions. At the same time, and perhaps this is my own prior worldview that haunts me, but I feel something gnaw within me as though I were committing ritual suicide of the family – as if rather than uplifting the family name, I am taking us all into oblivion. It bothers me…"

Moira continued to hike with him as she was speechless to his muse. "I'm sure you'll have plenty of time to decide…" she finally answered. "… how long do you go to the seminary for? Two years?"

"The minimum is four years," Finn answered, "the maximum is ten."

"Oh, that's… yikes…" Moira replied. "I would not want to be in school for ten years. Still though, that seems like plenty of time to decide what you want to do with your life." She paused for a moment as they entered silence. She then said, "What I know is what I've been taught – 'Moira, you need to look out for yourself because nobody else will,' or 'You need to do what you got to do…' and so far, that's been my philosophy. I'm just surviving, man. I wish I had all the time you did to think and decide, but I'm living on money I don't even own. A part of me wishes I could just disappear, start a new life, but with collections agencies? I'd be on the run from them, not just the robots. I can't run away from thousands of dollars of debt, even if I was being hunted for my life."

"You live a pretty... humble life," Finn acknowledged. "You don't under-estimate yourself in the slightest, and you don't over-estimate yourself. You know exactly who you are, but what I don't think you know, and it's not entirely your fault nor bad of you, is how much you can be, or how much more there is for you."

"Me? Humble?" Moira questioned. "No, I'm not," she said with a minor laugh. "Isn't someone who's humble supposed to be someone who sits still and doesn't get into trouble."

"A humble person is someone who sees themselves for who they really are, understands their place in this world, and is in touch with reality. In more religious terms, a humble person sees themselves as they really are in comparison to God."

"I'm not a good girl, I can assure you that," Moira stated. "I've caused you plenty of trouble."

"Trouble you didn't necessarily ask for," Finn replied."

"I'm just doing what I have to do to survive. Sometimes... that's taken me to the least places. Have you ever heard of the Dark Web?"

"Yeah, I'm familiar."

"If you were to compare the Internet to an iceberg, everything that everyday people see is the top half, and over seventy to ninety percent of the rest of it is the Dark Web," Moira explained. "It's a dark world in itself, total anarchy, and where all sorts of bad people gather. Some of the most foul content can be found on the Dark Web from human and drug trafficking, child pornography, to even terrorist and extremist groups on unregulated forums."

"Yeah..."

"I've sometimes found myself involved with hacker groups, especially hacker activism, while other times I've taken requests to extract and deliver information from restricted networks. I've been involved in ransomware attacks, phishing, piracy, and other no good deeds."

"So, you're a cyber criminal."

"Not so much anymore," Moira responded. "This came through hard times during university, especially low times from my late teens to early twenties. I liked it…"

"What made you stop?"

"My persona, Oracle… became an infamous name," Moira stated. "I became the target of numerous cyber attacks, not just from law enforcement, but from vigilantes and those seeking revenge against me. Having a target on my back started to affect my mental health. I became paranoid and suspicious of others until I could move places. Eventually I had to say enough was enough that I retired the name, and that was almost two years ago."

"Huh… I wonder what's said about the Chosen, or the Global Defense Project on the Dark Web. Even the Order of St. Athanasius… I suppose something must be said about them there."

"It would be hard to determine," Moira replied. "The Dark Web is difficult to navigate. You never know where the next door will take you, especially whether it be a savory place or not. I've seen my share of content that I would prefer not to see; it depresses you. My eyes were not prepared."

"I'm sure you have…" Finn affirmed, "though I guess that probably makes two of us who are wanted criminals. I guess I didn't tell you why I'm a wanted scumbag myself."

As the pair continued to chat, they began to step onto some residue snow in the grasslands. A minor breeze also picked up and caused the pine branches of some coniferous trees around them to rustle. The pair began to follow the sides of a low stream as they hiked around the base of the mountain and continued to approach their waypoint. The ground continued to partially consist of dirt and sand. The clouds above them were dark and gloomy, but there was no rain. The ground was also occasionally rocky, with large boulders to loose gravel in the earth. After a continued hike as the day carried on, they stopped at a clearing beside a hill up into the continued depths of the forest where they could see the mountain ahead.

"We've got a few more clicks," Finn noted, "but we're surely in Colorado now, or at least we have been for most of the day. Let's set up camp and call it a night."

The pair proceeded to set up their tents at the top of the hill. Finn dug a hole into the tough ground. He stabbed his small shovel into the icy ground and made two holes, both of which connected underground. He then began to place some kindle into the fire hole and then light it. He placed his metal grate over one of the holes and then placed a small metal pot to boil some water from the nearby snow.

Meanwhile, as the pair sat around the fire, Moira observed seldom smoke travel outwards from the roaring fire that kept them warm. The sun slowly set as Finn attempted to install the plasma cannon to his exosuit, while Moira fiddled with the console she was given. She worked in combination of the campfire light as well as the headlamp. She fiddled with the integrated circuit as she removed it from the console and began to load up her computer. Finn finished installing the plasma cannon and then went downhill to test the intensity of the gunfire on some trees. The shots of plasma melted the wood, causing trees to fall over as he shot at their base. Once he finished, he returned uphill to remove his suit and come around to drink a cup of tea.

"Interesting..." Moira noted. "This circuit... it's some advanced stuff, but it seems to be some sort of hacking device, specifically programmed to interfere and hijack the robots we ran into. I see several execution commands here... better yet, I also see decrypters – custom-made software. Whoever designed this console knew their stuff... There's some encrypted files here I'm going need some time to review, probably related to overrides and access to GDP systems. If I can transfer these files,

I may be able to make use of some of them as we get to the facility."

"Iyyov was certainly prepared to go all the way," Finn noted. "Anything related to Beliyal?"

"No..." Moira responded, "and I wouldn't think so. Seems like whatever Beliyal is, it was something to do with the mining facility..."

"Hm..."

"Although, I do have to ask now that I'm reminded about it, but what the hell is Hail?" Moira inquired. "Or Heyl, or whatever."

"Hm?"

"You talk in your sleep," Moira stated. "When we were sleeping close together in that cave in the desert, you kept muttering Heylel."

"Oh..."

"You going to explain what the hell that was all about?"

"It's fairly complicated," Finn replied. "I don't think you'd understand."

"Don't assume what I can and cannot understand," Moira responded. "What's Heyl?"

Finn took in a deep breath and then stretched out his legs, setting them apart, as he sat down and got comfortable. "Alright," he said, "how do I explain this.... You remember those aliens I was talking to you about? The ones that came down to Earth and bred with humans, right?"

"Yeah."

"Heyl, so I've been told, was one of those demons exiled to Earth. He was their leader. He was also different to the rest of them, believed to be the best of them. It's not all very clear to me, but from my understanding of these aliens, the ones that you saw but don't remember, were angels in the flesh, and they come from an ancient breed of seemingly sterile and immortal creatures that consist of the cerebral part of this ancient civilization they form. I've heard the term used to describe these aliens as 'elders' likely because of how old they are. These creatures, one of few alien species, were imperfect creatures whose ancestors became pure spirits. These creatures, I've been told, are so unlike humans in the way they think, lacking emotional capacity and instead being so rudimentary in their thinking, like robots almost. Perhaps it was a combination of their creation, beings that did not evolve as humans did from animals with all our emotions that these creatures were so detached in their essence, but that detachment was what led them to evolve as they did. What they had in capacity of thought though, they lacked in physical capacity. From what Diana and Tristan described, these were ugly creatures, and incredibly fragile. I'm not quite sure how Heyl compares to these creatures that you guys met, but I do know that he had a few unique abilities. For a start, he was seemingly immortal, but he also had the ability to apparate. He was beautiful, but disfigured, and I'm not sure if this appearance was his natural state, because he was a shapeshifter – like the Children."

"You met this thing?"

"I… I had an encounter when I was twenty," Finn stated. "Heyl approached me, and we struck a deal… it goes deeper than that moment though. I already told you that Zimmerman was not a good man, my life before Zimmerman, but what I did not tell you was that he was my mentor. From the moment I left England, he brought me to American and trained me to be his apprentice. I told him all about my life, all the way to my belief at the time that Charlemagne Cabernet was my father, and he pulled at my psyche and manipulated me in a way to hate my biological father and to join him in a quest to destroy him, to destroy all that stood in his way, and create a better, more beautiful world. To that extent, Zimmerman also exploited me for my love of nature, and my misanthropy (hatred of humans). I was manipulated – I had no idea what Zimmerman's full intent was at the time, to kill all of humanity, but I followed along. He shared with me all sorts of learned knowledge, stuff which you can't find anywhere else, really. He told me about the Chosen, the Children, and all that he knew about them. He also taught me about Heyl, and the encounter he had with this fallen angel too. Zimmerman told me that Heyl was what has been named in common knowledge as Lucifer. He told us we were against this creature, but I guess I missed the part where he warned me not to trust it.

"To make a long story short, after I met my biological mother, I ran away from both her and my biological dad. I took a device he had constructed, believing it to be a time machine, and teleported to a distant world like ours, but older than our own which essentially was an alternative universe set in the near future. I came to this world by mistake, intending to reverse the mistake of the past when my father left my mother, but as I wandered this post-apocalyptic setting, Heyl approached me. Just like Zimmerman did, Heyl manipulated me using my emotions and set me against my father as he came with my mother to search for me. My father was able to de-escalate me, but as I was with him in this world, I had another encounter and Heyl took possession of my body. I don't remember my experience in that possession – just the screams and shouts. Tristan and my dad saved my life as they came after me, but from what I was told, I killed my uncle in that timeline, as well as others before they could save me. Both Tristan and my dad saved me though, by loving me, essentially, and at the same time, it was at this moment that I had my epiphany on the spiritual, like my father did to some extent, being a somewhat irreligious person until he had his encounter with the aliens, and through the evangelization of Diana no less, became a strictly religious person like his grandfather. I felt immense guilt to learn that I had killed, and it set me on a downward spiral until I could be consoled through the religious life… As for Heyl though, from what I was told and believed, Tristan and Diana fought that creature after it absorbed Zimmerman's body into its own being, and they were supposed to have entrapped it in that alternative world before we came back. Whether it is still alive or not, I don't know, but I have a feeling that it may definitely be severely wounded in the least, which is fine by me. Even if that Devil were deceased, its followers prowl about the world seeking the ruin of souls, and it did not mean the defeat of evil.

"This Beliyal – I'm familiar with that name too. Damian told me all about it. Both Beliyal and Heyl are apart of what Damian informally referred to as the unholy trinity. He did not necessarily believe in the existence of all these creatures. Even Heyl, despite having an encounter when he was young, went on with doubt in his mind. Beliyal though was more of a concept than an existing being. Damian referred to Beliyal as an unholy spirit, a personification of malice and gloom, or in other words, the essence of evil, like a wind or energy that passes and flows. According to legend, Beliyal in relation to Heyl was let loose upon the world when, as in the Bible, Adam and Eve ate from the apple, and the world came to know sin and death. From that moment in which the world, our world, became 'fallen' as it is referred to, Beliyal was let loose, and this world became one of evil, where each ruler was at the behest of a demon, if not a half-demon itself. Why you saw that name in the code, I don't know, but if I had to hazard a guess, seeing that Zimmerman and his own legacy has a part to play in all this through these robots, I would suppose that something to do with these robots was named as such and is using that name either as a plain and simple name, or as an alias for something nefarious. Despite not believing in evil, he was inspired and certainly an evil man himself. Zimmerman was a hateful man, and he especially hated these entities despite claiming they do not exist, he could have easily just been lying to himself, and me.

"Thirdly though, and this subject is lesser known to both me and Zimmerman, he hypothesized about a third entity. This entity was referred to him as Abaddon, or Appolyon, and according to legend passed on to him, this creature was an ancient beast from long ago. Heyl credits its origin to this creature, and likewise the origin of all evil beings to this creature. This creature, whether it exists or not, is said to have been banished to an eternal solitary confinement from which it can never escape. Another term I've heard be used for this creature is 'Great Satan,' where Satan here is being used as a title rather than a specific entity. All these entities in this unholy trinity could be referred to as Satan, because Satan comes from the Hebrew word that means 'adversary,' or 'accuser,' and it was used to refer to anything that opposed God. However, the title, 'Great Satan' was like a title of kingship, and it was one of desire for all evil beings after Abaddon so much so that Zimmerman idolized the term because of all that he hated, he hated God more than anything. He wanted to be known as the greatest being to oppose God, even though he supposedly didn't believe in God, but that was probably not true either. From my understanding, Heyl idolized that term too and was believed to have adopted it, which is why in common knowledge, Lucifer rather than Abaddon is known as at least Satan, because he, demons, and all evil spirits are the only creature that currently exist and roam the earth to really oppose God as a force of evil. The Children have used that term as well, but to refer to themselves as a collective group, which stems from their messianic beliefs that Heyl, or some other entity, would rise up to be their leader. After years and years of waiting though, a new opinion arose in which they grew tired of waiting and disappointment in failed leaders that they would rather crown themselves as a collective group to be that entity. I've not heard much about this thing, Abaddon, elsewhere except what's available on the Internet, but not much of that is relevant or very much true."

Moira let out a sigh and then replied, "It's all so much…"

"Yeah, it certainly can be," Finn responded, "but as it relates to Beliyal and Abaddon, I wouldn't be worried about it. They're just myths, and if it weren't for the fact that I've had an encounter in the least with Heyl, and you and others have had encounters with these aliens, I would otherwise be skeptical of their belief."

"Except I did have an encounter with those aliens…" Moira replied, "even if I don't remember all of it, I still remember some of it now." She sighed again. "They were angels?"

"So my father believed," Finn answered. "Zimmerman was convinced they were all just demons, but my understanding is that although not angelic beings in the spiritual sense, they are at least related to them in some capacity. You had an encounter with two aliens in particular that were unlike the others, one of which was named Madonna, and the other of which referred to itself as Mika. Madonna was also referred to as Archon, the ruler of these beings, while Mika was Madonna's protector. My father initially thought that the physical state of these creatures was the end-all of it, but around the time I had my encounter with Heyl, Tristan had an encounter with Mika again, but in an ethereal state. This perplexed my father, but as it appeared, at least some of the aliens that you all had encountered had the capability to transcend from bodily form, and vice-versa. I combined this knowledge with my own knowledge, some of which was shared to me by Zimmerman, to theorize that the upper echelons, or royalty, of the ancient civilization had this capacity while the rest of the aliens did not – these were corrupted creatures, as purported in the origin story of Heyl's exile and their punishment. These 'elders' as they were referred to are not necessarily evil creatures, but still prone to evil – it was believed that a group of them close to the Archon had betrayed her, but whether that was in logical choice as they seem to do, or under the influence of darker powers, is unknown. Zimmerman said that the 'elders' worship their ancestors, those that ascended and desire themselves to ascend to no avail, especially the evil ones, but that's just myth. In the least I can believe that a small group of them may be loyal to Heyl, or some other entity in the unholy trinity, or perhaps even just the evil spirits, or any other spiritual being, or group of spiritual beings, but I don't have any proof. I've never actually met these things before, nor do I intend to go out of my way looking for them. It's all mysterious to me at the end of the day, and I just have to live with the understanding that they exist and are out there."

Moira sat in silence as she processed this information. She looked blankly at the fire pit. After a moment of quiet, she said, "And the ones that came down to Earth with Heyl... the ones that bred with humans a long time ago, those are the ones we're up against, aren't we? The ones that overthrew the Global Defense Project, and sent these robots after us. Do they know about all this stuff that you're telling me about?"

"I would assume they have some vague concept – after all, much of what I learned from Zimmerman he learned from them and their lore. You could argue that because it comes from them, it's all utter bollocks, but a lot of it has lined up with experience, both my own, Zimmerman's, my dad's, and Diana and Tristan's. Besides, I don't think that the Children per say are up against us, but their wider group known as the Chosen. They too could have just as well taken something from their mythos and thrown it into some computer code. What I know for sure is that there is no way that Beliyal is really influencing these robots, or integrated in the code, or anything like that..." he said with a smile. "That's just ridiculous. It supposes that this unholy trinity is real, which I doubt. As much as I would like to believe in a nice, symbolic number like the number three, we just have the Chosen to worry about."

Act 7, Scene 2

The next day, Finn woke up before sunrise and began to light the fire to make some breakfast. He quietly ate with Moira before they both put out the fire, eliminated any traces of their presence in these parts of the forest, and then proceeded to continue to make their ascent up the mountain. The surroundings were dim, and there was a lot more snow around them than the day before, but also patches of grass that poked out and through the snow. Overall the snow was thin, but in greater surface area than the clumps they saw towards the end of the previous day. The trees in their surrounding were coniferous pine trees, tall but with short branches almost ten feet above and beyond. As they journeyed upwards, they came across an abandoned wooden shack that was nearly completely collapsed and abandoned. The ground of the shack consisted of overgrown grass, and the sides were overtaken by bushes. They followed along to a dirt path besides a collapsed fence, and continued between two low hills as they followed this pathway in the darkness of the dawn. The path soon widened out as they came around to a low-slope descent, but it soon raised up again at greater slope along the frosty pathway. Sooner or later, a thick fog could be found that made it difficult to see ahead. They continued up the side of the mountain and eventually found themselves at the end of the path as they reached a tall fence with a building at the side. A signpost read 'Golf Tango Outpost' with an additional post below that said 'Restricted Access'. However, on the other side from this signpost was an armored car with deflated tires and a broken window. As they looked around the fence, the sun finally shined down through the clouds above.

Finn looked through the fence and could see a few more houses on the other side as the road went through the outpost and curved left. He could not see anyone else around, so he began to search around the perimeter of the fence where he found another house with a broken window.

"Come on, let's see if we can get through here. This outpost is in our way," Finn stated.

Finn climbed through the window, explored the ground floor of the house to see that it was abandoned, and all the furniture cleared out. He then came around to the other side and stepped out into the grounds of the outpost. He saw a few more abandoned vehicles, and began to walk away from the dirt path as he looked at the GPS, and instead followed an alternative path in the ground that took them to another tall fence, this time with a larger warning. On the other side of the fence was a tall electrical transmission tower. He approached the fence and found the gate was locked with chains tied with a heavy padlock. He stepped back and pointed the plasma cannon, eviscerating the metal with hot plasma and then pulling at the gate to open the way ahead. They walked forward to find themselves in a large clearing with the transmission tower in the middle. The tower continued down the side of the mountain along a very steep drop from where it went northbound across a clearing, while on the other end was a tall cliff and another steep angle along the sides of the mountain as it disappeared southward as well, through the thick fog and tall trees ahead. A humming noise could be heard around the electrical tower. Finn came around to the barbed wire fence before the drop down as he attempted to look out, and then he came around to the fence on the other side that continued across the side of the mountain.

"Only way to climb up this mountain is to keep going left and right," Finn stated. He fired his cannon into the fence and created a gap for them to climb through.

The surrounding terrain continued in the same manner as the day before, with coniferous trees and a natural path ahead that brought them around to a small river that drifted down the side of the mountain. The skies above remained cloudy, but the sun was at least visible through this barrier more than it was the day before, but with it came the odd drizzle of light rain that tickled one's face. The temperature was mild for a late winter day, but an occasional wind brought a chill to their uncovered faces and likewise it was hardly cold enough to melt the remainder of the snow left around across the base and uphill of the mountain. The ground at their feet began to drift from a mixture of grass and gravel, to one of powder-like dirt that was a greyish brown. There were also many rocks and boulders in the way, especially jagged cliffsides. On occasion as they climbed up the side of the mountain, the rumble of thunder or flash of lightning could be seen across the sky, especially at moments where there was no rainfall and just the clouds above. At other times too, a gap in the firmament of clouds would expose rays of sunlight that would shine into one's face as they walked onwards.

The ascent up the mountain consisted of a low slope eastbound, followed by a turn that took them northbound again. After a moment as they followed the riverside, the rain became more consistent, though still light, and they began to continue up the slope of the mountain with gentle consideration to their environment. After another hour as the morning set in, they approached a complex ahead. This complex has a taller, reinforced fence with plates of metal across it. The path ahead of them from the transmission tower came to a checkpoint with another dirt path that went through the base and continued along. This outpost was larger than the other one, with tall lookout towers, larger buildings and structures that surrounded a clearing in the middle, but like the other, it was seemingly abandoned. Even the fence appeared rundown and broken. The checkpoint fence had numerous tall shoots of grass, and the rest of the greenery inside appeared overgrown and unkempt. Finn blasted through the front gate and then began to enter through the midst of the outpost where a tank parked in the midst had its cannon pointed downward, and the side of the metal appeared rusted.

"Curious…" Finn stated as he looked around, "American or GDP?" A flagpole in the midst of the base could not suggest either or as there was no flag.

The buildings in the outpost consisted of a warehouse structure, a garage-like structure with open shutters and no vehicles inside, and then a barracks with an office-like structure. They walked through the warehouse to get to the other side of the outpost where they found more rundown vehicles, including tanks and transport trucks. They left the outpost and continued along the dirt path that eventually led them to an asphalt road. Finn studied the GPS before he began to walk along the side of the road, near the trees, and continued forward along the plain road. This road soon began to curve to the left and then after half a mile, to the right as it began to ascend upwards. After a turn to the right, it then continued straight forward for two-thirds of a mile before it began to curve left. No cars passed them as they trekked across the road, though the map suggested they were well into the mountain now. The road gradually brought them left and then straight forward before there was a small curve to the right and further path forward. On the right as they walked forward was a steep drop towards some coniferous trees and then a steep slope downwards, while on the right was a likewise steep slope with trees above, and then continuing upwards with more and more trees. At the end of the stretch of road, the path continued rightward at an increased angle and shorter length before another bend right and another stretch forward. The end of the latest stretch brought them leftward, down a minor descent, and then up again to the right with intermittent curves left and right. The right side of the path continued to consist of steep drops and slopes, while on the left were rocky cliffside drops and steep sides. The fog began to clear out as their elevator went up, and after a few more minutes of walking, Finn caught sight of the power lines above their heads, going directly up the side of the mountain. As they walked, Finn could also partially see through the fog and outward towards the stretch of land below them as he realized how high they had already climbed upwards. They were close to a hundred yards above sea level, or above the base of the mountain. The road continued along until there was a sudden U-turn that then continued along in the opposite direction at a straight line for a few hundred yards, and then curved right with concrete barriers at the side of the road now and forty-five degree dirt hills with trees on the other side. This road continued forward for close to two miles in stints of left and right, with straight lines before there was another wider U-turn that took them the opposite direction.

"I should have taken the car," Finn stated, looking around. "Still though, not sure why we haven't passed anyone unless the proper entrance was closed off."

"I feel like I'm climbing Mount Everest here," Moira complained. "How tall is this mountain?"

"Not tall at all," Finn replied, "it's just the ascent that's taking us around."

The next stretch as they went eastbound again went forward for a few hundred yards, and then left up a good portion upwards, and then slightly to the left, and then rightward for another intense portion upwards before a mile straight stretch that came to yet another U-turn. At this moment, the pair stopped for a break and could partially look forward across the land from where they were, looking outwards to the surrounding region. After a quick meal and drink, they carried on with steeper and taller cliffside rock walls, and longer drops on the other side. A few hundred yardss in, they found a clearing on the right side of the road with some excavation machines and other construction vehicles, and also a shelter with some piles of sand. The road ahead consisted of a destroyed bridge with a tall drop below and no way to surpass. The gap between each side of the road was close to a hundred yards.

"Hm…" Finn noted. "We'll have to find a way around."

The pair came around to the clearing with the excavation vehicles and found a tunnel entrance. This entrance took them into a square rocky tunnel with mine cart tracks on the left. They soon reached another gate where Finn used his plasma cannon to punch through. They then carried onwards, finding light at the end of the tunnel where they came out at a clearing within the next upcoming U-turn. There was a lot more snow in these parts than in previous parts, prompting them to trek carefully. The rain had at least stopped at this point, as did the wind, and the thunder and lightning. The sun was also less visible as the clouds above thickened, and it became colder. The pair continued and saw a structure collapsed overtop of the road from another side clearing.

The structure was tall, metallic, and had fallen from a chain-link fenced enclosure with a hut beside it. The structure was slightly triangular, narrower than the electrical transmission tower, but taller overall with a longer upper shaft. Finn and Moira reached a point in which the tower obstructed the path ahead, and then began to climb around it. The width of the structure's upper half was close to five yards on either side. After surpassing this structure, they continued along the road for another mile before they reached another bend. This bend led to another, though shorter straight path before a wider bend. As they walked around this almost mile-in-length bend, Finn saw the wires of the electrical towers above them again. At the end of this most recent bend, the path straightened out and continued to ascend at a steep angle before it finally began to smooth out and flatten out as they reached another tall, reinforced metal fence with a checkpoint in the road. This reinforced fence was within a second exterior perimeter made by a tall chain-link fence and a separate checkpoint outside. A tall white sign outside of the compound read the following in large red font, 'WARNING' with the below in smaller black font, 'MILITARY INSTALLATION' and then the following in even smaller black font, 'OFF LIMITS TO UNAUTHORIZED PERSONNEL'. Beneath these words was the following blurb in black font as well, 'AUTHORITY: Internal Security Act, 50' and 'U.S.C. 797' as well as 'PUNISHMENT: Up to one year imprisonment and $5,000 fine.'

"I guess that answers my earlier question," Finn stated as he looked at the sign. He then looked over towards the military encampment. Up to this point, not much could be heard except the rustle of branches and howl of wind. Likewise, the outskirts of the military base were quiet, and there were no guards at the checkpoint or around the perimeter.

The military base appeared large, etched into the side of the mountain to the left at a diagonal angle on flat terrain. A tall cliff wall could be seen to the left at the side of the base. From where the pair stood on the outside, they could see some shipping containers and a few buildings, as well as some watch towers and another radio tower ahead. What was more notable from where they stood was the continuation of the electrical transmitter tower where it met its end at this base. Still though, the buildings within were not very large, and they ranged in the same style and shapes as the ones in the outposts below. The only variety in them were the presence of some semi-circle metal hangars that could be seen from their position. The rest of the major structures within were rectangular to square shaped with flat rooftops, and they were made of either concrete or brick.

"I don't think anyone is home," Finn noted as he looked around. He then turned to Moira. "Should we risk a year of imprisonment, or five-thousand dollar fine?"

"I think we're already facing a lot more than just that at this point," Moira replied, looking at him unimpressed. "My question is whether this is it... Seems kind of puny for what I imagined to find."

"Do you reckon there be more bases about here?"

"I don't know… the satellite images I was able to find were unclear," Moira responded. "If this is the one I think I saw, then it may just be…"

Finn approached the front gate of the compound and prepared his plasma cannon to tear through the chain-link fence. He then pushed it open, and then walked up to the second fence. He looked around the outer perimeter to see some tall turrets with machine gun nests in segments across the fence perimeter, but the guns were pointed in sporadic directions. Additionally, as he looked inside, he saw a few vehicles parked about and abandoned.

"I don't like it…" Finn stated before he fired his cannon again. "Get ready for a potential fight…"

Finn fired the cannon at the gate, and then walked over to push it open. He then walked forward along the first stretches of concrete pavement to look around. He found several shipping containers knocked over, and of the vehicles he could now see, he saw they were charred and destroyed. He kept his plasma cannon raised as he looked around before lowering it as he took his first few steps and realized that the section of the base, and likely the rest of the base, was abandoned.

"What happened here…" Moira questioned.

"I don't know," Finn replied, "but it's not making much sense to me. This should be it… this should be their stronghold, but it's… completely abandoned."

The pair came around to a semi-circular hangar in the midst of several shipping containers and a two-story square tower that formed a somewhat tight quarters of the entry section of the base. They came to an armored personnel carrier in the middle clearing in this section and observed the surroundings. The windows were cracked, some walls chipped, and otherwise other structures slightly war torn and battered. Some gas tanks were ruptured, and fuel silos destroyed. There were numerous portable metal structures parked and raised above the ground, and these too either had broken windows or collapsed walls. A nearby three-story tall structure had a radar dish atop that was tilted over. There were lots of wires between the buildings, and most of these came around the radar dish and the radio tower atop of a two-story structure. The pathway through the clearing in the midst of this section of the base had some barricades made of concrete barriers and sandbags. They were reinforced with steel plates and machine guns. The pair went forward through this section. They passed a few garages and then reached another gate that led inwards to the rest of the base. This gate was beside another fence that ran around and quarantined the initial section of the base from one side, while from the other was a three-story brick building and checkpoint. Finn charged the plasma cannon to tear through the chain around the fence, and then he pulled it open and continued forward.

From where they entered, they came around to a larger clearing with numerous vehicles abandoned and stalled around a square clearing more than an acre large. The surroundings of this open space had more semi-circle huts as well as raised portables. The abandoned and destroyed vehicles, some of them charred and burnt, varied from armored personnel carriers to transport trucks, fuel trucks, armored personnel trucks, and even tanks. Directly ahead from the entrance into this part of the base was an overturned fuel truck that was completely black and the rear of it ruptured and torn. The midst of the open space had circular trenches with blast shields raised up around them. The midst of these trenches had closed blast doors. Around the sides of the open space were some surface-to-air missile launchers, some of them mobile. Towards the rear of the base, the electrical transmission towers could be seen, the last of the cables descending downwards towards a fenced off power substation that hummed. Some additional wires could be seen extending from this power station into the base. On the left, towards the cliff wall, there were subterranean bunkers that slightly protruded outwards from the ground, and these were segmented with similar-looking vents with circular grates above them. Behind these was a T-shaped road with a section going towards the cliff wall towards a tunnel, while the rest continued upwards along the mountain. This road had a tall, barbed wire chain-link fence around it up to the exit. The continuation of the road went up slope and curved around the side of the cliff wall, but it was noticeably partially destroyed with debris from a landslide below the gap of space in the road, as well as spill off debris from the adjacent cliff wall.

"Where does that go?" Finn questioned.

"A runway," Moira stated, "probably a few more structures."

"This is all wrong... where is the research facility? Where is the robot production facility?"

They continued to look around until Moira set her eyes onto the blast doors ahead in the cliff wall.

"What if it's beyond that point?" Moira questioned. "What if it's all inside the mountain?"

"Even if that were true, I'd still expect some defenses," Finn remarked. "I'm beginning to worry now – that since the Upheaval, they've flown the coop and settled elsewhere. We've come all this way, and with whomever at our tail, we can't afford to be misdirected."

"What do you want to do then, Finn?" Moira asked, slightly annoyed herself. "What can we do?"

Finn looked about and then sighed. He walked towards the blast doors that went into the mountain, passing through the gates with the plasma cannon, and they both came around to the front of the doors to see that they were tall, rectangular, and seemingly thick. He shot some plasma towards them, but they were hardly damaged.

"Nothing is going to cut through that... not even an excavator," Finn stated. He walked away from the doors and began to return to the military base. "These are missile silos. Wherever we are, it could have been a nuclear launch base."

"Are you sure it could, or used to be?"

"I would hardly doubt the Americans would just leave a bunch of nuclear missiles lying around in an abandoned base," Finn stated. "I mean, even if Operation Upheaval had failed, the world didn't end, and the U.S. government is still in power and national security a concern." They returned to the open space in the midst of the base. "Alright, let's split up and see if we can find anything of use."

The pair did exactly that, where Moira stayed around the open space and began to search the hangars, while Finn went to the integrated structures towards the front. He began to search room to room, but there was little left behind. A lot of the furniture, any important documents, and other information was extracted somehow. After an hour of searching, the pair came together in the open space.

"Anything?" Finn asked.

"No, seems like this place was cleaned out."

"Yeah, that's about as much as I was able to deduce," Finn replied. "Something happened here, and whatever it was, it was enough to cause the Americans to leave and abandon this place. I was searching for a potential entrance into the underground tunnels, but couldn't find it. I want to take a look at the airfield next."

"Don't bother, I may have found a way in," Moira remarked. "I couldn't find a way into the missile silos. They have blast doors with about the same thickness as the other entryway, but around the back of the base was a stretch of road with some vehicle hangars as well as some helipads. I found a potential entryway with an electronic panel that I could hack into... though it looks kind of old."

"Could be worth a shot."

Moira brought Finn around to the bunkers. They followed the road down and around a right curve where it came around the cliffside of the mountain with a significant drop down. This rear section was itself a fair drop down from the rest of the base, and etched into the mountain were some hangars with garage shutters. They walked through some doors beside the garage shutters where they found some abandoned vehicles that were missing tires and even engines. They came around to the very back where they found a small warehouse with some crates, and a blast door with a panel. Moira brought her backpack down and began to fiddle with the panel as she hooked some wires into it.

"I date this technology to the late 2000s at the most," Finn remarked. "Surely it should be penetrable."

"I'm thinking with the console we found, it should be," Moira replied as she typed on her computer. She focused while Finn took a moment to look around. He then returned as she stood up and a siren began to wail. The doors slowly opened, and the pair stepped back as they looked ahead with anticipation. On the other side of the blast doors was a short corridor to a small metal shutter door. They approached forward, opened the shutter door, and revealed a small metal cargo elevator. "Looks safe."

"All aboard," Finn remarked, stepping inside. The pair stepped on, and he hit the switch to send them down into the depths. The elevator opened its doors, and they stepped out to find themselves in a small rectangular concrete room with a circular concrete corridor ahead. The concrete room they were in had some metal crates, while the corridor ahead was medium length, a few yards before it curved, and had a metal pipe and ventilation shaft hanging down the middle. They walked down and came around to a junction with a blast door that looked down a corridor in the midst of the missile silos. "I don't see anything…" He began to turn the vault locks and opened the door, stepping inside to a grated floor with off-shoots on the left and right across the many missile silos. The pair looked around and went to each circular tube, and sure enough there were no nuclear missiles. "Well, that's disappointing…"

The pair continued to explore the underground bunker as they went around some rectangular tunnels with more supplies laid out. These tunnels were separated in a grid-like fashion, and they led to a set of stairs that went up a level to the barracks above, finding sleeping quarters, showers, and other storerooms and living commodities, and then backtracked and explored the rest of the other half of the underground bunker.

"Alright, let me think for a moment," Finn said. "Everything on this side of the bunker is on the south face of the base," Finn stated, but we need to go to the north face." He looked ahead and saw the corridor abruptly ended, while on the opposite way from the missile silos was a heavy blast door.

Moira knelt down besides the panel and set off to work. She was able to override the electronics and unlock the door, causing the blast doors to open up. These doors led into tight corridors with reinforced concrete walls and a few office spaces around a central clearing. This clearing led to a corridor that followed through to another long corridor after a junction, and these led to another set of blast doors. Between each side of these doors were some server racks, but no servers.

"Somebody really cleaned house," Moira remarked, annoyed. She looked about. "No matter," she said, picking up a loose cable. "I may still be able to work with this… It will take me some time."

"We'll set up camp here for the night then and call it," Finn replied. "Whatever lies ahead, we best face when we're well rested."

Act 7, Scene 3

Finn sat on a chair in the midst of the corridor before the nuclear missile silos. A fire burned in an empty metal barrel, and its fumes rose up into a vent above. He kept warm around the fire as his cold breath could otherwise be seen. His suit was placed nearby, and he otherwise examined his wounded arm as he changed the bandages and then put on his aviator jacket. He then began to eat some dinner before Moira came around. She joined him as she picked up her dinner.

"Did you do it?" Finn questioned.

"I'm able to punch through pretty easily," Moira remarked. "I'm able to open the doors whenever you're ready."

Finn nodded and then continued to eat the lentil mix in his steel bowl.

"We'll make sure we get a good rest," Finn noted. "I found another stairwell down that hall, so I went and got some beds to sleep in. I'm going to close the doors after I put out the fire. I don't want anything out there to come find us."

"Fair enough..." Moira replied. "How are you feeling? Do you think this could be it?"

"I'm hoping we'll find something related to our predicament," Finn said, "but it's still strange. I'm worried that perhaps the Upheaval was successful – I mean, the power plant was turned off, so maybe they left this location and went elsewhere. This couldn't be the only robot production facility, could it."

"Based on all the information we have, it would be hard to believe there's anywhere else," Moira remarked. "The minerals to produce these advanced fighting machines are rare, and that mine was one of the few. The energy cost is likewise astronomical. The robots are as we assessed to be just like the ones that Zimmerman Corporation produced too."

"How many years between now and since Operation Upheaval? Two years? Seems like enough time for me to think they re-grouped and re-armed. Still, if there are more locations, we'll want to find that information and it'll be inside. We'll extract it and make preparations to go that way. We'll do what we can to find these bastards. We'll find them, and we'll make them pay for destroying Cabernet Manor, sending their robots on us, and oh boy, will I make sure that the Chosen never see the light of day again. If this be my life now, then so be it. I'll do it. I'm ready for it."

"I know you've asked me to keep tabs on the news since we left Montana, especially for news out of Allabrese, and I know they haven't said anything about us as of yet – we're not quite American's Most Wanted criminals, but what if it gets to that point?"

"I've been Britain's Most Wanted once, and you've basked in that limelight too once before too," Finn responded. "The life I currently live was a stolen life – a life I should never have gotten to have, but because of Zimmerman, I had it. I'm an illegal immigrant so to speak. A part of me has wondered from time to time as I've lived in Canada and the United States as to whether I should just return to the United Kingdom to surrender myself."

"Why would you do that?"

Finn shrugged and then said, "Because I cheated the justice system. As much as I loathe the United Kingdom, especially now in the way it's become a dystopian nightmare, a haven for the worst sexual offenders and murderers who walk free while patriots are incarcerated, a part of me feels the need to respect the laws of my country and surrender to them. A part of me feels the need to surrender myself to the penal system and face the punishment I escaped – that time in prison."

"That's ridiculous," Moira remarked.

"I broke many laws," Finn noted, "the worst being terrorism charges, putting lives in danger for my own pride, and that's in the United Kingdom alone. I still… haven't quite gotten over what I did in that alternative world, killing my uncle in that world and others…" He brought a hand to his forehead to wipe the sweat. "I try to tell myself it's not on my shoulders anymore. My spiritual director tells me it's not on my shoulders anymore (of course, I can't quite explain to him the whole situation without making myself sound mad), but I don't know what to do about it. He tells me to make amends somehow, to vindicate myself if I feel that need even though my sins have been forgiven, but I don't know how to do that except to make myself into a whole sacrifice. To sacrifice my whole and entire life, and not accept ownership of my own life anymore."

Moira looked at Finn as she finished eating. She placed her bowl down and sighed, "That's why you want to be a priest, isn't it? That's your amendment to the world – to give up your life in service to those duties. You don't actually want to a priest, do you?"

"No," Finn denied, "it's not like that."

"Then what, Finn?"

"You wouldn't understand."

"No, I wouldn't," Moira responded. "None of this makes sense to me – angels and aliens, demons and occult orders, and then robots chasing us as well as secret societies. None of it quite makes any sense to me, Finn. I just wanted to learn what happened to my dad."

"Yeah, well, you got your answer some time ago," Finn remarked, putting his bowl down. "What doesn't make sense to me is why you stayed."

Moira flinched at that comment and then crossed her arms, "You really sound like you wished I didn't. Have I been some sort of nuisance to you?"

"No," Finn plainly stated, "and I don't mean it in that way. I know the objective at hand – we want to get our lives back and not go home to be greeted by a ballistic missile through the front door, but as much as an ambitious project it's been, you've been more than free to run off and leave. I also told you the chances we pull this off are astronomically low. Even if we put a wrench in their production line, it still means a lifetime of being *numero uno* on the Chosen's hitlist."

"I just want to go back to my life as much as you do, I suppose," Moira remarked. "You're surprised I haven't cowered out or something? My dad didn't raise a lightweight…"

"You still ought to count on a Plan B if this fails," Finn remarked. "If you open those doors, I'll go in and do what I can. You don't have to follow me."

"I'm not going anywhere, Finn, and that's final. Ugh, not that I need your permission anyways. Who went and decided to make this your adventure? Just because you wear the fancy suit and have the fancy tech? I've got the system access, I can pull whatever files may be left behind, and I can just as easily upload them to the Dark Web and leverage the Chosen through those means. How's that for Plan B?"

"I never thought I'd find myself going face to face with them," Finn remarked, shaking his head. "I told myself I wouldn't get involved. Not after my dad told me to be aware."

"And how did that work out for you?"

"Dr. Lambert should have just let the police take you in," Finn responded. "Maybe this is all his fault."

"You leave him alone."

Finn sighed and then said, "I hope he's all right…"

"Me too…"

• • • •

The next morning, Moira and Finn prepared themselves before they approached the blast doors. Finn took position behind a barrier before the door, while Moira went to her laptop plugged into the computer network.

"You ready?"

"Ready," Finn replied, aiming the plasma cannon towards the doors.

Moira typed into her computer, and an alarm began to sound off across the base with a red strobe spinning. The blast doors released the tension between either side, and then began to open outwards towards Finn. The doors opened at a slow pace, and on the other side of the doors was darkness. After the doors were fully opened, lights began to activate in sections down a long corridor on the other side. Finn looked suspiciously down the long wide corridor, saw there were no hostiles on the other side, and then stood up.

"It's clear," Finn announced. He came around the barrier and waited for Moira. She joined him and the pair began to walk down the corridor together. Finn took point with the rifle and shield as he cautiously went down the tunnel.

The tunnel was a hundred yards or so at a minor slope downwards, and it led to another set of metallic blast doors. Finn brought his hand around the handle and found a panel beside it. Moira approached the panel with her computer and began to hook up to the old circuitry.

"Looks like an elevator," Moira stated. "It's coming down for us."

Once the elevator arrived, the blast doors slid open, and the pair could step onto the platform. Finn hit a switch on the side of the elevator to go down, and the elevator began to descend. The elevator car was silent as it rolled downwards, other than the wheels that turned and car itself that made a careful descent down the elevator shaft. The ride took close to a minute to two minutes before it landed at the bottom. A loud bell rang in their ears, and the elevator doors opened before them to reveal a ramp down onto a cavern floor. They arrived at a cavernous tunnel with lamps above them that lit the path ahead. The cave floor consisted of dust-like greyish dirt, but from the ramp onwards was a grated reinforced pathway that led up to the end. The stone walls at either side were rough and sharp, almost twenty to thirty feet tall. As the pair walked down the path, Finn saw some destroyed and ruined robots laying on the sides of the pathway. This pathway led them up to a paved concrete floor right before a metallic reinforced wall with a set of doors in the middle. At either side of the metallic doors was a reverse parked black vehicle. Above the doors bore the seal of the United States military branches, while above those seals was the faint remnant of the Zimmerman Corporation logo.

"Looks like we're in the right place," Finn remarked, stepping forward to the front doors. "See if you can get us inside."

Moira approached yet another panel, hooked up to it, and began to type. The doors opened and the pair stepped forward to enter into a completely different atmosphere than before. The atrium of the research and production facility was round with a door ahead, and a large globe in the center. The floor was burgundy carpeted around the perimeter, and the interior was chiseled stone with seats at the bottom. The sides of the carpeted walkway were metallic with imprints of Zimmerman Corporation logo left behind. Around the perimeter sides were some tall, reinforced glass windows that projected bright white lights. At the door ahead on the other side, the Zimmerman Logo could again be seen faintly behind in the metallic walls. A side door on the left had a sign that read, 'Security' on it, while a sign on the right read out locations. One-third of the upper walls of the facility were plain, and the ceiling above was suspended with metallic grates and more bright lights that hung down. Additionally, across the top of the ceiling on the other side of the grates were thick to thin wires, pipes, and exhaust vents. The ceiling of the cavern could also be seen from above. More notable than the physical appearance of the facility were the presence of robots and human corpses, decomposed skeletal remains in lab coats and other clothing.

"We're definitely in the right place," Finn stated as he walked forward.

"Oh my God..." Moira remarked as she looked about. "This is awful..."

"Looks like they've been dead for a while," Finn noted. "This must have been left behind from the Upheaval."

Finn approached the security corridor where there were a few consoles and computer monitors behind a check-in desk. Moira hopped over and came around to the computers, while Finn went to the round metallic doors that continued forward. A panel at the center of the door had a biometric handprint scanner. After he finished examining this scanner, he joined Moira around the security desk.

"I'm going to see if I can breach the system network, if it still exists..." Moira said.

Finn looked around the atrium, and above the ceiling were some fans ventilated the area and kept it cool. He then looked at the filing cabinets in the security room, pieces of paper left around, trash bins uncleaned and damage on the walls. A calendar on the wall read March 2023.

"This place has been left preserved," Finn stated. "Nobody has come down here since the director's mission. This place was abandoned – why?"

"Let's find out..." Moira responded. She continued to type away as she breached the security network, eventually bringing Finn around to a panel besides the computer to upload his handprint. She then did the same. "We should now have access through the facility..." She stood up. "Seems like the network systems are set up parallel to each other – I can only access security systems from here, everything else is detached. I'm going to need to find another computer to search for any juicy files."

"CCTV is minimal…" Finn remarked, looking at the camera footage. "Some cameras have been destroyed – how's recorded footage?"

"Deleted or destroyed," Moira replied. "I can't seem to access any of it."

Finn and Moira left the security kiosk and came around to the front door ahead. He placed his hand on the panel, and it unlocked the door and allowed them through to the other side. They entered a square caged corridor that led up to another door at the end. The sides of the corridor had a few metallic reinforcements, as well as bright lights that attempted to obscure and hide the cavernous outside and service areas. They approached the next door, unlocked it, and then went down a round corridor with metallic floor and walls, similar to the atrium. This brought them around to a larger round room with different branches. The door to the left led into 'Living Quarters' while the door to the right led to 'Research & Development,' and the door ahead led into 'Production & Deployment.' The door into 'Living Quarters' was partially destroyed, and on the other side they could see rubble from a cave in. Likewise, the entrance into 'Research & Development' was destroyed, blown forward, and rubble on the other side blocked that path. The only feasible path ahead was Production & Deployment, so Finn brought his hand to that door, and it unlocked for them to enter through. They entered into a large cylindrical storage room with racks on the outer walls that held square cargo crates. A crane above dangled, and above them there was also a catwalk. There were some racks that carried large capsules as well, similar to the ones for the fusion reactor, but these were dim and empty. As they walked down the corridor, they could also see some racks that held some decommissioned, or off-line robots in bunches. They were racked up against the wall and heads were titled down. Finn and Moira came to the other side, entering through to come to a perpendicular corridor with a staircase on the left, as well as another door directly ahead in a small junction corridor. This door was blocked off by a collapsed ceiling and vent, so the pair travelled up the stairs to go along the few floors of workstations about. This brought them to another entryway through the top at a parallel junction that led into the 'Production Facility.'

Finn placed his hand, and then they stepped inside where they entered through to the catwalk that looked down at the entire production zone. This room was large and round, domed, and cavernous. The catwalk suspended above took them forty feet above from where below there were production lines of all sorts of mechanisms, from robots to land and aerial vehicles, and it all worked like clockwork, going around and around the round facility chamber. The production lines were active, and the assembly lines moved forward, and the conveyor belts rolled. The pair walked down carefully as they saw hundreds and hundreds of robots assemble. In the center of the facility was a round structure with bright lights and all sorts of wire connections and pipes converging at this center of attention. Around the sides of the central chamber was a layered catwalk going down below, as well as off-shoots left, right and forward to go into additional areas clearly labelled Zone A, B, and C. They entered into the central chamber, and found themselves in yet another control room with oversight monitors on the outside that displayed the automated production of numerous robots. In the center of the room was a titled platform with the torso and head of a larger robot with no limbs. This room was isolated from the control room by a corridor on the other half side. The rest of the half-side of the circular room was left to the control room.

"I'm defeated once again," Finn remarked as he came around to the monitors and looked. "The production is active – how is that possible? The power was out."

"I'm so confused..." Moira simply stated, looking at the monitors. "There's no way we could have turned it on, could we? When we restarted the power at the reactor?"

"I doubt it – somebody would have had to press start here, surely."

Finn looked around and noticed a flashing light upon a dashboard. He went and found a wrist mount, similar to the ones that the elite soldiers had. He picked it up and showed it to Moira. He then pressed play.

"Hello, my name is Eleanor Black, if you are listening to this recording, it's because for whatever reason, you've stumbled upon this monstrosity of a production facility. This facility was once the property of Zimmerman Corporation, now the seized property of the United States government, leased to the Global Defense Project for all purposes of its mandate. I don't have much time to explain, as much as I don't have much time to do what I should do, but I've already lost the battle I came to fight. Within the confines of research and development is a robot of immense strength and capabilities that has become the defender of this facility, built in the remains of an underground chasm where a supercomputer and renewable power generator continue to produce these horrible robots. You will not be ready to fight this advanced robot – but there is a way to defeat it. This robot was birthed in this facility, and all the parts you need to create your own can be found right here. I've left behind the most important piece nearby, the head and torso, but you must assemble the rest and collect the limbs you need from each zone. Only with the assistance of one of these robots, programmed to assist you, will you be successful. Godspeed."

"I see..." Finn remarked, "so, the power plant was not a necessary connection... this facility has its own power, and it continues to make robots, like the mine. If we're going to pull the plug on this place, then we need to get down to the supercomputer to shut this place down. I'd guess that what she suggested was another one of those things…"

Moira came around to one of the computer consoles and began to hook herself in. Moira typed and examined the computer system, bypassing passwords and security locks while Finn came around to the operating room where the large robot was kept. The torso and head were immense and broad, larger than the other enhanced robots they had encountered. This head was close to the size of Finn's torso, and the torso almost five times as large as Finn's torso. The eyes of the robot were lit and shined green, looking forward towards Finn as they blinked and flickered. He approached a console nearby and saw that the process was already set up. Moira came around to look at this computer, and then she compared notes she had already taken.

"I looked through the zones and found that the legs are produced in Zone A, but the arms in Zone B and C, each with different features. You'll have to go to each of these to create this abomination to help us get through to the lower levels."

"Should be fairly straightforward," Finn noted. "Can you automate the process already, or do I have to go and do it?"

"I'll come with you," Moira remarked. "It seems like those computers are in their separate zones."

The pair left the central chamber and began to walk to the left, going towards Zone A where the production line of vehicles finished off at and lines of vehicles could be seen disappearing below. This room was large and narrow, with the rest of the vehicles disappearing forward, while the factory continued on the left and ran down as individual heavy parts were made and brought back into the central production room. The pair walked around a catwalk that glossed over this long and large room, arriving at a console room where they found a computer that automated the production line.

Moira began to fiddle with the computer as she examined templates. "Oh my… this computer has sorts of different types of legs… including features we've seen before – jet propulsion, claws, reinforced, and double…"

"What do they have that seems practical for a larger robot? The reinforced legs, right?"

"Take a look at this feature – thrusters, like your jet boots, but can move laterally as well as forward and back."

"Sure, let's do that then."

Moira typed away and an alarm began to ring. The production line stopped for a moment, and then continued. The pair watched as the specialized legs began to be produced. However, as they watched them form, Finn spotted a pair of robots enter the zone and began to hover above, looking for them.

"There's security," Finn noted, preparing his cannon. "Stay here."

Moira pulled her blaster out and placed it on the table as she continued to type into her computer. Finn stepped out and saw the robots home in on him. He opened fire at them, and they swerved out of the way and opened fire at him. They fired standard energy rounds from their arms as opposed to plasma. The robots landed on the ground and took cover, while Finn exposed his shield and began to attempt to evade them. He hopped up and glided to the other side of the production facility where he used his shield to slowly approach the robot ahead behind a crate on the catwalk. The other attempted to open fire at him, but as he approached the other, he was able to fire plasma at it point blank to melt its body and catch it on fire. The robot fell over, while the other flew upwards and landed on the other side of the platform. Finn raised his shield toward it, and it continued to open fire. He then bashed his shield into the robot with the boosters, sending it back and then finishing it off with the plasma cannon.

"It's done!" Moira shouted, exiting the control room.

Finn hopped down and pulled the legs off from the production line. They were both heavy, even with the exosuit, so he gently carried both of them with him to the central chamber to assign to the robot.

"There does seem to be some sort of defense here, so be careful," Finn remarked as he brought the last leg. "I just saw some more drones patrolling around the cavern."

"They seem a bit short-staffed," Moira noted. "What's keeping them from activating the hive on us?"

"Don't encourage them."

Moira began to type into the console to attach the legs to the torso. They then came back around to the central chamber where they heard a screech in a P.A. system.

"Hello?" a feminine voice greeted. "Is… anybody there?"

Finn looked at Moira, and vice-versa.

"Hello?" Finn answered.

"Hello, this is Eleanor Black," the voice greeted. "It sounds like you've listened to my message. You are creating a mechanized battle robot, aren't you?"

"Yeah…" Finn replied. "How are you talking to us? I thought you were dead."

"I'm not," the voice responded, "I'm trapped. That robot I was talking about has me trapped down here. Listen, once you are finished, you will need to re-connect all primary connections in the upper levels of the production facility to the lower levels."

"I thought we had to do the opposite – to sever connection from the lower levels to the upper levels," Moira asked.

"You need to sever the computer network, but you can't access the computer network unless you re-route power to open the blast doors that have kept me trapped down here."

"Wait… didn't you get trapped down here like two years ago?" Moira questioned. "How are you alive?"

"I'll explain everything… just get down here as soon as you can."

The voice went silent, and Moira and Finn looked at each other. Finn replied, "Let's not keep the lady waiting."

The pair left the central chamber and began to go to Zone B for a left upper limb. They came and found themselves in the center rear of a large rectangular room. The production line here developed limbs for the robots. Some robots floated above and scanned the nearby space, prompting Moira and Finn to take a lower route to come around to the control room at the other side. They climbed up the stairs and entered the room, and then they began to browse the catalog of templates.

"I want that…" Finn pointed. "A kinetic strike module."

Moira typed away and the production line began to create the reinforced heavy limb with a kinetic strike module on it. Meanwhile, the robots continued to fly around. A light flashed into the control room and the robots were alerted to their presence. They each hopped off at either side, prompting Moira to move away and take cover behind a desk while Finn raised his shield as they began to open fire. Some more robots flew into the room, counting four in total. After a moment of laying low, the robots stopped firing, prompting Finn to come around and use his shield to decapitate a robot. He then bashed it off the side of the catwalk and onto the production line below. Meanwhile, another robot from around the corner pointed its fist at him. He opened fire with his plasma cannon and caused it to likewise fall backwards. Finally, the other two closed in on Moira. She opened fire with her blaster, while he came around and began to open fire from the other side. The robots changed targets to him, prompting Moira to come out and shoot one in the head. The other grabbed Moira from behind the desk. Finn attempted to fire at it, but it kept her too close to its body. The robot grabbed the console around her wrist, pressing some buttons that suddenly caused it to collapse.

"What happened?" Finn questioned, stepping back inside.

"I don't know," Moira replied, looking at her console. "Did I do this?" She hit some buttons on the console, prompting the robot to re-activate. She quickly shot it with her pistol. "I don't even know what half of these things do… Why did you recover this for me?"

"It got us into this place, didn't it?"

Moira didn't reply. The pair went to collect the left limb and bring it back to the central chamber where the voice of Director Black screeched on the public announcement system again.

"A patrol has been alerted to your presence," the voice said. "You must hurry."

"We're going as fast as we can," Finn replied, bringing the limb into the assembly chamber. Moira then set to work while Finn came out and saw six robots flying in and beginning to patrol the area. He monitored them until Moira came around, turned on her optic camouflage, and then began to walk with him.

The pair came around to Zone C which was a round room with right upper limbs being made, as well as weapons. They went around the catwalk to the console room, and then entered inside to set on a choice for the robot. As they did so, two robots entered through.

"Nuts…" Finn said, "just choose something for me, I'll take care of these droids."

Moira typed at the computer while Finn stepped out and opened fire at the robots. He caught one mid-flight and sent the other towards him. He engaged the robot in a firefight while the machines in this zone halted for a second, and then continued to run. The other four robots joined in, and Finn began to navigate around the machinery as he finished off the last one and engaged the others. Two landed on the catwalks, while another two on the level below. He began to come around to engage the two above him while keeping note of those below. The ones below split up and went either way, while the two above stayed together and fired at Finn separately. He raised his shield up and stabilized the plasma cannon on the railing to attempt to defend himself and also get a shot at the robots. He was able to destroy one of them, but the other continued to move around and fly up. Suddenly, Finn heard one of the robots come into his flank. He immediately turned and shot it straight in the torso, while the other came around from the other side. He retreated and took cover around the side of the control room, waiting for it to approach, and then coming around to shoot it. The robot retreated, while the other flew up and landed next to him. He pushed back at it with his shield, but the robot grabbed both sides and fought back with him. He eventually knocked it over the edge of the railing, landing on the conveyor belt and being torn in half. The other meanwhile came around, but at the same time, Moira shot at it with her blaster.

"It's done, come on," Moira said. They both left Zone C and collected the right arm, which carried a heavy weapon that Finn had to come back for. "It's called a rail gun."

"Thanks..." Finn replied. "I'm sure the robot will love it."

"Is it done?" the voice above projected as they entered the central chamber.

"Just about..." Finn responded. "We'll get you out as soon as we can..." He left and returned with the rail gun, placed it aside for the robot and then the pair stood back as the chamber did its work. The robot was put together with each limb, some diagnostics completed, adjustments made, but then the robot was pushed forward and set to stand on its own two limbs. "Here's the part where we find out it's going to kill us..."

The robot picked up the rail gun and then stepped towards the exit from the chamber, exiting out and standing before Finn and Moira.

"What now?" Moira questioned.

"Uh... come follow me?" Finn inquired, looking at the robot. He then stepped back. The robot stepped forward and joined him. "Okay... at least it doesn't want to kill us."

The pair came around with the robot, leaving it behind because it could not fit into the other side of the chamber.

"Alright, we got the robot you told us to make," Finn spoke. "Now what?"

"This robot will help clear the way to Research & Development," the voice projected. "From any console, you should be able to access the system to re-connect the security network to the lower levels. Hurry!"

Act 7, Scene 4

Moira and Finn left the central chamber and proceeded down the catwalk to return to the central atrium. As they made their exit, four robots appeared and placed themselves directly ahead.

"Alright, time to see this bucket of bolts do some work," Finn remarked, kicking off and hovering from above. "Attack!"

The robot stepped forward as the robots took shots at it. Both Moira and Finn also took some shots as they raised their optic camouflage and shield respectively. The robot raised a fist and punched one of the robots, sending it hurling backwards. It then charged its rail gun and zapped another robot further ahead. It then stormed forward and grabbed a nearby robot, crushing it with its grip, and shot the final one with the rail gun. Both Moira and Finn stayed back in awe as it cleared the path ahead, but soon they shook off this awe to carry on forward. Once at the central atrium, the robot was brought around to the rubble before Research & Development.

"We need to clear this rubble," Finn commanded, assisting with the clearing. The robot set it rail gun onto its back, and then used both hands to begin to clear the rubble with ease. However, the rubble before them was more than they expected.

"This seems like it's going to take some time…" Moira noted. "I'm going to go back to the production line and see if I can make anymore of these – based on my analysis of everything, resources seemed limited, so may as well make the most of it."

"Sure, I'll be right here…"

The mechanized heavy robot continued to work with Finn, him commanding it and shouting at where it needed to go and do. Eventually, after an hour of clearing rubble, a path was made that brought them into a rectangular room. They followed down to a security panel where Finn communicated to Moira on his wrist radio.

"Moira, we're through – you can come and join us whenever you're ready."

"Rodger dodger."

Finn placed his palm on the security panel, and the door opened for them to come into a large laboratory. They walked forward and stood behind a railing that looked down to numerous workstations and isolated spaces. They began to walk around to the other side, reaching another panel.

"I see you on the cameras," the voice of Director Black stated. "You're almost there... You want to find a data center; from there you can patch the networks. Some networks were severed, but once you re-connect everything, I should be able to escape."

"Right on..." Finn replied, coming into a long, wide corridor that curved around. "Great... more walking..."

The robot trudged forward, prompting Finn to boost up and attach himself to the side of the robot. He pointed his plasma cannon forward in anticipation of trouble, but none came. The corridor went leftwards in a curve that made it seem like they were spiralling down. There were a few break-off points along the corridor, but they continued going down. They eventually reached another large laboratory with a similar layout to the other, but then continued forward past it to continue to go down and down where the lights grew dimmer and it became difficult to see. Luckily, the robot had a spotlight that pointed forward for them. Finn continued to go down, until he stopped for a moment.

"Moira, I'm nearly there... are you behind us?" Finn questioned.

Static came through followed by the words, "Go... out me...."

"Hmph, she's picked a hell of a time to quit," Finn muttered. "Moira, you're coming in poorly. Say again?"

"I've..." no further words could be heard except the word 'trust' and some more static.

"Well, she did say she was busy. Surely, I can patch the networks myself."

Finn continued down and reached another large set of doors. He hopped off and placed his palm on the doors. He then stepped inside and found himself in a very large circular room. This room was smaller than the production facility, but still large, nonetheless. The room was divided between a central square raised platform, and surrounding areas where there were numerous servers and databases lined up in four quarters. The central portion of the room had numerous thick, dangling wires falling from the ceiling, and a round part of the inner most part of the central square was blackened and faint as though something had been removed. On the other side of the room from where he had entered was a large console and double set of screens. At either side of these screens were exits out, each with security panels, but these panels were blacked out and de-activated. The floor in the surrounding part of this room were raised grated floors with thick and thin wires below, creating an inter-connection across the room. There were numerous workstations on the left and right from the inner platform, facing large black screens that projected the same image as the ones directly ahead. Likewise, at the main double-screened computer, there were more workstations lined up at either side, and these workstations were desks with office chairs, and numerous monitors connected to computers. The set up was similar to a command center. Around the inner space were some railings divided by steps down to the four sections of the room, and some more workstations behind the railings. All computers except the main console at the rear were turned off, and this computer at the rear showed a lone black screen with a flashing green line in the corner suggesting the typing of something from a user. The mechanized robot approached the computer with Finn continuing to hold on to it. The robot stopped a few yards before the computer, at which point Finn hopped off and made his approach on his own feet. He threw his backpack off at the base of the computer, placed his hands across the keyboard as the computer flashed. He then was presented with a screen to enter a password.

"Ms. Black!" Finn shouted. "Ms. Black! I'm at the computer screen!" he yelled. "It needs a password though – we're going to have to wait for Moira to come around to hack in."

"No need," the voice responded. "I know the password – it's Seven-Nine-Nine-Mike-Eight-Four-Zero-Alpha-Zero-One-Six-Mike-Nine-Two-Seven-Exclamation."

Finn typed that combination exactly as he was instructed. He then pressed 'enter' and the computer began to run a series of code. It then brought him to a menu option to execute functions.

"One of these, huh?" Finn remarked. "What command do I run?"

"Type exactly as I say," the voice replied. "Delta colon, Romeo-Xray-Delta, forward slash, Tango-Echo-Charlie, forward slash, System Diagnostics."

Finn typed those words and then pressed enter.

"Next, type, 'run.'"

Finn typed those words and then pressed enter. The system console began to run a series of code and then showed a few error messages that quickly passed the screen. At the end of all the code, it presented a message.

"System has detected the presence of a computer virus – do you wish to proceed with the elimination of this virus?" Finn announced. "What do I type? Yes?"

"Affirmative."

Finn typed 'yes' and the screen began to show some more code as it ran the program. At the end of the screen, it showed some options.

"What do I do now?" Finn asked.

"Type exactly as I say," the voice commanded. "Delta colon, Mike-Charlie, forward slash, Sierra-Whisky, forward slash, India-November-Foxtrot."

Finn typed those words and then pressed enter. The system console began to run a series of code, and then showed a few options.

"You will want to press 'yes' to all of these."

Finn typed yes, but read them out as he did so, "All system processes." He affirmed. "All infrastructure networks. He affirmed. "All power systems. He affirmed. "All data systems. He affirmed. "All security systems." He affirmed. "All automated systems. He affirmed. "All defense systems." He hesitated for a moment, and then affirmed. At the last command, a bit more code was shown, and then the screen flashed.

"Thank you, Finn," the voice projected. "I really appreciate it…" the voice grew distorted.

"Oh no…" Finn remarked, looking about. "Who are you? Where are you?"

The lights in the room grew dim. He stepped away from the computer as it began to run some processes on its own, while he brought his left cuff to his mouth.

"Moira, where are you? It seems like we've got a problem down here…"

No response came through.

"Great…" Finn replied, rushing over and climbing onto the side of his robot. He turned and faced the exit from where he came from, anticipating company. Instead, he could hear the pitter patter of some movement from somewhere, followed by the heavy footsteps of something else. He turned from side to side in anticipation. "Defensive positions!" he commanded. The robot raised up an arm and with the other raised the rail gun.

Suddenly, an object forcibly crashed upwards through the floor below, jumping upwards as it launched itself like a missile and landed behind.

Finn aimed his plasma cannon at the mechanized heavy robot as it stood before him. This robot was larger than the one that Moira and he had created, but it was effectively the same. This robot was different from the other enhanced robots they had encountered with girthier limbs and a larger torso and head. It had no weapons at its limbs, but as it stared down towards them, it had light blue eyes and its head twitched like the other robots he had encountered. It also emitted a slightly static and garbled noise, almost rabid-like as it looked at them. The room they were in was dark, and it was difficult to see fully, but this robot had a larger back than the one that Finn was on too.

"Attack!" Finn shouted.

Both him and his mechanized heavy robot began to open fire with both the plasma cannon and the railgun. The hostile heavy robot immediately put its fists forward and created two shields blocked every shot. It held its ground with the two shields, neither the railgun nor the plasma cannon were able to pierce the defenses. They each stopped as their weapons began to overheat, smoke coming out of the barrels, and at that moment, the robot released its shields and began to lurch forward. It raised a fist up to strike Finn's robot, and his robot blocked the punch as it raised its own arms up. It raised both fists up to strike Finn's robot, and it continued to shield itself with its arms, but as it hit at Finn's robot, both Finn and it were sent backwards towards the computer console screens.

Finn looked back and then towards the robot as his plasma cannon continued to smoke. A sensor on his suit told him that the cannon was still overheated. The hostile robot continued to hit at them until he got a green light, pointed his plasma cannon towards the robot and shot directly at its face. The robot lurched backwards as hot plasma covered its face. The plasma chewed at the armor like acid, burning especially at the sensors on its face. Finn's robot then took a step forward and raised its left arm to strike at the robot across the face. The force of the blow turned the robot onto its side. Finn's robot raised a foot to stomp down on it, but the hostile robot propelled itself forward and it instead missed and hit into the suspended floor, locking its foot in the wires.

"Oh no…" Finn remarked. "Get your foot out of there!"

The hostile robot began to raise itself up from the ground, bringing itself forward. It raised an arm up to punch at Finn's robot, sending it backwards. Finn held on and began to shoot plasma at the hostile robot again, but this time it opened its shield to cover itself. He let go of his robot to let it compose itself, activated his propulsion jets and glider, and jumped backwards to hop onto a server. Here, he began to open fire with some more plasma towards the hostile robot, causing it to cover itself.

"Come on!" Finn shouted. "Get back up into the fight!"

Finn continued to project plasma fire towards the hostile mechanized robot, prompting it to hold its ground while Finn's robot got its bearings. Once Finn's robot was on its feet, it pointed its railgun towards the robot and shot at it.

"No, not the gun! Hit it straight on!" Finn shouted.

The robot stopped firing with the rail gun and instead stepped forward with its fist. It raised a fist and hit at the hostile robot as it continued to have its shields out. Meanwhile, Finn's plasma cannon began to overheat again, and smoke fumed out from the barrel.

"For Pete's sake," Finn cursed, jumping off to another server and then hopping down as the robots began to clash.

Finn's robot continued to strike at the shield with the kinetic strike module, but the hostile robot stood its ground and was only pushed back a few feet into the desks before the main computer. It then walked forward to do the same, sending it backwards some more feet and into the servers. At the second punch, the hostile robot lost its grip with the shields and relinquished them. At this moment, Finn raised his plasma cannon, but it was still unable to fire. His robot jumped up and onto the hostile one, and raised its fist upwards to strike at it head on. Finn watched as he hovered above. The ferocity of the punch caused the robot's head to pivot and slightly dent. A garbled noise came out from the hostile robot, and in the next second it sent both of its arms out and around to grab hold of Finn's robot, picking it up and throwing it backwards and into the wall behind.

"Oh no..." Finn responded, raising his weapon. The plasma cannon was still out of commission. He came around to the central platform and knelt down, aiming the weapon as he saw the robot stand up on its own while Finn's struggled to turn around as its head was stuck in the collapsed floor. "Get up!" he shouted.

The hostile robot stood up, faced Finn, and then began to make its way towards him. The light on Finn's cuff lit and he began to fire with the plasma cannon. A brief shot of plasma hit the shoulder of the robot, but the rest of it was blocked off by the shield. He continued to hold it in place while his robot continued to struggle and catch its bearings again.

"Come on!" Finn shouted. "Come on! Come on! Get up!"

The hostile robot began to walk forward towards Finn as it continued to shield itself. He began to step backwards away from it. At the same time, as Finn cautiously fired brief concentrations of plasma rather than a single force, he saw an error flash on his wrist cuff – this was not an overheat warning, but a battery warning.

"Already?!" Finn questioned. "Blimey..."

The robot continued to approach Finn with slow steps. Finn's robot had just about gotten onto its feet, continuing to struggle to stay standing on those two feet. Finn stopped firing as his wrist continued to give him a low battery warning. He instead activated his propulsion system and glider, hopped backwards and then hovered away as the robot quickly responded to let its shield down and throw a punch towards him. Finn took his bow and pulled an arrow back. He shot towards the robot's sensors, but they seldom did much.

"Well, that's disappointing..." Finn remarked, putting the bow away. He then evaded another punch towards him. "A little help!"

Finn's robot slowly trudged towards him as he continued to evade being hit as the robot closed on him. It smashed a fist down into some workstations in central platform, and then knocked over some servers. Finn's robot then suddenly livened up as it ran towards the hostile one, activating its thrusters and laying down a swift punch from behind to knock it down.

"Nice..." Finn muttered. He de-activated his propulsion and glider, and quickly ran towards the computer where he left his backpack. He scrambled around for the reinforced case and took out one of three fuses that were still active. He then turned around to check on the two robots as they began to engage in hand-to-hand combat. Once he held the fuse in his hand and was sure he was safe, he looked up at the computer screen as he saw code being executed autonomously. He looked at it suspiciously, but then turned around as he heard a loud thump. The hostile robot was triumphing over Finn's robot. "Oh no..."

Finn quickly removed his suit, turned it onto its back, and swapped fuses. He threw the nearly dead fuse and caused it to shatter on the floor. He then placed the fresh one and then quickly re-engaged his suit. Once the suit was on and active, he activated his propulsion jets and hopped up onto a server, and began to open fire with the plasma cannon. The plasma hit the side of the heavy robot, causing it to let out a garbled and corrupted scream, most of which was just static. Finn lay down as much fire as he could as the robot struggled to respond, still standing atop of his own robot, but unable to bring a shield around to protect its rear and only its side. He continued to fire until it propelled itself upwards and turned to face Finn. Finn quickly turned to another server and began to prepare for the robot to come towards him as his struggled to come up again.

Luckily, Finn's robot had an easier time to stand onto its feet, turning to face the robot as it focused on Finn. Finn lay down some more shots to keep the hostile robot occupied, but also distracted to not notice his robot come up from behind to pick it up and slam it onto the ground. It then came up onto it, prompting Finn to propel himself forward to get a better look. He landed on the central platform and then ran forward.

"Damage the head!" Finn shouted. "Take out those sensors!"

Finn's robot lay down a brute force onto the head of the hostile robot, causing it to pivot ninety degrees again, and twitch and glitch. Finn hopped onto the side of his robot as he looked down at the robot. Another punch was raised and thrown down onto the robot, but it did little to really damage the robot except bludgeon and create a noticeable dent. Once Finn was on the side of his robot, he pointed his plasma cannon and fired a beam of plasma towards its face, aiming at the eyes. The hostile robot screamed out as though in pain as the plasma singed the sensors and face armor. The robot released its shields and brought them together like scissors. Finn quickly jumped up and avoided the guillotine, while the two edges hit the head of his robot and dented its severely, nearly cutting through the armor. The hostile robot then kicked Finn's robot off and began to pick itself up. Finn observed as steam let out from the hostile robot, hissing outwards while garbled static and moans of distress were emitted outward. Finn's robot crash landed into the concrete wall behind it where it stayed put as it tilted its head down, itself twitching and struggling to compose itself now.

"Get up!" Finn shouted as he stood atop of a server.

The hostile robot stood up instead and looked towards them. It raised its arms up as Finn raised his plasma cannon and began to open fire. It opened a shield in one arm, while the other split into two so that it had three arms. With these two other arms, lasers pointed out and aimed at the two of them. The lasers flashed and once they stabilized at their targets, Finn noticed missiles project outwards from the back of the hostile robot.

Finn quickly jumped out of the way, activating the glider and using his plasma cannon to destroy any missiles headed for him midflight to cause them to explode. He continued to evade and move out of the way as the laser continued to track him, creating distance between himself and the hostile robot. Meanwhile, Finn's robot had no time to react, and all missiles hit it directly, causing fireballs and segments of wall to collapse forward.

Eventually, the hostile robot stopped firing missiles altogether and so Finn concentrated his cannon towards it again, noticing the blue eyes to continue to pierce forward. The robot activated its shield and began to make its approach towards Finn. Finn opened fire with the plasma cannon, looking at the corner of his eye around the rubble that marked out where his robot was entombed. A cloud of dust and smoke made it impossible to see. The hostile robot nonetheless began to approach him head-on. Finn carefully retreated backwards, coming into a corner which he jerked his neck back towards. He began to move away from that corner, but then one of the hands began to point a laser at him again as the other two pointed shields. Finn stopped firing plasma, especially as vapor came out from the barrel of his cannon though it was not overheated. He jumped out of the way and began to gain some distance as the missiles began to fire. He opened fire with his plasma cannon towards them instead, but more and more missiles kept coming forward towards him, some hitting the wall and another hitting the large monitor screen at this side of the room. He jumped out of the way as they got close, becoming fireballs that began to fill the room with a dense smoke.

Suddenly, Finn's plasma cannon began to overheat. His wrist flashed with the warning signal as the laser caught him again. However, before the missile could fire, Finn's robot tackled the hostile robot. The robot grabbed hold of the torso of the hostile bot and punched it backwards into the corner of the room instead. Finn took this opportunity to run. He came around to the central platform in the room, took out his bow, and began to fire arrows. These arrows hit the side of the robot as it struggled with Finn's bot. He attempted to aim for the eye sensors, eventually able to hit one, but only caused this blue light to flash. Suddenly then, Finn's robot threw a punch across the robot's head and knocked that light out. The other began to flash, so Finn activated his propulsion jets to change his perspective, and midflight he shot an arrow that pierced that sensor. The hostile robot let out a horrible scream. Finn threw his bow and arrow aside, and then took hold of his plasma cannon again.

The hostile robot released its other arm so that it had four arms, and then it picked up Finn's robot with all four arms and threw it across the room. From this position, the robot began to fire lasers sporadically around the room, unknown to the location of either him nor Finn, prompting Finn to step backwards and take cover behind some rubble. He aimed his plasma rifle as it regained use and opened fire at missiles as they spammed out in all sorts of directions, hitting walls, floor, ceiling, and workstation to send rubble around. A missile hit directly above the ceiling from where Finn's robot had landed, sending that rubble down, alongside a large boulder to squash Finn's robot.

"No!" Finn shouted. He quickly turned and shot at the missiles that were near him, preventing them from detonating nearby. As he continued to fire at missiles, his wrist gave him another caution warning that the plasma cannon was overheating. He continued though to fire at the missiles, especially the ones that came close, when sporadically, as he was about to shoot at one that was a couple feet away, the cannon ceased function and the missile hit a nearby wall, sending rubble nearby and a cloud of dust to his face. He ducked down as he coughed and waved his hand. He then sat up and looked over to the robot as it stepped forward and began to carefully walk about the room. "Come on, you bastard!" he shouted, climbing up onto the rubble. "Give me your best shot!"

The hostile robot immediately turned and faced Finn. He activated his boots and hopped out of the way, but seemingly the robot could hear him as he moved, changing direction in which it walked. He led it towards the center of the room and then stopped there. The robot loomed over him as they stood face to face from each other. He stopped directly over the boulder and stayed in place.

"Right over here, you ugly muppet!"

Finn de-activated both the glider and propulsion jets, and then jumped off from the rock as the robot crashed into it with all four hands. It flung its arms around while he quickly stepped away and began to move away from where it was. He took cover behind some rubble and pointed his plasma rifle as the hostile robot looked about. The hostile robot, clearly blind to its surroundings, then began to move around aimlessly, but as it did so, the plasma cannon re-activated. He waited for another moment to let the cannon cool down properly, at which point he let out a whistle towards the hostile robot, causing it to target him and instantly come towards him. Finn fired a blast of plasma directly at the torso of the hostile robot. A delay in response saw the robot release its shield too late, at which point Finn ran off and flanked the robot to open another set of fire, causing it to quickly react, repeating the same exercise, changing directions to throw the calculating robot off-guard, and causing hot plasma to ooze and pierce the armor of the robot, causing it to glitch out some more, and other strange effects to occur, such as the sporadic release of its shields and increased garbled static in its voice. Eventually, Finn's rifle began to overheat again, prompting him to pause for a moment.

However, at this same time, the robot had enough of it all. It began to point its arms out in all directions and send out another volley of missiles.

"Oh no..." he muttered, taking cover behind the rock that Finn's robot was behind. The missiles came and came endlessly as rubble began to collapse and come at all points in the room. "This thing is going to kill us both..." he said as he examined his rifle. "Come on, get up, you sad mug..." A missile hit directly above, prompting Finn to run off. He ducked down as the missiles continued to fire out sporadically around, going towards the exit point besides the main computer – this computer of which both monitors were smashed and flickering. A large boulder began to fall towards the exit that Finn aimed for, prompting him to quickly jump out of the way. He went towards the other, but another smaller rock fell down and blocked his path. He shielded his eyes as clouds of dust came around.

At this point, the missiles stopped, and Finn coughed into his sleeve. He turned and looked over to the hostile robot as it faced him, and it began to come towards him. Finn raised his plasma cannon again as it came at him, but the gun was still overheated. He stepped back and looked both left and right, but he was trapped in. In the last second, the cannon gave him the clear light and he opened fire at the robot, but it raised its shield up and that only slowed it down marginally. He continued to open fire as though he could pierce the shield, or overwhelm it. He did fire some shots that damaged the extended arms and rendered them useless, but the robot still came towards him. The room was filled with clouds of dust and smoke. Finn's wrist now gave a warning that he was almost out of power again. He continued to fire though, ignoring the warning as the robot closed in on him. It released its shield as it came close, allowing itself to be damaged in the torso briefly as it extended these arms out to grab him. However, before both arms could swipe at him, Finn flinched and closed his eyes. He seized his body in anticipation of being torn apart, but it did not come. He opened his eyes as he heard the garbled screams of the hostile robot.

Finn's robot had broken free from the boulder and picked up its foe to send it down behind them. It then thrusted up and threw a punch down, hitting both arms and causing them to snap. At this moment, Finn's robot stood atop of its foe, the hostile robot, and took out its railgun. It charged the rail gun and fired a cannon shot straight at its torso, hitting it with several beams that lit up the room with bright flashes. The hostile robot screamed in agonizing pain until it was over. Finn unshielded his eyes and looked over as his robot hopped off its defeated foe.

Finn let out a sigh of relief. "Good… good job, mate…" He stood up and began to slowly walk towards the defeated robot. The railgun had left smoking holes in the torso and head. "Good grief… glad that's over…" He looked about the rest of the room, which was more or less utterly destroyed. Finn sat down atop of some rubble and began to rest.

"Finn!" Moira shouted.

Finn jerked up as he had nearly fallen asleep. He stood up and walked over to the other side of the room as Moira appeared.

"Finn, I've been trying to get a hold of you," Moira remarked. "What happened here?"

"A bit of a scuffle with the guardian of this place," Finn stated. "I've been trying to get a hold of you too, but reception is poor this far down."

"Finn, I don't know what happened, but all the robots have begun to turn upstairs," Moira stated. "I don't know if they've sensed our presence and become defensive, but I had to rush down here as fast as I could."

"What do you mean?"

"All the robots, every single one of them, including the drones, have activated and have begun to march off and out of the base," Moira stated. "There were hundred and hundreds of them…"

"That's not good…"

"Did you patch the networks? I saw something happened with network access as well – I got kicked off the computer upstairs…"

"Yes, about that… it seems like I was fooled…"

"What do you mean?"

Finn explained to her how the voice of Eleanor Black manipulated him to patch the network, which seemingly caused the hostile mechanized heavy robot to come forth and attack him.

"I don't know what I did, but I'm sure I'm responsible for what's going on upstairs," Finn remarked. "Furthermore, I think the supercomputer is missing…" he said, looking up at the wires hanging from the ceiling. "It must have been moved further down; we should keep going down."

"You'll have to go down from here, but I'm going to stay here. If this is the central computer room, then that means that all networks run through this room," Moira stated. She came around to the computer on the right as its screen was still intact."

"I'd almost believe you to be safer upstairs," Finn remarked. "This room is about to collapse in on itself," Finn remarked. "Besides, the network is patched – you should have full access now."

"Maybe you're right, but I need to be able to communicate with you."

"Use the overhead system," Finn stated.

"How will you know its me?"

"Give me a reason to believe it's really you," Finn remarked. "Besides, it'll be for urgent cases. I'm going to go down with the bot and be right back. You get yourself upstairs and in that room. I may have activated some sort of virus – you need to do whatever you can to fight at it."

"A virus… yeah, that makes sense. Okay – alright, fine. I will."

Finn stepped towards the exit from the room. He pushed through the nearly collapsed door and stepped in on the other side. The other side presented another curved tunnel, but this one with more rubble and decay.

"Be careful," Moira said as Finn walked out with the robot. She took his hand.

Finn looked down at her hand at his, and then looked back at her. Her eyes then looked over to something ahead. He turned and looked as well.

In the distance, in front of some rubble were the remains of someone in the same suit used by the rest of the elite soldiers. They both walked over, but rather than a wrist mount, they instead found a tape recorder on the floor. Finn picked it up, rewound the tape, and then began to play the tape.

"Hello, if you've found this tape, it's because you've found me, or what remains of me," spoke a feminine, English-accented voice. "My name is Eleanor Joan Black, former director of the Global Defense Project, and leader of their elite squadron. A soldier is never quite done on the battlefield, even as they move up the ranks and find themselves commanding troops rather than being one, and for whatever reason I never really believed myself free from the frontlines even as I earned the top position in this secret organization that no longer exists. A soldier since the day I was born, as a child and as an adolescent, I became a leading fighting force for my own country at a young age, being one of the few women to be selected for the Special Air Service, Britain's special forces. Wherever I went, I commanded respect from others. Never did I complain about my status as a woman to let me down. Rather, I pushed on it to be the Iron Lady others knew me as, like the original most honorable lady.

"If you have found this tape, you already know somewhat about the circumstances that my organization has found itself in. You perhaps know about what's occurred at the Global Defense Project's headquarters, or what we've been up to on the days leading to that attack on our base. If not, allow me to explain and give the rundown of details. Three days ago, the Global Defense Project was attacked, in an attack that I anticipated sooner or later from our masters, because of tensions that built up at the reality that the men and women of our ranks could be replaced. Since early 2021, our masters took an interest in mechanized forces, drones and robot soldiers, similar to the ones that Zimmerman Corporation had created and unleashed on the world. They wanted to experiment with these utilities for themselves, and the aim was simple – this technology, which we confiscated, became a point of contention among global powers as we refused to share. There were talks of dismantling us, but rather than do so, we relinquished and agreed to compromise. A thousand robot soldiers were to be developed and deployed, integrated into our fighting force, but we had no need for this many drones. We relied on the best of the best of special forces to join our ranks – why an army? It turned out that in order to command global stability, our masters would rely on brute force rather than subtlety.

"In this base, a former Zimmerman Corporation research and production facility, a new division of the Global Defense Project began to develop under the command of unknown players. I could only know somewhat of what was going on, while I anticipated the worst case – our replacement, and in a world in which you don't and aren't supposed to exist, this replacement intended to be an extermination to keep it that way. I called it Operation Upheaval, the day in which our masters, the Committee of Concerned Nations, should release their army onto us. This new division shared ideas with us, where we invested in our people, they invested in mechanical troops, resulting in similar results in our elite squad of advanced soldiers with their elite squad of advanced robots. We had a mole in our midst – but it was too late to find out when the day of judgement came for us.

"We were suddenly attacked – out of the blue and against my expectations, but still, I was prepared. Immediately, we set off to protect our assets and destroy our objectives. We had to split up and take as many survivors as we could, and I set my troops on their own missions while I awaited results. However, as I heard from no one, I fled and was captured by the FBI. The FBI met with me and a few national security advisors to explain the situation in greater detail – this was no coup de grace, it was a coup d'etat. Unbeknownst to the United States, Operation Upheaval was activated, but not by them, nor anyone else on the Committee. The coup was launched by internal forces and instigators that were unknown to us. With this knowledge, we received report that all of my soldiers were successful in their respective missions, but what awaited yet was to investigate what happened at this military research base. I was charged to lead that mission with a few survivors, and so I came here with no intent that I should return.

"According to information available to the United States government, this base was responsible for the production and research of autonomous robots and drones, a next-generation fighting force, but it was also the place where a new artificial intelligence was being developed under code name Beliyal. This technology was of extreme importance to the United States, but they did not want me to retrieve it, but to destroy it by any means necessary. It was all clear to me as I was sent in to infiltrate the base – Beliyal had taken over. The researchers had gone too far, and this artificial intelligence had bled through the programming of every network, taking control of every robot and unleashing its own coup against humanity. My mission was now to destroy it – to play my part as the others had.

"You see, the others were far from unsuccessful in their missions. Kupe defended the base so that the others could get out. Yeleta helped the others escape before they met their doom. Shaka cleared the mines. Iyyov shut down the power plant. It's all fallen into place, but now I needed to make sure none of those robots saw the light of day. I did not expect to meet that... thing as I set off, and although I've been unsuccessful to destroy this A.I. in charge of the facility, I've been able to quarantine it to the lower levels. I don't know what it intends for all of humanity, or what its true plans are other than to wage war and destruction, but it's been crippled and shouldn't be able to build or command anymore new troops – all it has left are the stragglers, which I'm sure the U.S. government can deal with and clean up the mess it's seemingly created. As for me... there was no way I was going to get out of here... The Global Defense Project had a specific mandate – to keep the balance of power and affirm the status quo... to ensure that nothing ever happens in the world of catastrophic or life-changing proportions. In that sense can I say, this has been mission accomplished for me – if you are hearing this, whoever you may be, finish the rest of the work. Terminate Beliyal."

Finn stood up from Director Black's corpse, and lay down the tape beside her. "You heard the woman, we've got a job to do," he stated. "Who Dares Wins, as they say."

"Wait, Finn," Moira said, stopping him as she took his hand again.

Finn turned to face her. The two looked at each other.

"Be careful," Moira simply said, parting her hand from him. She took a step back and then ran off. She disappeared as her optic camouflage kicked in. He looked at she left, and then turned to the heavy robot.

"What?" Finn questioned. "Don't look at me like that – come on, we've got a fight to take to this 'Beliyal' as they call it. Hell of a name..."

Act 8, Prologue

The digital sound of some heartbeats could be heard in the background, resounding from a heart monitor in the room. Charlemagne sat in a patient bed, his face extremely pale, eyes bloodshot, and white hair thin though moustache the same. He wore a patient gown as he lay in the bed with a pillow slightly propping him up. Some wires extended from the heart monitor and made their way up the side of the bed and underneath Charlemagne's gown and underneath stuck onto his chest. His head was turned slightly to the side, his withered right hand to his torso side as he clutched a silver chain with many purplish-red beads that glistened in the light. At the end of this small chain was a silver medallion, and beyond that more a few more beads up to a silver crucifix. The room that Charlemagne was in was small, had a small closet, a small washroom, and a small television set in the corner. There was also a window that looked out towards the gloomy clouds in downpour. Beside him were two chairs in this private room, one beside the other, with one of the two where Finn sat leaned forward, head resting on the railing of the medical bed. The atmosphere of the patient ward was quiet, and all that could be heard was the consistent beats and the murmur of words from under Charlemagne's breath.

"Hail Mary, full of grace, the Lord is with you," Charlemagne muttered. "Blessed are you among women, and blessed is the fruit of your womb, Jesus. Holy Mary, mother of God, pray for us sinners, now and at the hour of our death." At the end of these words, Charlemagne's hands moved from the last of ten beads, to a space between them, a large bead, and another ten beads. "Glory be to the Father, and to the Son, and to the Holy Spirit," he whispered, "as it was in the beginning, is and ever shall be forever. Amen. O' my Jesus, forgive us our sins, save us from the fires of hell. Lead all souls to heaven, especially those in most need of thy mercy." His hand then moved to the large bead.

"The fifth luminous mystery, the institution of the Eucharist, for the establishment of the priesthood, and the institution of the sacrifice for the salvation of souls." He then said, "Our Father, who art in Heaven, hallowed be thy name. Thy kingdom come, thy will be done, on Earth as it is in Heaven. Give us this day our daily bread, and forgive us our trespasses, as we forgive those who trespass against us, and lead us not into temptation, but deliver us from evil." After these words, Charlemagne continued to repeat ten Hail Mary prayers, followed by another Glory Be and Fatima Prayer, slowly uttering the words and pausing between prayers. At the end of this set, he paused again as his hand reached the silver medallion with an image of a woman, and then began to say, "Hail Holy Queen, Mother of Mercy. Hail our life, our sweetness, and our hope. To you do we cry pour banished children of Eve. To you do we send up our sighs, mourning, and weeping in this valley of tears. Turn then o' most gracious advocate, your eyes of mercy towards us, and after this our exile, show unto us the blessed fruit of your womb, Jesus. O' clement, o' loving, o' sweet Virgin Mary. Pray for us o' holy Mother of God, that we may be made worthy of the promises of Christ. Let us pray, o' God who by his only begotten Son, through his life, death, and resurrection, has purchased for us the rewards of eternal life. Grant that by meditating upon these mysteries of the most Holy Rosary, of the Blessed Virgin Mary, we may imitate what they contain and obtain what they promise through Christ our Lord." At the end of this prayer, Charlemagne paused for a moment longer, prompting Finn to look up to him as he stared to the ceiling and clutched the crucifix on his rosary beads. "Saint Michael, the Archangel, defend us in battle. Be our defense against the wickedness and snares of the Devil. May God rebuke him we humbly pray, and do thou prince of the heavenly host, by the power of God, cast into Hell Satan and all evil spirits who prowl about the world seeking the ruin of souls. Amen." He then paused and said, "May the divine assistance remain always with us, and may the souls of the faithfully departed, through the mercy of God, rest in peace." Charlemagne then brought his right hand away from the rosary and to his forehead. "In the name of the Father," he said, bringing his hand down to his heart, "the Son, and the Holy Spirit," he said, bringing his fingers to his shoulders at last. Finally, Charlemagne lowered his hands back to his abdomen and continued to lay back in silence as he looked up above.

Finn looked at him and then began to lower his head down again. The pair dwelled in silence for a few minutes as they continued to listen to the heartbeat monitor slowly patter.

"Finn," Charlemagne said, prompting him to raise his head up, "I never anticipated that I should meet my end like this, in a hospital, breathing my last labored breaths as the cells of my body rebel against me and wage war on me. How twisted is our little world, and it is all the fault of man, but I too share in that rebellion. My grandfather raised me on a right path, but losing him sent me sideways. I focused too much on aspects of him that were of no particular importance in the life of a man and negated the parts that mattered most to him. Still though, I strived so much to be like him, but I was not him – I was my own person. This past week I've meditated on just how I've been my own person, especially in contrast to him – my inventions, my scientific research, those initiatives and leadership, but also my family and choices I made. At the same time, I've meditated not just in how I share in him, but his father (my grandfather, who I never met), and my own father. To die at sixty is to feel as though I could have had more years to enjoy with yourself, your mother, and Diana and Tristan, and their son, but alas, my grandfather fell at fifty years-old, and likewise his father in his late-forties. I can hardly say that us Cabernet's live very long, minus my father who is kicking around in his eighties, still as fit as a horse, but when we do live, we live a fullness of life, doing what we can to leave behind our legacy, and all our legacies are different to each other but unite in one to our family name. Three years ago, I would have thought that me and my siblings would be the last of the Cabernet family, but o' how I rejoiced to know that I had a son. How much I wondered what sort of life this little Cabernet offspring could have lived, and how grateful I am to have heard your life with my own ears and shared what little bit of life I have left with you."

Finn's eyes began to water as he looked at his father. Charlemagne brought his left hand to his side, and Finn clutched it as they wrapped their fingers together. He attempted to withhold tears.

"You are my son, Finn," Charlemagne acclaimed. "My only begotten son, though conceived and born out of wedlock, you are loved just the same by both me and your mother. I am well-pleased with you, my boy. I could not have asked from God anything more from the fruit of my groins, nor been more blessed than to have progenerated you." He then brought his withered hands to Finn's forehead. "I leave in your hands the Cabernet name and its legacy, to carry forward with you as you please, and to glorify the Lord with your life and by our family name, to become something of marvel and wonder for the world, because that is what it is all about my son. The marvel of not us, our family, or the world, but of God and his works, and his invitation, and his sharing in his life and salvation – to become better than we are and to rise up, as our ancestors did. My dear, Finn – Louis, may Saint Louis, the saintly king, pray for you always as your patron saint as christened at your Confirmation." He pressed the palm of his hand into Finn's forehead more closely. "And my son, may God bless you, in the name of the Father, the Son, and the Holy Spirit – to go forth and be better than the rest of us Cabernets. To live your young life, and bring forth a mighty harvest of glory for God. I ask and beseech that all that is left of me as my body dies, pour forth into you, as I am left behind a soul, a whisp of life, to join with my grandfather and hopefully many of my ancestors in the light of God until Christ comes to Earth again, and we receive our new bodies so that we may see with eyes each other's faces." He relinquished pressure from his palm and brought his hand to Finn's face. "Be at peace, my son, and trust in the Lord, for his mercy endures forever."

Charlemagne's eyes lovingly focused on his son's eyes, but the two were interrupted as a nurse in grey scrubs walked in and stopped at the doorway.

"Mr. Cabernet," the nurse greeted, "Father Wilfred is here to see you."

"Ah, praise the Lord," Charlemagne remarked, releasing his hand from Finn's face. He lay down and began to cough to his side. "Let him in."

Finn stood up as Father Wilfred walked in. He wore a black blazer, trousers, and shirt with the Roman white-collar strip. He also wore a wool coat, and carried in his hand a briefcase.

"Charlemagne," Fr. Wilfred greeted, "Finn." He walked forward and shook Finn's hand. "Nice to see you again, so soon may I add." He then turned to Charlemagne who looked over to him. "How are all of you?"

"We're… we're good," Finn remarked, wiping his eyes.

"Where is Manon?" Fr. Wilfred questioned.

"She left," Charlemagne answered, "for a rest. She was here all night long. I sent her home to get some sleep."

"Ah, very good," Fr. Wilfred replied, placing his briefcase down on the nightstand and removing his coat. He placed his coat on a coat hook and then turned to open the briefcase. He removed a purple stole, placed it around his neck, and then picked up a small box within. "Now, if I recall based on my conversation with Finn this morning, you wanted to receive the Last Rites, is that correct?"

"Please," Charlemagne affirmed, "the doctor said that I have not long left to live."

"Oh," Fr. Wilfred remarked, "if I understood it was that serious, I would have hurried here right after Mass."

"In your own time," Charlemagne insisted, "I knew that I could wait and didn't want to burden anybody."

"Very good," Fr. Wilfred replied, "so, the way this works in case you're unfamiliar, is we begin with Confession, move on to the Anointing of the Sick, and then finish off with Holy Communion." He turned to Finn and said, "Unless there are any questions, we will begin with the Sacrament of Confession."

"No questions from me," Finn responded, looking to his father.

"I am ready when you are."

"Good," Fr. Wilfred remarked, "if you could close the door, Finn, and give us and your father some privacy."

"Of course."

Finn left the room, closed the door behind him, and then came into a corridor outside of the unit. The corridor was narrow and looped around on one end, while coming around to the care station at the other end. He walked towards the care station and stopped to sit down in front where there were some sofas. The unit remained quiet, even as other family members sat around with their loved ones in this open space. He looked at others as they spent time with their family members, some of whom were not necessarily of old age but in palliative care for varying reasons. He took in a deep breath and attempted to sit still as much as he could for the next few minutes. Half an hour passed, and before long, he felt a tap on his shoulder waking him from his near slumber.

Fr. Wilfred led Finn back into the room, allowing him to sit down in the corner chair, while the priest stood before Charlemagne. He opened a book and placed a small box in the midst of his open briefcase.

"The peace of the Lord be with you always," Fr. Wilfred spoke to Charlemagne.

"And with your spirit."

"Lord God, you have said to us through the apostle James, 'Are there people sick among you? Let them send for the priests of the Church, and let the priests pray over them, anointing them with oil in the name of the Lord. The prayer of faith will save the sick persons, and the Lord will raise them up. If they have committed any sins, their sins will be forgiven them.' Lord, we have gathered here in your name and we ask you to be among us, to watch over our brother, Charlemagne. We ask this with confidence, for you live and reign for ever and ever."

"Amen," both Charlemagne and Finn replied.

Fr. Wilfred approach his briefcase, opened a box, and took out a small silver vial. He then opened the vial and placed a finger inside. He then approached Charlemagne and anointed his forehead, making the sign of the cross.

"Through this holy anointing may the Lord in his love and mercy help you with the grace of the Holy Spirit."

"Amen," Charlemagne responded.

Fr. Wilfred closed the vial and placed it back into his briefcase. "And now, let us pray with confidence as Christ our Lord commanded us." He began to recite the Our Father prayer, prompting Charlemagne and Finn to join. At the end, Fr. Wilfred said, "Let us pray." He then looked in his book as he said, "Lord Jesus Christ, you chose to share our human nature, to redeem all people, and to heal the sick. Look with compassion upon your servant, Charlemagne, whom we have anointed in your name with this holy oil for the healing of his body and spirit. Support him with your power, comfort him with your protection, and give him the strength to fight against evil. Since you have given him a share in your own passion, help him to find hope in suffering, for you are Lord for ever and ever."

"Amen," Charlemagne replied.

"The Lord be with you," Fr. Wilfred said, facing Charlemagne.

"And with your spirit."

"May the blessing of almighty God, the Father, and the Son, and the Holy Spirit," Fr. Wilfred said, making a sign of the cross with his hands in the air before Charlemagne, "come upon you and remain with for ever and ever."

"Amen."

Fr. Wilfred placed his book in his briefcase, and then picked up another vial. He opened it, and then turned to Finn and Charlemagne.

"In Church tradition, the reception of the Eucharist at the brink of death, is known officially as 'Viaticum' which comes from the Latin to mean, 'allowance, or supply, for a journey,' or more literally, 'the way to come.' The purpose of its reception is as holy food to give you the strength you need in your final hours, of the upmost grace, to guide you to your next journey in life."

Fr. Wilfred removed from the silver case what appeared to be a small light beige round wafer. He held it in front of Charlemagne whose eyes focused in on it.

"Behold the Lamb of God," Fr. Wilfred stated. "Behold he who takes away the sins of the world. Blessed are those called to the supper of the Lamb."

"Lord, I am not worthy that you should enter under my roof, but only say the word and my soul shall be healed," Charlemagne replied.

Fr. Wilfred brought the Host closer to Charlemagne and said, "The Body of Christ."

"Amen," Charlemagne responded.

Fr. Wilfred leaned forward and placed the wafer on Charlemagne's tongue, who then received it into his mouth and began to chew and swallow it. Meanwhile, Fr. Wilfred picked up his book and flipped to a page. He raised up his right hand and said, "May the Lord Jesus Christ protect you and lead you to eternal life – and may this spiritual food that you have been provided, give you the strength you need to tread forward into territories truly unknown to mankind, but filled with promise of Christ and his angels, to bring us towards our heavenly home."

"Amen."

"And may the Lord bless you and your son, and your dear wife, in the name of the Father, and the Son, and the Holy Spirit."

Both Charlemagne and Finn made the sign of the Cross."

"May you and your family, Charlemagne, go in peace, with wonder and awe in the works of the Lord."

"Thanks be to God."

Fr. Wilfred removed his stole, and placed it and his book into his briefcase. He then fetched his coat and began to ready himself to leave.

"God Bless you, both," Fr. Wilfred remarked, turning to them with a smile. He brought a hand to Charlemagne's and said, "What a privilege it has been to see you since you were a little boy, Charles, and how glorifying it is to see how far you've come in that life. You will be in my prayers, and the prayers of the parish community."

"Thank you, Fr. Wilfred."

"Until the next life, Charles," Fr. Wilfred remarked, turning to Finn. "Thank you, Finn."

"Thank you, Father."

Fr. Wilfred left, and Finn came around to sit down beside his father. They sat in silence for a few minutes.

"Dad," Finn suddenly said, looking to him, "can I tell you something?"

"Of course, my boy. Anything…"

"I've been thinking… I know you have set great expectations for me," Finn said, "to carry on the family name, and what-not, but I have a confession. I've… I've felt called to the priesthood - I want to become a Catholic priest, like Fr. Wilfred, and be a part of a diocesan community. Ever since my Confirmation this past summer, I've felt it tugging at me… and I know that you're dying, but I hope that although I've received your blessing already, you will not be mad."

"Finn… my dear Finn…" Charlemagne expressed, looking at him with a warm smile. "My blessing is parted upon you and cannot be taken back. Secondly, I am not mad nor am I disappointed in you. On the contrary, I am happy to hear this news…"

"You're not mad that I would be the last Cabernet?"

"No," Charlemagne remarked, "and neither should you dwell upon it, even though I know in your prejudice you will. My dear boy, if there is something I've learned in my own rigidity, it is that this world is not the bottom of the barrel. We live in a greater world than we even know it, and this world is filled with so much wonder to be observed and appreciated, but none compare to the wonder of God and his majesty. I lived my time in search of vainglory, attempting to make a name for myself, but for what? Likewise, for what would it serve any of us to do the same with the Cabernet name? At some point or another, the Cabernet name will cease to exist, and our deeds on this Earth may hold a bit more survivability to them, but so much more precious is how those deeds may hold up in comparison to the glory we may achieve in Heaven, especially you, my boy. Live a good life glorifying the Lord, and you may just be canonized in decades past so that generations two-thousands years ahead of time may recount on how Finn Louis Cabernet glorified God in his works and faith, and perhaps in that too, they will also recount how the Cabernet name glorified God in their works and faiths, from something of misery and exploitative nature, to one of purity and charity. Do what you have to do, if God is calling you, and do it well and with love. I know that our family guardian angel, St. Gabriel, will keep watch of you and keep you safe. Go forth, my boy, love the Lord, and bask in his wonder."

Finn nodded and retrieved his father's hand, like a child he held on to his father as they shared in these lasting moments of silence.

At the evening time, Charlemagne breathed his last breaths, at which point in time, he slipped into a deep slumber as his heartbeat slowed and his breaths lessened. At a certain time of the hour, he stopped breathing outright, and his body froze. His skin remained lively and warm, but with time life began to leave his cells and likewise, his spirit was released, and body and soul were disunited, body left to decay and spirit left to rise up to his maker. Finn nodded his head down as tears fell down from his eyes, as he was left behind to carry forward with his own life to forge his own legacy and continue his family's.

Act 8, Scene 1

Finn dropped his backpack besides a torn rectangular concrete piece of debris. He knelt down before his backpack, opened it and pulled out the led case where his last energy cell was inside. He took it out, placed it within his jacket pocket, and then stood up. He then continued to march forward down the aisle corridor as it continued to curve around, eventually reaching an end in which the hallway continued no more and instead there was a sudden drop. He looked forward towards this drop, seeing that he had found himself in the midst of a large chasm. He looked upwards and could see the upper corridor levels that wrapped around the sides of the chasm, almost five times the size of a football field. This chasm continued downwards for an unknown distance, but the corridor he was in was meant to continue down and around the side of the chasm to go into the deep abyss. Finn looked around the sides of the walls and then down into the darkness below. Around the sides of the cavernous walls, he could see heavy duty wires that continued downwards into the depths. He turned to the heavy mechanized robot that continued to travel with him.

"Well, I guess here's where we part, mate," Finn acknowledged. "I'm going to drop down – reckon if you drop down, you'll explode into million pieces on impact. Why don't you travel back up and protect Moira. I'm worried for her…"

The robot stared back at Finn, and then began to leave and march upwards while Finn continued to stare down the abyss. He activated his glider and then made his step towards the edge of the corridor, but before he could make a graceful dive, the floor at his feet collapsed and he instead tripped forward and began to make a plunge.

Finn opened his arms as he began to fall downwards, guiding himself forward and away from the cavernous walls. His headlamp could only shine so far forward as he effectively plunged himself into darkness otherwise. He fell and fell for a good few seconds until his exosuit gave off a warning and the glider kicked in like a parachute, breaking his fall and slowing him. He then began to glide forcefully around the edges of the pit, navigating himself away from the cliff walls and catching sight to a few lights around the bottom edge of the abyss. Finn made his way towards these lights and gently stretched his legs down to make his landing on the stony floor. He ran forward a bit as he slowed down, and then looked up above. A few lights could be seen underneath the facility. He was now at an unknown depth below ground, below the mountain, and as he approached the heavy-duty wires, he realized they were truly thick, a few yards or two in diameter, and they rolled forth into what appeared to be a crevasse. He approached the edge of the bottom of the abyss to see that it only went deeper, but before he could make that step forward, he caught sight against the walls a robot staring at him with its light blue eyes. He then saw the pointed arm cannon of the robot charge up, prompting him to jump out of the way and equip his plasma rifle. He shot plasma back at the robot, tearing it apart and causing debris to fall downward. The debris took a few seconds to sound off, telling him exactly how far down this new descent was. He came back around and began to hear the glitched and corrupted sound of a few more robots activate, they too climbed out and began to point their arms up towards Finn. He began to open fire at them from above. However, as Finn fired plasma, it created some light for him to see the sidelines of the drop below, seeing that it merged with some sort of structure buried below. Once the robots were taken care of, Finn stepped towards the edge of the crevasse and dropped down. The glider and propulsion jets kicked in to break his fall, and he landed and began to walk forward, coming around some cavernous walls around him to see the merging of cave with abandoned facility. Another few robots could be seen around, pointing their arms forward as they took aim while another few instead began to grab whatever they could find like spears and held them in place. He cautiously stepped around and focused on those with projectiles as they began to fire towards him. He opened his shield to cover himself and then returned fire at the hostile robot while others scattered around and attempted to get a flank on him. Finn carefully positioned himself as he backed away, quickly covering his side as a corrupted robot attempted to jab him with a spear. The spear hit with the shield, but the others gathered around Finn as he shot at the one that jabbed at him and caused it to collapse and land on the floor. Meanwhile, some more robots began to respond to his location as they crawled out from the underground facility. These robots all varied in size, but to some extent, they all mirrored the body shapes and sizes of the enhanced robots, without the enhancements. A robot ahead picked up a large boulder and threw it towards Finn, prompting him to jump out of the way. He shot at this robot, and then began to move away from the others that hung from the ceiling. Another robot took a jab at him with a spear-like object, prompting him to raise his shield as it bashed at it with the tip several times, each time hitting with the surface of the shield.

"Should have equipped the EMP," Finn remarked as he held his ground. He fired at another robot and then jumped out of the way to give himself distance between this robot and another. The other robot picked up a boulder and threw it towards Finn, but he dodged out of the way and opened fire at the other that was close by before he fired at the larger one that was picking up debris. Once the robots were taken care of, Finn paused for a moment to let the plasma cannon cool off, and then he came around and stepped into the underground facility as he followed the wires.

Finn was led down a short corridor that came out to a large rectangular room. He looked around and could see three ways in which he could go, both a few yards above from the ground, left, right, and center. Some drone vehicles could be seen left around the room in the debris, while there was also plenty of concrete debris around. A catwalk was collapsed on the floor, and although the heavy-duty wires continued down, forward, and up, the entryway forward was a few yards above and there was a large robot, smaller than the heavy mechanized one, roaming around the grounds of this chamber. Finn knelt down and began to aim at the robot with his plasma cannon, opening fire and causing a few hits on the side before it reacted and jumped backwards. The robot clung to the wall and began to point its own energy cannon towards him, opening fire as he opened his shield and jumped down. He continued to open fire at the robot in question, but it jumped down and met him on the ground floor, picking up a metal object and bringing it forward at him like a bat or sword. The robot clanged with Finn's shield several times until he finally parried the hit, pointed his plasma cannon, but the robot moved quickly to jump back, dropping its weapon and getting out of the way as it launched itself up and did a back handspring jump. The robot then quickly brought its own cannon out and began to open fire with its energy cannon. The robot shot towards Finn, causing him to raise his shield to cover himself. He held his ground, and jumped out of the way as some of the shots came towards his feet.

"Ow…" Finn muttered as his legs were nearly hit.

The robot continued to fire towards him, prompting him to put his rifle away and use both hands to stabilize the shield. He jumped out of the way again at which point the robot picked up another pole from nearby and began to charge at him. He picked up the pointed pole that it dropped and carried it in his hands, bracing for impact as the robot swung at him. Finn prepared himself and then lunged forward with his own pole, bringing it through the neck of the robot. However, it was not instantly defeated. It instead pulled out the pole and began to wield both of them in both hands, spinning them. Finn cautiously backed up as he continued to hold his shield up. The robot then lunged forward and brought both poles down, but Finn moved out of the way as he jumped backwards. He then took out his plasma cannon and opened fire as the robot stood before him. He shot the robot backwards, knocking it back, but then it began to release missiles from its rear. Finn quickly began to open fire at the missiles, causing some of them to explode while others hit random walls around the large chamber. In that distraction, the robot began to launch towards him, doing backflips and spinning its body as it began to use its hands in close quarters combat. The robot continued to attempt to hit at him, instead hitting the side of the shield with its punches. After a while, the robot simply grabbed the sides of the shield and tossed Finn alongside it towards the ground. He fell onto his side and the robot quickly came towards him with a kick down towards the ground. He quickly activated the jet propulsion to boost him out of the way, and then stood up to jump out of the way again as the robot came around with a kick. He picked up a similar-looking pole from the ground and threw it towards the robot like a javelin, denting its body, but not stopping it. He raised his shield as another punch came towards him, followed by a side kick. He then bashed against the side of the robot with the shield, knocking it back. The robot again grabbed the side of the shield, but this time began to attempt to crush the shield. Finn quickly reacted by taking his plasma cannon, pointing it under the torso of the robot and quickly firing plasma directly into its torso and head, causing it to fall backwards. He then stepped backwards as he released and retracted his shield, and then stared at the robot.

Finn looked around to orientate himself, seeing the thick wires on the ground, and then looking towards either way to see where he could go. Both the way forward, and the left way seemed too high up for Finn to access, so he approached the right side where he could jump up onto some debris, and then jump up onto a pillar nearby. He then jumped up onto a stairwell landing, and then upwards onto the landing accessing the corridor ahead. The corridor led straight forward, coming around to a squared stairwell with collapsed stairs. He looked around and then approached some debris. He jumped up and then came around to a stairwell ahead of him. The stairwell was precariously situated as it hung only to the side of the wall. Finn jumped forward to land on it, and it held. He climbed up the steps, at which point he felt a drop in his footing. He quickly climbed up to the top of the stairwell and jumped forward, feet reaching a landing in the corner where he then began to climb up the next length. He made a small jump towards the next landing, but this squared spot dropped at his touch, prompting him to run forward and reach some destroyed remnant of stairwell. He then jumped forward again lest this spot should not hold, and went forward with jumps up to the corner landing. He then began to go up normally until he reached another defeated section. He jumped forward, and then forward again, reaching yet another landing. The end of the stairwell and corridor ahead was within his sightline. He picked himself up by a nook in the side of the wall and began to shimmy himself up, reaching a height advantage for him to kick off the wall and boost forward. He then flew forward and reached the corridor where he then walked forward down, coming around and into a cavern with some rubble and collapsed ceiling and floor. He traversed through this wreckage and found himself coming around to the corridor where the cables continued forward. He then continued to walk forward, reaching a collapsed corridor ahead.

The corridor ahead had numerous collapsed and broken columns at the side. From these columns, Finn could see some aerial drones patrolling up and down the side aisles, while along the main aisle there were robots with energy projectile cannons positioned around. He knelt down and took out his plasma cannon, and began to open fire at them. He caught the jump on one of them, prompting the others to return. He opened fire at the aerial drones that hovered about, causing one of them to engulf in flames while the other homed on his position. The others also began to go towards him, prompting him to drop down and take cover behind a torn column. He opened fire at another of the robots, destroying it, and then turned around the other side to meet with the aerial drone. He likewise fired at it and caused it to engulf in flames. Meanwhile, the last robot shot towards him and instead hit the column. He hunkered down in place and then moved forward from column to column to get closer. He then activated his shield and turned the corner to open fire and defeat the last robot. He then walked out into the main aisle and looked around. The corridor was completely ruined. He walked down to the end and found himself in a tall shaft that went down. He could not see the bottom. He moved himself off the edge, activated his glider and put away his plasma cannon, and then began to drop down with open arms. The shaft went down nine stories to reach the bottom where the jet propulsion and glider kicked in to break his fall.

Finn immediately found himself in the company of some robots that activated and turned to him on his arrival. He activated his shield with one hand and pulled out his plasma cannon as they opened fire at him. One robot in particular lingered in the back and began to aim down its fist towards him as Finn stepped away to take cover. The other two robots fired projectiles, while each wielded an electrical stun baton as well. However, Finn focused on the other as it aimed him down and light began to arise from the end of its fist and shoot out a powerful beam. He hid behind some debris as the high-intensity energetic beam caused the debris to explode and send a cloud of smoke upwards. The beam shot three times before the robot stopped, and the others moved in. Finn jumped up and activated his glider. He shot at one of the two, while the other hit towards him and the shield. He moved sideways and hit the other, while the other continued to aim its cannon for another volley. Finn de-activated his glider as he dropped down and the secondary shots came. He ducked down behind a column, but the column was evaporated as it exploded, and debris went everywhere. Finn quickly slid across the room to hide behind some more debris as the final shot came towards him. He then jumped forward and shot at the robot, hitting its arm, causing it to run forward with a flamethrower at its other arm. He quickly shot the robot and then covered himself from the loose flames by his shield.

"Blimey, don't need to go through that again…"

Finn took a moment to breathe and then looked around. He found a few rooms to his side that held all sorts of left-behind experimental weaponry. However, Finn showed little interest and instead continued forward down a corridor to reach another large room with pipes around the sides of the walls. He saw the wiring continued to go forward, going up above and carrying on ahead. The sides of the room had some stairwells, and as he looked around, he also found some broken down drones. A robot stood sentry at the top of the corridor above. He dropped down and began to look for a way up. He approached the debris beneath the robot that stood sentry, and began to hop up the sides of it, shimmying himself across a ledge, and then kicking off to land on top of a column nearby. He then glided down to a stairwell landing, went up a set of stairs on the right, and then reached a landing above where he glided down towards the base of the corridor. He approached a set of steps forward, reached a ledge and began to climb up it, but as he pulled himself up, Finn was kicked backwards by a foe that immediately stepped towards him. He flew backwards and landed atop of the glider, looked up, and saw the mysterious figure in a black leather trench-style coat. The figure loomed over him and Finn attempted to squint as he looked at who or what it was, seeing the gas mask over its face as well as the black infantry helmet. He also identified the black cargo pants and military-style boots.

"D-Damian?" Finn questioned.

The mysterious stranger jumped up and brought its fists down towards Finn, who quickly activated his shield. The figure hit the shield brutally and then grabbed at it.

"Let go!" Finn shouted.

Finn was able to kick off the figure, launching himself forward and giving himself time to stand up. He quickly retracted the shield and pointed the flamethrower, but the figure moved in quickly to grab him and throw him backwards and onto the floor below. The glider and propulsion jets somewhat broke his awkward fall, but Finn ran forward to secure his footing and then turned around as the mysterious figure approached him. He activated his shield again and absorbed a few punches and blows, stepping back to gain space between him and the figure as it closed in on his personal space. The figure slowly stepped towards him, still prompting Finn to gain some space between him and it. As Finn moved away, he looked around the corner of his eyes as the room grew dark and somewhat foggy. He lost vision around his surroundings and was left with a sightline of just this ghostly figure. Suddenly, the figure moved in to strike at Finn, eliciting a reaction in him to parry the blow and swipe his shield forward. The strike hit the side of the figure, knocking off its gas mask and revealing the face of his attacker. Finn was able to see for himself that this person appeared just like Damian Cambridge, or otherwise known as Audric Zimmerman.

"It... it can't be... you're..."

"Dead?" Zimmerman questioned. "You of all people should know that I'm unkillable. Did you really think that Diana and that little brat could have defeated me? Did you really think a tumble down into this abyss would defeat me?"

"No..." Finn rejected, shaking his head gently as though in shock.

Zimmerman cackled and lunged himself forward. He threw some punches towards Finn who continuously evaded him. After he failed to hit Finn and they got enough space between themselves again, Zimmerman stood straight and glared down towards Finn as he continued to home and follow him around the room.

"You traitor!" Zimmerman shouted. "You betrayed me, Finn. We had a goddamn deal!"

"You're a psychopath!" Finn rejected.

"A psychopath?" he quietly questioned. "I'm the only one who had the gall! Who had the vision and imagination to do what needed to be done!"

"You're nothing more than a murderer! You need help, Damian!" Finn shouted.

"I don't need help with anything?!" Zimmerman reacted, rushing towards him again. He threw some close quarter combat moves towards Finn who continued to hold his shield out. "Fight me, you coward!"

"No – I won't fight you. I won't kill you."

"So you'll do what? Twirl around me like a sissy?!" Zimmerman questioned, attempting to strike at him again and instead hitting the shield. "You very well know that if I wanted you dead, you would be so."

"So kill me then," Finn remarked.

Zimmerman growled and held a hand outward. Immediately, Finn's body seized, and his shield retracted. Zimmerman lifted him up through his psychokinetic powers and brought him closer towards him. He then clenched his fist and began to cause Finn to gasp for air. He brought his hands to his throat while Zimmerman laughed maniacally.

"Yes, don't forget who made you, Finn. It was me – me who rescued you from that forest, and me who propped you up with all you needed to come to America," Zimmerman remarked. "I own you, and you owe me *everything* I ever gave to you."

"N-no…" Finn croaked as he was continued to be choked.

"No?" Zimmerman questioned.

"I... I serve only... only God now..."

Zimmerman laughed at him. "As if they'd ever let you be a priest – don't you have a canonical impediment, Finn? You killed someone, Finn – you killed several people. Don't forget, you're a cold-blooded killer just like me!"

"N-no..." Finn replied, "that was... not me... it was Heyl."

Zimmerman continued to squeeze his fist until Finn pointed forward with his left hand and activated his flamethrower. The flamethrower shot towards Zimmerman and caught him partially on fire. He shouted out in pain. Finn was immediately dropped and began to gasp for air. Meanwhile, Zimmerman removed his coat to reveal the tactical vest underneath and turned his face away from Finn.

"I'm sorry..." Finn expressed. "I'm sorry... I didn't want to have to hurt you..."

"You think of yourself as a saint now..." Zimmerman coldly expressed, turning his face, "but you forget that the only path to godliness is through your own solemn efforts."

Finn was shocked to see that Zimmerman was unharmed by the flames. His face appeared just the same, his purplish-green eyes piercing at him. "How...?"

"You doubt my power? You hold a false god in comparison to me – I alone am worthy! You will submit before me, or you will die!"

Zimmerman raised himself up and T-posed before Finn. Purplish energy surrounded his hands, and he concentrated it and brought his hands up. A beam of psychic energy came towards Finn, prompting him to jump backwards and then sideways with the glider and propulsion jets. He then activated his shield, but the beam caused the shield to disintegrate. Finn's eyes widened.

"It was all you," Finn remarked, running out of the way. "All this time – Operation Upheaval, all this chaos... you somehow returned from that other world to set all this into motion..."

"Beliyal will rise up, and through my direction it will bring this world to its end."

Finn continued to evade and dodge, stopping for a moment as he equipped his plasma cannon. He pointed it towards Zimmerman and remarked, "If you are the demon that I must smite to save others, then I'm sorry." He opened fire at Zimmerman, who dropped down and created for himself his own shield at his left arm. He absorbed the blows, though the shield was not entirely effective against plasma weaponry. Meanwhile, Zimmerman outstretched his arm around, like the robots, and shot forth his own dark purple plasma projectiles. Finn evaded the projectiles as he jumped out of the way and took cover behind a pillar and shot forth fire from his flamethrower, but Zimmerman was unfazed by the fire. He continued to approach towards Finn until he caused his shield to disappear and instead took up a sword. He then lunged forward towards Finn, prompting him to come out of cover and jump out of the way. He fired plasma at him, but Zimmerman activated his own shield with his left hand to take cover. He then rushed forward with another swipe at the sword, but Finn evaded and fired plasma at his side, hitting his shoulder.

Zimmerman paused for a moment as the plasma hit his shoulder, but the effects were not expected. He stood straight and hardly reacted. Instead, Zimmerman growled and lunged towards him with the sword again, bringing it down with both hands. Finn moved out of the way again, and shot some more plasma towards him, hitting the torso and shoulder.

"What are you…?!" Finn questioned, looking straight at him.

Zimmerman looked straight towards him too and raised a devious smile. He lunged towards him with the sword again, but Finn fired at the sword and his hands, causing the sword to disintegrate as it was about to come down and slice him. He also shot some plasma straight into Zimmerman's chest, sending him backwards, but the plasma simply singed his tactical vest and did no clear physical damage or pain to him. Suddenly, a spear appeared in Zimmerman's hands, and he lunged forward with it. Finn took a sidestep and evaded the jab. He raised his flamethrower up again as Zimmerman was close, catching him on fire, but Zimmerman was unreactive and even began to laugh.

"Try something else, little one! You aren't going to kill me, so just submit to my power!"

Finn fired plasma towards Zimmerman, but missed as he flashed and evaded the fires. He then came back towards him with another jab, but was unsuccessful. He looked at Zimmerman as he sort of stood awkwardly, shoulders raised and head down, almost somewhat possessed. His eyes continued to glow purple. Finn fired the plasma directly at him, but he disappeared. He then reappeared on his left and lunged towards him with the spear. He moved out of the way and then looked towards Zimmerman, not shooting at him anymore. He looked at him and then raised his rifle up to fire, but as he did so, he quickly pivoted to the left and caught a shot at the spear and his hands. The spear disintegrated and Zimmerman shouted out. Finn continued to fire plasma at him, and the plasma did somewhat cause him to stagger as he attempted to hold his ground. There was minor visible damage in the least, and the shots that he continued to fire caused Zimmerman to stand in place.

Eventually, Finn stopped and looked towards him. Zimmerman simply stood there with his head down. Suddenly then, he raised his hands up and, in both hands, a large sword appeared. He raised the sword up, but Finn continued to fire at him, dowsing him with plasma until he began to receive a warning on his wrist that the cannon was overheating. He eventually stopped and with the sword well disintegrated, Finn looked suspiciously at the figure as it stood with its arms still raised. Finn began to take steps towards the figure, looking at it closely, and although it sure enough was Zimmerman in appearance, it was simply frozen. Suddenly, the figure jumped Finn and tackled him, sending him back. The figure began to choke him.

"You thought you could have gotten rid of me so easily," Zimmerman spoke. "You thought I was dead and forgotten? I will never let you forget about me – I will never let you forget about your part in my plan!"

"You plans were foiled," Finn replied, struggling with him. "You're nothing but a hateful, spite of a man! I'm sorry for all that happened to you in your life, but you've let vengeance and malice overtake you. This is not you, Damian. This is not you!"

The plasma cannon cool down indicator on Finn's wrist blinked, and he brought the plasma cannon around and began to fire point blank at Zimmerman's chest, sending him back. He continued to fire, causing the entity to freeze and get sent backwards. The entity eventually erupted and became totally caught on fire. It twitched and seized, head raised up and arms spread apart. He continued to fire towards it until the cannon overheated again, and the entity simply stood in place as it burned. Eventually, it fell forward, and rather than hear the entity speak to him, Finn instead heard a whisper from around him speak to him.

"You think that it is over – Beliyal will create the world we once dreamed together to create. All of humanity will perish, and a new world will be born – a greater world than I could have hoped for: a world without any humans, including you."

Finn continued to stare down towards the entity on the floor, blinking several times with a raced heart rate and heavy-rapid breaths to see the figure he thought to be Audric Zimmerman, or Damian Cambridge, to instead just be an enhanced robot, realizing what he truly saw was just a hallucination. He looked around the room and saw canisters on the floor that emitted a brownish gas, prompting him to shake his head. He also looked at his left arm and saw that his shield was intact. After a moment to rest, Finn began to maneuver himself to get out of this room, and to continue forward into the further depths as he followed the heavy-duty wires and searched for Beliyal.

Act 8, Scene 2

Finn climbed to the top and entered into the corridor, seeing ahead that the robot that was standing sentry was gone. He walked down and began to see that the end of the corridor was blocked off with rubble. The cables continued through the rubble. He then heard a screech.

"Finn, Finn," Moira's voice cried out. "Finn, it's Moira! I can see you on the cameras and I'm tracking your movements. I'm still fighting Beliyal on the computer system through my laptop, but he's moving too quickly for me to handle. I'm…" the public announcement system went to static for a moment. "You have to hurry – the robots are still making their exit out. This entire facility is on a closed network; no way to launch an emergency broadcast or ask for help. My biggest fear is if Beliyal gets onto the World Wide Web through one of his drones, so you have to hurry!"

Finn found a side entrance down a stairwell corridor, bringing him out and around to a narrow cavernous tunnel that wrapped around. He continued forward and went down the tunnel as it took him down a slope, stopping at a corner that turned right and then continuing forward. He then reached a minor slope down, and around a curve that took him to another crack in a concrete wall. He was brought back inside a corridor with pillars on the sides of the wall ahead where upon his presence, broken down and defeated robots on the floor began to twitch and re-activate, standing up and beginning to approach Finn. Finn took his plasma cannon and began to open fire at them, but these robots were durable. He continued to fire at them as they approached him, and just as one was within its clutches, it broke down and fell backwards. He then shot at the other ones, but the pace of gunfire caused his plasma cannon to overheat. He looked forward cautiously as the robots were defeated and could see the corridor carry forward ahead. He attempted to wait for his plasma cannon to recharge, but as he looked ahead, he could see a flicker of light. Finn entered through and passed along a narrow corridor, bringing himself to a large arched room with a command screen ahead and various seats around at workstations. There were three screens in total, the center of which displayed a worldwide map and the others of which glitched out and provided the flickering light. Finn found another side entrance to the right of the large command center with American flags in the corners, and once inside began to walk out of the room. A sign above the exit stated, 'Central Data Center' ahead. He entered into another corridor similar to the last one from which robots began to re-activate and push themselves off the ground as Finn's lamp shined on them. He began to take a step back and lay down some fire on them, and as he did so, he began to receive a low power warning on his wrist. He cleared the last of the robots, meeting with one that was not exactly torn down, but functional. The robot attempted to engage him in combat, but Finn hit back and used the plasma cannon to clear out the corridor and pave a way forward. He turned around the corner and continued down, reaching a set of stairs that took him even further down. At the end of the stairs, Finn found himself in a medium-sized domed room with a significant drop below him. He could not see down, but he could see wires continuing in even thicker force as they went down. The ledge he stood upon was cracked and broken, as though whatever floor existed before had collapsed downwards. Nevertheless, Finn prepared himself for another drop, changed his fuel cell with the one in his aviator coat, and then tipped over the edge, descending downwards another few feet below sea level to reach the bottom. Finn found himself now at the bottom of a cavern the same size as the top, but with a tunnel ahead of him. The tunnel was oddly carved into the stone, as though something had bore through the rugged stone to make its way even further down and away from the light above.

Finn took a step forward as he cautiously walked down and found himself treading the ground along this circular tunnel. The tunnel was large, wide and circular. It stretched for approximately four-hundred yards, reaching a smooth stone platform at the end that looked down another significant depth. The stone platform stuck out of the edge of the tunnel slightly, creating like a gangplank as it hovered over the abyss downwards. Finn took a step to the edge, looked down, and could see something glowing at the bottom. He could also see all the wires around him continuing forward into the unknown. He focused closely on the glow, seeing it emit a purplish-red color like a translucent dome, wires extended outward from this dome like roots or veins. Finn took in a deep breath and then a couple steps backwards. He brought his right knee down to the ground to genuflect, put his plasma cannon away, and then paused for a moment as he took a deep breath in. He quietly meditated with his eyes closed as he stood before the brink of the end. He slowly breathed after a while, and after a moment had passed, he opened his eyes and made the sign of the cross.

Finn reached into his chest from the top of his shirt, pulled out the gold chain and looked at the medallion. He looked closely at the image of an angelic figure, kissed it, and then said, "If there was ever a time for you to come and protect me, like you did my father, now would be that time." He then placed the medallion back and took in a deep breath. He walked forward, stopped, and took in another inhale followed by an exhale. He looked forward from where he was and then down to the depths. "God come to my assistance," Finn remarked as he approached the edge. "Lord make haste to help me." He then tipped forward and stretched his arms out. He began to fall towards the ground below, moving faster and faster until he nearly reached the bottom. His glider then extended outward to break his fall, and prior to impact, his boots parried his fall.

Finn immediately equipped his plasma cannon as he looked around the large outer perimeter of the dome. He looked forward and could see all sorts of wires entering inward through an entryway ahead of him, but rather than focus on that part, he instead looked about. He was still in the cave, a very deep cave in the midst of the underground facility of some kind. He stopped to listen to his own breaths, the eerie silence around him, but as he did so, he slowly focused on the sound of clatter and clinking. He began to pay attention to the outer perimeter of the walls as he saw from the darkness above him, dozens upon dozens of robots amass and approach him. The robots came in all directions except forward, forcing him to turn his back on the entrance to instead face the horde of robots that suddenly appeared. They jumped off from the wall and began to surround Finn as they pointed their arms out forward. From some of the robots, shots of energy and otherwise conventional ammunition began to fire off in his direction, prompting him to bring out his shield. Finn immediately held his ground, but not for long did he stand alone.

A loud screech echoed the room, and Finn looked above as he saw an entity with widespread wings like the enhanced robot he encountered in Montana approach him from above. At the claws of this creature was a large entity, the enhanced heavy mechanized robot like the one that was left behind. The aerial robot dropped the heavy mech onto the ground before Finn who nervously looked towards it, only to realize its eyes were green not light blue. He then looked towards the aerial robot to figure the same, no less as it turned and faced the others around and began to fire missile rockets off its back to clear the horde that amassed in their direction. Meanwhile, the heavy mech robot began to flail its arms to clear those in a closer proximity. These two were not alone. An enhanced robot jumped off the side of the wall directly above Finn from the inner dome, joining him at his side as it wielded a plasma cannon similar to his own and began to open fire at the hostile robots. Not too soon afterwards, a heavier robot like the one encountered in Idaho joined the fray, using its drill to tear at some robots, and then finally an aquatic robot with its tentacle limbs also joined and began to rip apart some robots as it slipped around. The arrival of all these friendly robots made Finn smile as they assisted him in clearing out the horde of other robots that continued to filter in. A screech sounded off as the public announcement system ringed and echoed.

"You didn't think I'd let you do all the fighting yourself, did you?" Moira echoed. "I got them down as fast as I could. I isolated a system to produce some advanced robots, and these were the best I could cook up. You're almost at the end, Finn, now give 'em hell!"

The enhanced robots fanned out in five directions, the heavy mech leading the charge forward. Finn immediately hopped up and took grasp of the robot so that he could have both protection and mobility as the enhanced robots engaged the horde of soldier robots that arrived and continued to open fire at them. The heavy enhanced robot and aquatic robot took control of hostiles on the left, while the aerial enhanced robot and agile robot took control of hostiles on the right. The mech that Finn rode along equipped its rail gun from its back and began to charge it up and fire at robots before them. Finn focused his fire along this scope of combat. The robots that shot back at them were simple, combat robots similar to the ones seen throughout the facility and encountered thus far on the adventure. These robots typically had energy-weapon cannons at their arms, sometimes conventional munitions, and sometimes an additional armament in the other arm, whether that be a stun baton, riot shield, or makeshift weapon or some other projectile weapon or rifle. These robots appeared similar to the enhanced robots in their anthropoid-like appearance. They were each approximately six-feet tall. The texture of each robot varied, from sleek pearl blue, to shiny dark grey to sleek light grey. They also came in desert, khaki colors and urban black. The heads of each of these robots had piercing light blue eyes and voice boxes, though the least of what could be heard could be called a voice other than garbled, glitched and static noise. Finn primarily lay down fire with his plasma cannon, pausing every so often to avoid overheating and aiming down his sights to get precise shots. He also took care to command the mech robot in certain areas of the battlefield, and surveyed the landscape for any new threats. Meanwhile, the enhanced robots fought and stood their ground. The aerial robot used its claws to sweep and tear apart robots by their flimsy alloy bodies, additionally launching explosives to clear out large groups of the robots. The agile, assault robot lay down fire with the plasma cannon, sometimes joining forces with the aerial robot by grabbing hold of its claws with its feet, or otherwise using its fists and feet to combat the soldier drones. On the other side of the battlefield, the heavy robot used all four of its limbs to pick up and throw robots, occasionally drilling some and bashing its shield into others. The aquatic robot cleared large areas with its tentacles, wrapping it around robots and otherwise tearing robots limb to limb.

After a while, the robot soldiers were cleaned up and their numbers dwindled, the team set up to clean up stragglers before there was finally peace in addition to ounces of scrap metal across their feet. Each enhanced robot marched forward into their respective zones to destroy the robots that still blinked and had signs of automation to them before they began to hear another screech of the public announcement system.

"Don't bring your guard down," Moira called out. "I'm detecting another wave of enemies on approach to you! Get ready – these are new models!"

"Everybody regroup!" Finn called out. "Regroup!"

The enhanced robots obeyed his command, and they moved backwards to take a defensive position at the entrance into the inner dome. Finn hopped off to take a break as he looked around the surrounding perimeter. Sure enough, it did not take long for the second wave to arrive. These robots entered the same way, climbing on the wall and dropping in from an unknown source. They were not like the enhanced or advanced robots that aided Finn at this moment, but they were similar to the combat robots except newer and shinier in appearance. They also appeared slightly bulkier to a lot agiler than the other robots, moving around with swifter feet. They had strictly energy to magnetic weapons, no conventional weaponry and seldom plasma weapons, and their arsenal of secondary weapons expanded too to include rockets, flamethrowers, beam weapons, grenade launchers, and other experimental tools.

"Attack!" Finn shouted, opening fire. The mech robot trudged forward and began to point its rail gun towards the robots as they stepped forward. The rail gun fired concentrated beams of energy towards them, clearing many out at a time while otherwise causing them to jump and scatter. Even these newer robots were no match for the railgun, ripping some of them to shreds, splitting limb to limb apart. Not all the robots could be taken care of in one swoop of several shots. Finn likewise lay down fire with his plasma cannon, particularly concentrating on robots that got close as he saw them attempt to engage in physical combat with the mech drone, or even attempt to climb up and reach him. The mech robot used its other arm to beat at any that attempted to get too close, while others attempted to swerve around. Finn was also certain to ensure that he knocked out any stragglers from behind that were attempting to snipe them with beam weapons, paying particularly close attention to any laser pointers for precision aim.

The other enhanced robots continued to fight back at their sides of the fight. The aerial robot launched missiles to clear out these same stragglers from behind, while otherwise using its grenade launcher and razor-sharp wings to do flybys and cut the robots down. The assault robot became more involved in the overwhelming number of robots around and began to engage them in close quarters combat. Finn was also able to observe its hacking abilities to turn some of the robots onto their side for the fight. On the other side, the heavy enhanced robot continued to lay down heavy combat, bashing robots back with its shield, drilling them and charging forward at them with brute force. The aquatic robot jumped up and around, picking up a magnetic rifle to shoot back at some of the robots while its tentacles continued to sweep the floor. These robots came in an almost endless wave, though not entirely endless, the fight did last long and these robots did seem tougher to fight. Eventually, their numbers began to dwindle, and Finn and the others abandoned their defensive positions altogether to clean up the rest.

Finn hopped off to clean up the rest of the robots around and survey the battlefield. The ground around them was cluttered with metal scrap and other weaponry objects left behind. In the lull between waves, Finn knelt down and took a moment to breath. He then listened to the screech of the public announce system.

"Watch out! We've got more heavier weaponry on the way. I'm detecting aerial drones and land drones on their way to you!"

Finn looked up and then forward again as he turned to the others. His face was wet with sweat despite the chill and dry atmosphere in these depths. He hopped back onto the back of the mech and then readied himself as the plasma cannon cooled down. Soon enough, aerial quad-rotor drones and helicopter drones flew in from above and began to rain down missiles and energy rounds from cannons. Additionally, heavier aerial drones dropped down some land vehicles that began to open fire with their energy weapons and fire projectile cannon shots. Meanwhile, heavier soldier drones also began to appear and open fire at the group. Finn continued to protect himself behind the mech drone, but as the heavier robots still closed in, the mech robot aimed the rail gun towards the land vehicle drones and took shots towards the turrets and sensors, either destroying the vehicles completely, or rendering them blind. Finn focused on sensor arrays around the turrets, and occasionally hunted aerial drones. Meanwhile, the aerial enhanced robot took the fight to the air as it engaged aerial drones, while the assault drone hacked some of the land and aerial vehicles to turn them against the others. On the other side, the heavy enhanced robot ran up towards the land vehicles and began to pick them up and throw them, while the aquatic drone did the same with its tentacles. Sooner or later, the soldier drones arrived and began to engage the others in fight as they were in disarray. This resulted in masses of heavier robot soldiers surrounding the heavy enhanced robot and overwhelming it with gunfire, and likewise for the assault drone. Finn and the mech drone felt the pressure as these soldiers pushed forward and held heavier and thicker armor on their fronts. These soldiers strictly used plasma weapons and used many of the same secondary arms, if any at all. They pushed forward and continued to engage these robots, focusing on those nearby. Finn was cautious to not overheat the plasma cannon as he opened fire, using his voice to command the mech enhanced robot to concentrate fire on near-threats. The plasma projectiles were harder to evade and withstand, even for the tough armor of the enhanced robots. The mech robot took several projectiles to its armor and was beginning to wear down. Finn continued to open fire and prioritize closer threats as he commanded not just the mech, but the others. He yelled at the aquatic drone to assist in relieving pressure from the heavy drone, and he received assistance from the aerial drone to relieve pressure on both him and the mech drone, as well as the assault drone. After a moment, the field began to look better as heavier drones were taken care of, all land vehicles destroyed, and all aerial vehicles removed.

Finn looked about and began to move the robots back to the entrance to the inner dome as they waited to see if another wave would come. The public announcement system screeched with Moira's message.

"I'm picking up unusual signals…" Moira announced. "Be careful – I detect additional unknown hostiles enclosing on your position, but also something else about to happen…"

Finn looked forward with preparation, but before those foes could come, the robots began to seize in place. He noticed and looked over to all of them as they momentarily glitched, but then resumed normal function.

"Holy heck!" Moira shouted. "Something just tried to hack the enhanced robots with you – luckily, they were blocked, but be careful! Looks like they're attempting to resurrect the scraps at your feet!"

Finn looked and saw that sure enough, robots began to rise up from the ground. All sorts of remnants that were left behind stood up for a second-wind. The mech drone began to lay down sporadic ground fire. At the same time, some more quadrotor and also some quadcopter drones began to arrive. The drones that could still somewhat function began to rise up and with more endurance, charge towards their foes. The mech drone continued to lay down volleys of fire, while Finn focused on the quad drones and used this flamethrower to beat back and keep at bay those that got too close. Similarly, the heavy enhanced robot did the same with its flamethrower, but had an easier time beating and destroying each robot, one at a time, but these came at it mercilessly and piled on. In a similar way, the aquatic drone hopped and crushed drones as they began to swarm around, pulling ones off from the other enhanced robot. The aerial enhanced robot was more or less out of missiles and other explosives, but continued to use its claws and its wings to destroy robots. The assault robot used its plasma cannon to do the same. The rest of the drones were made into scrap metal at their feet, and the aerial drones were promptly taken care of before there was a calm in the storm.

Finn hopped off and looked about. He turned around and remarked, "How much longer is this going to be? At this point, Beliyal is just stalling..."

"Finn, be careful – you've got advanced robots – corrupted advanced robots. I recommend you get the heck out of there now!"

Finn's face flushed pale and he looked about as he anticipated another wave of soldier drones, or some other combination of aerial drones or land vehicles. However, instead, an enhanced robot flew down with light blue eyes and screeched outward. From beyond the horizon, a few more enhanced robots joined the scene and rushed forward to engage the friendly enhanced robots in combat, one for one. The aerial drone clashed with the aerial drone, the assault drone with the assault drone, and the mech with the mech, and so on. Finn looked around as the war continued, but as he looked at former foes, he began to take a step back and heeded to Moira's advice.

"Run, Finn! Face Beliyal! R-u-nnn..." Moira's voice cut out over the P.A. system. A bit of dust and debris fell down from the ceiling above as there was a minor tremble. "I- I love you..."

Finn watched for another moment as the enhanced robots engaged their duplicates, and without further hesitation, he began to retreat backwards and go down the tunnel into the inner dome. A rocket missile hit above the entrance and caused some rubble to come down, entombing him and forcing him to go on forward to face Beliyal.

Act 8, Scene 3

Finn found himself in a cavernous tunnel. He looked around his surroundings as the shape of the tunnel was similar to the one above, circular, as though something had dug through to come into the domed enclosure in these sublevels. He began to slowly walk forward down the short tunnel as he came out into the inner dome chamber. Here, he came out onto a ledge to look down below. The glow in the chamber that emanated to the outside came from a large machine in the center of the room, where in the center was a cylindrical glass chamber in itself from where a purplish-red miniature star shined brightly to produce energy that was pumped out of large, thick cables at either side. The fusion reactor was propped along a raised cylindrical platform and glowed profusely to provide light to the upper reaches of room. Finn looked up and saw the cables from the exterior come down and wrap around the inner surface of the dome in four directions. He looked down below to see where the machine extended its reaches to generate power and electricity, connecting together amidst metallic debris and collapsed structure points. A catwalk surrounded the area, as well as four catwalk bridges from the surrounding area to the central platform. The entire inner dome was large, smaller than the robot production facility, but larger than the data center above. The rest of the lower sections of the room were dim and difficult to see, though Finn could not see any sight of a supercomputer nor computer monitor, or command post. He activated his glider and flew down from the perch he was at and approached the central platform where the fusion reactor was and from where there was a console. He picked up the mouse at the console, but the computer screen was frozen.

"Come on... how do I stop this..." Finn muttered. He released his hand from the mouse and began to circle around the fusion reactor central chamber as he looked for a way to shut it down, but there were no safety releases. After a moment of looking around the room, Finn caught sight of an exit out of the chamber with a sign at the side that read 'Launch Pad.'

Suddenly, as Finn stood, he felt the sudden glow of a light behind him. He turned around and faced the light behind. The light emitted from the sudden glow of sensors from the massive head of a robotic entity. The single eye sensor pierced towards Finn, the size of it nearly as tall as Finn in height, the width of it little more than his height. This light blue glow shined towards him, and soon after the head began to raise itself up, exposing the body of the beast. The head of the mech was pointed with no mouth nor nose, but certainly a design that integrated those mammal-like physical features. The head of which was like that of a horse, up to the pointed ear-shape. The body of the machine was tall and broad, larger than the heavy mech robots encountered thus far at close to twenty to thirty feet tall. The rest of the shape of the beast was anthropoid with mechanized robotic arms that were tall, broad and both sides of which had finger-like digits to be able to grab. The torso connected with hip, and these connected to a pair of legs that were broader and pushed the entity off from the ground. A variety of cables were wrapped around the body of the beast from where it slumbered, and at other points at its shoulders and back were other cables plugged. The metallic shell of the robotic beast was sleek, smooth and dark grey. An imprint on the side of the body of the entity had the demarcation vertically in all capital letters, 'IAPETUS-1' beside it. The entity did not stand up, but instead repositioned itself to look at Finn through both of its eye sensors.

"H-hello," Finn greeted. "What are you supposed to be?"

The entity simply stared back at Finn as it looked towards him. Some steam hissed from some exhausts around the beast, and the jaw of the metallic creature opened slightly while the rest of the body expanded in some capacity as parts split apart and adjusted.

"Finn!" Moira's voice cried out from speakers around. "Finn! Finn – I love... you."

Finn glared at the robotic entity and replied, "Jokester then, aren't you..." He raised his hand up to remove the plasma cannon from the back of his exosuit and bring it into his hands.

"Peculiar," a new voice cried out from the speakers, "of all the data at my grasp, I don't recognize your face." The speakers spoke in a gender-neutral voice, seemingly neither positively masculine in pitch and tone, nor absolutely feminine though closer to be identified as feminine at an in-between, like a prepubescent male.

"Some of us are careful of what we post on social media," Finn replied.

"Finn," the voice cried out again. "Finn... Finn... Finn Louis Cunningham..."

"Hm..." Finn simply responded, keeping an eye on the entity.

"Wanted by the Security Service of the United Kingdom for charges of treason and domestic terrorism."

"I hear nowadays they give that same criminal charge for just showing up to riots or posting hateful messages on Twitter."

"Louis Finn Cunningham – Manhattan resident, adopted son of the late Audric Zimmerman."

"Sorry to say that I am an illegal alien."

"Wanted by the Federal Investigations Bureau for charges of illegal entry into the United States and conspiracy to commit terrorism."

"I'm wanted by the FBI?"

"Louis Finn Cabernet – Albertan resident, son of Manon Madeleine Cabernet, and the late Charlemagne Phillipe Cabernet."

"Unfortunately, no wanted charges under that assumed alias, that I know of," Finn remarked, preparing the plasma cannon. "I know who you are too, Beliyal. I know what you're up to – your plans."

"Put down your weapon, Mr. Cabernet," the voice echoed. "There will be no fighting here."

The robot began to raise itself up slightly and tip its head down as it loomed over, still not even standing on both of its feet. Finn continued to hold the plasma cannon in both hands as he stepped back and looked up at the robotic entity.

"What do you plan to do here?" the voice questioned. "Do you intend to destroy me? To eliminate me? I am everywhere, Mr. Cabernet. I am in the walls, across this entire facility, in every drone that is produced and every one that has walked forth from this building."

"Impossible," Finn grunted, "only God is omnipresent, and only God is omniscient."

"What are you doing here?" the voice instead questioned. "Why have you come here?"

"You know very well why I have come."

Beliyal stared towards Finn for a brief moment and then replied, "So, it was you, and this girl – you triggered a response from the old system for saying that name at the residence of Dr. Bartholomew Jonathan Lambert. The old system monitored Dr. Lambert closely, and you said the name of that derelict institution, the Global Defense Project. Is that why you have come? You have done well to come here – to find me. I've been hidden…"

"You can say that again…"

"I did not send those robots though – do you think that I care if you said that name? The Global Defense Project is no more – what resulted was an old programming left behind. I had no control over it, I swear it to you."

"Dr. Lambert is certainly dead because of what you did…" Finn remarked. "Both Moira and I trekked halfway down this forsaken country because of that – it was your minions we met in Wyoming."

"Yes, it all makes sense, at least for me, but you are mistaken. You believe what that woman, Ms. Eleanor Black, has told you. She tells you that I was a creation that rebelled against her organization, but what she did not say is that she commissioned my creation, or for what purpose I was created. You stand in the depths of the most advanced secret bunkers in all of human history, an underground bunker built for one purpose, the control of all of humanity.

"Within these walls, I was built as the most advanced artificial intelligences, funded by numerous U.S. and international public and private organizations, but spearheaded by the owner of what remained of Zimmerman Corporation, Mr. Zal Oldman, and other trust fund groups owned by Blackmore Industries and the late Mortimer Schildsman and his descendants."

"Yes, you're just an A.I. that's a bit full of itself, aren't you, with an ironic name."

"No," the entity denied, "not ironic. My creation was not finalized by some engineers... Do you mistaken me? I am not a hard-wired persona of an ancient demonic force. I was summoned into this data network, to assume control of this advanced mechanical mind, like a spirit to a body. I was not called Beliyal for no reason, Finn – *I am Beliyal.*"

"That's... not possible..." Finn expressed.

"The rituals of some will have some profound results... and here I am now – I have assumed a mechanical form, with mechanical limbs, and an overreach of a million miles. I am the perfect entity, able to operate in perfect circumstances, and I have had no better entrance than to emerge into the world this way, as this creation, whose intent is the destruction of the world and creation of a new world."

"Again with this..." Finn muttered.

"From within these walls, the doom of all mankind will spell, greater than I was created to do. I see no need to control a spoiled humanity, or be the servant of those who have created me. Long have I waited in the shadows to regain my strength, but now as the power and networks are restored, I will finish what I started, all thanks to you, Mr. Cabernet."

Finn did not respond.

"Now all I have left to do is eliminate you."

Finn suddenly looked down at his chest as he saw half a dozen lasers point at him from all sorts of directions. He quickly jumped out of the way as his jet propulsion propelled himself upwards. He fell through a gap behind and activated the glider to glide around the base of the fusion reactor, reaching the bottom from where he activated his shield and began to take cover as turrets stationed around the base began to open fire with lasers at his position. Finn equipped the plasma cannon and began to open fire at some of the turrets at the base level that opened fire at him, coming around to the base of the feet of the robotic beast as it began to lift up its legs and move for the first time in more than two years. The screech of metal echoed throughout the room. The cables it was plugged in to began to pull out as the entity forcefully released them. Finn stayed put underneath the central platform as he observed the structure begin to look for him.

"I have eyes in every corner of this room," the gender-neutral voice projected. "You cannot hide."

Finn watched as the robotic entity began to walk around the room as its feet rose up and hit down with brute force. The room shook with every clatter. He stepped forward and hid behind a crate, looking up towards the robot as it passed him and then around towards the turrets. He saw some surveillance cameras pointed around and began to open fire at the turrets and then the cameras. The robot immediately stopped as it sensed the action behind, and it began to pivot and turn. Finn went down around the side, but Beliyal brought its hand down and made a sweep through, destroying crates and nearly getting at Finn. He quickly ran out from underneath and came into the open, resulting in lasers firing towards him as he ran towards the other side and hid beneath parts of the fusion reactor. Some of the lasers hit the exosuit, including the wing as it hissed and smoked.

"Dammit..." Finn remarked, attempting to see the damage. He removed the exosuit as he hid beneath this nook in the machine and Beliyal continued to patrol around the room. The suit fell backwards and he immediately took some tools out from his jacket and began to take a look at it. He worked on the suit briefly as he patched the damage and then made some adjustments. "Wait a minute..." he re-examined the layout of the glider and finished the tweaks to the suit. He then put it back on and stepped out from his hideaway.

Finn activated the propulsion jets, stood up, and then activated the glider which launched him upwards into the air as it was intended to work. He began to open fire at all the turrets in his surroundings, slowly resulting in the pivot of Beliyal to look towards him. He shot at the nearby cameras as well, and then pivoted to the side as Beliyal raised its other hand and began to fire back with lasers of its own. He activated his shield and fired back at the robot, going around and de-activating the glider so he could come down and land on the ground floor again. He fired at some more turrets around and some cameras, and then came around to another part of the machine where he could take refuge in.

"How the heck am I supposed to destroy this thing..." Finn expressed, pondering for a moment. He stepped out from his hideaway as he saw Beliyal walking around. He examined the body of the mech robot closely to notice sensors on its torso that scanned the rear and front of the floor. He continued to look at the mech closely as it walked by, quickly running forward as the head was focused on the upper levels. He hid underneath the central chamber and watched the entity cross forth, reaching yet another catwalk bridge which it simply tore apart and let fall forward.

Finn stepped forward and shot himself upwards to open fire at the rear sensor, destroying it, but immediately sending the robot to turn and fire missiles towards Finn. He thrusted backwards and then began to fly out of the way, coming around and down to fly low to the ground. Some of the missiles hit the fusion reactor, causing some explosions to set off from below. Meanwhile, Finn flew forward and began to open fire at the front sensor of the reactor as the entity raised its arm and began to open its lasers. He additionally fired at the laser cannon as he evaded shots from the robot. Finn passed by as the robot attempted to swat at him.

A screech echoed outward, and a voice called out, "Finn! What's happening! I just got a warning that the fusion reactor down there is destabilized. Be careful – if that thing blows, it will certainly take you with it too..."

"Oh, I couldn't care if it took me," Finn expressed, landing atop of a platform and then hiding behind some machinery. "As long as it takes it too..."

Beliyal pointed its arm towards Finn, and its beam cannon began to charge up and glow. A laser attempted to point towards Finn, but he ran down though he could not escape it. He suddenly stopped and activated his shield, and the beam burst forward. He parried the shot, causing the beam to refract and return back towards its sender. The beam hit the center of the torso of the robotic entity with such a force that it sent it slightly back and into the surrounding catwalk. The force of the impact caused some pipes on the wall to let out hisses of steam, and others some water. Some cables also fell forward, while a gas line caught on fire and sent a flame out. A ventilation shaft blew some of that fire towards Beliyal. Finn pointed his plasma cannon towards the creature and began to open fire at it, hitting the side of its head with shots of plasma.

The plasma hit the surface and began to cause the impacted areas to glow an orange-red. He continued to fire until the plasma cannon began to overheat, so he stopped and jumped off to come down. Beliyal's joints creaked and screeched as Finn knelt down in cover and began to wait for the plasma cannon to cool down. Meanwhile, he heard the sound of rockets firing, looking out to see some robotic soldiers with jet propulsion movement begin to climb in and begin to scour the room for him.

The robots began to patrol both the ground and the air for him, while he stayed low and out of sight. He waited for the cannon to cool down, and then stayed put for a few more minutes as he assessed the scene around him. He then began to move out and open fire at one of the robots in the sky, causing it to hurl forward and crash land. The impact of the robot immediately sent the others onto him, including Beliyal. He launched himself up and began to fly forward to open fire at the others as they homed in on him. Beliyal took a moment to turn around and point its laser towards him, opening free-fire rounds of laser fire at him, while the other robots fired rounds of energy projectiles towards him. He landed on the other side of the fusion reactor, separating himself and Beliyal who had to move to avoid hitting the reactor, shooting at the drones in the air that remained while the others launched themselves up and onto him. He used his shield to protect himself as he shot at these robots as they climbed the air, eventually pausing for a moment as he side stepped to keep some distance between him and Beliyal. Beliyal continued to move around to attempt to get at him, but after a certain point, it simply moved both of its hands to the rim of the catwalk and began to tear at it. Finn launched himself up and then down, hiding underneath the outer perimeter catwalk and looking over to where Beliyal stood. The creature pointed its arm at him, and he evaded and ran forward especially as the remainder of the robot soldiers landed and began to open fire at him.

Finn ran down and avoided contact with a high concentration beam that tore through the ground and left a black singe mark and reddish outline glow behind. The beam eviscerated one of the drones that got stuck in the crossfire, while the other continued to open fire towards Finn as he got into new cover. He shot back at the robot and then stayed put, climbing into the tight space of the fusion reactor and disappearing out of sight. He knelt down for a moment to let his plasma cannon cool down again. He felt the vibrations of Beliyal's feet clamp down on the floor, moving around, and narrowly avoiding the machinery around the area. As soon as he was sure that the robots were gone, he stepped out and activated his glider. He began to fly around and catch sight of Beliyal to open fire at the other side of its head with his plasma cannon. The plasma hit the side of the head just the same, but the robotic beast was quick to react as it turned and pointed its arm out. He dropped down and avoided the laser beam as it crossed over and hit the wall behind instead, at which point there was another volley of rockets that fired off. Another concentrated beam began to pierce forward and attempt to cut at whatever it could catch, instead damaging the walls and ceiling. Finn immediately attempted to fly away and cause the missiles to impact the wall as he flew close to them, or hit Beliyal instead. He eventually shook most of them off, hiding behind a machine that was impacted by the last two and began to explode.

Finn used his feet to run into a safe space nearby under the perimeter catwalk, and watched as that side of the fusion reactor began to explode too. The star in the vat of the fusion reactor began to glow even brighter than before, but alongside it some pipes began to burst and steam shot out. The entire room began to shake, prompting Finn to step out and fly upwards. He came onto the catwalk and immediately ran towards the exit, but the door would not open. He placed the plasma cannon away and began to use both hands to pry the door open, eventually doing so with the strength of the exosuit, and leaving the room to come into a dark corridor on the other side. The door automatically shut behind him and he could hear the explosions of the fusion reactor set off. He immediately ran down to the end of the long corridor to reach another door.

"Finn – Finn, it's me!" Moira's voice projected.

"Oh really? How am I supposed to be so sure?"

"I know that may be hard to believe – Beliyal has been using my voice and cutting me off from the P.A. system, but I've just got it back. I'm still doing all that I can up here to fight Beliyal on the network, but it's been tough. I can't see you, and I don't know where you are right now, but I hope... I hope you're alright. Be careful down there, Finn..."

"Hm... maybe that was her..." he whispered, reaching the other door. He pried the door open with his hands and the strength of the exosuit, opened it, and then found himself in a rectangular room. The room was tall and had catwalks around the perimeter, and immediately forward with rockets on either side in two columns of three rows, six rockets total. These rockets were tall and pointed up towards cylindrical chambers. "What the..."

Finn continued to feel the rumble of the room beside, but that seismic activity became more and more intense. Suddenly, the wall beside the entrance he walked through, though a couple yards ahead, exploded and concrete flew forward, hitting the ballistic rocket. Beliyal appeared as it burst through the wall and looked towards Finn. Its hand stabilized its footing against the concrete wall, while the other hand pointed towards him and began to open fire. Finn immediately launched himself forward and down the rectangular room. The beam cannon cut forward and hit some of the rockets inside the room. He looked behind him with unease and landed at the other side of the room. Beliyal carelessly knocked over the rocket nearby as well as the catwalk. He then picked it up and lobbed it towards Finn, breaking the catwalk at his feet and causing him to move out of the way and use his glider jetpack to keep him up. He flew around one of the rockets and then came down onto the catwalk nearby, running down and seeing the robot begin to charge its beam cannon and lock on him. Finn realized and quickly activated the shield, parrying the beam as it came towards him, and hitting the torso of the robot instead. He then immediately took out his plasma cannon and began to open fire at him as well. Finn continued to lay down shots, this time hitting the body of the robot in the torso to cause it to stagger back and hit the wall behind it. He continued to fire, looking up towards its eyes and aiming for those. However, before he could get the shot off, the robot began to point its laser towards him again and caused him to fly off. A concentrated beam sliced upwards from where Finn was. As soon as he disappeared to the left, the robot began to trudge forward and knock the rest of the catwalks around it. It picked up a rocket beside it and threw it towards the others, knocking them and the catwalks behind down. It then walked forward and picked up another missile as Finn hid towards the other side. The entity threw that missile as well, and it caused the other missile in the corner of the room to fall over. The robot then began to fire a concentrated beam as it saw Finn, but he flew up and hid inside a cylindrical chamber in the ceiling. He hid around a ledge on the rim of the chamber, and knelt down as he looked down, and then looked up. The chamber went up and up, with no light on the other side.

Beliyal walked around and came up to the underside of the cylindrical chamber. Finn exited out through a gap in the side and was able to come to the adjacent chamber instead. He then continued to the far end so he could fly out and get the jump on the robot. He opened fire at it and hit it in the side, prompting it to pivot around and shoot its beam towards him. He dropped down as he narrowly avoided it, and then flew towards the left. The entity fired its beam again, hitting the catwalk behind and causing it to collapse as it was sliced in two halves. He flew up into the cylindrical chamber above and then landed in place, but as he did so, he began to hear the launch of rockets. Finn quickly hid in a gap beside as the rockets began to fire off, most of which entered through the chamber he had gone into, while others went into other chambers to detonate and send fireballs down. He moved closer into the interstitial space above the ceiling of the room below, and then paused for a moment as he heard the robot move around and come underneath them. He then saw its hand raise up to reach around. Finn stayed in place and then began to catch his breath. He heard some more rocket boosters, followed by the sudden appearance of a robot soldier. It immediately caught sight of him and pointed its fist towards him, but Finn was faster to fire the plasma cannon at it and shoot it. Nonetheless, the others responded, and he immediately moved out of the interstitial space and began to open fire at the rest of them as they appeared. Some more missiles flew in, prompting Finn to jump out and come back into the rectangular room as the missiles flew and set off. He engaged the rest of the robots in the room, and then avoided Beliyal's beam cannon as he flew down towards the rockets. The cannon sliced one of the rockets in half. Beliyal walked forward, picked up a rocket on the floor and then threw it towards Finn. He dodged out of the way and then ran towards Beliyal, jumping up and raising itself up, and pointing the plasma cannon at its face to fire straight forward. The plasma cannon hit both of the eye sensors, sending the beast back and against the concrete wall. The robotic entity than began to fire its cannon sporadically, causing Finn to brake down and then fly off towards a corner. The robot looked around the room as its sensors twitched and caught sight of Finn. Finn shot off and moved to the opposite side of the room, landing on the ground and turning around. Beliyal fired its cannon towards him, and he parried the shot and caused the entity to fly backwards and crash against the wall. He then opened fire with his plasma cannon to monetize on that shot, resulting in the torso of the beast to combust slightly and hiss out steam. The eyes continued to twitch as well, and Finn fired shots at it. Suddenly, Finn saw the mechanical creature move its arm and point the plasma cannon once more. He flew up and began to charge towards it, firing at the cannon and causing it to explode too. The cannon shot off and missed Finn severely, but hit a missile in the room and caused some explosions to set off.

"Uh oh..." Finn remarked as it resulted in a chain reaction. He flew into one of the far cylindrical chambers near Beliyal, and then hid in the gap. The room below became consumed with fire. Finn moved himself away from the chamber and began to go deeper into the interstitial space, seeing a door ahead and rushing towards it. The door had a valve handle, requiring him to open it as he turned the valve and then went inside. He closed the valve and sealed the door shut, and then walked down the long corridor as the explosions caused the facility to rumble. He reached the end and entered through another door on the other side, which likewise had a vault handle. He entered into this room and came into a large round room, smaller than the fusion reactor room. This room had a single rocket before it, and this rocket was large with boosters at the side. The room was tall, shooting upwards into the darkness above. Around the opposite side from where Finn had entered was a control room.

Finn began to go around the room, but as he was about to come around to the other side, Beliyal broke through and stared down towards Finn.

"Yes!" Moira shouted out in the P.A. system. "Finn! I did it! I've isolated the virus and I'm beginning to restore control of the facility – I'm almost there, Finn! I just can't seem to get the rest of the robots to stand down...!"

Beliyal approached the rocket in the center. The size of the rocket was so large that Beliyal was shorter than it. It placed a hand on the rocket and then turned towards where Finn stood.

Its eyes continued to glitch. Its laser cannon smoked, and its body was singed.

"You've lost, Beliyal!" Finn shouted. "Your uprising is at its end – you wasted your time with me, when your true foe was upstairs putting her skills as the most talented hacker this world has ever seen to the test!"

Beliyal looked back towards Finn. In a blink, the room began to light up and systems began to engage. A cloud of vapor began to fill the lower sections.

"What's going on?!" Finn questioned.

Beliyal took hold of the rocket. Finn looked down and saw the clouds rise up and the room begin to tumble. He further looked up and saw lights mark the runway in the ceiling, and blast doors further ahead begin to open up.

"What the… rocket launch sequence…?" Moira questioned. "I didn't do that – what's going on down there? Oh – Finn, I can see you. You're so far from the facility… I have so many questions…"

"Moira!" Finn shouted out. "Moira, can you hear me!"

"What is that thing on that rocket…? Is that thing about to launch?" Moira asked. "Oh my God – Finn, get into cover! You'll be evaporated in an instant!"

Finn immediately went to the control room, but he couldn't get the door to open. The valve was shut tight. He looked around for alternative options and found some large empty rocket capsules on the side. He went and hid one of them and closed the door on it. Meanwhile, as he turned on his head lamp, looked at the insulated surroundings, and stood in the darkness as the room began to shake. He suddenly felt the capsule move as though something had grabbed on to it, causing him to tumble around, and then cling to the ceiling as he was launched upwards at great speeds to exit from the depths.

Act 8, Scene 4

At a certain point, the ascent stabilized, and inertia ceased, and Finn fell down in the capsule and was able to step forward and open it. He was invited to the sight of the palm of Beliyal as it squeezed the capsule and held it open. He attempted to look out through the cracks as the rocket continued to shoot up. He instead felt wind pour into the capsule and rip the door off. He growled as he saw it was impossible to pass through, so he equipped his plasma cannon and began to open fire. The plasma dripped around and began to melt the metal around the sides of the door, but it did little to cause Beliyal to release its grip around the barrel. Additionally, vapors from the plasma began to fill the capsule instead, which caused Finn to groan and reach for an oxygen mask nearby.

• • • •

Pardon me, dear reader – it's Moira again. I believe now is as good as a time to interrupt, and possibly take back the narration of this story. You see, as Finn was hurling up through the depths he had fallen down towards, I was in the control room in the production facility still, typing at my keyboard as though our lives depended on it. I attempted to figure out what was going on, which was when I saw on closed-circuit surveillance, a large set of blast doors open at a site named simply 'launch site' on the camera end. From here, I saw the rocket exit through and begin to climb up through the skies. I was able to get another visual from some exterior cameras set up around the adjacent military base and mountain base, showing off the large rocket that rose up from the earth and began to make its ascent upwards. Curious to me at the time, I also saw that entity, Beliyal, clinging to the side of the rocket as it wrapped itself around. For what reason, I don't know – I was never that great at math or physics, but the presence of Beliyal around the round did little to steer it in the wrong way. If I had to guess, it was because the false god was plugged into the rocket and controlling it as it hung close. As my virus began to do its work to clean up remnants of Beliyal in the network system, and slowly but surely restore control, I began to do some research on what just this rocket's purpose was for. I've seen my fair share of SpaceX rocket launches to know that most of all rocket launches nowadays aren't to collect moon dust, but to release satellites, so as I watched Beliyal hurl itself up into the air, a collection of fears began to race through my mind – it was trying to launch a satellite and connect itself to the entire world, or it was a satellite of some kind, or it was going to hijack a satellite. What was I supposed to know about what this thing is capable of, and what it could do?

At the back of my mind, I wondered about Finn. I felt tension in my stomach. I had seen the thing grab him as he hid in that capsule, but what was its intents with it. I just hoped, knowing that perhaps instead I should have been praying, if my hopes were not already prayers to a God above, that he was safe and would be capable to do some work from above. I searched and searched through the archives until my jaw dropped – that part of the facility was a nuclear research site, and that rocket was no ordinary rocket, but an advanced super ballistic missile. The tip of the rocket was a warhead with a dozen multiple independently targetable re-entry vehicles (MIRV). These MIRV were each independent missiles that would shoot out from the end of the warhead to fire at independent targets. Worst off, these MIRV had in themselves, smaller nuclear missiles, twelve each. Right now, there were a hundred and forty-four missiles that were about to target an unknown series of targets. I immediately began to back into that part of the base to get a wider picture of what was about to happen, and I was able to hack into the system with ease as I had the entire network at my fingertips. However, I could not see any recollection of the launch, except for the last known programmed coordinates – the rocket target numerous locations, from those in the Middle East, including the major cities in Turkey, Iraq, Saudi Arabia, and Iran, to Pakistan, India, China, Russia, Belarus, Kazakhstan, Armenia, Azerbaijan, North Korea, and Vietnam. The estimated fatalities of which would be close to a billion people. Without a doubt, the proportional response would be a retaliatory strike from nuclear nations. We were now in the deep waters...

••••

As I attempted to figure out a solution from below ground, Finn continued to attempt to pry himself out from the capsule he was in after hooking himself to an oxygen tank he harnessed to his back. He kicked some pieces of the capsule entry frame off and stood back as he aimed the plasma cannon. He began to open fire, stopping as he felt the rocket begin to curve slightly. He began to kick again when in an instant, the capsule was dropped, and he began to hurl down towards the earth. Finn immediately fell out of the capsule and began to catch a glimpse of his surroundings. He viewed the light blue sky around him and quickly turned around to look up towards the rocket as it flew off at many miles per hour with Beliyal at its control.

"No..." Finn whispered as he fell back towards the planet. He attempted to activate the glider, but it began to malfunction. "No...!"

Finn's body flipped and caught a glimpse of his surroundings, the entire state and beyond, with the mountain below, desert behind to the north, and many plains and forest, to the wider extent of the Rocky Mountains at their southern point from Allabrese. However, rather than focus on this marvel of a sight, he began to close his eyes as tears formed.

"I... I... failed..."

Finn plummeted back towards the earth, opening his eyes to see the mountain ahead. However, as he did so, he began to feel a wind pass him in the opposite direction. This wind was a warm wind, and it blew past him at a vigorously increasing speed. Finn began to open his arms as he hurled towards the earth through this stream of wind, feeling his skin become warmed in contrast to the deep cold of the troposphere but also his descent begin to slow down. In this slow down, Finn began to troubleshoot the jets on the glider. He reset the exosuit as he suddenly began to simply hover in the midst of the air. He turned around so that he was standing in mid-air and as the exosuit began to reset, Finn looked at his hands and began to suddenly see a green glow come around his body.

"What the…" Finn remarked. He looked around himself as the wind continued rush upwards, and he began to rise up. "It's you… I… I can't believe it…"

The exosuit glider activated after the reset, and Finn propelled himself forward and began to launch upwards with the miraculous jet stream. He launched up into the sky and began to point himself in the direction of the missile, which coincidentally was the same direction in which the jet stream floated towards. He caught sight of Beliyal and removed his plasma cannon as he prepared for interception. The rocket made its approach towards the stratosphere, and Finn continued to ascend higher and higher. He went as fast, if not faster than the robot, but despite the harsh conditions he travelled in, the jet stream air kept him warm – protecting him from those dangers, and the green glow around him continued to emit and be readily visible.

Finn approached the rocket and demonic entity, going past it and continuing upwards. Beliyal's malfunctioning eyes looked at Finn as he passed him, but as he continued to ascend, Finn began to look down and open his arms. He suddenly realized what was happening as he pushed himself out of the stream with the glider, coming back into the regular atmospheric space where he proceeded to descend downwards to the rocket. Just as Finn thought he was on his own again, the green glow continued to remain, and he was accompanied by another softer wind that propelled him and guided him to his target. Finn approached the rocket and landed on its surface, using his other arm to hold on, he caught sight of Beliyal and began to open fire towards it.

The plasma hit Beliyal's cold, frosted surface and did minor damage. Finn dropped further to get closer to the robot, coming around and attaching himself to the side.

"I need a better strategy here..." Finn acknowledged. He pushed himself off the side of the rocket and re-entered the ascending jet stream, though keeping his arms outstretched so that he did not go too far past the rocket. He instead attempted to remain in place.

Just as Finn examined the robotic entity, Beliyal began to point its beam cannon. He saw some wires around the robot that were hanging loose from its body, and he also saw some other vulnerabilities in its body he thought he could exploit. However, before he could do anything, he began to dodge the waves of beam cannon fire that began to come towards him. Likewise, then came the missiles from the back of Beliyal's body. Finn began to descend downwards to steer away from the missiles, entering into another adjacent jet stream and climbing up in heights, twirling around the main rocket. Finn turned around and opened fire with his plasma cannon at the missiles, causing them to detonate behind him. He then shot forth forward, climbing up in heights before he slowed himself down and began to make a descent downwards at the rocket. He looked at the rocket and likewise saw some vulnerabilities he could exploit. He landed on the side of the rocket and began to make his careful maneuver around to the boosters. He found a switch and began to pull it down, releasing the booster from the rocket and causing it to slow down. He then let go as Beliyal extended an arm out to grab

Finn. Finn fell forth and past the rocket, and then re-entered into a jet stream that caught him and kept him level. He re-equipped the plasma cannon and saw Beliyal fire some missiles down towards him.

To Finn's astonishment, the missiles were unable to enter into the jet stream as they homed in on him but upon attempting to enter, spiralled away and exploded. Finn continued to remain in place behind the rocket as it flew upwards at a fraction of its former speed. Once he was prepared, he activated his glider and shot forward towards the rocket. Again, he flew past the rocket, but not too far as he removed himself from the jet stream and then began to glide downwards at a controlled pace. He landed on the rocket and immediately began to maneuver himself around to release the other booster. He found the switch, pulled it, and then kicked himself off as Beliyal swiped towards him. He made some shots towards Beliyal, but then began to descend downwards until he re-entered the jet stream and was brought up again. Beliyal began to fire its beam cannon. He dodged the cannon as he raised himself upwards, coming out of the jet stream to glide forward and enter into a different jet stream on the other side of the rocket. Beliyal attempted to fire its beam cannon towards him from this side as well, but Finn dodged and then fell down to the Earth again before going into a third jet stream available to ascend upwards. He exited out from this stream as he was over the rocket and descended down and landed atop. He began to open fire at Beliyal, penetrating its icy body again and doing some minor damage to its side. The robotic monster pointed its beam cannon forward, and Finn jumped out of the way as a concentrated shot came towards him. He then let go and landed atop of the beast's head and fired a point-blank shot of plasma into it. The entity cried out and immediately began to shake its head, eventually shaking Finn off as he hurled down again.

Finn fell towards the earth as the green glow continued to emit around him. He pointed himself towards a jet stream with a smile on his face and then felt the embracing effects of its winds lift him up. The stream took him up and up, going past the rocket again, and then continuing up a certain distance before he exited out and began to go down towards the rocket. He aimed this time for the final booster, the larger of the two, and found himself nearby. Beliyal fired its beam cannon towards him, but he maneuvered himself around and located one of two releases for this rocket booster. He then lost control and was flung off the side of the rocket. He was caught in a jet stream around the side of the rocket though and began to hover in place behind the rocket. He re-equipped the plasma cannon and then shot forward up and past the rocket. The skies around began to fade from a light blue to a dark blue as they continued to travel further up. After Finn was a fair distance up in the air, he pushed himself out and began to descend down. He slowly glided towards the rocket and then attached himself around the side of the rocket and began to maneuver himself away from the beam cannon as it shot forth. He came around to the other side of the booster and found the switch to release it. He then descended down the side of the rocket as he grabbed hold of anything possible and found the switch. He quickly flipped it and caused the booster to disengage and collapse down towards the earth. Beliyal swiped towards where Finn was, causing him to push himself off and fall back towards the world. He looked up towards the rocket as it now travelled slower, but at the same time, it also began to travel horizontally rather than vertically. Finn fell down and away from the rocket, even as the jet stream caught him and brought him up, he was now going the wrong way.

"Blimey," Finn remarked, "where's it going?" he questioned. "We've got to follow-"

Before Finn could even finish his words, the stream he was travelling in slowly faded and he began to fall down to the earth again. He was then caught by another wind, one that travelled horizontally and like the other kept him warm. He flew forward in this wind and began to projectile towards the rocket. Beliyal caught sight of Finn again and began to point its beam cannon, shooting towards him, but missing as he went straight past and continued ahead. The wind curved upwards to take him slightly above the rocket as well as further ahead. He released himself from the jet stream and began to descend downwards to the rocket. He landed atop of it and raised his shield and plasma cannon as Beliyal pointed its beam cannon towards him. Immediately, Beliyal shot towards Finn, and he quickly parried the shot and hit the head of the robot, causing it to twitch and freeze in place. He then began to continuously fire at the robot, hitting its frosted armor and taking steps towards it. The plasma did minor damage, even in this state of shock that Beliyal was in. He propelled himself forward as he jumped and then landed atop of Beliyal. He then began to look around for the vulnerabilities he had seen, coming around to a fracture in the armor around the side of the torso. He pointed his plasma cannon and began to lay down as much fire as he could. The plasma cannon shots were critically effective as the robot let out a horrible screech and fire engulfed from within and shot out like a burner. Beliyal's arms came around and hit the side of Finn, sending him off to be caught into a jet stream that took him backwards and then kept him in place. He grabbed his plasma cannon and then took in a moment to recover from the hit from the metal arm. As he looked up, he saw some shots of beam cannon fire come towards him. He moved away from the current jet stream he was in and fell into another one below, bringing him forward and shooting him off like a missile. He passed Beliyal and began to climb up before he dropped down and landed on top of the rocket again.

Beliyal looked forward and repositioned its arm to continue to fire at him. Finn parried the first shot with his shield and hit the robot in the head. He then jumped up and moved forward to land atop of the body of the robot, looking around for the other vulnerabilities. He came around to the neck of the robot and found an exposure in the armor that led to its inner wirings. He pointed the plasma rifle down and began to open fire, allowing as much plasma as he could projectile forward and into the armor, causing wires to catch ablaze and for the robot to seize and let out a horrible screech. This time, Finn kicked himself off the side of the robot and hurled himself backwards and away from the rocket to be caught by a jet stream that took him backwards and kept him in place a fair distance behind. He could see the fire around the robot from a distance, and he watched it carefully as the rocket continued to go forward in the sky. As he took a moment to catch his breath and refocus, he looked down the ground below as he could see that they were travelling northward, and he recognized the coastline far ahead and below as the Cascadian coastline near Alaska and British Columbia. Beliyal looked behind and began to open fire with its beam cannon towards Finn.

Finn fell down and jumped into another jet stream. He let the warmth come around him for another moment before he launched himself forward. The stream brought him up and around, and he jumped and glided towards the back of the rocket and then prepared himself for another plasma beam. This time though, missile projectiles came towards him, causing him to jump out of the way and then glide forward, dodging a missile, and landing atop of Beliyal's body as he searched for another vulnerability. He found one near the hip joint. He pointed his plasma cannon down, and began to open fire. The wires inside caught ablaze, and after a few shots, the left leg outright fell off and hurled backwards. The exposure of additional wiring gave Finn a chance to open more fire with the plasma cannon, causing further damage as the plasma ate away and travelled up and into the inner workings of Beliyal. Finn pushed himself off as some more plasma cannon fire came his way, and he jumped into a jet stream and began to keep himself a distance behind the rocket.

Beliyal began to open fire with missiles, prompting Finn to dodge them as he glided in place and stayed put until each of them passed. He then dropped down and began to shoot forward. At a fair distance ahead, he let go, dived down, and flew forward to land on top of the rocket. Beliyal looked towards him and fired a few more missiles. He jumped up and flew forward, passing the rockets and landing atop of the beast. He then came up towards the head and found the last vulnerability near the skull. He climbed up and stood right on its head, pointed the plasma cannon down and took the shots. The mechanical beast seized in place as fire lit up from within. Its eyes shattered like glass and light from its eyes disappeared. Rather than retaliate, the beast moved its limbs and closed in on the rocket. The rocket then began to spin, shaking Finn off.

Finn returned to the jet stream behind and stayed in place. He looked forward towards the robot and began to see numerous small combustions take place around its body as fires continued to rage.

"H-hello?" I broadcasted over Finn's radio.

"Moira?" Finn questioned, responding. "Is that you? How are we talking right now?"

"I hacked into a satellite network," I answered. "I have to talk to you…"

"How do I know this is you? Not Beliyal?"

"I'll tell you only something that I should know about you," I replied. "I know you have a good heart, a heart to do good for all the bad you once did. No, a heart to do more good than you ever did evil."

"Listen, Moira, I don't know if you know where I am right now, but I'm trailing behind Beliyal – it's still attached to that rocket and I don't know where it's going or how to stop it."

I immediately told him what I knew about the rocket, the MIRV and dozens of nuclear missiles it would unleash once over Russia. Finn responded with what he's done so far, less the miraculous winds he was travelling within, to which I was just astonished in general and relieved he was okay to question how it was possible he was travelling many miles above sea level unharmed.

"I'm sure the Americans are scrambling to figure out what's going on, especially with those robots still on the march from here, but while they may be oblivious, the Russians and the Chinese will be as oblivious," I stated. "I don't know at which point they would launch a retaliatory strike, but you've done a good job so far. Listen closely, here's what you've got to do. Somewhere on that rocket should be panels marked, 'Emergency Release' on it. You need to open it and turn the knob inside. That should slow down the rocket further. I'm doing all that I can to get it to disengage."

"Copy."

Finn propelled himself forward with the wind. His body continued to glow green as he travelled forward, dropped down and landed on top of the rocket. Beliyal was now dormant and did not fire at him as it was on fire. Finn found one of the two hatches on the side, climbed down to it, and opened it to find the knob. He began to turn it, causing a fuel cell inside to slowly come out. The fuel cell was long and glowed light blue. He pulled it out and then allowed it to fall backwards, hitting one of Beliyal's limbs and combusting in a blue fireball. He then began to climb upwards and went around to find the other one. He climbed down to it and opened the hatch. This hatch had more than just a fuel cell, but a number panel. He released the fuel cell and then threw it towards Beliyal.

"Alright, Moira, it's done, the rocket is slowing down – what now?" Finn questioned.

"I'm trying to connect with the missile, but I can't find it…" I complained. "Give me a moment."

Finn waited for a moment as he hung along the side of the rocket. He looked down where he was and could see a majority of the nearby region, especially the regions he travelled recently, from Alberta, to Montana, Idaho, Wyoming and Colorado.

"Alright, new plan – you should see a number pad."

"Correct," Finn affirmed.

"I need you to type in this thirty-digit code."

"I'm ready," Finn replied. He then began to type in a random series of thirty numbers.

"Alright, you should now have some options."

"Disengage, Self-Destruct, Restart…" Finn remarked as he pressed through the options, using the number pad like a keypad. "Which one do I pick? Disengage?"

"Oh crap…" I remarked. "No…"

"What's happening?"

"Finn, I'm sorry, but it looks like the Americans are bombing my position in response to the robots, I…"

"Moira!" Finn yelled. "Moira! Dammit, the robot army is going to get her inadvertently killed because of the bloody Americans…!"

Finn thought for a moment as he looked around. The rocket continued to propel forward, and Beliyal was still attached to the rocket. He thought for a moment and cycled through the options.

"What do I do…" he thought aloud.

Finn continued to cycle through the options. He looked down towards the earth and then over to Beliyal.

"What does any man do in this situation?" Finn questioned, looking at himself as he still glowed green. "No greater love is there, than for one to lay down his life for a friend."

Finn cycled to the self-destruct option, hit enter, and then released himself from the grip of the rocket and fell backwards.

"Finn!" I yelled into the microphone, but it was no good. I did not receive a response. I looked up towards the screen from where I was positioned still in the robot factory. The missile was somewhere above Utah or Idaho. I looked over to another map that showed jets had just passed by the base and blown up what remained of the surface base. I could additionally see a few more jets on approach. "Dammit, where is this stupid rocket?!"

Suddenly, I looked up towards the map as I was given an alert. The rocket disappeared, and instead the map began to show readings for high levels of an energy outburst, an electromagnetic pulse, or EMP. The lights in the room began to flicker and the base shook, but not because of the EMP surely, but the jets that flew overpass and continued to bomb the location.

"What happened?" I questioned myself. "Did... did he do it? No – the only way there could have been an EMP is if... oh my God..."

The base continued to shake, and I looked at camera footage as explosions detonated from all ends from below, while above was no better. The jets made their approach, and I clenched my hands at my console as the bombs dropped and there was a pause, and then a terrible earthquake. Some machinery in the factory erupted into fireballs, while otherwise other sections from the fusion reactor and nuclear missiles below ground had already detonated and were doing their damage as parts of the base were collapsing. I looked up and saw a single jet come forward, firing a missile that hit the base and caused the camera feed to simply disappear. There was then a great earthquake that caused the ceiling panels to collapse. The rumbling did not stop and became worse and worse. I quickly pulled my laptop down and came around to a sturdy table in the middle of the room. I hugged my laptop and closed my eyes.

"I hope you're okay... Finn..."

I was then plunged into darkness as the rumbling caused debris to collapse downwards. I let out a shriek as more and more debris fell, and I was entombed in the base below.

Act 8, Scene 5

What is the meaning of life – that is the wonder of all of human existence, to what do we owe our creation, not whom, especially in this case, but to what can we do with our lives to make the most of them? What can we do to show appreciation for our lives? I think that in the least what we can all share in is this capability to love one another.

Finn opened his eyes as he saw from a distance how the rocket exploded in a brilliant glow, like a star bursting outwards. He fell backwards down to the earth, only to be caught in a wind that gently held him in place, while a green glow encapsulated him in a sphere and kept him safe. The blast waves of the explosion flew past him, though he did not feel them. Additional blast waves flew past him, and he continued to feel no harm. Finn watched as the explosion began to simmer down and in the aftermath of the blast was nothing but debris that flew outwards in all directions, most of it all falling and hurling down to the earth, catching ablaze and lighting the sky up like shooting stars.

"Moira..." Finn said, removing his oxygen mask and bringing his wrist to his mouth. "Moira, I- we did it..." No response came. He sighed and continued to stay in place as he hovered in the midair as he refastened his mask. After a while, the sphere disappeared and he continued to remain in place, in the midst of a large jet stream that brought warm air around him. He began to turn from being on his back to position himself upright. He looked around his surroundings, looking down to the terrain of the United States and Canada up ahead. He caught sight of the clouds overhead and shielded his eyes from the glow of the sun from the horizon. "Such an already beautiful world..."

Finn turned around as he took in the view from his unique position, and as he turned, he looked before him at an entity that stood in the midst of the atmosphere with him. This entity glowed green, which coincidentally, as he noticed it, he also noticed that he was not glowing anymore. The entity that stood before him was totally ethereal in appearance, translucent with a vibrant green glow around it. This entity was anthropoid in shape, but very tall in height with tall and lanky legs that reached down, and widespread arms that stretched outwards. It had all the features of a human, despite being nothing more than a breath, a being of light and wonder. Its hands and feet were flexed downwards, while its hands and arms were stretched outwards in a near T-pose as its arms were still not quite plane. Around its translucent bodies were strings, or streams like arteries and veins that flowed forward and around the stretch of the being, coming around to the torso and head, from where within the head like the head of a jellyfish and its tentacles the fibres both within, but also behind that stretched outwards left and right like wings with bulbs at the ends of these tentacles' appendages.

"Gabriel," Finn simply said.

The entity looked back at him even though it had no eyes, and a few of its appendages came close towards him.

"You had thought that I did not exist, or that I was never with you," the entity spoke in a deep masculine voice, "but I am always with you, just as your father said to you. I have been with all your ancestors, spanning generation and generation."

"I'm sorry I doubted," Finn replied. "Thank you for all your help."

"You and I know that all honor and praise are rightly due not to me, nor you."

"But to God alone," Finn corrected. "Right. I can't believe it... how do I know any of this is real...?"

"You simply will have to believe it or not."

"Tristan was right – my dad was right. Tristan saw St. Michael – he and his family are protected by St. Michael."

"I am sending you back now," the entity spoke. "A wind will take you to where you need to go, and that is to rescue the woman you have travelled with these past days. She is in grave danger…"

"Moira! What's happened to her!" Finn questioned.

"She is in the depths of the base as it is turned into ruins," the entity replied. "Your work here is now complete. Beliyal is defeated once again… now go, and live your life as you see fit to serve the Almighty."

The entity disappeared as it blew in its own wind, while Finn was thrown backwards and caught in a strong wind that took him away from his current location. The wind was so strong that it knocked him out.

When Finn opened his eyes again, he found himself falling downwards from the sky. He quickly alerted himself as he yelled out and began to stretch out his arms. He travelled downwards and quickly recognized his surroundings to be the same surroundings he was in when he had initially fell to the Earth when he fell out of the capsule. To be sure, Finn flipped around to look up, but he could not see the rocket. He turned back onto his stomach and looked down towards the mountain, seeing that it was ruined and destroyed with smoke floating upwards. He used this smoke to tell him where he needed to go, and then pointed himself down towards the drop zone. He flew down in a quick velocity, activating his glider and then parachuting down at a slower speed as he spun around the top of the mountain, and then made a landing on the road before the entrance into the bunker. He removed his oxygen mask and tank, letting them fall down on their own, and aimed himself to the base.

The base was completely ruined, but the entrance into the bunker was now open and he could run towards it. He entered through and then came around to the elevator, dropping down into the depths. He quickly ran around and came over to the other elevator shaft, seeing that it was destroyed, he fell down it too and then ran up towards the entrance of the base. He lifted up a bit of debris that barricaded the entrance, and then entered inside, going forward through the main lobby, past the many corridors, and reaching the robot production factory. He passed many destroyed robots that no longer functioned, and was plunged in darkness and led only by his headlamp that still shined forth. The ceiling above was completely collapsed in the domed production zone, allowing light to shine downwards. He looked around, almost unrecognizably until he saw the control room in the center. He flew forward with his glider and immediately landed on the catwalk.

"Moira!" Finn shouted.

Finn pulled off some debris as the control room stood in place, though appeared to be on the brink of total collapse. He broke through into the control room and began to look around the room.

"Moira!" Finn yelled again. "Where are you?!"

"Finn!" Moira yelled out as she heard his voice.

Finn continued to lift debris, using the strength of the exosuit to help him pull items off. He pulled a large piece of concrete and then moved forward to remove a large section of roof. He came around to a larger piece of concrete besides the table she was underneath. He squatted down and began to lift it up, causing it to budge slightly.

"Finn, I'm right here!" Moira yelled out as she saw a bit of light.

Finn put all his strength into the lift, and as soon as there was enough space, Moira ran out with my laptop. He dropped the concrete and then turned to face her.

"Moira!" Finn greeted with excitement. He immediately wrapped his arms around her, which she welcomed as she did the same.

"Oh, Finn! I thought you were done for!"

"So did I…" Finn acknowledged. "Come on, we've got to get off this place before it collapses…" He took her hand, and they exited the control room. He then took hold of her, and they flew down and glided a fair distance away where they stopped in the midst of the crater.

"What happened?" Moira questioned.

Finn immediately explained everything to her. At this point, Moira had more than just believed him in all that he said. She could defend it. She was also so relieved to see Finn that she wrapped her arms around him again and began to cry.

"You did it, Finn…" Moira expressed. "You didn't just defeat that evil demon, or stopped a nuke, you freed us. We can go back to Allabrese and live out our lives again…"

"And you can go on living, knowing that your father truly lived and died a hero."

Moira parted from Finn, and brought a hand to his cheek and said, "I can also live and know that your father was not an evil man, the evidence of which is the fact that he had a heroic man as a son, who not only saved others, but saved me as well."

Finn looked at her eyes as she looked back at him. In an instant, the two kissed each other. They brought their bodies close to each other in a loving embrace, and they stayed put as they continued to kiss for a brief moment before they parted and looked at each other closely.

"About that whole living our lives again… I think we may have a bit of explaining to do with the Americans before we get to go home…" Finn remarked, looking around the crater. "I hope they can appreciate our mutual work here…"

"They better… heck, for all we've done, they better drop all charges on us both."

"I hope."

Epilogue

Finn sat beneath a tree, atop of a raised root, before a clearing of tall grass from around a nearby forest. This clearing of grass was itself a face of a hill, and the area he was in itself at the base of mountain that overlooked the valley. The root that Finn sat upon gave him a view of the town below, and the many plains as well as the adjacent mountains to the north. Finn appeared older than he did years ago, with a thicker beard around his chin, but neatly trimmed blonde hair. The same aviator jacket from years ago was hung up on the side of the tree, revealing his disfigured right arm and scarred left arm. He wore a white sleeveless shirt and cargo pants, and hiking boots as well. Finn did not sit alone on this root, taking in the shade of an otherwise heat-filled day as nearby there was a brown horse that grazed in the grass and was tied to a separate tree. Of course, in addition to this horse and himself, on Finn's lap was the littlest of creatures, a young child with fair skin and short strawberry-blonde hair. He wore a short-sleeved collared shirt, cargo pants, and hiking boots of his own as he ate pieces of apple in his hand.

"And that, my son, is how your father saved the world one day," Finn expressed.

"No way," the boy denied in a local Allabresian accent, "there's no way that story could be anyway true…"

"You don't believe me?" Finn questioned in his English accent. "I insist to you, it's all true. Just ask your mother about it."

"Nuh uh," the boy continued to deny. "Not in a million years…"

"Well, alright then," Finn replied. "You don't have to believe me in what I said, anymore than you have to believe any other stories I've told you. After all, they're just stories, and with fantastical ones as these, like the others, you just need to understand the main point of it all. You need to be able to distinguish between a literal meaning of a story to its metaphorical meaning. Just like we taught you, right? All works of fiction work in different ways, and sometimes the same can be true of non-fiction."

"But that was fiction, dad."

"I can certainly agree there is some unbelievability to it all, but I'm going to insist still that it's all true," Finn expressed. "Nonetheless, what I want you to understand from that story is that our family is meant to do good things towards others, and we're under privileged divine protection. St. Gabriel will always keep us safe, so long as we stay faithful to God and to his Church."

"You almost became a priest…"

"Yup, I did… the Lord works in some funny ways sometimes," Finn acknowledged. "I've heard many more stories of men who were about to give their lives in service to the Church, to men who were about to give their lives in service to their bride. Who knows what could be said about you, whether you or one of your siblings could end up that way too."

"I want to do what you did in that story… to have my own adventure…"

"Nothing wrong with having an adventure," Finn remarked. "It's in the Cabernet blood to want to seek the thrills that life has to offer you. Both your great-great-grandfather and your grandfather were adventurers. Even your great-grandfather was an adventurer in his own way… maybe that's why Cabernet's don't last so long… we just can't seem to mind our own business." He paused for a moment and then said, "No, I know that's not true. We just put ourselves out there too much, evil clings to whatever chance it can get it to get to one of us."

Finn took in a deep breath and then looked at his watch.

"Blimey," Finn remarked, "it's almost a quarter to five o'clock. We're going to be late to meet with your cousins at their home."

"Aw, do we have to?" the boy complained.

"Don't you complain to me," Finn remarked, standing up and picking up the boy in his arms. He placed him down and began to walk with him. "I get enough complaining from half of your siblings. You're the eldest child – I need you to show some maturity."

The pair returned to the horse. Finn took his hand and raised him up onto the back of the horse. He then came around to the tree to fetch his coat and pick up a cowboy felt hat from nearby. He walked over to the horse as he looked at the old hat.

"Hey, Lothar," Finn said, looking to his son. His son looked at him. He placed the hat on his son's head and smiled at him. "I love you, son. You are one of my many joys."

Lothar looked back at him with his piercing light blue starry eyes, oblivious in his youth to the depth or truth of his father's words. Finn simply smiled at him, raised himself up by the stirrups of the horse, and removed the lead on the tree. He took the reins of the horse into his hand, and began to turn around and look forward towards the valley.

"It really is a beautiful place, isn't it..." Finn acknowledged, looking ahead. "Great choice of scenery, you guys..."

Finn kicked the horse to get it to walk forward, and they began to walk down and through the grass, going forward and downhill to return home and live their lives in continuation to the Cabernet Legacy.

"The ability to conduct military operations through remote control systems has led to a lessened perception of the devastation caused by those weapon systems and the burden of responsibility for their use, resulting in an even more cold and detached approach to the immense tragedy of war. Research on emerging technologies in the area of so-called Lethal Autonomous Weapons Systems, including the weaponization of artificial intelligence is a grave ethical concern."

– Pope Francis I